James Stoddard's debut novel, *The High House* won the Compton Crook Award for best Fantasy novel by a new author, placed in the Locus Top Ten for best SF/Fantasy book of the year, and was named one of five finalists for the Mythopoeic Award, an award given to works reflecting the spirit of the writing of C.S. Lewis, Charles Williams, and J.R.R. Tolkien.

His short stories have appeared in prominent science fiction and fantasy magazines. *The Battle of York* was selected for inclusion in Eos Books' *Year's Best Science Fiction 10; The First Editions* appeared in the *Year's Best Fantasy 9* anthology, published by Tor Books.

As a labor of love, Stoddard has retold William Hope Hodgson's epic adventure, a tale of terrible danger, breathless battles, and the enduring power of love.

Walk with Andros on the battlements of the Great Pyramid; journey with him into a land of endless night, where giants and monsters await.

With nothing but his own skill and courage, he must pass beyond the darkness, beyond the Watchers and Forces that threaten both body and spirit, to find his one true love, the woman he has sought throughout the ages.

THE NIGHT LAND

A Story Retold

JAMES STODDARD

and

WILLIAM HOPE HODGSON

This is a work of fiction. All events portrayed in this book are fictitious, and any resemblance to real people or events is purely coincidental.

THE NIGHT LAND, A STORY RETOLD

Visit www.tinyurl.com/james-stoddard to learn more about the author.

A Ransom House Book
Printed in the United States of America

First Edition 2011

ACKNOWLEDGMENTS

This version of The Night Land would not have been possible without the help of a number of people. I would like to thank Howard Fisher, Marquel White, and the other members of the Write Right Writers' Group for their thoughtful critiques. I am especially indebted to Lon Mirll, Kreg Robertson, Scott Faris, and Joe Justice for their advice and friendship, and to Jamie Herring, whose enthusiasm for the book meant more than she could possibly know. Andy Robertson was especially kind, reading the entire manuscript and clearing up several key points. I am also grateful to Jason Mills, who I contacted out of the blue with the insane proposal of doing an audio recording of a rewrite of a relatively obscure novel with little hope of compensation. That he was willing to lend his considerable vocal talents to such a lengthy and dubious enterprise bespeaks a generous heart and a love of Art for its own sake.

This book can only be
dedicated to those who have brought
The Night Land
to the public eye over the years:

To H. C. Koenig,
who championed its cause

To August Derleth and Arkham House,
who published the first American hardback edition

To Lin Carter and Betty Ballantine,
who introduced the first mass market paperback

To Andy Robertson, who
created The Night Land website
and publishes original anthologies based on the book

THE DREAMS THAT ARE ONLY DREAMS

"This to be Love, that your spirit to live in a natural holiness with the Beloved, and your bodies to be a sweet and natural delight that shall be never lost of a lovely mystery . . . And shame to be unborn, and all things to go wholesome and proper, out of an utter greatness of understanding; and the Man to be an Hero and a Child before the Woman; and the Woman to be an Holy Light of the Spirit and an Utter Companion . . . unto the Man . . . And this doth be Human Love . . ."

". . . for this to be the especial glory of Love, that it doth make unto all Sweetness and Greatness, and doth be a fire burning up all Littleness; so that did all in this world to have met The Beloved, then did Wantonness be dead, and there to grow Gladness and Charity, dancing in the years."

INTRODUCTION

The book you hold in your hand is a masterpiece. At least, I hope it is *still* a masterpiece. It is a tale of adventure, a novel of both fantasy and science fiction, and more than anything else, a love story. William Hope Hodgson (1875-1918) wrote professionally for only eleven years before a German shell ended his life during World War I. In that time he produced numerous short stories and four extremely imaginative novels. Of the four, *The Night Land* is surely the most ingenious. The book was praised by such diverse sources as C.S. Lewis and H.P. Lovecraft. Lovecraft commended its ". . . sense of cosmic alienage, breathless mystery, and terrified expectancy unrivaled in the whole range of literature." *The Bookman*, a leading journal of its day, said, "Mr. Hodgson gives us the most touching, exquisite. . . romance that has ever been written."

Unfortunately, a book that should be considered a classic is mostly unread and forgotten, for Hodgson chose to write it in a difficult, archaic style. Editor Lin Carter, while praising the book when he oversaw its paperback publication in 1972, said, "*The Night Land* is a work of sustained imaginative vision without equal in literature, but it is dreadfully overwritten, overlong, and verbose and repetitive to the point of shameful self-indulgence."

That this novel should survive, despite its many faults, is an indication of the power of the narrative.

I first got the idea to rewrite *The Night Land* more than ten years ago. I began by rewriting the book, paragraph by paragraph, but soon discovered that Hodgson's prose did not hold up in a direct "translation." I grew bolder and began adding dialogue (Hodgson had none), character motivation, and even brief scenes not in the original volume, but necessary to support the logic of the story line. I was forced to name the main character, who Hodgson left nameless. I have divided the book into more chapters than in the original, breaking the action at various points to slow the relentless pace, and have renamed several chapters to avoid giving away the plot. Despite the many changes, I have striven to use Hodgson's thoughts (sometimes only bare hints) to recreate his world. Everything I have done has been for a purpose. Although I have served as second scribe, all of the genius belongs to William Hope Hodgson.

James Stoddard
Ransom Canyon 2010

The charred fragments of the story we now call "The Night Land" were discovered in an iron box in the burned ruins of an ancient country residence in the County of Kent. Nothing else survived, nor does anything remain around the manor except a stand of ancient oaks and a small, family cemetery.

I

MIRDATH THE BEAUTIFUL

"And I cannot touch her face
And I cannot touch her hair,
And I kneel to empty shadows—
Just memories of her grace;
And her voice sings in the wind . . .
And I answer with vain callings . . ."

It was the joy of sunset that brought us together, as I walked alone, far from home with my oak staff in hand, pausing often to view with wonder the clouds forming, row upon row, the battlements of evening in the sweet, gathering dusk of the year 1827.

The last time I paused, lost in solemn glory of the coming twilight, I heard to my right, beyond a gap in the hedge bounding the country road, the din of strident voices, some low and coarse, but one higher, as of a person in distress. I stepped through the hedge gap to find three men confronting a woman so lovely I knew her at once as the maiden acclaimed throughout the County of Kent as Lady Mirdath the Beautiful. Until that time, I had heard of her only by reputation, for though the estates of her guardian lay next to my own, I had often been abroad, and when at home had immersed myself in studies, riding, and physical training, the last of these such a constant passion I do not boast to say I have never met my equal in strength or speed.

Because of my conditioning, I did not hesitate to place myself between Lady Mirdath and her assailants, and with my oak staff raised, warned them to withdraw. I am not a small man, and at first my unexpected appearance and sheer physical size must have startled them, but after a mo-

1

ment, they recovered their courage and ran at me without a word, knives gleaming in the dusk.

I stepped briskly forward, eager for the attack, while behind me sounded the shrill call of a silver whistle, as Mirdath summoned her dogs and household servants. Even as she did so, I drove the end of my staff into the stomach of one of the attackers, dropping him to the ground. Without pausing, I gave another a sharp rap on the head, surely cracking his skull, for he toppled instantly to the earth. The third, who was nearly upon me, I met with my fist, nor did he require a second blow, but went down to join his companions. Seeing my enemies defeated, proud of my easy victory, I turned to the lady and laughed at her look of astonishment.

My mirth died in my throat, however, as she said, "You are either Hercules reborn or a strongman escaped from the circus. Do you thrash villains as a regular practice, or is it a natural gift?"

Her question deflated me somewhat, and before I could find anything close to a response, three enormous boar hounds, drawn by Mirdath's whistle, bounded up and encircled me, fangs bared; and the lady spent several uneasy moments keeping them off me, while I, in turn, prevented them from mauling the unconscious thieves. Just when the dogs had settled, shouts arose and lantern lights came bobbing through the woods, marking the arrival of the footmen of the house, who came armed with cudgels. They too were as baffled as the dogs by my presence, and if Mirdath had not stepped between them and me, I would have been mobbed.

"Who are you?" their leader demanded in a Northumbrian accent, his gaze taking in my face and the men upon the ground. "What are you doing out in the woods?"

"Why, John, don't you recognize him?" Mirdath asked. "It's Andrew Eddins. He has saved my life."

The servant's tone immediately softened. "My pardon, sir. Sir Alfred has told the Lady not to wander alone, but she's a stubborn one. When we heard her whistle, we were terrified for her safety. What would you like done with these rogues?"

The assailants were gradually groaning their way back to life, and I ordered them taken into custody to be presented next morning to the magistrate. As the servants secured the thieves, I removed my hat. "Would the lady care

2

to be escorted to the safety of her door by a circus strong-man?"

Despite the danger she had faced, Mirdath blushed and gave a brave smile. "I fear I have embarrassed myself in my excitement. When I saw you leap from the hedge like an ancient hero, you seemed more dream than reality; and I hope you remember that I called you Hercules at first. Please forgive me and say we shall be friends."

"How did you know my name? We have never been formally introduced."

"Some of us do not spend our days locked away in our manors or traveling abroad. We snoop instead."

"Is everyone in the county watching me, or is it just you?"

She smiled. "The rest of the spies are busy elsewhere, so you do not receive the attention you deserve, but I have often seen you riding your horse past our manor and have inquired concerning you. What a beautiful stallion you have! You and I are actually third cousins, you know; Great-grandmother Agnes was Lord Charles Eddins' sister, and you must call me Mirdath, since we are related and you have just saved my life."

She grinned mischievously. "For shame, sir, in not visiting us before. You must present yourself to my guardian tonight to make amends for your neglect."

"I will do so," I replied, keeping my voice steady, for though I had defied the assailants without a quaver, the face of Mirdath, seen so near, took my breath away. She was tall and slender, though I was a head taller, and the rumors could not begin to match her beauty. More than this, it impressed me that she could face danger one moment and stand joking the next.

She led me back through the breach in the hedges and we walked together down the road. "This gap is my own special secret," she said, giving me a sidewise glance. "You must promise to tell no one, for my maid and I, disguised as village lasses, sometimes slip through it to attend country dances."

Not being a man for flattering words, I said nothing, though I thought it unlikely that any disguise could hide that lovely face. But in that I was wrong, as I would eventually discover.

At her manor, she presented me to her guardian, Sir Alfred Jarles, an old and respected man I knew in passing because of our adjoining estates. There, she praised me to my face, and Sir Alfred thanked me profusely, proclaiming me an eternal friend of the house. I dined with them that evening and afterward walked again on the grounds with Lady Mirdath, who seemed more familiar to me than any woman had ever been, as if we had always known one another. It became our constant delight to discover how much we had in common. But that night, I soon perceived she was most fascinated by how easily I had overcome the three assailants.

"Are you truly as strong as you seem?" she asked me.

When I laughed in pride and embarrassment, she clutched my arm to discover my strength for herself, then released it with a gasp.

"A circus strongman, indeed," she said. "You must spend little time in reflection."

I chuckled. "A polite way of calling me empty-headed. I study more than you might suppose. I do enjoy physical activity and rambling outdoors, but have done extensive reading in the sciences, especially biology. I love learning about nature."

"Then we share that passion as well. It seems you are not only a protector of women, but a scholar, too."

But if she took pleasure in my strength, her beauty, glimpsed between the shadows of the candlelight at dinner, likewise amazed me. Were it only that, I would have been amply infatuated, but our shared interests and her cleverness and easy laughter left me twice enchanted.

We wandered through the woodlands all that evening, lost in conversation, unaware of the passing of time, until there arose the shouts of men's voices, the baying of dogs, and the gleam of the lanterns. I stood perplexed, until Mirdath gave a sweet laugh, perceiving that we had stayed so long Sir Jarles had feared once more for our safety.

Such was the way of our meeting, the flowering of our acquaintance, and the beginning of my love for Mirdath the Beautiful.

***

The following days passed in a delightful haze, for from then on I wandered every evening along the quiet country road leading from my estate to Sir Alfred's. Entering through the hedge gap, I often found Lady Mirdath already walking there, accompanied, at my request for her safety, by her boar-hounds. Strolling together, we shared the things that have always fascinated me—the mystery of twilight, the glory of ancient woods, and the splendor of night. She seemed to enjoy my company, though she had a mischievous streak and sometimes teased me relentlessly, as if to see how much I would bear.

One night I came to the gap in the hedges just as two country maids were leaving Sir Alfred's estate. I nodded a greeting, intending to continue through the gap, but as they passed they curtseyed with unusual grace for provincial girls. On a sudden intuition, I drew near enough to peer at them through the fading light. Though I could not be certain in the dimness, I thought the taller might be Mirdath.

"Who are you?" I demanded.

In answer, she only simpered and curtseyed again, keeping her head down, leaving me in doubt. Knowing Mirdath's impish nature, I decided to follow them. They hurried away, as if fearful of my intentions, and I pursued at a distance to the village green, where a great dance was being held. Torches, plunged in the ground in a circle, lit the night for miles around, sending the shadows of the trees bobbing in imitation of the scores of dancers. Barrels of ale were set out on long benches, and a fiddler stood upon a low hill, playing a tune. Half the county must have been there. Since I was the only one dressed as a gentleman, I felt the eyes of many upon me, and the crowd parted as I advanced.

Though the two joined the dance, they avoided the torchlight, keeping only one another for a partner. By these signs I was convinced this must be Lady Mirdath and her maid. I approached the taller woman, bowed, and said, "May I have this dance?"

"I am promised, sir," she said, in a voice similar to but somewhat unlike Mirdath's. I caught a glimpse of a grin beneath her bonnet, but before I could get a closer look she gave her hand to a hulking farm lad, who danced her round the green. She was abundantly punished for her deception; it took all her skill to save her feet from his clumsiness, and when the dance finally ended she excused herself as quickly as she could.

Despite the darkness and her disguise, I was convinced of her identity. I strode across to her and whispered, "Mirdath, this is scarcely proper. What would Sir Alfred think? Quit this nonsense and let me take you home."

Her eyes flashed in the torchlight in response, and if I had doubted her identity before, I did so no longer. She stamped her foot in fury, turned from me, and hurried back to the farm lad. After suffering another dance with him, she bid him escort her and her maid part of the way home. Another young lout, his comrade, accompanied them as well, while I trailed a discreet distance behind. No sooner had they left the light of the torches than the lads, ignorant of the true rank of their companions, tried to put their arms about the ladies' waists.

Lady Mirdath cried out in alarm and slapped her escort so violently he recoiled, but then, cursing loudly, came at her again. He seized her by the shoulders, trying to kiss her while she screamed my name and beat at his face with her fists. Her struggles would have been useless, had I not been close, but I caught the poor lad and struck him once, less to hurt him than to teach him an unforgettable lesson. He folded and I cast him to the side of the road. The second boy, hearing my name and probably knowing my reputation for strength, released the other woman and ran for his life.

In my anger, I caught Mirdath by her shoulders and shook her soundly. "What were you thinking?"

I was breathing hard and my expression must have looked dreadful, for she appeared terrified. My temper is one of my worse faults, but her fear shamed me into regaining my composure.

"Walk down the road ahead of us," I ordered the maid, my voice trembling with rage.

After the woman complied, I said more softly, "Mirdath, why do you do things like this?"

She spoke so quietly I barely caught her words. "Perhaps because I want someone to stop me."

We returned to the manor without another word. Mirdath kept close to me, as if both comforted and embarrassed by my presence, and I led her through the hedge gap and back to the Hall, where I bade her goodnight at a side door for which she had a key. She replied in a subdued voice, acting almost as if she did not want us to part.

Yet when we met the following day, she taunted me all through dinner, little jabs that burned like tiny brands. Finally, around dusk, when we were alone in the Music Room, I asked, "Why are you being so spiteful? Is it because of last night?"

"Have I been cruel?" she asked.

"You know you have."

She looked down. "After my parents died and Alfred became my guardian, my moodiness often surprised him. Sometimes he took me rowing out on the pond in a little boat. We would spend the whole day together. Those were happy times for me. We laughed and played—he can tell the most wonderful stories—but when we speak of it now, he says that toward the end of the day I would invariably start an argument. He thought it was because I was afraid to love him, lest he die, too."

"An understandable reaction, I suppose, but it won't bring you much happiness."

"No," she said, her face growing gentle. "Come, let me play my harp for you."

All that evening, to make amends for her cruelty, she played the favorite melodies from our childhood, and by the time I left I loved her even more.

That night, escorted by her three boar hounds, she accompanied me to the hedge gap, but being unwilling to leave her alone in the darkness, I followed her unobserved until she returned to the safety of the Hall. As she walked home, softly singing a love song, one or another of the dogs ran back to me and nosed against my hands, but I quietly sent them off again. I did not know whether she loved me or not, though I believed she felt some affection for me.

***

On the following evening, I went to the gap somewhat early, and to my surprise found Lady Mirdath talking to a well-dressed man with the air of the king's court about him. When I approached, he did not step aside to let me pass, but eyed me insolently and stood his ground.

"Pardon me," I said, the way being clearly too narrow to accommodate us both.

Though he looked directly at me, he refused to budge. My pride rose at his ungentlemanly behavior. Regardless of his rank, I would not be mocked in my own country, not before Mirdath. Determined to teach him a lesson, I picked him up by the shoulders and set him to one side.

To my pain and astonishment, Mirdath turned on me, her face red with rage, "How dare you manhandle my friend, you—you bully! I have been so mistaken about you! How could you? How dare you?"

I stood stunned before her assault. For her to humiliate me, her true friend and cousin, before a stranger, surely meant she did not love me. Too deeply wounded to argue, I bowed low to Mirdath and the man, who really was slight of frame. He had weighed nothing at all when I lifted him. "I . . . apologize. The Lady is correct. I should have been courteous from the start."

Having somewhat repaired my error, I turned and stalked away, leaving them to their happiness, my own sight blurred by despair and anger. In my anguish, I walked a good twenty miles before returning home. I ate no supper that night, and got little sleep. For days afterward, I remained despondent, for I was so desperately in love with Mirdath, and my entire spirit, heart, and body ached with the sudden, dreadful loss.

For a long week I took my walks in another direction, but by the end of that time could not resist following the old way in hopes of catching a glimpse of her. In reward, I saw all a man ever needed to fill him with jealousy, for as I approached the gap, I found Mirdath walking beside the well-dressed man, his arm around her. Since she had neither brothers nor young, male relatives, I knew they were lovers. Yet the moment Mirdath saw me, she acted ashamed, for she shrugged off her companion's arm and curtsied to me, her face glowing crimson. Not knowing what to say, I bowed low and passed on.

"Andrew, wait!" Mirdath called behind me.

I turned only long enough to say, "There is nothing to wait for, nor any reason to ever pass this way again."

I did not linger for a response, but even as I turned back I saw the man put his arm around her once more. Perhaps they watched me as I departed, stiff and desperate, but I did not look back again.

For an interminable month thereafter, I avoided the gap, my love and hurt pride raging within me. However, pain shapes a man's character, and at the end of that time, thinking myself reconciled to the loss, I began taking my walks past the gap again. I never saw Mirdath, though one evening I thought she must be nearby, for one of her boar hounds bounded out of the woods and onto the road to nuzzle my hands. I waited a long time after the hound left, but caught no sight of her, and so continued on again, my heart heavy.

I threw myself into my studies and physical conditioning, and rode my black stallion around the county for hours. Like many young men of my station, I thought much of myself, and the idea of Mirdath rejecting my advances for such a slight man, regardless of his position, baffled and wounded me. I had yet to learn that living invariably cures vanity, and that no one passes through this world without undergoing humiliation.

Two weary, lonely weeks passed, and I grew sick with longing. By the end of that time I resolved to enter the grounds surrounding the Hall to try to catch sight of her. Having made my decision one evening, I went out immediately, and entering the gap, came by a circuitous route to the gardens around the Hall, which I found brightly lit with lanterns and torches, and filled with a throng of people eating and dancing at a costume ball. A sudden, horrid dread pierced my heart that this might be Lady Mirdath's marriage dance, but I soon dismissed the notion, for I would have heard the announcement of a wedding. Then I remembered this was her twenty-first birthday and the end of Sir Alfred's guardianship. In fact, I had received an invitation several weeks before, but had dismissed it as a polite gesture on Sir Alfred's part.

Had I not been so heartbroken, I would have enjoyed seeing that spectacle. The revelers danced on one end of the wide lawn opposite lines of bronze and silver lamps, and lanterns twinkled among the trees and leaf arbors, reflecting their starlight off the silver and crystal adorning a magnificent table spread with all kinds of food.

I caught my breath as Lady Mirdath stepped out of the dance, dressed in an exquisite, blue gown, her golden hair falling about her shoulders. Despite her beauty, to my eyes she seemed pale in the looming lights. No sooner did she take a seat than a dozen young men from the great families flocked eagerly around her. She looked exquisite in their midst, but somewhat pensive; her glance drifted away so often that I soon realized she must be looking for her absent lover. I could not imagine why he would desert her on such a night unless he had been called back to the court.

As I watched the young men fawning about her, I burned with a fierce, miserable jealousy. How I longed to step from concealment, to pick her up and carry her away, to take her to walk with me in the woods as in the former days, when she, too, seemed close to love. But what was the use? Clearly, it was not they who held her heart, but one small man of the court. So I stood and watched and did nothing until my misery drove me back to my house.

I avoided the gap for three miserable months after that, but by the end of that time, unable to bear not seeing her, I found myself standing before it one evening, at the spot where I had first, on a single night, both met Mirdath and lost my heart to her. Trembling with eagerness, I peered across the sward lying between the hedgerow and the woods. I stayed there a long time, waiting and watching hopelessly, until something soft brushed my thigh. My heart leapt when I discovered one of the boar hounds, for I knew, with agony and anticipation, that Mirdath was near.

As I waited, my heart pounding in my chest, I heard a low singing among the trees, faint and filled with sorrow, and knew Mirdath wandered alone in the dark with her dogs, murmuring a broken love song. Despite the way she had treated me, hearing her in such grief awoke my compassion. Though I yearned to comfort her, I did not dare move, but stood motionless in the gap, my soul in turmoil.

Presently, her slim white figure slipped from among the trees into the twilight. She came to an abrupt halt, and staring all around, gave a muffled sob. A sudden, unreasonable hope filled me, and leaving the gap, I rushed to her side, calling softly, with eager passion, "Mirdath! Mirdath!"

I came to her, while the hound, supposing it a game, bounded beside me. Without thinking, only craving to ease her pain, I held out my hands to her. She rushed into my embrace and remained there, weeping. When she finally fell silent, a sweet peace swept through me.

Suddenly, she relinquished her embrace, slipped her hands in mine, and raised her lips to me, so that all at once I knew she loved me.

That was the way of our betrothal, simple and wordless, yet adequate, except that love always gives more than mere adequacy.

She soon freed herself from my arms, and we walked home through the woods, holding hands like children. After a while I gathered my courage and asked her about the man of the court. She laughed sweetly, but refused to answer until we came to the Hall. When we arrived, she led me into the Greatroom, where another lady sat demurely embroidering, though her eyes betrayed a hint of delight at seeing me.

With an impudent curtsey, Mirdath said, "Sir Andrew, this is the Lady Alison."

"My pleasure," I said, bowing slightly, though the looks the two exchanged confused me.

Mirdath suddenly laughed so impishly she grew breathless, swaying a little with the effort, her cheeks red. "There is only one thing to be done," she cried, reaching above the fireplace to retrieve two pistols from their rack. "Andrew, you must challenge her to a duel to the death."

I stood in astonishment, while Alison kept her head down over her work, her frame, too, shaking with suppressed laughter.

"I don't understand," I said.

In answer, Alison looked full into my face, and I exclaimed in astonishment, for her features were those of the man of the court. I looked helplessly at Mirdath.

"Oh, Andrew, forgive me," Mirdath said, no longer laughing. "I have played a cruel joke not only on you, but on myself, and have paid a dear price. I have learned my lesson not to tease. Alison is my best and dearest friend. For a wager, she disguised herself to play a prank on a young man who wanted to marry her. When you happened along and treated her so forcibly, I lost my temper, forgetting you thought her a man."

"So that was it?" I asked. "My bullheaded jealousy?"

"And my foolishness," Mirdath said. "After that, we decided to punish you by fanning the flames, and met every evening at the gap to play at lovers, so you would see us. But when you appeared, I suddenly regretted our plan. I had not admitted, even to myself, my. . . feelings for you. Seeing the suffering on your face, I drew away from Alison, but when you bowed so coldly and refused my call, I grew angry and vowed to punish you even more. Oh, Andrew, forgive me!"

I laughed. "I refuse to. I intend to remain by your side day and night, haunting you for your devilry."

Filled with gratitude and mad delight, I took her into my arms, and we danced around the Greatroom while Lady Alison whistled a tune.

So all ended well, despite the stubbornness and inexperience of youth. Mirdath and I were never apart thereafter, but wandered together rejoicing in one another's company.

We were alike in a thousand ways, for we loved the splendor of gray evenings, the gathering darkness of dusk, the silent shining of starlight, the soft turning of the clouds by night, the faded colors of pastures in moonlight, the whisper of the sycamore to the beech, and the slow, somber rumbling of the sea. We listened to the thunder and watched the soft rains.

We were married in the spring. She looked radiant in her bridal gown, slender and lovely as Love itself—the curls of her hair, her wonderful eyes sober and sweet, her full lips, her mischievous smile, her slender hands, the grace of her every move—this is only a hint of my beloved's charms.

***

Mirdath, My Beautiful One, lay dying, and I had no power to hold back death's dread intent. In another room, I heard the thin wail of the child, and its crying woke my wife back into this life, so her pale hands fluttered desperately on the covers. I knelt beside her, taking her hands gently into my own, but still they moved helplessly, and she looked at me, unable to speak, her eyes pleading.

I left the room and called softly to the nurse, who brought the child, wrapped in a long, white robe. When Mirdath saw the baby, her eyes filled with a lovely light, but she still moved her hands weakly. I took the infant in my arms and the nurse stepped from the room. Sitting gently on the bed, I held the baby near Mirdath, so the tiny cheek touched the white cheek of my dying bride, though I kept the child's weight off her.

Presently, Mirdath tried to reach for the baby's hands, and I turned our daughter toward her and slipped the tiny fingers into the weak hands of my love. I held her above my wife with infinite care, so Mirdath's dying eyes looked into the eyes of the baby. In but a few moments, though it seemed in some ways an eternity, Mirdath closed her eyes and lay motionless. I gave our daughter to the nurse, who stood in the next room, then closed the door and returned to the bedside, so we could share those last seconds alone together. Mirdath groped along the covers, and I took her pale fingers into my own clumsy hands.

After a little while, her eyes opened, quiet and gray, but a little dazed. As she rolled her head on the pillow, the confusion left her expression and she looked at me clearly.

I bent close to her and her eyes begged me to take her into my arms for those final moments. I lay gently upon the bed and lifted her with all my care until she lay comfortably against my breast, for love gave me skill to hold her, even as it eased her pain in the short time remaining.

So we were together, and it seemed Love made a truce with Death around us, leaving us undisturbed, for a peace fell upon my heart for the first time after many weary hours of pain. I whispered my love to her, and her eyes answered. The strangely beautiful, terrible moments passed into the hush of eternity.

Suddenly, Mirdath whispered something. I leaned my head down to hear as she spoke again. "My Hercules. My circus strongman."

I tried again to tell her how much I loved her, how much I would always love her, but even as I spoke the light left her eyes, and My Beautiful One lay dead in my arms . . . My Beautiful One . . .

II
THE LAST REDOUBT

Since Mirdath died and left me alone in this world, I, who once cherished her sweet companionship, have suffered a longing such as words can never tell. I have tried to continue my studies, my riding, and my physical training, but it all seems empty now. Mostly, I spend my hours sitting beside the hedge gap where we first met, remembering our moments together.

In the last few months, however, a miraculous event has given me hope, for in my dreams I have been transported into the future of this world, where I have witnessed strange and marvelous sights, and known once more the joy of living. Though I do not know if anyone will ever read it, I must write the story down, if only to ease my yearning for my beloved. If anyone does read my account, they will certainly disbelieve it. I scarcely believe it myself, and sometimes think grief has robbed me of my sanity. But if you read with an open mind, putting aside your doubts, you will gaze with me into the very portals of eternity.

From the time the dreams began, they continued night after night, always opening exactly where they ended the night before. They did not seem like dreams to me, but rather as if I woke in the far future. A gray mist always obscured my vision when I first arrived, but it soon faded, leaving me in a land of darkness lit here and there with miraculous sights; for the sun had died and everlasting night lapped the world.

From the moment I entered the dream, I possessed a complete set of memories of the Night Land, as if I had lived there all my life. In my earliest vision I found myself an adventurous, if hesitant, sixteen-year-old named Andros, standing at one of the windows of the Last Redoubt, high up in a four-sided pyramid of gray metal forged to protect the last millions of the world from the Forces besieging them, a structure rising to a height of almost eight miles and holding one thousand three hundred and twenty floors, each containing a city. I do not know its location, except that it lay in a tremendous valley.

I stood upon the One Thousandth Plateau, looking through an odd spyglass to the northwest, studying the hideous, but completely familiar landscape I had observed all my life. The window, made of a transparent substance much thicker and more durable than stained glass, rested in a recess the inhabitants called an embrasure. Thousands of embrasures covered the shining gray metal walls. The spyglass was a rectangular box that gave off a slight hum, set upon a pole with not one, but two lenses, one for each eye. Thin points of golden light burned within it, and its range could be adjusted by a thin lever.

In my right hand I held a copy of *Ayleos' Mathematics*, a book with a yellow metal cover, for as Andros I had always loved the art of numbers, particularly geometry. There is such certainty in mathematics; the world may change, but a seven is always a seven, and when added to two invariably makes nine. As a child I assigned personalities to the first ten numerals: 1 was strong, 2 friendly, 3 wicked, 6 funny, and so on. I even devised rules to explain how their personalities produced the correct answers in addition, subtraction, multiplication, and division. To me, working with numbers was glorious sport, particularly the number seven, who I considered a good friend. Any time I was presented with a difficult decision, I could escape to mathematics for a pleasant hour. Often, after doing so, I would return to my troubles and immediately see the solution. But perhaps an interest in geometry is not surprising for one raised in a pyramid.

Because of my mathematical propensity, as I stared through the spyglass I could recite the name and distance of every object in sight, as calculated from the pyramid's *Center Point*—a mysterious strip of polished metal rumored to have neither measurable length nor breadth, installed within the Room of Mathematics where I carried on my daily studies.

In the wide field of my glass, my eyes first fell upon the bright glare of the fire from the Red Pit shining upward against the underside of the vast chin of the Northwest Watcher—The Watching Thing of the Northwest: *That which hath Watched from the Beginning until the opening of the Gateway of Eternity.* So Aesworth, the ancient poet had written.

To my amazement I suddenly realized the bard was incorrect, for deep within my soul I saw, as dreams are seen, the sunlit splendor of the past. Thus, even as I, Andrew, dreamed of the future, the youth in the embrasure remembered his former existence, though it seemed to him a vision old as the dawn of the world. I looked back upon my life as Andrew Eddins as if seeing dreams my soul knew as true, but which appeared as a far vision, hallowed with peace and light. Since I had often demonstrated a knowledge of antiquity that perplexed the men of learning of that age, I cannot claim to have been completely unaware of the past before then, but from that moment my memory of the lost eons grew tenfold.

The knowledge struck me with such force that I groaned and fell to my knees, overcome by the power of the revelation. I knelt there, stunned by all I knew and guessed and felt, overwhelmed most of all by the memory of Mirdath. As I recalled the way she had sung to me in the days of sunlight, my longing for her reached across the ages, and for the first time I understood the emptiness that had haunted me even from my childhood.

"Are you ill, Andros?" a voice asked.

I looked up to see the ancient, friendly face of Cartesius, my mentor and friend, who had taken me under his protection after my parents died six years before.

"Why are you up so late?" I asked, avoiding his question as he helped me back to my feet. "It's past the fifth hour of sleep."

"I can sleep later. A waste of time, sleep. I haven't slept in . . ." he blinked in thought, "forty-two hours. There is too much to do. The Thing That Nods has changed the angle of its movement by point three degrees. We can see a fraction more of its face, if it is a face at all; the scholars are in furious debate about it. The whole tower is astir with excitement. According to the Records, such an event last happened four thousand seven hundred and twenty-six years ago, when Olin was Master."

"After all these centuries? How extraordinary."

"Precipitous times, indeed. Who knows the ramifications?" He smiled happily, his eyes lost in distant horizons, and then, remembering himself, made his expression stern. "It is extremely serious, of course. We are gauging the rest of the land, to see if any reactions arise. So far, we show a twelve percent increase in movement around the Giants'

Kilns, but nothing more. We are watching the points of the compass steadily, though I just sent most of my assistants to bed—for some, exhaustion overcomes passion. A pity they lack fortitude."

He paused, his eyes suddenly focusing on me. "But you were distressed when I first approached, and now you are trying to divert me. What is it, Andros? How can I help?"

I sighed. "It's hard to explain. I've . . . seen something."

"Something unusual, by your demeanor. A vision?"

"I think so."

"Tell me all about it. Leave out no detail, no matter how small. We shall find the significance in the insignificant."

I smiled at his old turn of phrase. A brilliant man, Cartesius served as the Master Monstruwacan within the Tower of Observation located at the pinnacle of the pyramid, where he and his fellow Monstruwacans observed everything that occurred within the land, peering into the darkness to extend their knowledge, always seeking new information despite being thwarted by distance—the plain of the Night Land remaining always beyond their reach. Their main duty was to watch, measure, and record the movements of the monsters and beasts besieging the Great Pyramid, so that should one merely sway its head in the darkness, every detail was noted. The name Monstruwacan itself, in the language of the people of the pyramid, literally meant *Scholar of Monsters*.

Though snow-haired with antiquity, Cartesius stood straight and unbowed, his dark eyes shining. He wore a perpetual stare, as if peering through the Great Spyglass had fixed his expression.

He had noticed me in my youth, for I possessed that rare talent my people call the Night Hearing, a gift so uncommon that out of all the pyramid's millions, only I showed any degree of skill in its use. I could detect, with better accuracy than the recording Instruments, the invisible vibrations pulsing continually through the eternal darkness of the ether.

"I have seen the past," I finally said.

His hoary eyes grew bright; he gave a happy smile. "Tell me."

The words tumbled from me as I related everything I knew about the lives of Mirdath and Andrew. As I spoke, I expected Cartesius to reprove me, for I mentioned grass and trees, oceans and wind, and most of all, the glorious, golden sun—things the people of the pyramid considered only myths—but he kept a respectful silence.

It took more than an hour to tell it all, and when I finished, my voice choking with emotion, tears glistened not only in my eyes, but in his as well. "Is it all a fantasy?" I asked. "A delusion?"

The Master Monstruwacan sat upon a gray stone bench, his hand upon his bearded chin, his eyes lost in the fantastic world I had described. He cleared his throat. "You have certainly experienced something. Nor do I think an Evil Influence has affected your mind. How extraordinary if it is true! And how sad."

I gave a sigh of relief. Even though, through experiments and the refinement of mental arts, the people of the pyramid spoke comfortably of concepts beyond our present understanding, as we of this day hold beliefs our forefathers would have considered lunacy, still I feared my story too bizarre to be taken seriously.

"This strange gift you have, Andros," Cartesius said, "you have always known many things about the ancient Days of Light. How I have laughed to see you confound and anger our scholars. How they long to believe you, even when they cannot accept your stories."

"But this—" I said. "It seems inconceivable! Can a man live again?"

"I do not know. I have never heard of such a thing, but life is filled with unusual and wonderful events. I am perpetually astounded that we exist at all. How can I say something is impossible simply because it has never happened before? Every action must have originally occurred for the first time. I therefore grant that though your experience is unlikely, it is within the realm of the possible. I believe you."

"Thank you." My voice almost broke in gratitude.

"You need time to understand the revelation. Once you absorb it, you must record everything—the tiniest bit, the merest speck. You must draw the shape of every leaf, show the precise color of the sky—a thousand things. Fear nothing and tell all! That is the way of the observer. Then I will set the Monstruwacans scouring the ancient histories —a man could spend a lifetime studying all you have just told me. If only I were young! It makes me long to leap to the annals, to brush the dust away, to blow back the debris and look for correlation." A fire rose in his eyes. "This is even more important than the movement of The Thing That Nods! I must go to the Hall of Records at once. There is one volume, yes, I see it clearly in my mind. I will rouse all the Monstruwacans from bed—they've had at least an hour's sleep; it should be sufficient. We must discuss this. We must correlate. We . . . must . . . correlate!"

He leapt to his feet, eager as a hound, and sped a dozen steps before abruptly turning.

"Forgive me, Andros. I forget the human in the hunt for the unknown. Will you be well, my boy? I can stay if you like."

I managed a smile. "I just need time to think."

His eyes focused gravely upon me; I felt him studying me with the meticulous scrutiny usually reserved for his work.

"Yes," he finally said. "You do need time. You must weep and laugh, grow angry and mourn, to prevent the vision from overwhelming you. But you will prevail, Andros. I see it. You *will* prevail. Come to the Tower of Observation if you need me."

As he vanished from sight, the thought struck me that I would not be the one to correlate my story with the Records. I did not need to; I had seen the past and knew the truth, but I loved my wise, old friend for believing me. Then the revelation overcame me again, and I sat and wept, clutching my copy of *Ayleos' Mathematics*, consumed by my memories of Mirdath.

***

After a time, when I could no longer bear contemplating my former life, I turned from the haze and pain of my memories back to the embrasure and the inconceivable enigma of the Night Land, for none of the inhabitants of the citadel ever wearied of looking upon its dreadful mysteries. The old and young, from infancy to death, watched the black monstrosities of that fearsome country, which only our Great Pyramid, the last refuge of humanity, held at bay. But now I saw the familiar things with new eyes, from the perspective of that ancient gentleman, Andrew Eddins, and it shook me to my core to see my impressions of the world so altered. For the first time, it seemed overwhelming to think of an entire planet bereft of light, spinning through the unending darkness of a starless sky, the only illumination the unearthly fires dotting the landscape.

Nearly overcome by this new-found sense of horror, I looked again at the Red Pit and the Northwest Watcher. Slightly more than fifty-three miles separated the pyramid from the Watcher. The creature could be seen from such a distance both because of the height of the redoubt, and the Watcher's enormity, for it stood twenty-six hundred and seventeen feet tall—almost half a mile. Its form was so cragged it might have been mistaken for a mountain if not for its brooding mouth and hollow-eyed, unswerving stare. It possessed neither arms nor legs, and its whole body cascaded downward from its head in irregular terraces. The long, sinuous glare known as the Vale Of Red Fire, a valley of flames, lay to the Watcher's right, and beyond the creature's bulk stretched the dreary, shrouded leagues of the Unknown Lands, across which shone the cold light from the Plain of Blue Fire.

On the very borders of the Unknown Lands, there ran a range of low volcanoes, which lit up, far away in the outer darkness, the Black Hills. The Seven Lights shone there, which neither twinkled nor faltered through eternity, and which even the Great Spyglass could not see clearly, since they stood over one hundred and sixty miles away. Neither had any adventurer ever returned to tell of them; if he had, a record would have existed within the Great Library, which held the histories of all who ever risked not only their lives, but their spirits, by venturing outside the pyramid, for the accounts of the Last Redoubt did not deal with mere thousands of years, but with millions, dating back to what we called the mythical Early Days, when the sun still gloomed dully in the twilight sky. Of all that occurred before that, only legends remained.

As I read over what I have just written, I nearly despair, for in trying to describe the world I have seen, it seems I have set for myself an impossible task: to portray a land of such vast proportions, such darkness, and such looming, hideous evil. I seek to describe the indescribable. My descriptions fail; my pen falters. Yet I must make the effort, if only for my own sake.

To my right, to the north, the House of Silence stood upon a low hill about seventy-five miles away. Many lights gleamed within it, but no sound ever came from it. It had remained unchanged through uncountable epochs—always the unwavering lanterns shining from beneath its sloping eaves and twisted windows, but never a whisper our listening devices could detect. Our people considered this House the greatest peril in all the Night Land. From my earliest childhood, perhaps because of my Night Hearing, I feared it more than any other aspect of that terrible country, for I often thought I felt the evil seeping from it, reaching toward the pyramid. It was as if some fate awaited me concerning it, and a violent trembling would seize my entire body if I stared too long into the beckoning blackness of its enormous, arched doorway.

Beside the House of Silence wound the gray, shimmering Road Where The Silent Ones Walk. We knew almost nothing about the Road, which passed around the eastern and southern sides of the pyramid before finally vanishing in the west. Many scholars believed that, of all the structures surrounding the pyramid, only it had been built by human hands. And on this point alone a thousand books have been written, all contradicting one another, as is the way of such things. It was the same with every other monstrous creature—whole libraries had been penned on every aspect of the Night Land, and millions of such volumes had molded, forgotten, into dust.

I stepped out of the embrasure. Because of the lateness of the hour, the wide corridor in which I stood, banding the One Thousandth Plateau, lay deserted save for a watchman riding the moving road spanning the width of the passage. Seeing this familiar scene from Andrew's perspective, I hesitated, for I could not help but wonder what he would think of it all, especially the traveling roads we called *migrators*, which ran around the outer edge of each of the plateaus. The One Thousandth Plateau stood six miles and thirty fathoms above the plain of the Night Land, and stretched more than a mile across. Numerous doors and passages lined the corridor's inner wall, and though most of the pyramid was made of shining gray metal, throughout the ages artists had painted colorful scenes along the passage, so that as I stepped onto the migrator, I rolled past brilliant depictions from the history of the One Thousandth City, and portrayals of battles with the monsters of the Night Land. The ceiling, which hung twenty-six feet above me, had always provided ample space before, but now, remembering the blue dome of the ancient sky, I felt confined.

In a few minutes, I stepped off the migrator at the northeastern wall, where I gazed through another spyglass at the

Watcher of the Northeast—called the Crowned Watcher because a blue, luminous ring hung in the air above its vast head, shedding a strange glow downward over the monster's dreadful folds. The light revealed its enormous, wrinkled brow, but left all the lower face in shadow, save the ear, which belled out from the back of the head toward the redoubt. Past observers claimed to have seen it quiver, though no living person had ever witnessed it. The night hid its body, but ancient travelers' accounts claimed it stood like an enormous idol, its shoulders tapering down in a severe angle, its distorted hands hanging to its sides, its lower body a shapeless mound of darkness.

Beyond the Northeast Watcher, close by the Road Where The Silent Ones Walk, lay the region called The Place Where The Silent Ones Are Not, so named because the Silent Ones were never seen there. The Giants' Sea bounded the Road upon the far side, and beyond the sea ran another, smaller road called The Road By The Quiet City, which passed beside the unwinking, haunted lights of a deserted metropolis. We had never, in hundreds of thousands of years of watching, ever spied signs of life along its empty avenues, nor had even one of its lights ever faltered throughout that time. Its towers and domes rose, row upon row, into the sky, strange sculptures dotted its high roofs, and sweeping stairs wound between the buildings, as if it had once been home to a noble race.

Close beside the lights of The Quiet City lay the impenetrable void of The Valley Of The Hounds, home of the monstrous Night Hounds. Beyond that, obscuring all the east, hung a tangible, absolute darkness we called The Black Mist.

As I rolled on the migrator through the quiet Hours of Sleep, making a circuit to see each section of the Night Land, I heard a far, dreadful sound down in the lightless east, and, presently, again—a cackling laughter, deep as low thunder among the mountains. Because this came at random intervals from the Unknown Lands beyond the Valley Of The Hounds, we named that distant, unseen region The Country Of The Great Laughter. Despite having heard it many times, it always made me uneasy, a constant reminder, even in the redoubt's depths, of the horrors assailing earth's last millions.

Again, I was struck by the contrast between my life and my vision of the world before the sun failed. How strange a man Andrew Eddins seemed to me, who could, on whim, ride a horse through forests and glades! How different and yet how similar the two of us were, he with his interest in nature studies, I with my fascination for mathematics, he loving an outdoors I had never seen. I knew my environment had made me more thoughtful than he; I lacked his quick temper but shared his impulsive nature. He seemed the strangest of creatures, a great hulk of a man compared to the size of my people, so alien as to be almost beyond my understanding, and yet, at the same time, a part of myself.

Stepping off the migrator, I gazed at the translucent cover of one of the pyramid's millions of interior lights. Though I understood the simple principle that powered it, the part that was Andrew, who lived in a world of torches and candles, looked upon it with awe.

I sat down on a bench, overcome once more, thinking of that whole lost world. How unfair it seemed for my people to suffer imprisonment when humanity had once roamed the whole world. I put my hands over my eyes, as if to blot out the vision, but in the darkness I saw only a tall, gray-eyed lady, wearing unfamiliar garments.

After all these ages, where are you? The thought came unbidden, and I looked up, suddenly struck by the notion that if I had returned to life, perhaps Mirdath might do so as well. The idea filled me with excitement, but dismayed me too, for if she lived among the millions of people in the pyramid, I did not know how I would ever find her. Undoubtedly, she would look completely different, even as I, Andros, looked different from Andrew.

The Laughter sounded again, rousing me from my reverie. As it died away into the eastern darkness, I rose and looked through the spyglass, knowing Andrew's memories would alter my perspective. I focused on the crater of the Giants' Pit, lying south of the Giants' Kilns. Titans tended these Kilns, enormous, bulging cylinders casting a red, sporadic light. The illumination threw wavering shadows across the mouth of the Pit, and the giants could be indistinctly seen crawling along its rim, performing unfathomable tasks. We neither knew what they did to the Kilns, nor why they did it, and this was but another of the mysteries of the Night Land.

To the back of the Giants' Pit, between it and the Valley Of The Hounds stood a vast, black Headland. The light of the Kilns struck the brow of the formation, revealing forms constantly approaching the illumination, looking over the edge, and swiftly returning to the shadows. Throughout our recorded history, never had an hour passed without at least one of the creatures emerging. Because of this, we marked the region on our maps as The Headland From Which Strange Things Peer.

I could write for hours about all the examinations, observations, and speculations spent on the Headland alone. The Monstruwacans possessed thousands of images comparing the creatures who came to peer, and still no one could say what they were, or how many. For a brief period of time in my childhood, Cartesius thought he had positive proof that they were all actually a single being, returning again and again. It is impossible for me to convey how much excitement the discovery caused throughout the pyramid, or the wild theories that arose from it, but in the end, the information proved contradictory, and the Monstruwacans were forced to admit they knew no more than before.

Far closer than the Headland, running straight before me, was The Road Where The Silent Ones Walk. As I had done countless times before, I searched it with the spyglass, for the sight of its sojourners always stirred my heart.

Soon, alone in all the miles of that night-gray road, I saw a quiet, cloaked figure. As was the way of those beings, it was shrouded, and looked neither to right nor left. Legends said the Silent Ones would not harm a human, so long as one kept a fair distance from them, but I could not help but shudder as I watched him leave that part of the Road lit by the light from the Three Silver Fire Holes and pass into the shadows.

Far beyond the Fire Holes fluttered The Thing That Nods. I gaped at it a time; it had indeed turned a fraction more of its face toward the pyramid, and though its features remained indecipherable, I looked upon it in fascination. No one knew what it was, or why it moved; like so much of the Night Land it remained a dark and unfathomable enigma.

To the right of The Thing That Nods, but nearer, rose the vast bulk of the Southeast Watcher—the Watching Thing of the Southeast. Though the fires called The Torches, burning to either side of the squat monster, were

easily a half mile away from it, they cast enough light to illuminate the beetled head of the unsleeping brute. Its body
hung behind it in a mound resembling the distorted form
of a frog. It seemed to rest its weight on its deformed,
splayed front legs. Regardless of how many times I had
seen it, it always brought a shudder to my soul, and I soon
looked away, following the Road as it swept farther on to
where it wound close by the Dark Palace, and then farther
on, passing around beyond the mountainous bulk of The
Watcher Of The South—the greatest monster in all the visible Night Lands. My spyglass showed it clearly: a living
hill of watchfulness, brooding squat and tremendous,
hunched over the pale radiance of the Glowing Dome, its
mouth gaping open, its eyes staring vacantly ahead.

Much had been written concerning that odd, vast Watcher, for it had come out of the blackness of the Unknown
Lands of the south a million years before and had drawn
steadily closer through twenty thousands years, but so
slowly no one could perceive its movements in a single
year. Yet it did move, and the Monstruwacans had recorded every foot of its progress.

After it had come quite far on its journey to the Last Redoubt, a Glowing Dome had arisen out of the ground before it, halting its advance, and from that time on, through
countless ages, the Watcher had stared over the pale glare
of the Dome toward the pyramid.

Because of the rising of the Dome, many scholars wrote
essays suggesting that even as the Forces of Evil were un-
leashed upon the last age of mankind, so other Powers of
Good, incomprehensible to the human mind, arrayed themselves to battle the terrors. But the Glowing Dome was not
the only evidence of such Powers, as I will later relate.

Of the coming of the monstrosities, we knew little, for
the evil began before the histories of the Great Pyramid
were written, before the sun had even completely faded.
We believed the trouble arose in the legendary Days of the
Darkening, when ancient science disturbed powers beyond
the earthly plane, allowing the monsters and Ab-humans to
pass an unseen barrier previously protecting mankind.
Grotesque and horrible creatures materialized to assault
humanity, while those entities lacking the power to assume
physical form grew into Forces capable of influencing and
destroying the human spirit. As civilization degenerated
into lawlessness, the surviving millions banded together in

the twilight of the world to build the Last Redoubt.

Later, through hundreds of thousands of years, mighty races of dreadful creatures, half man and half beast, appeared. They warred against the pyramid, but were driven back time and again, with much slaughter on both sides. After many such attacks, the people tapped the energy flowing through the earth and erected a circle of power around the redoubt. Then, after sealing the lowest half-mile of the pyramid, they found peace in what was the beginning of an eternity of quiet waiting for the time when the Earth Current would fail.

Through the centuries, the creatures glutted themselves upon any who dared to venture outside the sanctuary to explore the Night Land. Of those who went, few returned, for eyes peered through the darkness, and Forces of Evil moved upon the face of the earth, keeping vigil with senses superior to those of humankind.

As the eternal night lengthened across the world, the power of the evil ones grew, and new and greater monsters developed, bred out of space and other dimensions, attracted like infernal sharks by that lonely hill of humanity. Giants arose, fathered by bestial humans and mothered by monsters, and various other creatures appeared, bearing human semblance and cunning, so that some of the lesser brutes possessed machinery and underground chambers for warmth and air.

I listened to the sorrowful roar rising continuously over the Gray Dunes from the Country Of Wailing, which lay midway between the pyramid and the Watcher Of The South, then I took the migrator toward the southwest side. As I rode the traveling roadway, I watched the panorama of the Night Land, a landscape vast as a nation, through the passing windows.

Leaving the migrator, I looked from a narrow embrasure far down into the Deep Valley, four miles to the bottom, where boiled the Pit Of The Red Smoke. The mouth of this pit extended one full mile across, and the smoke filled the Deep Valley at times, making it appear as a glowing red circle amid dull, ocher clouds. Since the smoke never rose much above the valley, it left a clear view across to the country beyond. There, along the farther edge of the Valley, the gray, quiet Towers, each nearly a mile high, shimmered wickedly.

Beyond these, to the southwest, loomed the enormous

bulk of the Southwest Watcher, a creature shaped much like a gargoyle with shoulders held high as if in a perpetual shrug. The Eye Beam projected from the ground before it —a single ray of gray light shining on the monster's right eye. Because of the illumination, that eye had been scrutinized through thousands of years. Some believed it looked steadily through the light at the pyramid. Others, thinking the ray the work of the Powers of Good, argued that it blinded the Watcher, preventing it from seeing the redoubt clearly. Whatever the case, as I watched through the spyglass, it seemed the brute stared, unwinking, as if fully aware I spied upon it.

I have told of the five great Watchers surrounding the redoubt: the Watchers of the Northwest, Northeast, Southwest, Southeast, and South, each keeping silent, immovable guard upon the pyramid. Despite their motionlessness, we knew them as mountains of living vigilance, filled with hideous, steadfast intelligence, ever ready to destroy us should our defenses fail.

To the northwest of the Southwest Watcher, extending an unknown distance, lay a region called The Place Where The Silent Ones Kill, so named because ten thousand years before a group of adventuring humans left the Road Where The Silent Ones Walk and were immediately destroyed. Only one survived to tell the tale, though he died soon after, his heart frozen. Our scholars could never explain this strange account, but it was written in the Records along with the testimonies of those who examined the body.

In the very mouth of the western night, far beyond The Place Where The Silent Ones Kill, glistened the Place Of The Ab-humans, where the Road Where The Silent Ones Walk was lost in a dull green, luminous mist. We knew nothing of that region, though it stirred the imaginations of our greatest thinkers. Some believed it to be a place of sanctuary, differing from the Last Redoubt as we of this day suppose heaven to differ from earth. Those who held that view thought the Road might lead there, if only the Ab-humans did not block the way.

Finally, my observations came full circle, back to the Red Pit and the Northwest Watcher. Between all the Watchers, the monsters, the flames, and the terrors, countless fire-holes pocked the surface of the Night Land. From where I stood, they appeared as pin-points of light across the dark plain. As a boy I had often tried to count them, but they were too numerous.

***

I have described something of that land, and of the be-sieging Watchers and terrors that waited for the hour when the failure of the Earth Current would leave us defenseless. I stood, quietly gazing, lost in wonder both at my own dark world, and at the forgotten days of sunlight. Sometimes I glanced upward to the gray, metal mountain rising mea-sureless into the gloom of the everlasting night, or down-ward to the sheer sweep of the grim, metal walls, more than six full miles to the plain below. All around the base of the pyramid, which was five and a quarter miles each way, ran the great circle of light generated by the Earth Current, bounding the edifice for a mile on every side and having the appearance of a transparent tube. This, we re-ferred to simply as The Circle. None of the monsters could cross it, because it created what we called the Ether Bar-rier, an invisible wall of safety. The vibrations from the Barrier disrupted the minds of the monsters and lower man-brutes, and created resonances to protect us against the Forces capable of attacking our souls. A Force of Evil could only penetrate the pyramid if an inhabitant dabbled in matters that left him open to its dreadful influence.

I could never look at The Circle without thinking of my parents, who had helped maintain the pyramid's mech-anisms. They and their fellow workers had been required to perform a full survey of The Circle once every six months. A young member of the team, either through fool-ishness or carelessness, stepped across the Barrier and was attacked by a monster. When my mother and father rushed to his aid, the beast killed all three. I was ten years old at the time, and saw the entire episode through a small spy-glass.

As I stood thinking of my parents and Mirdath, I real-ized that in both instances death had stolen my loved ones while I helplessly watched. Leaning against the embrasure, overtaken by the losses of two lifetimes, I stared out into the night.

III
THE QUIET CALLING

Upon turning seventeen, every child in the Great Pyramid is required to spend three years and two hundred, twenty-five days traveling from floor to floor through all the cities of the redoubt, spending one twenty-four hour period in each. I greatly enjoyed this journey and met many I might have learned to love, if there had only been time. Most I never saw again, for though the whole population traveled up and down the pyramid with an almost obsessive passion, there were so many millions and so few years. During my sojourn, I continuously watched for someone who might be Mirdath reborn, but as time passed I grew discouraged, for it seemed to me our souls would be drawn to one another if she were in the redoubt.

As I journeyed, I heard a rumor of another remnant of the human race living in a second refuge located somewhere in the night. As was often the case, though its existence was confirmed by hundreds of ancient works stored in libraries scattered throughout the cities, those scholars who bothered to read the Records remained skeptical, but from the moment I heard the tale of a second refuge, I thought it must be true. Having discovered no sign of Mirdath in my own pyramid, I believed she must be elsewhere, perhaps in that other, hidden sanctuary. I found myself constantly listening for her with my Night Hearing. Though I had not heard her voice for an eternity, it sang sweet and clear in my memory, as if she slept within my soul, whispering to me out of the eons.

When I came of age at twenty-one, my journey through the cities ended, and like many young men, I did not know what I wanted to do with my life. I considered becoming an instructor in mathematics, but I preferred applying my knowledge rather than teaching it to others, and was therefore overjoyed when, because of my gift of the Night Hearing, Cartesius offered me a post within the Tower of Observation. Such an appointment was the most coveted in all the pyramid, and I arrived at the tower grinning with pride, my yellow copy of *Ayleos' Mathematics* tucked under my arm.

As Cartesius's ward, I had been to the Tower of Observation often, but had never lost my sense of awe. It stood at the pinnacle of the redoubt, overlooking the Night Land from a height of nearly eight miles, two miles higher than that of my native city of Ogygia at the One Thousandth Plateau. Although the tower was less than a hundred yards in any direction, its embrasures covered the entire surface of the walls, giving one the impression of floating high above the plain of the Night Land. The Instruments clustered in the center of the chamber, a mass of crystals, pulsing lights, and controls. In many ways, the Tower of Observation was like the bridge of a warship, for the Master Monstruwacan had many forces at his disposal. The Instruments were as old as the pyramid itself, though some had become neglected and fallen into disrepair.

The most important Instrument of all was the Great Spyglass, an apparatus that took up as much space as the rest of the equipment combined. It bore little resemblance to the spyglasses of the nineteenth century, its main mechanism being a multi-faceted stone, pure as the clearest diamond, filled with shimmering light. Connected to this gem were hundreds of tubes running up to the ceiling and back down again beside the embrasures. The tubes, each of which contained a pair of eye slits, normally rested about seven feet off the floor. Whenever a Monstruwacan needed to look through the Great Spyglass, he simply seized one of the tubes and pulled it down to the proper level.

A low, pleasant hum constantly filled the tower and the air tingled with a slight electrical tinge. Monstruwacans shuffled back and forth, studying various portions of the Night Land, bending over their Instruments or hovering over one of the many breathing bells scattered across the chamber. Despite the air being pumped throughout the pyramid, the atmosphere in the tower sometimes grew rare, making the breathing bells a necessity, and clouds billowed from them with a soft, continuous hissing. I adored working there, where I could see the Night Land through the clearest eyes in the world.

***

If I had debated the scholars before my awakening, I did so even more afterward. I often sat half a day telling tales that sounded like fables, entrancing their hearts while angering their intellects. But Cartesius listened to anything I had to relate. Sometimes, after speaking for hours in the Tower of Observation, I glanced up and found all the Monstruwacans gathered round, their observations and recordings forgotten, their Master too enthralled to notice their negligence. When Cartesius finally roused himself, he would scold his assistants, scattering them, bewildered and thoughtful, back to their work, but they were always eager for more. The scholars outside the Tower of Observation were the same; though they scoffed and argued, they would have listened to me from the first hour, the start of what we still called the *day*, to the fifteenth, the beginning of the Hours of Sleep. Occasionally, I found some who believed my tales, and a faction eventually rose up that later became more numerous, but regardless of whether they believed or not, everyone loved to hear, and I could have spent all my time telling stories.

Because of this, I became famous among the millions of inhabitants, for the people passed my tales down through the cities, even to the farms at the lowest tiers of the Underground Fields lying a hundred miles below the redoubt. There, supervisors and workers alike gathered eagerly around me whenever the Master Monstruwacan and I descended on business concerning the Instruments and the Earth Current.

***

I had worked in the tower less than a year and was at my post at the fifteenth hour, pondering my lost love and my memories of the past. As a young man might, I had fallen so deeply into my meditations I almost fancied hearing my Beautiful One whispering in my ear. As I stood gazing out at the Night Land, communing with my own thoughts, there arose a real whisper, beating on my Night Hearing.

I staggered as one struck. Through five long years, since my awakening in the embrasure at sixteen, I had listened. Now, out of the everlasting darkness, through all the eternal years of my lost life, the call came. I knew it instantly, but because of my rigorous training, did not reply using my name, but sent the Master Word through the night, projecting my thoughts in the manner taught to every inhabitant of the pyramid. If my caller were human, she would be able to hear and respond, but if this were a false message intended to deceive my soul, sent by cunning monsters, Evil Forces—or as was often suspected—by the House of Silence, the creatures would be unable to repeat the Master Word. I do not know why this was so, except that we considered the Master Word holy, possessed of a power proven through all the everlasting ages. Even now, in my journal, I will not dare to reveal the sacred Word.

As I stood trembling, trying to control those emotions that destroy mental reception, the throb of the Master Word swirled around and around my spiritual essence, beating steadily in the night. Though I had no evidence that this might be my lost love, I replied with all my will, *Mirdath! Mirdath!*

At that moment, the Master Monstruwacan approached me. "Andros, the Instruments have detected the faint pulsing of the Master Word. Did you—" Seeing the intensity of my expression, he fell silent.

I listened with my spirit a long while before returning his gaze.

"What is it?" he demanded.

"A voice from the darkness."

"Do you still hear it?"

"No. Only a sense of faint, happy laughter."

***

According to the law of the Pyramid no one can enter the Night Land before the age of twenty-two, when—if a person wishes to make the journey—he receives three lectures upon the methods of survival, the use of weapons, and the dangers, including a strict account of the mutilations and atrocities done to other adventurers. If the candidate is judged sane and still wants to go, the people consider it an honor for him to add to the knowledge of the Great Pyramid by making the journey. A small capsule containing a fast-acting poison is inserted beneath the skin of the traveler's inside left forearm, so that, should he become entrapped by a Force of Evil, he can save his spirit from destruction by biting the capsule and taking his own life.

From the moment I heard the voice, I began planning such a journey. Everywhere I went, I listened for that quiet calling. Twice, I sent the Master Word throbbing solemnly through the everlasting darkness, though I dared not do so any more than that without further information, for we did not use the Word lightly. However, I often projected my thoughts outward, crying Mirdath's name. Sometimes I thought I heard a feeble thrilling of the ether, a whisper so faint even my Night Hearing could not catch its meaning, either sent by one with a weakened spirit or by an Instrument powered by insufficient Earth Current. This continued for many days, leaving me anxious from constant listening.

One day, as I stood by the Instruments in the Tower of Observation, the ether stirred around me. I instantly made the Sign for Silence, and the Monstruwacans throughout the tower emptied their minds of all thoughts, bowed over their breathing bells, and stood motionless.

The gentle thrilling returned, breaking into a clear, low message. *Andrew!*

Hearing my ancient name shook my soul, leaving me trembling with excitement. I replied with the Master Word, sending the ether rippling with the force of my response. A long silence ensued.

Finally, I discerned a calling so faint even the Instruments could not have detected it, followed by the heavy, throbbing reply of the Master Word. I hurried to the Instruments and used them to accentuate my own powers of thought. *Mirdath.*

Andrew, the night replied. I could scarcely breathe. To steady my emotions, I took deep swallows of air from a breathing bell. As soon as I had composed myself, I remembered those about me—and with the link fully established—signaled the Monstruwacans to return to their duties so the Records would not lapse.

Beside me stood the Master Monstruwacan, quiet as any apprentice, waiting with slips to make notes, keeping a strict eye upon his assistants to prevent anyone from disturbing my concentration. For a precious hour, I spoke with that woman out in the darkness of the world, who knew my name from ages past.

Are you really Mirdath? I sent into the night.

A brief silence followed, as if she collected her thoughts, but her reply nearly broke my heart. *My true name is Naani.*

For an instant I could not think of a reply. *But you called me Andrew!* I finally protested.

As a child I read a book that is very dear to me, the story of two lovers, Mirdath and Andrew. When I first

*called and you replied with her name, I thought it might
be some sort of test, and answered like the woman in the
book.*

For a moment, a haze of sorrow blinded me; all my
hopes were dashed and my ancient love forever lost. Yet, I
was puzzled as well. Although all the history of love is
written by one pen, it seemed an enormous coincidence
that Naani's book should mention Mirdath and Andrew,
names unfamiliar to that age. More than that, amid my
pain, Naani renewed my hope, for she replied, almost wistfully, *Somehow, I thought your voice would be deeper.*

Why would you expect it to be?

I sensed bewilderment from her. *I don't know. I wonder
now why I said it.*

*Perhaps the man in the book was described as having a
deep voice.*

I don't think so, she said. *It was a foolish comment, for
which I ask your pardon.*

I did not reply at once, but my hopes were raised, for in
the ancient days I possessed an extremely low voice. Further questioning only confused her more, and I soon let the
matter rest.

Although it shows how much my soul longed for my
lost love, it was strange for us to talk about so trivial a subject when our communication represented the breaking of
as much as a million years of silence. Already, the news
was being relayed from city to city throughout the pyramid
by way of the Hour Slips, a sort of paperless printing press
with the daily tidings appearing on enormous crystals scattered throughout the cities. My contact with Naani filled
the accounts, with every inhabitant anxious to learn more.
The authorities had suppressed the news of her first brief
message, dismissing it as the delusion of an imaginative
young man—no doubt my tales of the sunlit days made
many think I suffered from hallucinations—but with the
Instruments confirming the communication, there could be
no question. In that one moment I became more renowned
than in all my life before.

Naani and I spoke a long time, and her words verified
the accounts of some of our most ancient Records. She
told of dwelling in a three-sided pyramid, a mile in height
and three-quarters of a mile along its bases, built, according to her people's accounts, upon the shores of an enormous sea whose waters had long since evaporated. Her no-

mad ancestors had raised the pyramid in the twilight of the ancient world to escape the predations of the growing tribes of half-human monsters. The man who had designed her redoubt, and who led a group of four million to construct it, had once lived in the Great Pyramid, but had been exiled after rebelling against the authorities of the lowest city. The construction took many years, the builders living together in a camp and keeping continuous watch against assailants. They tunneled miles beneath the surface to tap the Earth Current, raised the pyramid, built Instruments, ordained Monstruwacans, and for many generations communicated every day with our own citadel. Even though her people had not spoken to us for generations, they still called their pyramid the Lesser Redoubt.

Eventually, their Earth Current began to fail, causing us to lose contact when they could no longer power their Instruments. Hundreds of generations passed in silence, while the Earth Current continued to fade. As it deteriorated, their numbers dwindled.

I interrupted her at this point: *Even without your Instruments, some must have been born with the Night Hearing. According to our Records, we have heard the Master Word at various times. That, more than anything else, kept the reports of a second pyramid alive.*

She explained that the Master Word was agreed upon and made holy between the two redoubts during the early days, and some of her people had indeed possessed the Night Hearing, but because of the weakening of the Earth Current, which caused their population to diminish to less than ten thousand over the centuries, none had been born with the gift for a hundred thousand years. This had changed in the last two decades, when the current unexpectedly increased. As a result, their young people had ceased growing old before their time and their birth-rate had risen.

This all happened about the time I was born, Naani said. *I am the daughter of the Master Monstruwacan, and as I grew older, my father realized I possessed the Night Hearing. When the people learned of my power, a new interest arose in the ancient, forgotten Instruments, and we searched until we found the plans to restore them to order. We prepared an Instrument, and I was given the honor of being the first to call across the darkness, to discover if any other members of our race still lived.*

35

She paused, and I sensed her trying to contain her emotions. *The first time I called, there was a multitude gathered around me. No sooner did I send out my thoughts than I heard the Master Word. When I reported this to the others, some wept, some dropped to their knees in prayer, and some stood silent, but all urged me to continue. I spoke the Master Word and heard you respond using the name of Mirdath, but when I tried to answer, the Instrument failed.*

We worked frantically to restore its power, but it took us several days. During that time I discovered I could hear the Master Word surrounding me sometimes, even without the help of our machines, but I lacked the ability to answer. The name you used reminded me of the book, so I found the volume and read it over and over. I seem to be drawn to it, though reading it fills my soul with a strange melancholy.

Perhaps because you find it familiar?

I do not know. I contacted you again after we repaired the Instrument.

I pondered all she had said, and remembering how I had often heard a vague stirring of the ether, knew it must have been Naani using her untrained mind.

We spoke a great while, and many times in the following days, concerning our lives within the two redoubts. After so long a separation, our cultures were similar in many ways, but quite different in others. Food was scarce in the Lesser Redoubt, though Naani's people had not realized it until the revival of the Earth Current partially restored their appetites and vitality. Our men of learning understood how the soil could lose its nutrients, and we recommended various methods to accelerate the restoration process.

As might be imagined, the story of our conversations, along with countless comments, were published in the Hour Slips. The libraries brimmed with people pouring through ancient Records that had been either forgotten or disbelieved for centuries. I was so besieged with questions from the curious that if I had answered them all I could not have found time to sleep. Endless stories were written about me, most of which I ignored. Of what I did read, much was pleasant, but some was so absurd it angered me.

I suppose if my work had not kept me so busy, such recognition might have made me vain, but I was always occupied either listening for, or speaking to, the Lesser Redoubt. If anyone noticed me standing in communication, they plagued me with questions, so I spent most of my time within the Tower of Observation, where the Master Monstruwacan maintained a strict discipline.

In the days following our first communication, an ancient and evil deception soon resumed, in the form of calls for assistance from ones claiming that the Lesser Redoubt had fallen into danger. When I replied with the Master Word, I invariably received no answer, and when the Lesser Redoubt heard my transmission and contacted us, they always contradicted the false reports. By this, we knew the monsters and Forces of Evil were aware of our contact with the Lesser Redoubt and sought to trick us into leaving our sanctuary. Such deceptions were familiar to us, but they now became more frequent. If not for the sure test of the Master Word, which was too holy for the Forces of Evil to utter, many of us would doubtless have been lured to our destruction.

If anyone from our present century ever reads my narrative, it should show them something of the terror of that time and give them a quiet gratitude to God that we do not suffer as humanity shall yet suffer. Of course, the people of the pyramids, to whom it was the normal way of life, did not think of it as suffering, and I have come to realize that mankind is capable of persevering, and of even learning wisdom, in the most desperate of circumstances.

***

Through all the Night Land the monsters and Forces began to awaken; the Instruments constantly registered increased levels of power at work in the darkness, and the Monstruwacans kept an unceasing vigil, lest any movement go unrecorded. A sense of change, of wonders abroad and wonders to come, filled the whole country. Cartesius, as excited as a boy, scarcely slept at all, and could be seen at any hour hurrying from Instrument to Instrument, eyes glittering.

From The Country Of The Great Laughter, the Laughter sounded incessantly, like murderous, heart-shaking thunder rolling over the lands out of the unknown east. The Pit Of The Red Smoke filled all the Deep Valley with crimson, the haze rising above the edge and hiding the bases of the Towers upon the far side. Around the Kilns to the east the giants gathered, and enormous balls of fire erupted from the tops of the Kilns themselves. From the Mountain Of The Voice, which I have not mentioned before, but which stood southeast of the Southeast Watcher, I heard the calling of the Voice for the first time in my life. Though the Records mentioned it, it had seldom been heard through the ages. It was shrill—strange and distressful and horrible all at once—as though an enormous woman, filled with an unnatural hunger, shrieked across the night. As with everything else outside the shelter, we had no way of knowing the meaning of all this activity, but it made us uneasy. In my few hours of leisure I consoled myself by working problems out of *Ayleos' Mathematics.* Only my beloved geometry drowned out the sounds of the Laughter and the Voice.

Other ploys were used to entice us into the Night Land, as when a call warned that a band of humans, faint with hunger and in need of aid, had escaped from the Lesser Redoubt and were approaching. Again, the creatures failed to respond to the Master Word. This came as a great relief, for until we knew it was a false message, it filled us with anxiety.

I spoke with Naani at all hours. I soon taught her how to send her thoughts without the use of the Instruments, though I was careful not to allow her to exhaust herself by overusing the power. Because her health, like that of all her people, was deficient, her messages remained faint except when she used the Instruments. Apart from this, her Night Hearing was keen, and I suspected it might someday exceed my own.

Through our many hours of conversation, our spirits drew ever closer, and though we seldom spoke of it, we both shared a deep sense of familiarity, as if we had always known one another. And this, as might be imagined, thrilled my heart.

IV
THE EXPEDITION

One night, toward the end of the sixteenth hour, when I had nearly fallen asleep, the ether stirred and Naani's voice sounded so clearly I thought she must be using the Instruments to amplify her thoughts.

What's wrong? I asked, for the hour was late. *Has something happened?*

She ignored my question, but her words set my soul trembling.

Dearest, thine own feet tread the world at night—
Treading, as moon-flakes step across the dark—
Kissing the very dew to holier light . . .
Thy voice a song past mountains, which to hark
Frightens my soul with a lost delight.

I was dreadfully startled, for I recognized the words as a poem I had written to Mirdath after her death. My thoughts churned; the strength poured from my limbs. At last I managed a stammered reply: *Where did you learn those lines?*

She did not respond except to repeat the verses across the long dark of the world, but I knew beyond doubt that she must be my lost love.

"Mirdath!" I cried her name aloud even as I sent it with all the force of my mind. I gasped for breath and called her over and over, but the voice that was both Naani's and Mirdath's only repeated the poem again and again. The eeriness of it soon left me disquieted; I began to wonder if I were listening not to a human, but to a ghost speaking from heaven.

Her voice gradually faded to spectral silence, and though I called for many hours, she did not answer. At last, exhausted, I threw myself on my bed and fell into a fitful sleep.

When I woke, I could not understand what had happened except to believe that after her death Mirdath's spirit

39

had watched me write the poem. Overcome by the implications, I began trembling again. As soon as I regained my composure, I called Naani three times in succession, and the throbbing of the Master Word soon surrounded me.

Here I am, Naani said, her voice weak as always unless she used the Instruments. If she had not utilized them the night before, her Night Hearing was surely far more powerful than she realized.

Where did you hear the poem you quoted me last night?

What poem?

I faltered, surprised by her response. *You called me in the Hours of Sleep. You kept repeating the same lines over and over.*

Did I give the Master Word?

No. But the things you said . . . My thoughts drifted away in perplexity.

I slept through the night, she said, *though I did have a strange dream about a poem and a tall, dark-haired man dressed in ludicrous clothing. I started to laugh at him, until I saw how sad he looked. Then I pitied him and drew forward to comfort him, but he ignored me. Using an odd writing instrument, he began jotting down a poem, and even though I didn't know the language in which he wrote, I understood its meaning. When I awoke, I had forgotten all the verses except for the first line with Mirdath written above it. I suppose I dreamed the name because you used it when you first called me.*

Tell me what the line said, I ordered, scarcely able to control my excitement.

Dearest, thine own feet tread the world at night, she said, *but that is all I recall.*

It was enough; and with a burning in my soul, I blurted, *Treading, as moon-flakes step across the dark.*

I heard her mental gasp and sensed her shock even through the distance. Phrase by phrase I finished the remainder of the verse, and as each line beat against her spirit I sensed it rousing her memory with the violence of a blow. The impact of so many recollections left her speechless for several moments, but at last her voice swirled all around me, halting and thick with emotion.

Is it true? Am I Mirdath? Am I truly she, Andrew?

Her use of my old, familiar name wrenched a cry from my throat. The blood pounded in my ears; my concentration failed and I could scarcely reply.

You are my Mirdath, I finally managed. *My Mirdath.*

And you, she said, with a tone of finality, *are my Hercules, my circus strongman.*

I broke into tears. I am not ashamed of it; it had been so long since she left me. We wept together, our joy and sorrow intermingled, our spirits finally meeting across the everlasting night. We spoke of all that had been, slowly at first, then with gathering fervor, until the memories came rolling over both of us, making our time as Mirdath and Andrew seem like only yesterday.

***

Once we knew we had once been husband and wife, Naani and I longed to see each another again, a desire that nearly drove me to despair. Our situation seemed impossible, for none of the scholars in the Great Pyramid knew the position of the Lesser Redoubt, and the Records held only vague references suggesting that it lay somewhere between the northwest and northeast. Nor were we able to find anything to tell us the distance between the two structures. Beyond even these obstacles, there remained the peril of the Night Land and the desolation of the Unknown Lands beyond.

Naani and I often discussed the location of her pyramid, but the only information her people possessed was a dim legend that the founder of the Lesser Redoubt had come out of the south. However, they had noticed that the needle of their ancient compass never remained steady, but always swung in an arc between north and south, which caused them to guess that the powerful pull of our Earth Current affected it, drawing it away from magnetic north. If this were true, the Lesser Redoubt lay north of the Great Pyramid. The evidence, though intriguing, was too insubstantial to risk a human life.

I convinced the Monstruwacans to bring our own compass from the museum, but it reacted as it always had, spinning when we stirred the needle without stopping anywhere at all, the flow of the Earth Current from the fissure beneath the pyramid pulling it from the north and sending it wandering. I stood in a small, well-lit room with several of the Monstruwacans, watching it turn around and around.

The Master of Metaphysics guffawed, "This device never pointed any direction at all! A fantasy, that's all it is,

41

or an ancient toy."

But I watched it with the minds of both Andros, who could not help but concede the Master's point, and of Andrew Eddins, who remembered a more ordered world.

"If the compass never worked," I said, pointing toward the cardinal points etched upon its plate, "how did our ancestors know to name the directions? And if the sun and stars never shone, why do we still keep the days of the week, the months, and the years? They used this compass until they tapped the Earth Current, when it quit working."

The Master chuckled. "You're only guessing. No one knows how the ancient traditions arose."

"I do, for I remember the twilight."

***

Though Naani longed for me to come to her, she forbade it out of fear for my safety, saying it was better to commune in spirit than to risk life and soul in a foolish attempt to find her through the darkness of the dead world. Despite her warnings, I would have gone anyway if I could have only discovered the direction and distance of her redoubt.

The Master Monstruwacan did notice that I instinctively faced north whenever I sent my thoughts into the night. We tried various experiments together, covering my eyes and spinning me around to confuse my sense of direction, but I turned northward every time, and was incapable of speech if forced to face any other way.

"I will write a study on your turning to the north," Cartesius said.

"Fascinating reading, that," I replied, feeling sullen at having learned Naani's experiments had not achieved similar results.

Cartesius did as he said and the study passed from the Tower of Observation to the Hour Slips of all the cities, where it became immensely popular. Everyone read it, and flurries of discussion swept through the redoubt, which only shows how fascinated our people were with anything pertaining to the outside world. Cartesius and I received so many messages we could not read even half of them. At times I enjoyed the attention, but it often made it difficult for me to live an ordinary life.

Even as I struggled to find some way to reach Naani, a terrible thing occurred. I was taking my turn at watch beside the Master Monstruwacan in the Tower of Observation during the Hours of Sleep, when the ether suddenly thrilled around me and Naani spoke in my soul.

As soon as we exchanged the Master Word, I asked, *What's the matter?*

Her voice came so faintly I could scarcely understand her. *We are in terrible danger. The Earth Current has failed! Father tried to reach you by the Instruments, but when you didn't reply he woke me to see if you had heard us.*

I hadn't heard anything! How did this happen?

We have been so happy, Andros. Now, sorrow has made us old in a single hour. Everyone fears the surge in the power of the current was its final flicker before the end.

Even as we spoke, Naani's voice grew fainter. There was nothing I could do, but we talked through the remaining Hours of Sleep, two lovers who might soon be forever parted.

When the cities woke, the news surged through them, leaving our populace anxious and concerned.

***

A month passed, while Naani's voice grew ever fainter, until I could hardly understand her messages. I treasured every word, and could neither eat nor sleep for my dread of our inevitable parting. Cartesius, fearing for my health, warned that if I became ill, we would lose all contact with the Lesser Redoubt since the Instruments could no longer detect Naani's messages. This goaded me to try to maintain a routine of rest and nourishment, but it was hopeless, especially when I learned that the monsters of the Lesser Redoubt had sensed its weakness and were gathering around it, awaiting the time when they could overwhelm its defenses. Two days later, Naani told how an Evil Force had assaulted the minds of some of the people. Under its influence, they had opened the gate and fled into the night, where they were all slain. Many of their souls were undoubtedly lost as well.

Our scholars attributed the ability of the Evil Force to strike inside the Lesser Redoubt to the failure of the Earth Current, the lack of energy sapping the people's vitality. In only a few weeks their appetite for food and drink deserted them, along with their will to live, which was soon accompanied by an overwhelming dread of death.

Upon hearing this news, my people began considering the eventual failure of our own Earth Current. The subject filled the Hour Slips. Most wrote to assure the populace that we faced no immediate danger, though some wrote foolishly, warning of impending peril. The accounts were also full of the imagined terror of our poor brothers and sisters out in the darkness of the world, facing the end which must come to all. I could not bear to read any of it.

Our people wrote poems and songs to the Lesser Redoubt and contrived ridiculous rescue plans that no one put into effect, which only shows how easily people love to speak from a position of security. But more and more I considered going into the Night Land, for even if I achieved nothing but my own end, I preferred a quick death to my lingering heartache.

One night, in the eighteenth hour, Cartesius woke me from a restless sleep.

"The ether is filled with a tremendous disturbance," he said. "I need you to listen for the Master Word. We thought we detected it, but it is too faint for our Instruments."

Even as I sat up in bed, the Word beat all around me, much stronger than I had anticipated, followed by: *We are coming! We are coming!*

Fear gripped my heart, for the message seemed to originate nearby.

I called with the Master Word and received no answer at first, but then the faint voice of Naani responded.

Are you safe? I asked. *You haven't left the pyramid?*

I am well, but was awakened by the sound of many voices. Are you coming to our rescue?

The hope in her voice pierced me to the heart. *You mustn't depend on that. I don't want you to torture yourself with false hope. I am not sure about the source of the voices, but the Monstruwacans will never allow anyone to leave the pyramid until we discover your location. Go back to sleep. I will tell you when I know more.*

We said little else, and when I finished, I turned to the Master Monstruwacan, who waited beside my bed.

"What is it?" he asked.

I began rapidly pulling on my clothes. "The Master Word was sent from somewhere nearby."

"Impossible!"

"It's true, and I don't think they used an Instrument. I

44

sensed many minds calling in unison."

"We have to reach the tower."

As soon as we arrived at the Tower of Observation, we used the Great Spyglass to search the Night Land. For several anxious moments we saw nothing, for the country was enormous, but when we turned the glass to the pyramid's base we spied a large body of armored warriors passing over The Circle beyond the safety of the Ether Barrier, marching toward the darkness, the strange fires, and the hidden mysteries of the night.

I exchanged a look of horror with Cartesius; I had never seen his eyes so wide with fear. We stared at one another, speechless, then he recovered himself and called to one of the Monstruwacans in a soft, earnest voice, "Send word to the Master Watchman. His guardianship is violated. Some of our folk have left the pyramid."

I could scarcely comprehend the enormity of the offense. No one ever entered the Night Land without notice being given to all the people, nor without a posting of the Full Watch by The Portal, for we opened that enormous door only with lavish ceremony. Neither did anyone ever leave the pyramid without passing a centuries-old Rite of Preparation. This law was so strict that a set of metal pegs still remained on the inside of The Portal where our ancestors, in the early days of the redoubt, flayed a disobedient man alive and stretched his skin there as a warning. Every child knew the story.

We soon heard from the Master of the Watch, who had responded to Cartesius's message by leading a company of the Central Watch from the Watch Dome to The Portal, where he found the Gate Warden and the Evening Watch gagged and bound. Upon freeing them, he learned that at least five hundred young men and women—probably from the upper cities judging by their large chests—had assaulted the Watch and escaped into the night through the Eye Gate in the top of The Portal. Some of the Watch had tried to sound the alarm, only to discover the mechanisms sabotaged.

"Is there anything we can do?" I asked Cartesius.

He shook his head, looking older than I had ever seen him. "Nothing," he murmured. "They can be neither helped nor recalled, unless they choose to return themselves. So brave . . . so brave . . . but so foolish! Do they really think they can rescue the inhabitants of the Lesser

Redoubt?"

"What will happen to them if they return?" I feared they had broken the law beyond forgiveness.

"That is the least of it. If they make it back, they and those who aided them will have to be punished, of course, but nothing we could do would be as terrible as what they may face out there with their unprepared souls. Bad enough the monsters, but if a Force of Evil finds them. . . And we dare not even call to them without alerting the whole countryside."

News of the young warriors' journey swept through the cities of the Last Redoubt. The people of the south rushed to the northern sides, for The Portal was located in the northwest plane of the pyramid. Since the travelers had turned north after crossing The Circle, they were visible from both the northeast and northwest embrasures, and everyone in the redoubt wanted to see them. In addition to the spyglasses posted at many of the embrasures, every human owned a portable version, some hundreds of years old, some as old as ten thousand years—all handed down through many generations. Others were newly made, and of unusual and exotic designs, for our people were obsessed with constructing such instruments. Watching the monsters was our greatest sport, an insatiable fascination that followed us from birth to death. The embrasures were never entirely deserted.

Although I did not understand exactly how the spyglasses worked, I knew they used energy from the Earth Current to gather and focus light, for no ordinary lens could have penetrated the sheer darkness of the Night Land. They were oddly shaped devices that fit close around the forehead and left a slight tingling sensation at the eyes.

We had other means of observing, including huge Viewing Tables scattered throughout the cities. These utilized a method I can only compare to what we of the present age call Camera Obscura, but many times larger and low to the floor, so ten thousand could sit and look down on them from raised galleries. Unfortunately, these did not show the Night Land as clearly as the spyglasses.

From the time the travelers left the pyramid, onlookers thronged the embrasures and Viewing Tables, anxiously awaiting word. Sometimes we saw the company plainly, other times they remained lost in the grotesque shadows of the Night Land. According to our Instruments and my Night Hearing the monsters and Forces of Evil remained unaware of them, and we began to hope that tragedy might be miraculously avoided. Three days and nights passed, and I scarcely slept at all, for as I sat in the Tower of Observation I knew there were mothers and fathers keeping vigil below me at the northern embrasures. With a strong enough spyglass, they might even be able to see their children's faces. Their combined sorrow, which I could sense with my Night Hearing, drove through me like a spike. I could not bear to rest while they suffered, not when my unique gift might aid them by sensing things undetectable to the Instruments.

It encouraged us that the company kept a semblance of order. Through the Great Spyglass, we could see by the rising and falling light of the volcanic fires that they had food with them, and that they ate and slept at regular intervals and posted a watch whenever they halted. During their brief rests, they sat in circles among the shadows, facing outward. Any time they could, they stayed hidden within the moss bushes growing throughout the region. They seemed to have appointed commanders, and we later learned that their leader was a young man named Aschoff, an exceptional athlete from the Nine Hundredth City. They also each carried a weapon called a *diskos*. Every adult in the Great Pyramid was trained to use one from earliest childhood. The warriors had broken countless rules in obtaining their armaments, which were stored in every tenth house of the cities under the care of Charging Masters. The weapon did not shoot, but used a sharp disk of gray metal spinning at the end of a metal rod, charged by the Earth Current. So powerful were the devices that they could cut a man in two with a single stroke. They looked somewhat like battle axes, with handles that could be extended.

The company angled northeast to avoid the Vale Of Red Fire, keeping about seven miles away from it. This brought them dreadfully close to the Watcher of the Northeast— the Crowned Watcher—and I could sense the rising anxiety of the inhabitants as the company approached that dreadful mountain of vigilance. Cartesius ordered his Monstruwacans to scrutinize the Watcher's left ear, which belled out from the back of the head toward the redoubt. According to our Records, if it began to quiver, it meant the Watcher knew of the company and was alerting the

Forces of Evil throughout the Night Land. Since the blue ring of light suspended above the creature illuminated its ear, we could detect its slightest motion, and I spent many hours at the Instruments studying it. Like me, many of the Monstruwacans never left their posts while the young warriors remained outside, for this was the very purpose that the Order had originally been formed, and everyone was needed to monitor the Night Land for changes.

Finally, after many uneasy hours, relief swept through the pyramid as the youths passed beyond the Northeast Watcher. They must have grown overconfident after eluding the danger, however, for they began to travel more quickly, with less stealth, and were soon sighted by a band of wandering giants.

As the entire pyramid watched, the company formed a long line, with a space between each to give them room to use their weapons. They scarcely finished their preparations before the giants were upon them—twenty-seven in all—impossibly huge, like monsters from the ancient world, all covered with hair like crabs. When the flares of distant fires threw their fierce light across the darkness, the Great Spyglass showed the creatures so clearly that I could see the sweat streaming down their bodies.

A terrible battle ensued. The travelers broke into circles around each of the giants and attacked from every side. I could scarcely bear to watch as many of the young warriors were torn to pieces, yet was unable to avert my eyes from the grim spectacle. At times, I glimpsed the sparks from the weapons and felt the ether stirring with the passing of the slain, though the miles of distance prevented their screams or the roar of the monsters from reaching my ears.

The fight did not last long. When it was over, the dead giants formed twenty-seven hills where they had fallen. The leaders of the company sorted out their followers, and through the dim twilight I managed a rough count of our losses. The giants had slain about two hundred, leaving three hundred youths standing. Knowing the Great Spyglass could see what lesser lenses could not, Cartesius allowed me to send word through the Hour Slips.

I watched as the warriors cared for their wounded. They separated about fifty from the others, and while the main company continued their march toward the Road Where The Silent Ones Walk, these began to make their way back toward the pyramid. They approached slowly, stopping often because of their injuries.

For the slain, there would be neither burial nor ceremony outside the pyramid, for the law was clear: *Leave the dead where they fall lest the living be lost.* So there they remained, subject to the scavengers of the night. However, this was not as great a sorrow as it might otherwise have been, for the people of the pyramid held a strong belief that the body was merely the shell for the soul.

It distressed us greatly when the two hundred and fifty survivors did not abandon their quest, but continued into the Night Land. Despite our apprehension, we were gratified that our children were willing to go on after such a terrible battle. It occurred to me that while their mothers wept, their fathers' hearts must have swelled with pride. This, at least, postponed their pain a time.

We now had two groups to watch, as the wounded youths slowly returned, many helping one another. Excitement and concern swept though the Great Pyramid about who were among the wounded, who among those who continued, and who lay quietly among the dead. Pleas for information poured into the Tower of Observation, but even with our superior lenses we could not help, since the company did not stand out in the glare of the flames the way the giants had, and the youths' faces were only plain when the light from the fires flared high or when the company passed close to the innumerable fire-holes scattered across the region. Even if I had seen them clearly, I could not have identified them, for the inhabitants of the redoubt were so numerous no one could know even half the leaders of a single city.

Not long after that, one of the Monstruwacan's shouted across the chamber, "We are recording an Influence!"

Cartesius ran his hands across his face and murmured, "What will save them now, I wonder?"

At the same instant, I sensed the rising of a malevolent intelligence in the ether. There could be no doubt; one of the Forces of Evil was moving across the land.

***

The rulers of the cities had met during the first hours of the emergency, and as a result, ten thousand men and women soon assembled beside the Room of Preparation.

Throughout the Hours of Sleep they underwent the spiritual and physical rites called the Brief Preparation, in order to be ready to help the wounded once they drew closer. The next day, while the ten thousand slept, a hundred thousand more readied their weapons.

Meanwhile, the main company drew close to the Road Where The Silent Ones Walk. Having learned their lesson from the giants, they traveled slowly, with great caution. This gave the people of the pyramid little comfort however, because of the approaching Influence, which the Monstruwacans believed came from the House of Silence, though without seeing anything tangible through the Great Spyglass, we had no way of knowing the form the Force of Evil might take.

Eventually, the company marched upon the gray surface of the Silent Ones' Road, which turned slightly north. The House of Silence stood upon a low hill to the right of the Road, many miles beyond the young warriors, its twisted gables and open doorway gaping at them.

By this time the wounded had come within fifteen miles of the Last Redoubt. The news swept through the cities and weapons were issued to the ten thousand who had undergone the Brief Preparation. I descended to the ground floor to watch them come down. No one dared to approach or to speak to them, for once made ready they were considered holy.

The people of the redoubt thronged around the main lifts to watch the descent of the ten thousand. These lifts, the largest in the pyramid, were two hundred yards square. Dozens of them clustered along the center of the structure. The floors of the lifts, and of the surrounding area for several hundred yards, were made of a material clear as glass, but stronger than iron, allowing the population to flock around the shafts and watch the warriors descend. They came down, their faces determined, their gray metal armor dull in the lights, each man armed with his diskos. A longing to accompany those warriors shone in the eyes of the young men and women, but the older ones, understanding the peril not just to body, but to spirit, stood pale and sober.

It may seem strange to those of our present age, that this people, with the knowledge of eternity to aid them, lacked weapons to kill at a distance. The Records showed that the pyramid once possessed terrible energy cannons capable of

50

slaying from twenty miles away—I have even seen some
of these displayed in the Museum of Antiquities—but they
fell into disuse more than a hundred thousand years before
because they wasted vast quantities of the Earth Current,
were ineffective at close range, and served only to stir up
the more distant Forces and monsters. Nor could they
harm such Evil Forces as the House of Silence and the
Watchers, whose vast power surrounded us constantly.
Though always armed and ready, we preferred to keep
quiet, to leave the Night Land undisturbed, and to live
from generation to generation in relative peace and security. I have often pondered how limited resources, either in
chemistry or the Earth Current, reduced the people of the
pyramid to a simplicity of living not unlike that of the ancient world.

***

As required by law, word soon passed through every
district that The Portal would be opened. Each city sent its
Master, clad in gray armor and carrying his diskos. These
formed the Full Watch, which along with the Watchmen,
numbered two thousand.

At the prescribed hour, the Master of Metaphysics
dimmed the lights in the Long Causeway, keeping the
glare from shining through the open gate into the Night
Land, so the Watcher of the Northwest and other denizens
would not see humans leaving the pyramid. Despite these
precautions, we could never know whether the vast, hidden Forces of Evil were aware of our actions. All who entered the night lived with this doubt, their only solace being in the Rite of Preparation, and the Capsule of Oblivion
embedded in their forearms.

The ten thousand marched quietly through The Portal
into the darkness, and the Full Watch stepped back from
them and silently saluted with their diskoi. Those who
went returned the salute, their weapons raised, then vanished into the night.

The Portal shut behind them with only a soft tapping
sound, leaving we who remained to wait and watch and do
our best to comfort the spouses and children of the departed.

I returned on a small lift to the Tower of Observation,
where I looked out into the Night Land and saw the ten
thousand. They halted at The Circle, arranged themselves,

51

and sent a few warriors across the Ether Barrier to scout their way. Without wasting time, they crossed the protective shield of The Circle and entered the land of darkness. Since The Circle was attuned to affect the brains of the denizens of the Night Land, humans could cross it without first deactivating it.

I watched the ten thousand for a while, then turned my attention to the two hundred and fifty still traveling the Road Where The Silent Ones Walk. I could not see them at first, for the Road seemed empty, but finally I spied them clambering back onto the way. They had left the Road to avoid a Silent One, who I could still see passing along some distance south of their position.

For three hours I split my vigil between the youths and the ten thousand slipping forward to help the wounded, who were now about nine miles from the pyramid. The two groups soon spied one another, and I sensed in my spirit the relief of the youths, an emotion mingled—despite their wounds and weakness—with the knowledge of their failure and disobedience to the ancient laws. The ten thousand soon reached them. They placed those most seriously injured on slings, turned the party more quickly than might have been thought possible, and rushed back toward the Great Pyramid. I happened to be standing close to the Instruments used to record the noises of the Night Land just then, and I heard the Night Hounds baying in the east. I then understood the rescuers haste.

I swept the Spyglass toward the Valley Of The Hounds. The beasts, which were already less than ten miles away, approached at a shuffling gallop. They were large as horses, with thick gray coats and yellow eyes. Their heads were similar to a Great Dane's, except the pointed ears were taller, and the jaws many times more massive.

To my astonishment, as I swept my glass back toward the rescuers I noticed the enormous belled ear of the Northeast Watcher quivering. I had no doubt that it had spied the travelers, and was signaling their location to all the dwellers of the night.

One of the Monstruwacans rushed to the Master, his eyes glassy with shock. "The Instruments—" His voice broke, but he recovered and continued. "According to the Instruments, a new Force approaches, different from the one we detected earlier."

Another Monstruwacan, standing beside me, turned

back to the embrasures, and overcome with emotion, shouted to the travelers, "Hurry! You must hurry!"

Others, forgetting themselves in their concern, did likewise, but their voices could not carry to the ears of the ten thousand.

"Monstruwacans!" Cartesius's deep baritone rose above the clamor. His followers grew quiet. "Collect yourselves. You have your work. Every eye open! Every heart calm. The most minute observation may prove invaluable. Serenity through scrutiny."

The Monstruwacans obeyed, but I knew Cartesius well enough to see he was as anxious as any.

Using the Great Spyglass, I searched until I sighted a tremendous Mound in the shape of a black mist, coursing over the land from the direction of the Plain Of Blue Fire.

"Master!" I called. "Over here!"

The Master Monstruwacan looked through one of the numerous eye pieces. After a moment he called to the man who had given the report: "What do the Instruments show?"

"The Influence is drawing closer. It travels swiftly."

I watched in terrible fascination as the Mound passed down into the Vale Of Red Fire, which stretched all across that portion of the Night Land. It remained hidden so long I hoped it might not climb from that hideous pit, but at last it rose on the other side, and then into open country. Its speed increased so much it passed half way across that region in less than a minute.

"What is it?" I asked the Master, though in my heart I knew.

"A Force of Evil," Cartesius said. "I can wait no longer."

He moved to the controls with a speed I thought impossible in such an elderly man. His hands fell upon the Home Call, and an enormous roar, the sign of imminent danger, reverberated from the base of the redoubt. This alarm, which had not been activated in hundreds of years, had originally been used as a homing beacon in ancient times when flying ships traveled the earth.

With my Night Hearing, I perceived by the emotions of the ten thousand that they already sensed their peril. There came the dreadful moment for which the commander had long been prepared. Though some later questioned his decision, he acted according to his orders, with both wisdom and courage. Without the Preparation, the youths lacked any protection against the assault of the Force of Evil. Even from a distance, the Mound could seize their souls. Those Prepared could resist such an assault until the Force was nearly upon them, though even they would eventually be compelled to preserve their spirits by taking their own lives with the Capsules of Oblivion. Knowing this, the commander lifted his hand and signaled his followers to kill the youths. This was done with rapid, merciful strokes. The anguish that racked the inhabitants of the pyramid was nearly more than my Night Hearing could bear, and I was driven to my knees. The pyramid actually trembled with the people's combined cry.

When I recovered, I seized the spyglass again and looked back toward the Mound, which was almost upon the company, a hill of blackness rushing toward them like an approaching storm.

Suddenly, a miraculous event occurred, for just when the men were about to be forced to swallow the capsules, a faint light, like a crescent moon, arose. It grew into an arc of dim, copper fire that arched above the ten thousand and the dead. The Mound quavered and halted, then retreated back into the darkness as rapidly as it had come, driven away by one of the legendary Powers of Good.

Once it was gone, the men rushed toward the Last Redoubt, while the protecting light remained all around them. Before they had reached safety, however, the Night Hounds were upon them.

The pack, numbering at least a hundred, loped out of the darkness, tall, powerful creatures running with heads bent low. As they approached, the warriors drew three paces apart, to leave room to swing their diskoi.

A tremendous battle ensued beneath the glow of the crescent light, for though that radiance could protect their souls, it could not defend them against physical danger. The warriors fought with the handles of their diskoi at full length, the spinning disks shooting glistening wheels of fire.

All around me, I sensed the emotions of the inhabitants. From thousands of embrasures, they watched, wept, and watched again. In the lower cities, the onlookers reported hearing the crash and splinter of the armor as the hounds darted back and forth, rending even metal with their massive jaws. Throughout the battle, the ten thousand stood firm until they cut the last of the hounds to pieces, but it was no easy victory; seventeen hundred warriors died at the monsters' fangs.

At last the weary band struggled back to the pyramid. Because they were so close to sanctuary the commander had broken the law requiring the dead to be left on the field, and had ordered all the slain, including the youths, carried to the redoubt, a decision that was never questioned. They returned weeping, but the people met them with silent reverence. Throughout the pyramid, the cities mourned, for no such disaster had occurred for thousands of years.

The travelers bore the youths to their mothers and fathers. The parents thanked those who had risked their lives to save their children's souls, but the slayers kept their faces shrouded and their identities concealed. For such was the law.

***

The deaths of so many of the ten thousand served as a fresh reminder of the Night Land's terrors, and no one spoke any more about helping those who remained outside. It was just as well, for the company traveling the Road Where The Silent Ones Walk was far beyond our assistance.

Though the Mound had retreated, our Instruments still detected an Evil Influence abroad in the land, which the Monstruwacans feared might now be directed toward the remaining adventurers. When the Instruments suggested that it emanated from the House of Silence, we became even more anxious. Our machinery could not completely confirm this, but I felt certain the House was the source, for I could sense the malice radiating from it.

The travelers, who had reached a point where the road wound almost straight north, were only a short distance from the House, and the Instruments soon showed an increase in the Influence's power.

"We should use the Home Call again," a Monstruwacan suggested. "To warn them."

"Not yet," Cartesius said. "Not until absolutely necessary. The land is already wary. If other Forces learn of more humans traveling outside . . ." He fell silent.

I could not help but agree, for the aura of vigilance emanating from the country nearly overwhelmed my Night

Hearing, and a deep roaring echoed almost continuously across the land.

"Could we use the Set Speech, instead?" I asked.

Cartesius lifted one eyebrow. "Bless you, my boy. I had nearly forgotten it! Who among us is proficient in its use?"

The Monstruwacans exchanged timid glances. At last, old Toniff cleared his throat. "I trained on it when I was young, but it's been many years."

"You must try it," Cartesius commanded.

Toniff rose and hobbled to the ancient Instrument used to send the Set Speech, which was a language still taught to every child in school. It used flashes of light in various order and duration to represent the letters of the alphabet. The Instrument was connected to a series of blinking emerald lights on the top of the Tower of Observation.

As Toniff fumbled with the controls Cartesius muttered to me, "When this is over, remind me to begin training every Monstruwacan on the Instruments we seldom use. Knowledge must not be lost through my negligence. We also need to go back through the Records, to insure that we have clear copies describing the functions of every Instrument. Continuance through diligence."

We sent the message repeatedly, urging the youths to return home, but we could not see the travelers well enough to know if they read it. Whether they did or not, they did not change their course.

A day and night passed, while all the millions peered with speculation and dread into the Night Land. The youths traveled at a tremendous pace along the Road, eating only once and going without sleep, so that we knew they must be nearing exhaustion. Their relentless gait made us suspect them of having fallen under the dominion of a powerful Force. Our Instruments supported this, for from its first detection the Influence steadily increased in strength, until all the night pulsed with its dark malevolence.

During the eleventh hour I saw the youths suddenly break from the Road Where The Silent Ones Walk and rush toward the House of Silence.

"Cartesius!" I cried.

"I see it." He did not hesitate then, but sounded the Home Call again. As its bellowing voice filled the Night Land, he also sent a message in the Set Speech, urging the youths to either resist the calling of the House, or to save their souls from falling under the dominion of the Force by taking their own lives.

All around me I felt the fear and pity of the redoubt's millions, who knew the significance of the Home Call, and who understood that the Master Monstruwacan was pleading for the youths' spirits. The prayers and empathy of so many millions, focused on a single objective, created a vast, spiritual noise quite plain to my Night Hearing, a powerful counter-force that filled the night. As that supplication radiated through the darkness, the warriors halted their headlong flight and stood milling in confusion, as if having recovered their senses.

A tremendous roar issued from the pyramid, the cheers of the millions looking out from nearly six hundred thousand embrasures. The shouts rose through the metal frame like the blast of a tremendous wind, but the victory cries came too soon; the rejoicing broke the power of the counter-force, and the Influence within the House regained control of its victims' minds. They began to run again.

The cheers ceased; the pyramid fell silent. Sorrow and horror filled the ether.

In that moment a wonder occurred: billows of mist suddenly rose before the travelers, shining with a pure white fire that was also somehow cold, for though it burned directly before the youths, it did not illuminate them.

"Something fights for them," Cartesius rasped. "A Power of Good."

Everyone saw the mist, for the people of that age possessed great spiritual sight, but I think I saw it more clearly than any, both because of the power of the Great Spyglass and the special gifts associated with my Night Hearing.

"Master," a Monstruwacan called, "the Influence has ceased! The Force from the house has been cut off!"

My heart filled with hope and trepidation. I sensed the same in all the millions around me.

"Send the Home Call again!" the Master ordered, his voice heavy with passion. "At once!"

Once more the great voice filled the countryside, accompanied by a message urging the youths, for the sake of the love of the mothers who bore them, to save their souls by hurrying back to the pyramid while the Power kept the House of Silence at bay. It was impossible to be certain at such a distance, but I thought some glanced toward the pyramid. Then, I saw their leader, Aschoff, waving his arms to call them to attention. This courageous young man then unwittingly caused his comrades destruction, for he stepped forward and leapt into the billows of the shining barrier of fire. The mist shrank and flickered out, and Aschoff of the Nine Hundredth City ran once more toward the House of Silence, his followers close behind. They soon reached the low hill and ascended to the horrid House —two hundred and fifty young men and women, with wholesome hearts and spirits, their only fault the natural rebelliousness of youth. They reached the doorway that histories say *hath been open since the Beginning.*

A hush fell over the pyramid as the mothers and fathers watched their children pass beyond human ken over the threshold into the cold, steadfast light. I could hear the silence welling through the redoubt, broken only by the dull throbbing of the Earth Current and the tapping of the Instruments. Even the Night Land itself fell into a strange hush, a quiet brooding more terrible than all the roars proceeding it.

A cold fear clutched my heart. I could no longer detect the travelers with my Night Hearing, as if in passing into a Silence beyond understanding, they had simply ceased to exist. I suddenly longed for the normal noises of the Night Land—even for the far echoing thunder of the Great Laughter, or the whining from the southeast, where the Silver Fire Holes opened before The Thing That Nods—or the baying of the Hounds, or any of the dreadful things that normally passed through the Night Land. They could not have offended me as the silence did.

***

This was not the end of our sorrows concerning the lost youths, for a day later, during the ninth hour, we saw something that we had read about only in histories, though we dreaded that it might come.

Cartesius woke me from a sound sleep. Like the rest of the Monstruwacans, I was exhausted after my long vigil in the tower. I stumbled up, groggy as a drunkard, mumbling my questions while the Master urged me to haste. He did not take me immediately to the lifts, but led me to the nearest embrasure. Even before we reached it I felt an unusual stirring of the ether, unlike anything I had ever experienced before.

"Down there," he said, "just in front of The Circle."

I squinted at the plain below. Figures stood there, lined up as if in formation. I gasped and rushed to the nearest spyglass.

They stood in their armor, their diskoi by their sides, their faces pale and filled with anguish. Though I could not identify them by sight, I knew these were the lost youths.

"If only they had died," Cartesius said, his head in his hands.

They were ghosts, for their forms shone with a dull, gray light and wavered insubstantially, as if the barest wind—had there been any—might have disbursed them. I could partially see through them to the plain beyond. They gestured toward the pyramid, motioning for those within to come out. With my Night Hearing, I heard them calling, urging their parents to leave the safety of the redoubt.

When I told Cartesius, he said, "We know. The Instruments detected it. The Master of the Watch has already doubled the sentries at The Portal."

"What can I do?"

He looked bleakly into my eyes. "Perhaps with your Night Hearing you can tell us. Are these truly the souls of our children or an illusion sent to confuse us?"

I am an honorable man, but I wanted to lie at that moment, because I knew whatever I said would be reported in the Hour Slips. "It really is them. I don't understand their present state of existence, but they are suffering. I can feel it. They suffer as no living person has ever suffered before."

He nodded heavily. "I see." He turned away. "You can go back to bed. That is all I needed."

"Cartesius?"

He turned back.

"Don't tell them about the pain."

He nodded again and departed.

For three days the phantoms stood beckoning on the plain. When no one responded to their pleas, they abruptly vanished, never to be seen again. Though our scholars held many opinions on the matter, none really knew if those souls captured by Evil Forces remained eternal prisoners, were ultimately destroyed, or finally escaped to paradise. Whatever the case, those that had questioned the commander who had ordered the other youths slain questioned him no more.

***

All during the time we had watched the travelers upon the Road Where The Silent Ones Walk, I had occasionally sensed the thrilling of the ether and the beating of the Master Word, but it was always faint. Though I could not decipher Naani's messages, I tried to send back words of comfort.

When the ghosts vanished, I fell into deep despair, driven by my helplessness against the Forces and monsters of the Night Land. Not an hour went by without my thinking about Naani. I tried to find respite in calculations of geometric shapes, but even mathematics could not divert me.

Ever again the faint call came, but never Naani's voice speaking in my soul.

V
PREPARATION

The end of the slain youths and the seventeen hundred heroes came a few days later in the Country of Silence, the lowest of all the Underground Fields. It spread a hundred miles in every direction, with its domed roof arching three miles above, as if its builders possessed a racial memory of the sky. The history of the construction of the Country of Silence was recorded in seven thousand and seventy volumes, one for each of the years spent in its making. Like the great Egyptian pyramids, generations had lived, labored, and died without seeing the end of their work, but it had been shaped and hallowed as an act of love, rather than through the efforts of slaves. Seven moons, lit by the Earth Current, set in the dome in a circle sixty miles across, bathed the whole region in a soft, holy light. In such a place anyone could weep without shame.

In the center of the country stood a tall hill crowned by a huge dome covering the fissure from which the Earth Current poured; its golden light could be seen from anywhere in the land. A narrow path called The Last Road led up to the north side of the dome to a door named, simply, The Gateway.

Throughout the Country of Silence ran long roadways, winding past memorial statues and tablets. Temples of Rest, surrounded by the soft chatter of waterfalls, lay scattered along the roads. To walk alone in that land was to wander once more among the mysteries of childhood, and those who came there returned to their cities renewed, filled with peace.

In my boyhood, I had rambled weeks at a time through the Country of Silence, carrying food with me and sleeping among the memories, for my soul was drawn to the resting place of the heroes of the past. In the end, I always found myself standing on the Hills of the Infants, small rises where I could hear, above the noise of the bubbling fountains, a peculiar echo like a little child calling over the slopes. I never knew how this was done, but it must have been the work of a long-dead craftsman. The hills were covered with countless memory tokens dedicated to the infants who had died through the ages, and I often happened upon a mother, sitting alone or in the company of others, mourning her child.

Such was the quiet wonder, the holy splendor of that vast country, hallowed for generation after generation to memory, eternity, and the dead.

The people bore the bodies of the young warriors into the Country of Silence, and Cartesius and I, along with a hundred million others, came to honor their memory. The bearers placed the slain upon The Last Road. The road, which was actually a *migrator*, lumbered forward, carrying first the dead youths through The Gateway, then those who had given their lives to save them. As the first bodies vanished into the dome, we all fell silent until we heard, rising from the direction of the Hills of the Infants, a distant wailing like a rustling wind. We, in turn, took up the song, for it was the soft mourning of the entire multitude. The melody passed in a wave among the people, then ended in a profound silence as the last of the dead rode into the brilliant light of the dome, where they became one with the consuming fire of the Earth Current.

When they were gone, a memory token was placed in a triangular cluster for each of the slain, and a representative from every city that had lost one of the ten thousand rose and charged the pyramid's artists to create beautiful sculptures to their honored dead. Then the millions sang a song thousands of years old, a loud, triumphant hymn of honor, while the swelling of underground organs rose from the earth below, like thunder from the deep. The refrain reverberated through the Country of Silence, then fell away, leaving only faint echoes passing over us, dying in the distance.

With the ceremony done, the people drifted over the Country of Silence to visit the markers of their ancestors, before entering the lifts and returning to their cities.

***

There was no more talk of helping the people of the Lesser Redoubt after this, though the thought of Naani's people dying unaided only added to our sorrow. I realized then how foolish I had been in hoping that a secret expedition could rescue the inhabitants of the Lesser Redoubt. How often I had imagined stepping through the darkness to Naani, arms outstretched, our souls recognizing one another from ages past! But it was all nonsense. It haunted me that my love might, at any moment, be suffering beneath the hand of a foul monster; I grew nearly mad with worry, and struggled against the urge to seize my diskos and rush into the night.

I often sent words of comfort and love to Naani, warning her not to be lured into leaving the safety of the redoubt by false messages, but it was a dreary effort, directing my thoughts into the darkness without ever hearing a response. Sometimes the ether stirred weakly around me, and I thought I caught the faint call of the Master Word. Though this gave me hope that Naani lived, it also kept me in a constant state of anxiety. Every day my heart grew more restless; life seemed vain and empty. I tried to throw myself into my work, and at night, when I could not sleep, I sat staring blindly at the formulas in *Ayleos' Mathematics*, gaping at them without understanding, too distracted to apply myself.

To add to my apprehensions, a voice disguised as Naani's began speaking to me, only to lose its power to respond when I gave the Master Word. It usually remained silent only a short while before calling again. This occurred time after time, both during the day and in the Hours of Sleep, until it nearly drove me to desperation. Regardless of how it tempted me, I refused to speak to it, fearing it might snare my soul. Its voice tainted my spirit; after its calls I found peace only through prayer, contemplation of noble tales, and thoughts of my sweet and holy love for Mirdath. Finally, I learned to rebuke it by sending the Master Word with all the strength of my will. Only then could I find a few hours of serenity.

I ate little and grew thin. With the comfort of my mathematics denied me, I found solace in vigorous exercise. During those times, my old life as Andrew seemed quite close, as if his pleasure in physical strength had become my own. I would run along the outer ring of the One Thousandth City until exhausted, then sprawl in a heap beside one of the embrasures. Only then would my mind be free. Cartesius chided me gently, but there was little he could say, and little I could do to change my longing. Finally, I suppose out of desperation, he suggested I search through the Records, to see if I could find anything useful.

I took to the task at once, as it put action to my anxiety.

Cartesius helped me as well, both out of sympathy and from his natural thirst for knowledge. One day he brought me an ancient book plated in metal, with runes engraved upon its cover.

"I found this stored in a section of the library last visited ten thousand years ago," he said. "It is very old, a remarkable find. I've only read a bit of it, but enough to know its value. I intend to send copies to the scholars of every city, but I wanted you to see it first."

I took it gingerly, but found its pages, a remnant of a forgotten science, as fresh as the day they had been printed. Over the next few days I poured over its contents.

Much of it concerned a tale I had read before in various histories of the ancient world, a narrative most of the learned discounted as myth, though I had always liked such accounts, perceiving a yolk of truth within their outer shells. However, the version in the metal book was written in a different manner from any of the others, as if quoting from witnesses to the actual events. It told how, many eons before, tremors racked the world, opening a tremendous chasm a thousand miles long, so deep its bottom could not be seen. The oceans rushed into the rift with a power that shook the continents, and for weeks heavy mist and torrential rain brooded over the entire world. Toward the book's end, written in a style different from the first, it depicted a time countless centuries later, when the rift had become a huge chasm passing west to southeast, then turning north, a hundred miles deep and approximately a thousand miles each way. The sun shone in its western end, casting a red gloom down one leg of its length.

Though this seemed the stuff of romance, I, with my memory of the sunlit age, did not discount it so quickly. Instead, I theorized that one of our oceans must have been drawn into the fires at the earth's mantle, causing horrendous destruction.

The final author of the text lived in an even later time. The sun sputtered, and the surface of the earth grew cold and inhospitable, but the great chasm, tamed by the handling of eternity, had become a deep valley, large enough to hold seas and mountains, with beckoning forests and hills in places, and fire pits and poisonous clouds of sulphur in others. It was a primal world, given to warmth and life, with enormous beasts, the descendants of birds and mammals, dwelling in the forests.

Men struggled to survive during that time, and a hardy race of humans eventually descended into the valley. They were builders by nature—the book called them the Road Makers—for they constructed roads everywhere they went.

For many generations they built the roads downward, yet it took them centuries to reach the bottom of the valley. They fought and conquered the behemoths living there, then built cities, which they connected with their roads all the way to the north turning, which they called the Great Bight. Beyond the Bight, where the sun could not penetrate, lay darkness and shadow, but even that did not prevent them from continuing their roads far into the north, past fire pits rising from the earth's core. Eventually, however, the monsters dwelling in the shadows of the towering cliffs drove them back to the red glow of the western valley.

They returned to their cities, where they lived in peace for perhaps a hundred thousand years, growing ever wiser and more cunning, but in the end they dabbled in matters best left alone, and inadvertently opened a way for Forces from beyond our dimension to enter the world.

As the centuries passed, the sun waned until all lay in perpetual dusk. In those times, the twilight fell upon the people's souls as well, so they embraced depraved and shameful customs, and consorted with the Evil Forces. As a result, monsters from the west attacked many of the cities. An age of sorrow and struggle followed, which destroyed many, but refined the spirits of those who fought for good. A leader arose, Gosil of Geddon, who led the people in a war against the monsters and scattered them up and down the valley. Envisioning that the Forces of Evil would grow stronger with the coming of eternal night, Gosil conceived a plan to build a place of refuge.

Over many years, his people constructed a great house, meant to hold the world's millions, but the plan failed, for the structure could not protect the humans against the Forces of Evil. Gosil and his followers abandoned the house and journeyed farther south, where they built the Great Pyramid.

The Master Monstruwacan and I believed the words of the book. By its description, we knew that the surface world, lost a hundred miles up in the night, contained no life, for none could survive in that frozen desolation. We also assumed that the Road Where The Silent Ones Walk must have been built by the Road Makers, and that the House of Silence was the original sanctuary made by Gosil.

"According to the account, our pyramid was built in the southeast portion of the rift," Cartesius said, "just before the valley turns north at the Great Bight. That suggests Naani's pyramid must be either to the north or west. The road going to the Place Of The Ab-Humans might lead there."

"That isn't where I would search first," I said.

"Legends suggest that something extraordinary lies in that direction."

"I know. But I'm almost certain the Lesser Redoubt is north of us. Naani's people claim their founders came from the south. It *feels* like she calls from the north."

Cartesius sighed. "A man might wander a thousand miles wrong and never find it. It's all too uncertain. We need more research. Surety through study, as we say."

"Not just study," I said. "Sometimes action must suffice."

The Master Monstruwacan shook his head, a touch of alarm in his eyes. "No, Andros. Not without more information. Do not even consider it. The darkness is too deep; it would swallow you up."

I fell into a brooding silence, the book lying open in my lap, thinking of those vast cliffs all around us, hidden by the darkness. Still, we had always assumed we lived in the depths of the world, though those who thought of such things generally believed the pyramid stood in the bed of an ancient sea, with its sides gradually sloping away from us. Myriad other theories existed, of course, as is always the way when facing the unknown, but I trusted the account in the metal book. It was, at any rate, only the scholars who pursued such concepts; to the average person, the thought of the upper world, or of any other condition than that in which they lived, seemed mere fantasy. To them, everlasting night, distant figures, terrible monsters, fire-holes and Watchers—all the mysteries of the Night Land —were the normal way of things. Only children believed the ancient stories.

***

Despite Cartesius's counsel, from that moment I thought of nothing but going to find Naani. I finally made my decision when I awoke from a troubled sleep to the sound of her voice, anguished and beseeching.

Andros. Oh, Andros! Can't you help me, as you did when the three rogues attacked me? My Andros.

I sat up in bed and answered with the Master Word, which was returned, but almost too faint to hear.

Through a long hour, I called into the night. I sent her reassurance and begged to know what dangers she faced. I trembled with excitement; I was nearly beside myself, but I heard her voice no more, save for a weak murmuring of the ether.

"I will not wait!" I cried at last, raising my hands above my head, palms outward, tears rolling down my cheeks. "Upon my honor, I won't abide here while you perish. I will not wait!"

But the darkness gave no answer.

Knowing my course at last, I dressed swiftly and rushed to find the Master Monstruwacan. I woke him from a sound sleep, but he rose quickly. We sat together in his little study, he with his night robe about him, his ancient eyes filled with a dread I did not, at that moment, understand.

I told him what had occurred, ending with, "I won't suffer in silence any longer. I'm going into the Night Land, to either find Naani or meet a swift end to my torment."

"No, Andros," he said, his voice quavering as I had never heard it before. "No. You are overwrought. We will meet tomorrow and search the Records anew. We will seek other ways. We need more information. We must find the particulars. I know a room, filled with Records untouched by generations—we will look there. Yes. There are certain volumes—just sitting here I can think of a dozen. You should go to bed. I will rouse you early. We will find something soon. I'm certain of it."

"Master, I must go," I said quietly.

"No. No. I won't allow it. You cannot go. Tomorrow we will look into the Records. We will find—"

"No!" I cried. "No more Records. I am going!"

"You are not! I forbid it. I am the Master. I forbid it. Do you hear me?"

For perhaps the first time in my life I had raised my voice to this man—a man whose commanding presence had always compelled me to obedience. It terrified me to have done so. We stood glaring at one another.

"You are the Master," I managed, in a lower tone, "but you cannot prevent me from doing this. I am of age. I have the right."

For an instant I feared that he *could* prevent me, that he would call the City Watch and have me restrained. He possessed great authority within the pyramid. But he only sat, defeated, his face haggard in the dim light.

When he spoke his voice was gentler. "This is not a story, Andros, where all turns happy in the end. The task is too great. You will be lost, like the others. You mustn't go."

"How can I stay? Has anyone ever lived and loved in one life, and awakened in another to find his love alive? Do the Records report such a thing?"

He shook his head. "No. I have searched the accounts since you first told your story, but have found nothing."

"Then this is my destiny. Can't you see?"

He sat silent, marshaling his thoughts. "Who am I to say if you are destined or not? But I don't want you to go, Andros, out there, into the dark." He suddenly drew his hands to his face and sighed into his palms. "Even before your parents died, I knew you were different. I was so proud of you when you showed signs of the Night Hearing. But this—this, dear Andros! I do not want you to leave. I do not want to be without you." Tears suddenly filled his eyes, and his voice broke. "The night will be darker with you in it."

"I know," I said, patting his ancient hand, scarcely able to control my own voice. "You have been as much my father as any I can remember. You took me in, taught me. I can't begin to repay all I owe you. Let me go. Don't make this more difficult."

In that moment I think he saw my resolve, but the young, caught up in their own will, can never understand the full measure of their elders' pain.

He wiped the tears from his eyes. "But you've lost weight. How can you go into the night without your full strength? You should wait, to regain your vitality."

"I will go as I am," I said gently. "I may be lean, but I have never been stronger. It will help protect my soul—aren't the Three Days of Preparation intended to harden the spirit against Evil Forces? I have prepared longer than anyone."

"The physical is only *part* of the Preparation. You will

also be told the full dread of the Night Land. There are horrors—oh, Andros, there are horrors not told to the young—mutilations, abasements of the soul that shake the heart if but whispered. They are kept in books few men have read, books locked in the chambers of the Master of Preparation. Even I do not know all . . ."

I rose. "Tomorrow, I intend to find out. I will send a message to the Master of Preparation this evening. Will you accompany me to the rite?"

He turned his head down into the shadows, his face stern once more. "I have . . . much to do tomorrow. There are charts to study. We are reviewing our survey of the Giants' Kilns. Let us say farewell and be done with it."

"Very well," I said, stiffly. "Goodbye, then."

He did not escort me to the door, and I left feeling like a traitor.

***

When morning came, if I may refer thus to the brightening of the lights within the Great Pyramid, I woke to find the Master Monstruwacan standing by my bed.

"Cartesius! I thought—"

"Shhh. Do not say it. Only forgive an old man who thought to spare himself pain. I have spoken to the Master of Preparation myself. Dress quickly and we will go."

I cannot express my surprise and joy at finding him there. If I had been more than half-awake, I would have wept. I did as he commanded, and we soon found ourselves standing before the door to the Room of Preparation.

"This is farewell," he said. "When next I see you, you will be holy, untouchable."

"Cartesius, I'm sorry if—"

He suddenly hugged me fiercely. "I love you, Andros. God protect you in the night."

Only then, I think, did I realize what I was about to do, but I put on a brave face and entered the chamber, leaving him alone outside, an old man, watching me with troubled eyes.

I stayed in the Room of Preparation for three days and nights. I saw things there that made me wonder why anyone ever willingly entered the Night Land. Still, the natural inclination of youth is to seek adventure. I cannot regret this trait; it would be a terrible grief if humanity ever lost it.

On the fourth day the Master of Preparation brought my armor. He set it on a table, then stepped back in silence, for with the Full Preparation done, it was forbidden for anyone to either speak to me, or even approach.

I dressed myself, first in a special, close-knit body vest designed to protect me from the bitter cold of the Night Land, and then in the armor. Over this I wrapped a heavy gray cloak around my shoulders and across my hip. I carried a scrip of food and drink designed to sustain me though many weeks, with a Mark of Honor stitched upon it.

Once dressed, I picked up my diskos and silently bowed to the Master of Preparation as he opened the door of the chamber. To my surprise, I discovered a crowd waiting beyond the door, in violation of the laws of the redoubt. Only then did I realize how my story had spread throughout the cities.

The Master of Preparation signaled for the masses to stand aside, so I could walk untouched among them. The crowd parted in eerie silence, and as I stepped through the door I saw the halls filled with people all the way up to the main lifts. I entered a massive lift alone, while everyone watched me through its clear walls. It felt strange to have so many eyes upon me; literally thousands massed around the shaft as I descended the long miles. Though they remained silent, I felt the ether surging with their sympathy and good will.

At last I reached The Portal, where I found the Master Monstruwacan waiting, dressed in his full armor, his diskos in hand, surrounded by the Full Watch. We stared into one another's eyes in silence, and I bent my head in respect. I do not think I ever loved him more than in that moment. He raised his diskos in salute, and then I passed toward the door.

The lights dimmed to prevent their glare from shining in the Night Land once the door opened. As a final honor, they did not open the Eye Gate which stands within The Portal, but swung wide The Portal itself, through which an entire army could have passed.

I will never forget the silence and the eyes of the two thousand of the Full Watch upon me, their diskoi raised in salute, as I lifted my own diskos, reversed in answer, and entered the night.

VI
THE NIGHT LAND

As I walked away from The Portal, not even the rigors of the Rite of Preparation could steel me against the shock of finding myself, for the first time in my life, outside the pyramid. My feet had never trod bare earth before, save in the safety of the Underground Fields; my eyes had never gazed, unhindered by embrasure glass, upon the bleak horizons. I began trembling uncontrollably and broke into an icy sweat. I cannot describe how deeply I was affected, for until that moment, entering the Night Land had seemed more dream than reality.

I suddenly longed to return to my place beside the Master Monstruwacan within the Tower of Observation. Of all the millions, I would miss him most; truthfully, I missed him already.

Between my homesickness and fear, I dared not look at the redoubt, not while the ether stirred all around me with the hopes and blessings of the millions at my back.

I glanced around, half-expecting to be immediately attacked by a monster, an irrational fear, since I still stood inside the protection of The Circle. When an assault did not come, I took several deep breaths to calm my racing heart. The cold night air tasted sharp on my tongue and burned my lungs. It was heavier than the air in the One Thousandth City, but this was not surprising since the atmosphere of every city was slightly different, with more contrast between the higher and lower levels. People often migrated from city to city for health reasons, and in some extreme cases, even dwelled in the depths of the Underground Fields.

I soon reached The Circle, which lay a mile out from the pyramid. From a distance, its haloing brilliance had made it seem much larger that it actually turned out to be—a clear tube slightly flat on top and less than two inches thick. Though I knew it conducted enough power to generate the Ether Barrier which kept the monsters from reach-

71

ing the pyramid, it looked dreadfully fragile curving around the redoubt.

How often as children had my comrades and I watched from the embrasures, each hoping to be the first to spy some creature peering from behind The Circle, competing with one another to see who could spot the most gruesome beast of all. Such brutes often came there, only to slink back into the night, driven away by the radiance and the barrier's invisible vibrations. What a strange game we played, shuddering behind our jests, quaking inwardly beneath our laughter, secretly grateful for the protection of the metal walls.

As I remembered the beasts peering from behind The Circle, their heads thrusting out of the darkness, I instinctively stepped back, where I remained for several moments, calming myself, recovering my courage. Then I turned toward the pyramid to bid a final farewell.

I gaped when I saw it, for it is one thing to live within a vast edifice and another to see it from outside. I understood at last why it had attracted the attention of so many monsters, for it spread before me, a mountain stretching measureless into the night. In school I had learned that each of the four sides contained three hundred thousand embrasures, but looking upon those windows for the first time, I realized the scope of the architect's design. The lowest tier started a half-mile up, with multiple tiers running, row upon row, above those. The light shining through them made them visible for many miles, distinguishable at first as individual windows, then blurring together with distance, merging in the upper reaches as a constant, glimmering fire, a shining peak dwindling into the heights of the black heavens.

I soon recognized the shadowy shapes clustered around the embrasures as the countless inhabitants. I could see them clearly in the lower levels, though they looked minuscule compared to the windows themselves.

My eyes roamed back up the great slope of gray metal toward the Tower of Observation, where a star of light crowned the pyramid's summit. I could picture Cartesius already returned to his place, bending the Great Spyglass upon me. I raised my diskos to him in farewell.

A dim murmur filled the night. Seeing the people in the lower embrasures moving back and forth, I realized they thought I had meant my salute for them. As they shouted and waved, their combined voices resonated through the walls of the sanctuary.

I felt small and unworthy standing there. As foolish as it may sound, after so much being made of my leaving I suddenly pictured how ridiculous I would look if some creature killed me the moment I left The Circle, and I vowed to at least be out of sight before I died. Realizing that the longer I stayed the more I increased my danger, I raised my diskos again, this time reversed, which was more respectful, and turned my face up toward the Tower of Observation, so my friend and mentor would know I thought of him in those last moments.

Perhaps the invisible millions in the upper cities thought my gesture intended for them, for a faint, far murmur, as of a distant wind, flowed down from the heights.

As I lowered my diskos and turned away, the voices fell silent. I felt a slight twinge of pain in my forehead as I stepped across The Circle and passed through the Ether Barrier into the solitude of the Night Land. I decided not to look back for a long time, for fear of weakening my resolve. The ether surged all around me with the good wishes of the multitudes, so that it seemed as if they journeyed with me. This both comforted and concerned me, for I feared it might alert a Force of Evil to my presence, but there was no way to stop them. Neither could they prevent it themselves, since so many people concentrating on a single event always caused such a disturbance.

I hurried into the darkness without considering my direction, until I came to myself and remembered my plan of travel. I wanted to avoid the region where the youths had gone, since its occupants would probably be on the alert. Instead, I intended to journey northwest, to circle behind the back of the Northwest Watcher, past the Plain Of Blue Fire, and then straight north, keeping a significant distance between myself and the House of Silence. Despite making my trek longer, this seemed the most prudent course.

As my first fears of being in the Night Land subsided, I began to notice my surroundings, which took on a new perspective now that I no longer saw them from the pyramid's heights. I journeyed across an enormous plain, bare in some places and covered in others with the gray, rush-like vegetation we called moss bushes, which grew from one to five feet high and smelled dank and rotten. Scattered fires dotted the area. It amazed me how little I could actually see. The Road Where The Silent Ones Walk had vanished beneath the horizon. I thought the red glow lighting the eastern sky must be from the Giants' Kilns, though both it and The Headland From Which Strange Things Peer were hidden. Behind me, to the southwest, the Pit Of Red Smoke loomed beside the Great Pyramid, its fires turning the face of the redoubt crimson, the smoke of its burning billowing high into the air. For the first time, I realized the sheer size of the valley where the Pit lay. Even the word, *valley*, does not begin to describe it, for though we called it the Deep Valley, it was actually an enormous rift.

I felt some relief that the House of Silence also lay beyond my sight, but in the distance the distorted head of the Northwest Watcher peered above the horizon, its twisted features seeming to stare right at me over the glow of the Red Pit. Every time I looked at it, tremors of fear ran through me, beginning at my chest and passing through my body. With the heightened perception of my Night Hearing I sensed the Watcher's presence brooding over the land in unsleeping vigilance. Whenever I could find cover, I slipped from moss bush to moss bush to conceal myself from its eyes.

Although the Red Pit and the Plain Of Blue Fire were also hidden, their lights intermingled across the northern horizon, creating hues varying from silver to crimson. Where their illuminations met, they turned the sky the color of blood. A line stretched across to my right, radiating from the Vale Of Red Fire. Farther right of that, many miles away, I could see the upper torso of the Watcher of the Northeast.

Far behind me, I heard occasional shrieks from the Country of Wailing. These maniacal cries had been terrible enough when heard from the safety of the pyramid. Now, they were almost unbearable. More than anything, my new perspective filled me with awe for the sheer vastness of the land, and I dared not think about it too much, lest my fear overwhelm me.

I began passing some of the scattered fire-holes—pools of bubbling, burning liquid of various sizes and shapes, lighting the surrounding rocks in circles that narrowed and widened with the rise and fall of the flames—but I avoided approaching any too closely for fear of what might lurk around them.

Since I assumed the journey would be a long one, I decided to walk at a moderate speed, keeping a regular schedule in order to maintain my strength. I hoped such caution might also prevent the monsters and beasts from noticing me. To this end, I decided to eat every six hours, three meals per cycle, and sleep from the eighteenth to the twenty-fourth hour.

But I broke my own rule immediately, for I was far too excited to sleep until the exhaustion of creeping and hiding from the eyes of the Northwest Watcher forced me to halt at the twenty-first hour. Neither did I eat in all that time, for the thought of food nauseated me. Only when I began stumbling in fatigue did I look for a place to rest.

Eventually, I noticed a small fire-hole similar to those I had passed earlier. Despite the protection of my armor, the chill of the night had seeped into my bones, and I longed for a bit of warmth. I soon reached the hole and found it deserted and comparably cheerful, a circle only a few paces wide, full of a dull, bubbling fluid emitting a sulphurous smoke that drifted straight up into the windless night. A hot spring steamed a few feet from the fire, its waters heated by the flames.

I sat beside the hole and placed my diskos on one of the flat rocks surrounding it. My weariness fell upon me all at once, and for a time I simply sat and stared, too tired to either eat or drink.

During my journey, except for my brief glimpse at the Pit Of Red Smoke, I had not dared to look back at the Great Pyramid. When I finally did, I was both cheered by the sight of it and discouraged by its proximity, for it seemed to have scarcely shrunk, as if I had hardly traveled any distance at all. The hopelessness of my task momentarily overwhelmed me, but my despair eventually passed, leaving me to ponder the sight of the redoubt towering into the night sky, as formidable as any of the monsters besieging it. The crimson light from the Pit Of Red Smoke reflected off the gray metal of the southwest face, making it look like molten iron.

Sitting there, I suddenly remembered that in my former life there had been stars in the sky. The recollection struck me with the full force of a revelation; I could scarcely understand why I had never thought of it before. This sent me into a flurry of speculation; even with the death of the sun, I could not think of any reason for the loss of the stars. The only explanation I could conceive was that something in the upper atmosphere blocked our sight. This, in turn, made me wonder if the sun had truly gone out, or if, dimmed by age, its light hidden by whatever concealed the stars, it still shed a little heat onto the world.

My weariness kept me from dwelling on this for long. Instead my mind turned to all the millions watching me. I made no sign to them, for it seemed absurd to be constantly waving farewell, but it was odd, feeling so alone with so many eyes upon me.

Knowing the Master Monstruwacan must have watched me through every hour of my journey, I realized what a bad beginning I had made by walking past my endurance. How he must have scolded me from his seat within the tower! This thought stirred me to open my scrip and remove my travel rations: three pale tablets that I ate at once. Despite their size, they provided a nutritious meal, but left the stomach feeling empty. I produced a long tube from my scrip and squeezed a few grains of a golden powder into a metal cup. Upon contact with air, the powder fizzed and became liquid, swirling up to the rim. I drank it with some trepidation, since it was so different from my normal sustenance, but despite being bland, it proved nourishing, if not as satisfying as I would have liked.

Without those peculiar foods, my journey would have been impossible, for there was nothing to eat in all the Night Land, whereas I could carry enough supplies within my scrip to last weeks. According to our Records, we had developed the powder and the tablets centuries before, during a period when the crops in the Underground Fields temporarily failed.

As I drank my meal, I went over the equipment I had brought, laying the objects side by side upon the flat rock. Besides the scrip and diskos, I had a pouch containing several useful tools and the only personal object I had brought with me, my battered copy of *Ayleos' Mathematics*. I opened its yellow cover and thumbed through the pages. I did not know why I had brought it; I had a vague notion that its formulas might be useful in some way, and I thought I could keep a journal of my travels in the blank pages at the back. Whatever my reason, it comforted me to hold it there in the darkness, knowing these were the same equations used from time immemorial. I tucked the volume gingerly back into my pouch.

There was also a compass, hand-made by the Master Monstruwacan—so I could finally test whether it indicated direction outside the redoubt. Since I remembered using compasses in my former life, I felt confident it would work, but when I set it down, it spun wildly, presumably still too near the fissure containing the Earth Current.

It pleased me to think of my mentor watching me test the device; since the light was good around the fire-hole, I thought he could see, though I could not be certain. Having used the Great Spyglass countless hours, I knew the wavering fires and rising smoke often gave observers an unexpectedly clear view at times and an unanticipated obscurity at others.

After observing the compass a while, I returned it to my pouch. I considered beginning my journal, but it seemed pointless to do so, since the whole pyramid had seen my progress, and the Monstruwacans were recording my every move. Actually, I was too exhausted to do anything but lie down beside the fire-hole, wrap my cloak around me, and compose myself for sleep. I kept my diskos beneath my cloak, taking comfort from its cold metal.

As I drifted into slumber, a vague surging of the ether reminded me that the whole redoubt watched over me, their hearts stirred by how fragile I must have looked, sleeping like a baby among the horrors of the world. I slept better knowing they watched, but was uneasy as well. I thought of Andrew, striding boldly between the hedge gap to face Mirdath's assailants. I was twenty-one years old, ten years younger than when he had first met her; sometimes I thought of him almost as a mentor. Would I face danger as bravely as he, or would I turn coward? How strange it felt, wanting to measure up to the man I once was.

My last hazy thoughts were of Naani, and I spoke to her in my dreams.

***

A tremendous noise shook me from my sleep, and as I came to my senses, I caught the last reverberations of the Home Call. Without hesitation, I slid from beneath my cloak, my hand on my weapon.

Seeing nothing but the shadows around me, I glanced quickly at the pyramid, hoping for some sign to indicate what had forced Cartesius to risk alerting the Forces of

77

Evil to my presence. I knew without doubt some terror approached, and I shifted my gaze back and forth between the Tower of Observation and my immediate surroundings, while my whole body trembled with fear and excitement.

Far up in the heights, I saw the darting, emerald flashes of the Set Speech. For an instant I was too panicked to decipher their meaning and had to force myself to concentrate. The message warned of a monster crawling toward me through the low moss bushes at my back.

I dove into the vegetation to my left and crouched in hiding. My heart pounded in my chest; sweat broke across my brow. I gripped my diskos.

No sooner had I taken my place, when a Gray Man, twice my height, slipped with serpentine grace out of the bushes beyond the fire-hole. It squinted as if half-blinded from the glare of the flames, and kept its head, which wove from side to side like a viper's, almost level with the ground. I doubt it saw beyond the fire at all, for it soon slithered back among the bushes, only to poke its head out at another place.

It did this three times to my right and three to my left, each time laying its head against the earth, its shoulders hunched, thrusting its jaws forward and turning its neck with the instinctive movements of an animal. Every time it vanished into the bushes, I thought it had seen me and was planning to seize me from behind.

Finally, it moved away, as if preparing to depart, passing around the circle of the fire-hole and vanishing at the spot where it had first appeared.

I drew a ragged breath, but remained crouched, watching and listening while my pulse hammered in my temples. As the moments passed, my breathing grew steadier. The night lay quiet.

Just as I was preparing to crawl away from the spot, I heard the voice of the Master Monstruwacan calling to my soul in the barest whisper.

It circles behind you!

My skin crawled. The beating of the Master Word following the message left no doubt that my old friend, knowing of my Night Hearing, had used the Instruments to send a warning.

I leapt from my position into another clump of undergrowth and crouched again, watching all around, trying

78

despite my anxiety to keep my ears and spirit open to both the Monstruwacan's warnings and my enemy's approach.

The slightest rustling drew my eyes to the right. An enormous, gnarled hand parted the bushes behind the place where I had previously been. Gray eyes peered out, the gray head followed, and the Gray Man rushed forward.

Even as it pounced, I leapt, swinging my diskos with all my strength. The weapon spun, emitting a sparking fire, as if alive and thirsting for blood. I struck the creature across the neck, decapitating it.

The Gray Man writhed in its death throes, uprooting the bushes all around. I backed away and crouched to watch it die, my eyes fixed in morbid fascination. In all my life, this was the first thing I had ever killed, and it surprised me to see the creature so easily slain.

When at last it became still, I strode to the far side of the fire-hole and stood with my diskos held high and spinning, discharging fire so my people would know I had destroyed the beast, in case the shadows had hidden our battle. Perhaps this sounds barbaric, but I was elated with victory; despite my fear, I had not panicked or run away in terror, but had stood and fought. I had passed my rite of initiation into the Night Land. And beyond even the relief of having accomplished that, the acclaim of all the millions pulsing around me made me feel as if I were not entirely alone.

At that moment I longed for the Master Monstruwacan to speak again, to share my triumph. Of course, he did nothing so foolish, for every communication threatened to alert the Evil Forces of my presence.

When my elation passed, I found myself trembling all over. At last I gathered my wits and checked my chronometer. To my dismay, I found I had slept ten hours. I vowed never again to repeat my mistake of traveling to the point of exhaustion.

Circling the fire-hole, I grabbed my cloak, gave one more glance to the pyramid sloping up into the darkness, and continued my journey. It may seem foolish to say I held my diskos with new respect, but having seen its power, I now thought of it as a trusted companion. For the first time I understood the generations-old restriction forbidding anyone from handling another's diskos, a ban prompted by the belief that the weapon would not only prove unresponsive to a stranger's touch, but harmful to anyone who insisted on using it. Perhaps the ancient knights felt the same way about their swords. Because of the prohibition, every man and woman carried their diskoi with them on The Last Road in the Country of Silence, where the weapon was given back to the Earth Current.

After my encounter with the Gray Man, I became skittish, constantly glancing over my shoulder, pausing at the slightest sound, and seeing assailants where none existed. In addition, I grew faint, having once more played the fool by not eating breakfast. Realizing my mistake, I sat down in a clear spot among the bushes, where I chewed the three tablets and drank the water made from the golden powder. I forced myself to rest as well, occasionally glancing at the lights of the Great Pyramid, so close but so unreachable. I remained vigilant, listening with ears and soul and keeping my diskos across my knees, but nothing approached.

As I sat there, the sheer enormity of the Night Land seemed to seep into me, a country so huge I could travel across its surface, surrounded by every manner of horror, and still escape detection because of its sheer size. The thought both comforted and disturbed me, for if the land was large enough for me to go undetected, how could I ever hope to find Naani and the Lesser Redoubt?

Such despairing thoughts were not for me, however, and to escape them, I soon climbed back to my feet and continued walking for six hours to the north and west. In my concern for Naani, I decided not to travel so far northwest, but to save time by keeping more to the north, even though it brought me closer to the Northwest Watcher. This was a rash decision, for if that grim behemoth saw me and signaled a Force of Evil, I would die a terrible death. But the heart is an unruly organ, given to sudden terrors and inexplicable foolishness. It could be that an Evil Influence affected me at that moment; I do not know.

I went another six hours before halting to eat, traveling cautiously and staying among the moss bushes whenever I could find them. Sometimes I was forced to cross bare patches of stony ground where choking sulphur roiled in heavy clouds along the earth. Though I tried to watch in every direction, my eyes were drawn more and more toward the Watcher of the Northwest, whose unholy presence filled all that part of the country. A growing suspicion rose within me that it already knew I was there, a misgiving that drove me to crawl from bush to bush to escape its sight. The sharp stones cut my hands at first, until I remembered the armored gloves in my belt. Again, I lamented my lack of experience in not thinking to wear them before.

Eighteen hours after my battle with the Gray Man, I began to search for somewhere to sleep, and soon reached a place where the land, shattered by subterranean pressures, made a steep descent. I lay on my stomach on the ridge line and peered down the cliff-side a long time, searching for danger. Seeing none, I rose and walked along the rim until I spied a narrow shelf jutting out of the rocks a few feet down. Being both hard to see and to reach, it seemed to offer some measure of safety. Nothing could come at me from below without a difficult climb, and I would hear any monster approaching from above and could escape by slipping to the bottom of the cliff.

More than once, I nearly fell climbing down, but when I reached the bare ledge, its relative safety comforted me, for the rocks overhung it in such a way that drawing close to the wall made me invisible from above. If I leaned out slightly, however, and looked back, I could still see the top third of the Last Redoubt, its lights shining through the darkness. I glanced up at its summit, where the Master Monstruwacan might even then be focusing the Great Spyglass upon me.

I ate my dinner, and being bone-weary, lay down on my left side, my back against the rock, my head upon my pouch and scrip, my diskos against my chest, my cloak covering me. The moment I composed myself for slumber, two things occurred to me: first, that to judge by my grumbling stomach, the tablets and powder were not particularly filling; second, that I had miscalculated my meals. Despite my plan to eat three times in twenty-four hours, I had actually had four meals, once at waking, then once every six of the eighteen hours.

"What a fool!" I whispered. "Was anyone ever less prepared? An idiot and a glutton, that's what I am. But at least I know I'm not starving . . . even if it feels like I am."

I chuckled. For some reason this lifted my spirits—so far I had made error after error, yet there I was, still alive. I decided to continue eating four meals, since that seemed to fit my schedule, but to use only two tablets each time. That sobered me somewhat, since it meant living on even less, but thankfully, my anxiety for Naani had kept me from eating much during the last month, and my stomach had already shrunk. Small comfort, that.

"Tomorrow, meals will be lean," I murmured, through half-closed lids. "Lean, lean, lean." I drifted into a watchful sleep.

***

I awoke, and finding nothing to fear, looked at the dial of my chronometer. My unconscious mind had followed my instructions well, rousing me after little more than six hours. Groaning, I pulled myself to my feet and ate two of the tablets. Already, I longed for solid food—my stomach gnawed on itself—but I drank some of the water, which helped ease the pain. I wound my cloak about me, put my diskos on my hip and my scrip and pouch in their places, and peered over the ledge into the night. Seeing neither brute nor monster, I glanced at the Great Pyramid, which still looked quite close because of its colossal size. The sheer solitude of my journey seemed suddenly overwhelming, so that I descended the ledge quickly and strode away, trying to leave my homesickness behind. I soon became aware that I was being careless, however—and remembering my previous errors of the day before—slowed my pace and took my diskos in hand.

Having always seen the Night Land from the pyramid, I was fascinated by the shifting patterns of my changing perspective, which revealed new details in every monstrous form. This proved more than a little confusing, and I found myself having to constantly regain my bearings.

At the fourteenth hour, I drew nearly parallel to the Watcher of the Northwest, which stood about a mile to my right. It had been visible from the pyramid's base, though I had traveled over fifty miles to reach it. Up close, it's sheer size terrified me as I crawled among the moss bushes, glimpsing it between the fronds. Rearing before me, a living mountain, it seemed a completely different monster than the one I had always known. I was amazed at the way its chin projected toward the Last Redoubt, like a jutting cliff hollowed at its center, hanging before the flames of the Red Pit, scorched by their crimson glow. With its scored face it resembled less a living creature than a sculpture, worn by the eons.

In my fascination, I soon found I had crept closer than I intended, and for a moment all the terrors of childhood engulfed me. My courage abruptly failed; I could not go on, but lay upon my stomach, scarcely able to breath. But when the Watcher did not notice me; when its titanic head did not swivel around, as in my fear I imagined it might, my terror faded. I realized how small I must be to such a one, hidden as I was in shadow and the thick shelter of the bushes. Growing bolder, I peered between the vegetation to try to see the creature more clearly, for I lay closer than anyone had ever been.

It rose into the night, jet black except where the light of the Red Pit colored it. It seemed rooted to the earth; I could not imagine such a mass ever advancing. Lumps, indentations, and warts large as houses covered it. Where the light touched it, the lumps stood out on its hoary face like the mountains of the moon.

I lay watching it a long time, until I became aware of a stirring in the ether. A wave of anxiety, created by the combined concern of my people, washed over me. Fearing the Watcher might sense their passions and guess the cause, I began crawling away from the behemoth at an angle. When I had gone a few hundred feet a mist seemed to lift from my mind. I suddenly felt the Watcher's silent, steadfast intellect pulsing all around me, and realized the beast not only knew of my presence, but sought, with infinite patience, to lure me to my destruction. Only my Night Hearing had saved me, for without it, the emotions emanating from the pyramid would never have brought me to my senses.

Hearing a creaking sound above me, like stone grinding against stone, I glanced up at the Watcher's brooding face. An icy tremor ran through me, for the titan's head turned the merest fraction, and the soulless disks of its eyes looked full upon me.

I began shivering so uncontrollably I could scarcely command my own body, not out of fear, but from the weight of that awful gaze bearing upon me. I put my head down, not daring to meet those terrible eyes, and attempted to crawl away. My trembling grew to the intensity of seizures; I collapsed, writhing, while the Watcher's will pressed upon me, seeking to shake me to pieces.

For what seemed an eternity, I thrashed about, unable to proceed, caught like an insect on a pin. Despite my terror, I forced myself to concentrate, first on my right hand, then my left, willing them to push my body up. I drew myself to a crawling position, then dragged my knees forward, one leg at a time, all the while shuddering like an epileptic. I returned my attention to my right hand, and thrust outward, then did the same with my left. So I went, step by infinite step, for two miles, body quivering, bones rattling. During my struggle I became aware of a peculiar din, which I dimly recognized as my chattering teeth.

The pressure abruptly ceased, leaving me gasping, heart hammering, every muscle aching. I kept on for another mile, not daring to look back. When I had put some distance between myself and the Watcher and could no longer sense its dreadful influence, I went more swiftly. Yet, many hours passed before I left that mountain of vigilance, and I often glanced behind me, fearing the Watcher would send an Evil Force in pursuit. I do not know what saved me from destruction as I lay beneath its scrutiny, unless it was the Rite of Preparation. It seemed as if the Watcher tried, almost casually, to destroy me, and finding it could not do so easily, decided I was not worth the effort.

At the eighteenth hour, I stopped to rest. As I ate, I studied the Watcher's pitted, humped back. Its vast shoulders rose into the night, black and ravaged, silhouetted against the shining of the Red Pit. Although I could not be certain, I thought its head had returned to its original position. I pondered the way the brute had studied the Great Pyramid through all the eons—steadfast, silent, and alone—beyond mortal comprehension.

The Vale Of Red Fire ran out of the Red Pit toward the east, a bloody gash across the earth, miles long, much wider than I had ever imagined. I turned back to the north, where I could finally see the beginnings of the Plain Of Blue Fire, which had been hidden behind the glow of the Red Pit during most of my journey. Beyond that, distant volcanoes glowed, and the Seven Lights glistened upon the Black Hills. I shivered as I saw the upper windows of the House of Silence standing on a low hill many miles northeast of my position.

I ate and rested for a few minutes, and then, unable to sleep until I put further distance between myself and the Watcher, I continued for six more hours, at which time I came to the Place Where The Silent Ones Kill. Since I intended to circumvent that infamous plain, and was half-starved for warmth and light, I set off toward a cluster of distant fire-holes burning to the north.

Bare rock covered The Place Where The Silent Ones

Kill. As I crept through the vegetation bordering its east side, I watched for any sign of a Silent One moving across that quiet, rocky plain. With the exception of the House of Silence, this region terrified me more than anywhere else in the Night Land, and had done so from my earliest childhood. A cold, gray light, diffused and dismal, overspread the whole country. The illumination possessed strange properties, for those who stared into it perceived moving shadows, never clearly seen, always at the edge of perception. Whether this was caused by some atmospheric trait, or by the clouding of human reason, no one knew.

Because I dreaded this place so, I slid quietly from bush to bush, my eyes fastened on the dim light of the plain to my left. I often thought I glimpsed a Silent One, standing motionless, watching, only in the next instant to see nothing at all.

As I crept among the moss bushes, I pushed the fronds aside and found myself at the edge of a clearing. From my vantage, I could see the vegetation growing again only a short sprint away, if I dared take the chance. I licked my lips, debating between this and bypassing the empty plain by following the curve of the foliage east for several hours, a course that might take me into even greater danger.

After searching the plain a long time without seeing any sign of life, I decided to make the run. As I half-rose out of the bushes, it seemed my eyes were suddenly opened to something waiting in the wavering light.

I dropped back into concealment, cold sweat on my brow, and peered once more between the fronds. Instantly, out of the gray luminance a long line of lofty figures appeared, shrouded from head to foot, facing me in watching silence. I felt naked before their gaze; I knew my death, or worse, had come. My limbs stiffened and would not obey my commands.

For long moments, I dared not move, as if their eyes pinned me in place. After what seemed an eternity, when the Silent Ones did not approach, I realized I was safe as long as I did not step across the barren plain of their dominion. Mustering my courage, I crawled back through the bushes, and after gaining some distance, began to circle around that country of gray light. I felt no relief until I bypassed the Silent Ones completely and reached a place where I could stand again and travel more easily.

I pressed on through the twenty-fourth hour, heartsick

and homesick, weary beyond hope—gripped by a fear the Silent Ones would send some monster in pursuit—so unnerved that despite my exhaustion, I dared not rest. Only the thought of Naani's last, despairing message drove me on.

By this time, I was shaking from the cold. The farther I traveled, the deeper the chill seeped into my bones, until I had but one goal, to reach the fire-holes to the north and sleep before their flames.

As I approached the fires, I rallied somewhat and increased my pace. I drew near enough to the first blaze to see that its light rose out of a deep hollow among the moss bushes, making it what we called a fire-pit rather than a fire-hole. The surrounding vegetation, which was easily five feet high, prevented me from looking down into the hollow.

Being desperately eager to reach warmth, I traveled with more haste than care and soon reached the top of the pit. The climb proved more difficult than I expected, because the soft ground gave way in places. The bushes grew tallest at the rim, perhaps somehow nourished by the flames. I parted them and looked into the crater.

A thunderous voice filled the air, deep, husky, and horrid, brimming with an indescribable evil. I drew back, startled, instinctively clutching my ears, every nerve taut, afraid to go forward or back, trembling like a hare caught between musket and hound.

The voice bellowed again and was answered by another. At first I thought they had seen me, but I soon realized they were conversing among themselves. Their words rose, slow, brutish, and hoarse, from the hollow.

They spoke a while, then fell into a long silence, during which I considered the best way to escape. I shifted my position carefully, wary of the rustling bushes giving me away. Thinking it better to know my enemies' location before I moved, I parted the fronds the merest inch and peered down into the pit.

A large flame burned at its center, and scores of holes covered the slopes surrounding the fire. Enormous men lay burrowed in the holes, sleeping with only their heads or legs protruding. Three more giants, each larger than an elephant, with stiff red hair and large festering sores, sat around the flame.

I had caught them in the middle of skinning the carcass

of one of the Night Hounds, but during my brief glimpse, they sat motionless, listening, peering stupidly at the ground, the sharpened, bloody stones in their hands forgotten. Panic filled me, for I knew they suspected my presence. To be seen was to be destroyed. In my haste to withdraw, I loosened a stone; it rattled down the hollow.

Immediately, the three monsters turned their heads upward. They seemed to stare directly at me through the vegetation.

I backed away, making even more noise than before, unable to tear my eyes from those of the titans'. Their orbs shone red and green, like the eyes of animals. A roar arose from the pit, a turmoil like the cries of all the devils in hell. The hollow came alive with giants, as the sleepers woke, crawled from their dens, and lumbered up the sides toward me.

As I retreated, the soft ground gave way beneath me, sending me tumbling into a hole among the bushes. Earth and rock collapsed over me. At first, as sand and ash filled my throat, I tried to scramble out, but then realized I was completely hidden. A bit of air reached me through cracks in the covering stones. I lay still, trying neither to cough nor breathe.

Monstrous footsteps shook the earth all around. At any moment, I expected my hiding place to collapse, suffocating me, but though the rocks quaked, they held firm. I heard running and shouting all through the night and the sound of bushes being uprooted. Sometimes the giants seemed directly above me, sometimes far away. At last the tumult drifted off to the south.

I dared not wait too long in the hole, for fear of the titans' return, so when I heard their voices dwindling in the distance, I pushed my way out. That proved a struggle in itself—the weight of the earth was nearly more than I could lift—but I finally pulled myself into the night air, thankful for my salvation, but terrified of being discovered. I crawled through the moss bushes on hands and knees for three long hours, traveling northwest as fast as I could go.

Exhaustion finally overtook me, and I collapsed among the vegetation into a hard sleep. I had journeyed twenty-seven hours, neither eating nor drinking during the last nine, and I lay there, alone among the bushes and stones, a morsel for any creature that might happen upon me.

VII
DOORS IN THE NIGHT

I woke ten hours later, unharmed but stiff in every joint, nearly frozen from having failed to cover myself with my cloak. My stomach ached with hunger.

Before rising, I pulled myself to a crouch and studied my surroundings until I was certain that nothing stirred. By stamping my feet and swinging my arms back and forth, I soon restored my circulation, then sat down to eat, my cloak about me, my diskos at my hip.

"A feast," I murmured. "Congratulations, Andros. You have earned four tablets and two cups of water."

I ate, staring at the Northwest Watcher's back. The lights of the redoubt burned like beacons through the dark. I was so hungry my meager fare seemed a banquet, and despite my aching muscles the meal put me in excellent spirits. The fact I lived at all seemed utterly miraculous, and I rose cheerfully and set out again toward the northwest. So content was I that, to my chagrin, I caught myself whistling unconsciously under my breath, an act I discontinued at once.

I walked twelve hours, eating and drinking twice during that time, thankful for the surrounding silence which I hoped meant that I would not see any further terrors for at least a few hours. This was a particularly dark part of the Night Land, a bleak country empty of fire, warmth, or vapors, apparently shunned by all life, and I kept my bearings only by watching the cold, distant light of the Plain Of Blue Fire.

A story persists among the chronicles of the Last Redoubt, a legend handed down through countless generations, believed by all the children and many adults. Those scholars seeking to verify the stories generally accept three first-hand traveler's accounts from the Records. Each describes mysterious Doorways in the Night, ruptures in the ether, opening and closing on horrors beyond mortal comprehension. Most people believed that the Doors were remnants from the days when humans accidentally opened gateways into other planes of existence, allowing the Forces of Evil into the world. The accounts varied in their details, with only one exception: those who survived hearing the phenomenon were convinced their comrades had suffered not only death, but destruction of the spirit.

My ordeal began when I heard a soft creaking like a door opening, followed by a moaning hum just above my head and slightly to the left. Though quite close, it also seemed to come from a great distance, as if from a realm never meant for human hearing. The sound was unmistakable. I have no way to explain it, except to say it was unlike anything I had ever heard or wanted to hear again, and I *knew* beyond doubt that this was a Night Door.

A horror gripped me, akin to the dread I felt before the Silent Ones, but immeasurably different and immensely worse. I instinctively removed my right glove and bared my arm, ready to bite down on the Capsule of Oblivion hidden just below my skin, to take my own life for the sake of my soul. Though I loved my existence, I knew only death could save me if whatever lay beyond the Door chose to strike.

I dropped to the ground and began crawling toward the right, away from the sound, supporting myself on one hand while keeping the capsule poised close to my jaws.

Waves of weakness and nausea swept over me, as if an icy wind flowed from the open Door. My teeth chattered uncontrollably, as they had when facing the Northwest Watcher, and my heart throbbed so painfully against my chest I thought it would burst. I kept glancing up over my shoulder, but could not see anything in the absolute darkness.

The noise abruptly died away, but I crawled for another hour, the capsule ready, my whole body quaking not just from fear, but from my exposure to unearthly Forces. Twice, I became physically sick.

Finally, my heart slowed and my spirit grew easier, though chills and nausea still wracked my frame. If the Door had opened immediately above me instead of to the side, I would surely have been lost.

No sooner did I think I was safe than I heard the sound again, far in front of me. I concealed myself as best I could among a few scattered boulders, and made a wide circle to avoid the source. Since I had been straining to listen, I was far away when I heard it, and managed to evade it before it could harm me.

At the eighteenth hour, I stopped to rest. But when I tried to eat, I gagged and could not keep anything down. I felt unclean, befouled in both body and spirit. I lay down in the hollow of a solitary rock rising above the moss bushes, threw my cloak over me, and fell into a dreadful slumber filled with nightmare shapes and fumbling hands —the kind of dreams normally brought on by fever.

When I stumbled to my feet six hours later, I felt little rested, but my stomach was better and my strength had returned. Though I still remained in a lightless region, I caught the glimmer of fire-holes to the north, and beyond them, the mysterious shining of the Plain Of Blue Fire. Behind me, for the first time, the Great Pyramid seemed far away. This surprised me, since I had spent the day before crawling through a circuitous route, but I suppose I had reached a point where the sum of my travels affected the redoubt's apparent height. Had I felt better, I would have tried to calculate the effect of distance on perceived size, but even mathematics held no appeal for me just then.

I wondered if any animals or half-men had ever lived in this part of the Night Land, and if so, whether they had been driven off by the Doorways, the lack of heat, or a combination of the two. Whatever the case, I stayed alert, stopping often to listen for the sound of creaking portals. My vigilance proved futile, however, for I heard a Door opening right behind me, as if I had just passed beneath it. As the portal widened, the buzzing din of the alien eternity lying beyond its threshold increased.

Perhaps it opened by chance; perhaps my passing disturbed a Force of Evil. Whatever the case, no sooner had I heard the sound than my former weakness returned worse than before. I dropped instantly into a creeping crawl, willing my muscles to press on against the power that sapped my life.

The moments seemed like hours; I faintly saw my hands moving before me, as if I watched them from a distance. I forgot all about the Capsule of Oblivion; all thoughts except escape—or death—were driven from my mind.

Eventually I got away, though feeling even more ill than I had before. I have no idea why I was spared, for if it had chosen to take me, I would have been easy prey for whatever stood beyond the Door. Perhaps the Rite of Preparation helped me more than I knew. Whatever the case, I did realize one thing in comparing my encounters with the Doors to my confrontation with the Watcher of the Northwest: despite the horror of the Watcher, its power rose from a cold, calculating intellect. Though it might be able to summon a Force of Evil, it was not, itself, such a Force. But whatever waited behind the Doors possessed the power to enslave the soul.

I crawled as far away as my strength allowed, my eyes blurring, my whole body aching. When I could no longer continue, I dropped to my stomach and wrapped myself in my cloak. Despite having traveled only a short distance that day, I fell asleep where I lay and did not wake for seven hours.

***

I rose to a throbbing headache, but was able to eat and drink, and soon felt well enough to continue north toward the fire-holes. After the traumas of the previous day, my courage failed me; I jumped at every sound and glanced constantly over my shoulder. At times, my own breathing even startled me. I had fits of trembling.

After going only a short distance, I thought I heard the sound of another Door. I stopped, hid myself, and listened for a long time, my nerves screaming at me to run away, to avoid encountering that terror again. At last I decided I must have imagined it, for the noise the portals made was as plain as the hiss of a viper—one can fancy a hundred serpents in the Underground Fields, but the sound of a real one is unmistakable. Still, I could not make myself go forward, but lay frozen, unmanned, my mind empty of everything but dread. It took several moments to muster my courage enough to begin crawling again toward a nearby fire-pit.

After my experience with the giants, I approached the fire cautiously. It lay in a shallow hollow, and I peered through the bushes a long time, making certain it was deserted before I descended. Once down, I sat beside the flames, my back to a tall boulder. The bubbling pit cheered me after my long march through the darkness.

"Andrew would have liked this," I murmured, as I watched the gases within the pool build, escape with a soft grumble, then fall silent only to begin building once more. "He loved the things of nature. He would be amazed at all I've seen."

I picked up a pebble and rolled it in my hands. "How long," I asked the fire, "have you murmured here alone? Half of eternity? Andrew would want to know."

The blaze turned the sides of the hollow crimson crackling its reply, but I did not understand. The hollow was a lonely place, but I was glad just to sit with my back against the sheltering stone and let the bubbling fire melt the residue of the Doors from my spirit. The rock, which stood like a sentry above me, was hot, and its heat warmed my heart. Because my mind for some reason focused on my former life, I took comfort just then from the borrowed recollections of Andrew's horses. I thought of noble Battalion, my black stallion: his silken coat and coarse mane, the velvet softness of his nose, the noise of his hooves on English roads, the way he blew and snorted on cold mornings. I could almost smell the scent of him. How Andrew loved that sturdy beast! It was good to think of horses there, amid the desolation.

After some time, I stirred myself, as one stirs the embers. I ate and drank, and fell asleep where I was. I had walked less than twelve hours since my last slumber, but was exhausted, and dreamed no dreams at all. After so much danger to body and spirit, those few hours of rest were my salvation. Without them, I could not have gone on.

When I awoke I felt stronger than I had in what seemed many weeks; I rose, prepared my meal, and climbed the far slope of the hollow toward the north. More fire-holes stretched before my path, like a line of torches leading me on to the Plain Of Blue Fire.

Perhaps it was wishful thinking, but I was convinced I had left the Doorways behind. My heart felt lighter; I remained alert, but no longer glanced constantly over my shoulder. After walking three hours, I drew close to another fire-pit, and being chilled, decided to risk approaching it. I paused at the edge behind the safety of the moss bushes and surveyed the area. A burning jet of gas stood at the pit's center, surrounded by scattered boulders, but the hollow was otherwise empty. I scanned the sides without seeing any cavities a monster could use for a den. After a moment's hesitation, I decided to descend. The sides of the pit were steep, and it took several moments of careful climbing to arrive at the bottom.

I reached the pit and stood warming my hands, grateful

for the heat. The crackling fire seemed almost homey to me; a picture of Andrew and Mirdath's hearth drifted through my mind, and I sighed in a mixture of longing and contentment. After a moment, I turned my eyes to my surroundings. On the rock wall, my shadow danced with the rising and falling of the flames, fluctuating from the shape of a giant to the squat body of a dwarf. When I glanced at the floor, I noticed that the ground on the far side of the hollow was covered in an unusual, yellow-tinged sand rather than bare stone. The fire's glare kept me from seeing it clearly, so I circled the pit to examine it more carefully, having no fear or thought of any sort of danger.

When I reached the other side I discovered a curious, shiny substance spread across the sand. I came closer. As I stooped to examine it, it moved.

I leapt away, diskos raised. Hearing the sand stirring at my back, I glanced quickly behind me. The sand writhed, rising and falling; serpentine forms shivered and curled beneath its surface.

As I hesitated, uncertain which way to go, the ground beneath me heaved, buckling upward, nearly knocking me from my feet. The whole surface of the fire-pit was in motion; I suddenly realized I was surrounded. Animal instinct took over, and I sprinted across the shifting sand to the edge of the hollow. The sides at that point were too steep to climb, so I turned, my back to the wall, diskos ready, not knowing what new terror I was about to face.

Slowly, ponderously, a Yellow Beast, like a living hill, lifted itself off the ground, sending sand sifting downward. It had a segmented body made up of three sections, the back two rounded like those of an ant, the front elongated, giving the impression of a broad, blockish chest. Its face was like that of a horse, but with wide jaws and the heavy tusks of a boar. As it rose, it unfurled dozens of clawed tentacles. It gathered its multiple arms to itself, and stretched three of its members toward me.

I swung the diskos with all my might, severing two of the tentacles. The third instinctively withdrew, but I stepped forward and lopped it off, leaving the stump wriggling on the sand. The creature gave an eerie, high-pitched shriek, a cross between the buzzing of an insect and the scream of a child. This was not the end, however, for it charged at me with ferocious speed belying its great size, using its tentacles like the legs of a spider.

I leapt back and retreated along the edge of the fire-pit, trying to avoid the claws. Four times I dodged it, but the monster was far faster than I. It caught my heel, causing me to stumble. I grasped the rock side with one hand, barely keeping my balance, but by then several claws had seized me. The creature was unbelievably powerful; I could not break its hold. One of its members held my diskos arm, keeping me from using my weapon.

In desperation, I reversed my course and charged straight at the beast. It had bent all its efforts toward pulling me toward it and was unprepared for my change of course. Its claws slipped from me. As I drew close, it tried to reach me with its gaping, yellow mouth. I ducked; its gnashing jaws closed a fraction of an inch from my head, and then I was under its heavy body and arching legs.

Its whole form was covered with huge, spiny hairs so sharp they would have cut me to pieces if not for my metal plating. Poison oozed from the spines in huge, shiny drops, venom so lethal its stench burned my nose and throat. It fell dripping and hissing onto my armor. The creature heaved itself to the side, trying to bring its legs around to grasp me, but I thrust upward with my diskos. The blade spun, roaring in its thirst for death, sending out a wheel of golden fire beneath the yellow body of the beast. It cut through the creature's abdomen, spilling pus and entrails on the ground.

The monster screamed and leapt back, knocking me away. I was half-blinded by blood and muck, and before I could see again, it darted in and seized me with two of its claws, pinning my weapon hand to my side and bending me over as if to break my back. I felt my armor straining; I nearly fainted from the pain. With a desperate effort I reached across my body, seized my diskos with my left hand and struck at the tentacles. It was a weak blow, but the weapon did most of the work.

The Yellow Beast threw me across the hollow. I landed at the edge of the fire and tottered precariously, the bubbling, roaring pit gaping before me, the heat of its flames singeing my brow. With a savage wrench, I pulled myself back from destruction.

When I turned, I found that my blow to the monster's body had finally taken its toll. It had collapsed, its legs crumpled beneath it, its body churning up the sand in its death throes. This was fortunate, for my own strength was gone, and I could not have withstood another attack. I fell to my knees, helpless, my breath coming in gasps.

Eventually, I recovered enough to examine myself. I was bruised all over, but otherwise unwounded. A sharp, hairy claw gripped my right ankle, but my armor had protected me from its sting. I kicked it into the fire with my other foot.

Though the Yellow Beast no longer moved, I still dared not approach it, so I retreated to the far side of the hollow. After regaining my composure, I decided I would never be able to rest until I washed the monster's taint from me.

My whole body aching, I climbed out of the hollow, back into the night, to search for one of the hot springs I had passed. I soon found another hollow containing three small fires with a steaming puddle bubbling beyond the third.

Before entering the hollow I walked all along its topmost edge, looking for danger. Seeing none, I made a spiraling descent, examining the ground from every angle to avoid encountering another spider-beast. Just as I was about to strip off my armor so I could wash, a small serpent struck at my foot. I jumped back, startled. My nerves already frayed, I darted back in with my diskos, killing the snake in a blind fury. For some reason, the thought of dying at its fangs after surviving the spider-beast infuriated me. I checked my foot, but my armor had protected me once more. Still, I no longer dared remove my clothes.

Finally, I tested the water temperature, and finding it bearable, laid my scrip, pouch, cloak, and diskos at the edge of the pool.

Feeling I had taken every precaution, I stepped daintily into the puddle and immediately plunged several feet into what proved to be a deep well. The hot, sulphurous water covered my head, burning my eyes and stinging my nose. Choking, I thrashed my way back to the surface, half in panic, half afraid of being seized by an inhabitant of the pool.

I clambered onto firm ground, and scooted back from the water in case I had awakened a lurking beast. For a few moments I watched, diskos ready, my wet body trembling in the chill air.

When nothing appeared, I began to laugh—softly, so as not to arouse danger—but deeply, nonetheless. After so many precautions I had overlooked such a simple thing. I could have drowned! If any ever read this account, they will probably think me foolish. So be it! I wonder if they could have done as well in such darkness and danger? But I laughed until my bruised sides ached. Better that than weeping.

Eventually I noticed the sulphur had washed the muck from my armor, to say nothing of my face and hands. Neither had the chemicals burned me. I returned to the pool and scrubbed first my diskos, then my cloak, scrip, and pouch.

By the time I finished, my teeth were chattering from the cold. Knowing I had to get warm immediately or risk becoming ill, I approached the nearest of the three fireholes, only to find it guarded by a score of small serpents. When the other flames proved the same, I took my belongings and returned to the hollow of the Yellow Beast. With its guardian destroyed, I doubted that anything remained to harm me. I sat before the fire on the side opposite the carcass, watching the steam rise from my armor and cloak as the heat dried them.

Afterward, knowing I would find nowhere as safe as that hollow, I resolved to put my disgust in my pocket, as the saying goes, and sleep there. I ate and drank, and after examining the monster carefully to insure it was dead, made a comfortable bed in the sand with my cloak wrapped around me and my diskos cradled to my chest.

Before I fell asleep, I glanced around, and for the first time perceived that the depth of the hollow and the distance from the Great Pyramid blocked my home from sight. This affected me more deeply than I would have suspected, making the night seem abysmally forlorn. I laid my head back on the pouch that served as my pillow and turned my thoughts toward Naani, but that only made me anxious for her safety. I tried thinking about horses again, but visions of the Yellow Beast kept lumbering through my mind.

Finally, I fell asleep pondering the Insoluble Conundrum, an equation for which there was said to be no solution. In my student days in the pyramid I used to spend hours brooding on it. Numbers rose and fell in my mind, and as my thoughts grew more hazy it seemed if I could but solve the Conundrum, it would show me the way to Naani.

VIII
NIGHT HOUNDS

I awoke seven hours later, my muscles so sore and uncomfortable from my battle that I could scarcely rise. Despair had overtaken me while I slept, for I had dreamt of the sunlit lands, and the dreams only served to remind me that I slept in darkness, woke to darkness, that darkness covered the whole world. I began to feel the strain of my isolation; I wondered how it would affect my mind.

I drew a ragged breath and stood, which made me wince in pain. I forced myself to exercise until I grew more limber, then ate breakfast and shuffled into the dark.

I encountered nothing dangerous until the second third of the day's journey, when two shining men, seemingly made of pale mist, appeared far to my right. Though their bodies scarcely seemed to move, they advanced rapidly across the countryside, figures easily forty feet tall, but without thickness, like paintings passing through the night.

I hid in the bushes and watched them go by about two hundred yards from my position, quiet as vapor and no more substantial. They came out of the north and soon vanished into the darkness of the south. If they saw me they showed no sign. I did not know whether they were good or evil, but I recognized them as the Mist Men mentioned in the ancient Records. During my time in the Tower of Observation, I had sometimes glimpsed such vaporous beings, though always too far away to be clearly seen. Now, as I watched them passing, it occurred to me that perhaps these were the visible shapes of some of the Forces abroad in the land. But this was only idle speculation.

A wave of melancholy passed through me; if I was witnessing phenomenon my people considered fables, I must be far from home, indeed.

That day, I passed seven large fire-pits and two small ones. I always approached them carefully, for living things often dwelled around them, such as the enormous man sitting before the flames of the sixth fire-hole, his knees drawn up to his chin. He had a long nose, bent downward as in the illustrations of goblins. His huge eyes darted back and forth, reflecting the firelight, the whites appearing and vanishing. Despite his human features, he was not really a man, and his bestial odor filled the hollow. I slipped quietly away, looking always over my shoulder.

At the eighteenth hour, I began searching for a safe place to sleep. Since many of the fire-holes were inhabited, I decided to avoid them, so I lay down among the moss bushes, but slept only fitfully in the bitter cold. I woke several hours later, stiff and shivering, and had to beat my hands together and stride back and forth to restore circulation to my limbs.

I soon reached the northwest border of the Plain Of Blue Fire. The Plain, which I kept to my right, was not a proper flame, but a cold, blue glow, eerie and dreadful, floating just above the ground. In its dismal illumination, the near-by moss bushes looked black and twisted. Despite its seeming transparency, it blocked everything behind it, including the Great Pyramid. My people could no longer see me. A loneliness, worse than before, fell on my soul.

From the time I drew abreast of the Plain Of Blue Fire, I crawled on my hands and knees. My journey took me quite close to it, and though I could see nothing within its blue folds, I heard peculiar voices calling to one another across its breadth, as if spirits wandered blindly within it, vainly seeking one another throughout eternity.

For three days I crept beside it, keeping as much distance as possible—usually about two miles—for I felt it must be linked either to Evil Forces or unknown monsters. Though I had to crawl, I kept a good, steady pace, sometimes feeling like a machine plodding through the darkness, sometimes like a beast of burden placing one foot in front of the other. At the eighteenth hour of each journey I slept, the first time beneath a thick bush, the second upon a high ledge of a lone rock protruding among the vegetation. No harm came to me, except from the cold, but the blind shining of the Plain prevented me from catching even a glimpse of the Last Redoubt.

During this time I realized how remiss I had been in not keeping a record of the details of my journey, so at the end of each trek I started sketching maps and writing a few short lines in the back of *Ayleos' Mathematics*.

I passed thirteen fire-holes and ten fire-pits, but saw no

living thing in any except one inhabited by creatures similar to scorpions, only more squat and thick. They were as large as my head—miserable bed mates for any man.

In the sixteenth hour of the third day's journey I passed beyond the Plain Of Blue Fire and spied the Great Pyramid again, looking quite small far behind me and to my right. Only my caution kept me from cheering at the sight of it. I did, in that moment of weakness, break my promise not to signal to my people, and in a bare place between the weeds I held up my diskos in salute. Shortly thereafter, I felt a disturbance of the ether and knew someone in the Tower of Observation had glimpsed me and sent word through the Hour Slips to the inhabitants.

I pictured the millions rushing to the embrasures, flushing with disappointment when they could not see me; only the Great Spyglass could focus so far. But how sweet it was to sense their prayers and good will surrounding me, wrapping me in love and concern. I wondered if Cartesius had been the one to first see me.

Even though I relished their regard, it was foolish to have signaled to them, for their combined attention might attract the notice of an Evil Force, of which I most feared the House of Silence now looming in the distance. Realizing my error, I turned and hurried away. The stirring soon ceased.

Close to the eighteenth hour, hearing the sound of falling water, I discovered a hot fountain boiling out of the rocks in a column thick as my body. A stream flowed from it, plainly visible by the flickering light of the numerous surrounding fire-holes. A trail of steam hung above it, colored crimson by the firelight, a rather pretty sight amid the bleakness. I followed its winding way through the moss bushes, testing the water temperature as I went until I reached a point where it had cooled enough to touch without burning my hand. Sitting on a small boulder, I took off my boots and bathed my aching feet in the warmth. Such comforts were hard to find in that harsh land, and I sighed in gratitude. Then, with the air of one contemplating a stay in the best room of the One Thousandth City, I considered how nice it would be to find a place among the moss bushes to retire for dinner and slumber.

No sooner did I think this, when I heard the distant baying of a Night Hound, rising northwest of the Plain Of Blue Fire. Though I still sat beside the smoking river, I no longer felt its warmth. An icy fear spread over me.

"Is it me it's after?" I whispered, my voice hoarse from disuse.

Still I remained, unmoving, listening, my feet yet in the stream. Out of the night the howling came again, from what seemed less than a mile off. And with a dead certainty, I knew the brute was tracking me.

It is difficult to describe my sense of helplessness, for where, in all that country, could I hide from an animal large as a horse, with the jaws and nose of a hound?

I scrambled to get my boots back on, and though I fumbled in my fear, was soon up, diskos in hand, my gear upon me. Though I tried to think, no plan would come, and I turned in a rapid circle, muttering, unable to decide anything. Then I forced the panic down, forced myself to concentrate.

An idea came to me, and I immediately ran down the middle of the stream, which was about ankle-deep. Before I had gone far I heard the hound baying again, even closer.

I thrashed furiously through the water for more than a minute, until the moment when I thought the beast must have reached the place where I had entered the stream. I slowed to a quick walk, going as silently as possible to keep it from hearing me.

As I glanced from side to side, I imagined seeing a Night Hound in every shadow, but at last I heard it again, baying a short distance away. I sank down into the knee-deep water and turned on my stomach, letting the stream cover me. With only the top of my head and my eyes exposed, I watched until I saw the hound approach. The steam made its shape hazy, but I could still see it, a black, monstrous form, powerful as a stallion.

I did not watch as it streaked past me at a lumbering gallop, for I ducked my head below the surface and held it there until my lungs were fit to burst. And when I raised up again, I struggled to breath as softly as possible. I could not see the Night Hound, but I heard it whining among the moss bushes, tearing them under its paws as it darted back and forth.

A silence soon fell, but I dared not move. If the water had been cold, I would have frozen to death. The moments passed; I listened to my heart pounding against my armor. The steam rose upward, vanishing into the black sky.

Just when I thought the hound had gone, when I was

about to stand up, I heard it running toward me again. It passed so swiftly I had no time to duck, but instinctively froze where I lay. It tore the ground and bushes in its passing—clods of earth and stone splashed into the stream.

Then it was gone, and I heard it baying farther and farther away, its cries growing ever more dim.

I rose, determined to put some distance between myself and the beast. I kept to the stream. Whenever I stopped to listen, I could hear it baying, far away.

I slogged down the stream for twelve hours, my body taut from watching and listening, the hound baying ceaselessly. The water seeping into my boots grew gradually colder. And after all that time, when I thought I might finally be safe, I raised my eyes from watching for danger along the banks, and found myself approaching the House of Silence.

It had always been my intention to remain as far from that dreadful structure as possible. Instead, the hound had driven me right to it, for the stream intersected and followed the Road Where The Silent Ones Walk almost straight to its door. I left the water, which had become unbearably cold, and crept into the moss bushes.

No sooner had I done so than the hound quit howling, a silence that startled me at first, making me think the beast was close enough to see me. But then I remembered that its last cries had been far away.

"Go find a rabbit," I muttered, then chuckled quietly, for a rabbit was a memory not of that life, but of my earlier one. Because of my lack of sleep, I found that far more amusing than it really was, and snickered awhile, my hands over my mouth to contain my mirth, like a madman in the night. Perhaps, by then, the constant darkness and terror had made me a bit insane.

I crept through the vegetation, angling toward the west to leave the vicinity of the House as quickly as possible. But after less than two hundred yards, the bushes ended at a plain of bare rock. My heart rose in my throat as I gazed at it. I could not cross that emptiness, naked for all the Night Land to see, especially not so close to the House of Silence.

By lifting my head as high above the moss bushes as I dared, I discovered that the vegetation grew only in a narrow band running alongside the Road Where The Silent Ones Walk. This left me no choice but to follow the Road for a time, even though it bent inward to the north, drawing so close to the House of Silence that the shadow of the stark, steep hill on which the structure stood overshadowed it. The House loomed before me, brooding over the whole land, a gargantuan structure as large as the Great Pyramid. The dismal, disconcerting lights shone steadily at its portals; the uncanny stillness surrounded it. We think of silence as an absence of sound; this was Silence Manifest, a palpable hush guarded for all eternity behind that ominous doorway.

I crouched wet and cold among the bushes, held there by terror, loathing, and solemn wonder. If, as the legends suggested, humans had built the House as a first attempt at a sanctuary, Evil Forces had warped its original design. It bore some slight resemblance to a Victorian manor, though one of unfathomable proportions: gables crowded its sloping roofs, vacant windows stared out, turrets and towers overtopped its immensity, yet all were twisted, misshapen, the angles and lines alien. Over all loomed the gaping mouth of the doorway, wide enough to consume a multitude, yawning miles high to meet the tattered eaves.

Of all the people of that time, perhaps only I understood the magnitude of the structure's corruption, for I remembered noble houses surrounded by green lawns and wide forests, wholesome homes built with care and filled with love. The contrast sickened me; sometimes the contradiction between the beauty of the past and the gloom of the present was overwhelming. As I looked up at the House, the terror in my soul chased away any thought of my physical discomfort. I remembered how short a time had passed since Aschoff had led his followers through that immense portal. I looked in vain for signs of their passing, but the House had swallowed them, leaving no trace. As I have said, I had feared this place all my life, perhaps because I sensed the full measure of its malice through my Night Hearing. Now, crouched before its door, it seemed the surrounding night suffered under a quiet, terrible anguish, as if hundreds of tormented souls wandered those halls, seeking an escape they would never find. Any moment I expected to see silent, agonized figures peering out the windows or passing between the door posts. None ever appeared; only the silence held reign.

Creeping, hiding, often halting, quaking in fear and gathering new courage, I pressed forward, my eyes fixed upon the House. It took five hours of following the Road before I came clear of that dreadful place, five hours that seemed an eternity, for the torment of those imprisoned within its walls beat incessantly upon me, until I wanted only to lay down and die. Why I survived, I do not know. I doubt I escaped the House's attention. Perhaps the souls it had recently stolen satisfied it. Perhaps the Rite of Preparation protected me. Perhaps it thought me beneath its notice.

As the road passed around to the north, I began to make better time through the undergrowth, despite being forced to detour to avoid bare patches on the plain. The hours of sleeplessness began catching up with me; my mind droned; I stumbled as I went, half in the trance of a sleepwalker. Still, I dared not stop. Chilled as I was by my wet clothes, I would die unless I found a source of heat.

As I passed just north of the House, something happened that gave me the strength to continue: the beat of the Master Word suddenly broke all around me, as if I had crossed through a barrier. At first I thought it a delusion brought on by fatigue, but I stopped, straining to hear. Through my weary mind, I realized that not only was the message genuine, but that its lack of intensity indicated that it came from the Lesser Redoubt rather than the Great Pyramid.

When I concentrated, I recognized the faint voice of Naani, crying out in supplication. It shook my soul; I wanted to leap to my feet and run to her, but I kept still, listening to hear more.

Several anxious moments passed, but no further message came. Despite my fear for her safety, I felt a measure of justification in my decision to travel north, for I had apparently been journeying toward her all along. It also seemed that the House of Silence had served as an obstruction, preventing her weak signals from reaching me. I guessed Naani had called to me often, perhaps with the same measure of despair.

This brought new meaning to the name of the House of Silence, for it had raised a wall of silence between the two redoubts, and might even have been responsible for breaking the contact between the pyramids centuries before, following the waning of the Lesser Redoubt's Earth Current.

This call, coming when it did after so much hardship, gave me a burst of strength. Despite my weariness, I steadied my gait and concentrated on listening for her cry.

Presently, I spied a fire-pit about a mile to the west. So encouraged was I, and so determined to reach a dry place in order to continue my journey to save my beloved, that I vowed to kill any monster I found lurking in the hollow.

Despite my bravado, a moment later I dropped to my knees to hide among the bushes as one of the Silent Ones, ten feet high and shrouded to its feet, appeared along the Road to my right. I crouched low, but after a moment's hesitation, parted the vegetation and watched it approach, its movements quiet and without haste. As it drew nearer, I sensed the aura of its cold intelligence, and suddenly knew that it was aware of my presence. A trembling overtook me. It looked dreadful in its silent shroud, drifting across the Road without any noticeable movement of its legs, like a ghost-ship sailing over the sea.

I dropped to my stomach and covered my head, knowing I could not escape it. But the next moment, its presence seemed to fade. When I glanced up, I saw it had already gone past my position, and was continuing down the Road. Like its fellows in the Place Where the Silent Ones Kill, it seemed to think me beneath its concern. A sudden, intense respect for it swept over me, and even a peculiar compassion for the silent, lonely beings who I thought might not be intentionally malicious. But this did nothing to lessen my fear of them, for I suspected that if it had chosen to do so, the Silent One could have slain me with a thought.

As soon as it vanished, I hurried toward the fire-pit, keeping hidden as much as I could, but often forced to scramble across short, bare clearings.

I slowed when I reached the pit and crept around it, scrutinizing it for danger. It lay, like so many of its kind, in the bottom of a deep hollow in the rocks. After assuring myself it was deserted, I descended and made a careful search among the boulders. It appeared sweet and warm, without serpents or giant scorpions.

I stripped both armor and undergarments away, and stood naked in the hollow, too cold and weary to feel vulnerable. Still, I kept my head about me, knowing I should not remain defenseless too long. It was a pleasant place, the surrounding rocks holding the heat, turning the pit into a mild oven. I wrung out my clothes and spread them on a nearby rock, then massaged my limbs to restore circulation. While my garments dried, I ate and drank and examined the contents of my pouch and scrip. Because of their tight seals, both remained dry despite the drenching.

As warmth returned to my limbs, my lack of protection began to bother me, and I strode nervously around the hollow carrying my diskos. I turned my garments over several times to help them dry, while the steam rose off in clouds. Under such heat, they were soon ready, and I felt much better once I had my armor back on. Though I hated to leave the warmth of the hollow, I dared not trust to its safety; I had not slept in over thirty-seven hours and was still recovering from the bruises earned in my battle with the Yellow Beast. As weary as I was, I knew I would never hear an approaching enemy. With diskos in hand, I climbed back out to find a place to sleep.

After a short time I discovered a hole in the base of a tall rock formation rising out of a field of moss bushes. I thrust my diskos into the cavity and triggered it. The sparking light of the spinning disk showed the hole to be empty and dry, and I climbed in feet first. My new bedroom, which was just wide enough to accommodate my shoulders, angled twelve feet into the rock. Though I have never liked close places, I curled up with the contentment of a fox in its den. I thought only a moment of Naani before slumber took me.

***

I awoke ten hours later, feeling sore but much stronger. Peeking out, I saw nothing to alarm me. Since I had gone so long without eating on the previous day, I ate four of the tablets before continuing on my way.

I soon drew close to where the Road curved slightly to the west. I was tempted to walk upon it instead of on the stony ground, but did not. At least I could go comfortably upright most of the time, for the land lay peaceful all around.

After traveling twelve hours, I noticed the earth sloping steadily downward, and the distant fire-holes lying far below told me it would continue to do so for many miles. I kept to the north and soon reached the end of the Road Where The Silent Ones Walk. This surprised me greatly. Somewhere in the back of my mind I suppose I thought— since it came from the darkness and went into the darkness —that the Road would continue forever. I should have known better, having read the metal book, but humans, despising change, always believe things will remain constant. So it came to me as a great revelation, and I stood examining the way the Road ended—not in a precise boundary as if the workers intended to stop there—but faltering, the material swirling down into the earth from the Road's normal elevation and spilling across the bare slope. Its color changed, too, for it lost its gray sheen and became brown as the surrounding rocks. And it seemed to me that its builders must have been driven from their work all those hundreds of thousands of years before.

I tried to memorize everything I saw, and made notes in the back of *Ayleos' Mathematics*, for if I managed to return to the Last Redoubt, the Monstruwacans would want to know every detail. I had a sudden longing to share this information with Cartesius; I smiled, thinking how it would send him rushing back to the Records, seeking confirmation.

A glance back at the pyramid left a hollowness in my chest, for I could now see only the highest lights on the Tower of Observation. This momentarily confused me, until I realized my descent down the slope had hidden the redoubt from view.

With the loss of the Road, which I had followed many miles, I found myself somewhat adrift, for I now stood in an unknown part of the world, farther away from the pyramid than any had ever gone before. Or if someone had reached this point, he had not returned to tell of it.

The time had come for a final parting from my home, and I realized it would now be as if I walked entirely alone. But at the same time I felt the ether stirring with the emotions of the millions, who must have received word of my position from the Tower of Observation. So we pondered one another across that vast, foreboding expanse.

I had passed the last fire-hole—there were no lights or flames before me, and I could not help the tears that sprang unbidden to my eyes as I looked into the absolute darkness to the north.

As an escape to pain, it occurred to me to test the compass. I was just drawing it from my pouch when the beating of the Master Word suddenly enfolded me. I stood dumbfounded, then gave a choking sob, for though I could not tell for certain, it seemed to flow up that terrible slope, out of an eternity of night.

I nearly responded without thinking, to tell Naani I was

coming, and only restrained myself in time, for had I done so all the Evil Forces would have known of my presence. Instead, with my whole body trembling, I listened in vain for another message.

Finally, I stirred and glanced around. The compass lay forgotten in my hand. I looked at it and gave a barking laugh. It pointed steadily and continuously to the north.

My courage rose; my chest heaved with gratitude. I took one last long look at the Great Pyramid, burning the sight of it into my memory, but giving neither sign nor salutation. Then I turned and went down into the dark.

IX
THE GREAT SLOPE

As I entered the darkness, the night that wrapped itself around my soul filled me with a terror akin to a child's fear of entering a blackened room. I could see nothing before me, and after traveling only a short time, nothing at my back, for the Night Land vanished as I continued my descent. When the darkness surrounded me completely, I was nearly overcome by waves of panic. I halted, dropped to my knees, and hugged the earth, scarcely able to breath, wishing for a light I knew would never come.

There I remained several minutes, my heart pounding. My head grew light and I may have fainted, though I am not certain. At that moment I became as great a coward as any man who fled a battlefield. In the back of my mind, I knew Andrew would be ashamed of me.

To combat my terror I mentally calculated the square roots of various random numbers. Gradually, the fear passed. I felt the sharp stones beneath my gloved hands, hard and real.

I'm still alive. Even in the dark, I am still alive.

Despite this realization, I stayed there, not knowing how to go on. I might have remained forever, I suppose, except I was suddenly struck by the irony that for all their science and mechanisms, the people of the redoubt no longer possessed lamps. A pyramid full of lights, yet no one owned any form of portable illumination. It seemed so strange, sitting there, remembering how common such devices had been. I particularly recalled, in my life as Andrew, using one old, red lantern as a boy; in my mind I saw the spots of rust along its top and remembered its weight as I carried it. For some unfathomable reason, this gave me courage, for I knew men had walked in darkness before and found ways to conquer it. I rose and went on.

With my fear suppressed, I faced a new trial, for in such a night nothing seemed real, and I soon lost all sense of self. Often, I imagined that I no longer walked the earth, but stepped across an endless void. This impression seldom lasted; invariably when my thoughts wandered, I kicked a jutting rock or stumbled over a boulder. But without light, I made less than a mile every two hours.

After continuing in this manner for what seemed a lifetime, I sat down upon a boulder, breathless from anticipation of danger, uncertain whether I was even going in a straight line. As I thought again of lanterns, it occurred to me that I could use the diskos as a light source, letting it spin occasionally to illuminate my way. It was an awkward plan, for I would be announcing my presence across the slope, but I seemed to have little choice.

I activated the weapon. Its hum seemed so thunderous and its light so dazzling that I stood half-blinded, overwhelmed with fear in its fading afterglow, my every muscle taut in anticipation of an attack. When none came, I rallied and tried the diskos again, having been too startled the first time to notice my way. I let it spin for a few seconds while I looked around. Nothing lived, nothing moved; the bare stones stretched before and behind. The light faded. I walked through the darkness until I could bear it no more, then triggered the weapon again. I wanted to use the diskos continuously, but since it was not made for that purpose I feared I might exhaust its power, especially since I did not know how it would react so far from the Earth Current, the source of its energy.

It is amazing to what we can become accustomed. I walked across that rocky slope alone, absolutely blind save when I employed my weapon. Then the lightning flashed all around, accompanied by the low hum of the spinning disk, and the bare stones rose before me in a circle of light. I dreaded using it, for I never knew what danger might appear. At any moment, I expected to face some horror from the night. Only my love for Naani drove me on.

After six long, bitter hours of this, I sat down in the darkness and prepared my supper by feel. I had traveled a total of twenty hours. After eating, I wrapped my cloak around me, placed my scrip and pouch beneath my head, and with my diskos in hand, fell into an uneasy slumber.

Five hours later, something woke me. I gripped my diskos, raised myself on one elbow, and listened a long while, but heard nothing.

I debated making a bit of light, but if anything was near, I would be revealing myself. Finally, I decided that was better than uncertainty, and I activated the diskos several times. During the brief flashes, I spied only the craggy ground, though my imagination and a hulking boulder caused me to waste unnecessary power.

With some relief, I let the light die and sat down to prepare my breakfast. It occurred to me again how odd it was not to be able to see the moon and stars in the sky. Through Andrew's memories I recalled Orion, the tiny Pleiades, the Swan, and ominous Scorpio—I thought of the former beauty of the moon in all her phases. It is difficult to describe my feelings—it was as if I recalled a fairy tale, a far off vision, though one I had seen with my own eyes. It filled me with a wistful sorrow for all the lovely things now passed away, leaving only the emptiness, the dark, and me fumbling for my cup.

Since it was not in my nature to brood, I soon rose, diskos in hand, and began making my way once more down the slope. Throughout that day, I felt uneasy, as if something followed me. I paused often to listen, and occasionally used my diskos to light the way behind me. Once I thought I saw a creature as cragged as the stones around it, crouching at the edge of the light. In my surprise I released the trigger, plunging all into darkness again. I instantly reactivated my weapon and stepped forward, but if something had been there, it was gone, leaving me doubting whether I had seen anything at all.

In the early part of the seventh hour, after I had rested and eaten, I stepped into a small hole and tumbled across a sharp boulder. The fall shook my whole frame and took my breath away, so I had to lie, nearly helpless, gasping for air. Without my armor, the rock would have ripped me open.

When I could speak once more I lay muttering, cursing the rocks, the darkness, and my own clumsiness. My ribs hurt, but did not seem broken.

"Being foolish," I whispered. After only a brief time in the dark, I had taken up the habit of talking to myself in a kind of shorthand. "A moment's fall, a broken bone—die here alone—no one to help Naani. Must be more careful. Hands and knees are the way to go, feeling my path. Won't need the diskos as much—save power—mustn't overuse the weapon. Can't see with it half the time, anyway."

When I was strong enough to continue, I began crawling along, ever downward, feeling my way as I went.

I crept all that day, and though it was laborious, creeping through the Night Land had hardened my muscles to the exercise of going on hands and knees. The lack of things to think about bothered me more—my mind wandered in widening arcs, sometimes I dreamed of my life in the pyramid, sometimes of my existence in the world of the past. The memories began to wind together, until I pictured Mirdath's face with Naani's voice, or thought our little house, where we had spent such happy hours together, stood in the middle of the Night Land, with the Watchers peering through our windows at the fire in the hearth. I tried to concentrate on my mathematics, especially on the problem of the Insoluble Conundrum, but the formulas slipped away.

I whispered as I went, a ghost among the rocks. If there is a purgatory, it surely resides among the crags of that barren slope.

After crawling for eighteen hours, without bothering to trigger the diskos I felt around in the darkness for a level place to rest.

"If there are monsters, let them come," I whispered, casting away enough stones to make a reasonably smooth bed. I ate and composed myself for sleep. My last conscious words were: "Something follows—I've felt it all day. Something follows." It was true, but I was too weary and discouraged to care.

Despite my exhaustion something roused me twice. I raised myself on my elbow, and listened, but could not discern anything, and both times I eventually returned to my troubled slumber.

At the sixth hour, I awoke abruptly, even as on the day before, certain something was near. I listened in vain for a long time, my diskos ready, but when I detected nothing, I rose without making any light, ate, packed my gear, and continued crawling through the darkness.

That day passed much like the one before, except that in the eighth hour, when I reached out my hand to take another step, I encountered empty space, and fell forward on my stomach, my armor rattling against the stones. I felt around and discovered a pit before me, stretching in both directions. After a moment's debate, I decided not to risk waking any inhabitants by using my diskos, but crawled to the left, keeping the pit at arm's length, but feeling for it occasionally so as to remain parallel to its edge. Once, as I did this, a cold hand clasped my wrist.

I shrieked in fear and hammered at my assailant with my diskos, which I had been carrying in my left hand. The spinning disk severed a long, gray arm, lean and gnarled as an oak branch.

As I leapt to my feet, diskos still whirring, I looked down into the pit and saw its entire bottom churning as if filled with serpents. No sooner did I back away than an army of arms reached over the lip, writhing in a long line along the crevice edge as far as my light could show, fingers flexing in their hunger to grasp me. I could not tell whether they were attached to a body.

I stood in a crouching stance, trembling in fear, awaiting their assault. They strained toward me, but seemed unable to leave the pit. As soon as I realized this, I sprinted as hard as I could go around the crevice, keeping my diskos lit. I put several hundred yards between myself and the den, then stopped, panting, my finger still on the diskos' trigger. I could not bear to face the darkness again without knowing if any more such pits awaited me.

"Won't do," I finally said, sitting back on my haunches in the middle of the circle of light. "Won't do. Too slow. Need a plan. Need a rock and a rope. If a boy has no cord about him, shall not the same be said of a man!" The last was an old saying of my people.

The endless solitude had dulled my thinking, but at last I removed the strap from my pouch and tied a stone to one end of it. The strap, being long and thin, suited my purposes well. Since I could no longer use the strap to carry my pouch, I buckled the pouch to my scrip. With much trepidation, I doused the light. I held the end of the strap and cast the stone before me as I crawled along, so I could tell if any pits lay in front of me.

If my trek had been monotonous before, this proved even worse, throwing the stone, crawling to it, and throwing it again, like an animal lured forward at the promise of reward. Despite that, I felt elated; for perhaps an hour I chuckled in a rasping whisper, gloating over my presumed cleverness.

I made up snatches of song about crawling down to see Naani, though sometimes it was Mirdath, and little verses about numbers. I sang in a buzzing whisper to the beat of the rock and the four thumps of my hands and knees on the ground. For a time I counted the casts, but lost track, began again, then forgot about it entirely.

I slept at the eighteenth hour, and was again awakened by something just before the sixth hour. I rose uneasily, knowing there was something near me in the dark, but when I triggered my diskos, I saw nothing but rock and stone.

During my journey that day, I felt a change in the air, which seemed to be growing warmer and heavier. When I attempted to put powder in my cup, the increased oxygen augmented the chemical reaction, making it foam over the rim.

I fastened on this change as something to occupy my mind during the monotony of the trek, and spent several hours, between throws of the stone, brooding how the air in Andrew's day must have been like this, not thin and keen like that found around the pyramid. The atmosphere of the Night Land did not extend far up, but hung in a narrow band close to the earth, so that even the upper stories of the redoubt rose above the breathable air. For this reason, the higher cities were sealed from the outside. I cannot recall whether the pyramid was also closed at its base, though I seem to remember that we drew our air from the Underground Fields. If so, I assume we used some method to exchange our atmosphere for the air outside, though there may have been some kind of advanced purification method, instead.

I realized, perhaps for the first time, that the inhabitants of the pyramid had much larger chests than the people of Andrew's time, with the features of those of the upper cities even more pronounced. Because of this, anyone could identify what part of the pyramid a person came from by his appearance. According to the Records, concern over these differences once resulted in a plan to shift people up and down throughout the redoubt. Since the inhabitants preferred living in the city of their birth, the edict had failed, though a remnant of it remained in the law requiring every young person to spend three years and two hundred twenty-five days traveling from city to city. In this way, they not only learned the customs of all the cities, but could try the air at every level and find the atmosphere that best suited them.

The lack of atmosphere in the Night Land accounted for the absence of birds or other flying creatures, though our Records mentioned tremendous flying brutes that had roamed the land with mighty leaps in ancient times.

When I had first decided upon my journey, some of the Monstruwacans had foolishly suggested using the small flying vessel kept beside the models of the ships in the Museum of Antiquities. This particular craft, made of the same enduring gray metal as the pyramid, glistened as if new, and was even in working condition. We soon discarded the idea, however, for no one had flown the vessel for more than a hundred thousand years, or even practiced using it. I had read the ancient *Book of Flying* and knew the difficulty of learning to pilot such a ship. I also doubted if the air of the Night Land would have supported it; if so the ancients would never have abandoned using the craft in the first place. Neither did I want to hang in the night for all the Forces of Evil to see, with the sound of the engines announcing my presence to the whole world.

From my reading of the Records, I suspected that, countless centuries before, a band of brave adventurers had sent their flying machines leaping over the edge of the upper world, descending the hundred miles into the great Rift where I now walked. I imagined them spinning downward, seen from above for perhaps ten or twenty miles and afterward lost in the depths. These courageous scouts must have led the way for the nations that became the Road Makers, who built the paths that brought the earth's inhabitants into the Rift.

I muttered such things to myself as I went, in a fever of what I thought to be inspiration, though in fact it was the ramblings of a tottering mind. I considered how all the world seemed to go in a circle, the Road Makers deserting the ruined earth to fight the monsters and beasts of the Rift, rebuilding civilization anew only to have it gradually cut off by the Forces of Evil; the people forced to retreat first into the sanctuary that became the House of Silence, then into the Great Pyramid, where ancient machinery such as the airships that had brought them into the Rift sat, unused, their workings forgotten. I thought of kingdoms and nations rising and falling, and imagined myself part of that cycle, treading an eternal ring through the darkness.

Rousing myself from my reveries, I triggered the diskos. To my dismay, I discovered I had been crawling in a circle over the rough stones, wearing them away with my armor.

***

Three more days passed. I had descended for six endless

114

days and nights, and for all I knew, would continue in blackness forever. I whispered continually, a little crazed, deprived of everything save the darkness and the hard ground beneath my hands and knees.

"The heart of the world," I whispered, over and over, to the beat of the cast stone, as I thought of how I traveled far below the level of the redoubt, deep in the depths in the monstrous night. "Going down, going down to the heart of the world. No end to it. No end at all."

I began to believe I had died and was suffering an eternal punishment; the stones beneath my hands reminded me of Sisyphus. Of all the people of the world, only I remembered that ancient tale; only I remembered the Greeks at all. I became maudlin about it. "Greece is gone. All her glory faded into the night. She had no pyramid for refuge." Tears filled my eyes. "And I am pushing a stone down a slope, seeking my Mirdath." So my two identities became confused in the darkness.

Abruptly, I sat down, staring in astonishment, for I saw a faint flickering, so far away I thought it my imagination. When it flashed again, I rose to my knees and gawked, like a stranded sailor gaping at a sail. At first, I refused to believe it, thinking, since it came and went so quickly, that my eyes were playing tricks. I held my breath, waiting. When it sparked again, it seemed alien to me, as if in my stumblings I had lost the *concept* of light. But at last I realized it was truly there. I began to laugh, and rising, wobbly and stiff, sprinted madly toward it.

I traveled less than a dozen steps before I stumbled over an upcropping and fell hard on my face. I lay still, gritting my teeth and groaning until the pain passed. Finally, I climbed back onto my hands and knees and crept along with bruised and aching limbs. An hour or more I traveled, often raising my head to look for the faltering illumination. Though I expected to reach it any moment, I journeyed six full hours before drawing near.

As the flame turned the night to twilight I began to hear a distant piping sound. I stopped, crouching and wary, and waited several moments, but when no danger approached, I continued on my way. The sound became increasingly louder as I went.

Even when I came close, I could not perceive the source of the light, for several enormous rock formations blocked my view. I veered to the left for a half mile to circle them.

The piping grew, a whistling, festive tumult.

Finally, I knelt among three boulders and peered out into the mouth of a tremendous gorge created by the narrowing of the sides of the Rift. The light revealed a stark cliff climbing into the shadowed heights to my right, and when the flames flared up I could also see the wall of rock to the left. For the first time in my life, I beheld the boundaries of my world. I stared in awe, knowing from my reading of the gray, metal book that the crags extended upward for many miles above me.

I had reached the end of the Great Slope, but not the end of my descent, for the gorge continued its decline, though more gradually than before. Multi-colored fires shone far down its length.

Moving almost numbly, I pressed onward, walking upright, and passed between two tremendous boulders. For the first time I could see the flame clearly, gushing from the earth, massive stone outcroppings standing like giant sentinels around it. The sound, as I had already surmised, came from burning gas exiting the earth. The flame danced and swayed enormously, sometimes dipping as low as a hundred feet, sometimes rising three hundred yards. At its peak, it lit the far side of the gorge, which was easily seven miles away. It laid the whole gorge before me, wild, stark, and empty, filled with bare stone and distant, winking fires.

As I gaped at that gargantuan flame, the only man to see this wonder for thousands of years, the madness that had overtaken me fell away like a discarded cloak. Here was a light to pierce the darkness, though it burned in a place lonely as a distant sphere. It seemed eternally holy and significant to me. Gradually, I realized how strange my thoughts had grown. As the light burned away the last traces of my foolishness, a deep peace filled my soul. I remained there a long time, drinking in its radiance, thinking nothing, absorbing its brilliance.

With my mind once more my own, I shook my head and continued past the blue, flaming fountain, which lit my way for many miles. After so much darkness it delighted me to see my shadow rise and fall, leaping with the fire. I turned often to watch the blaze. It filled me with hope, this light that had not failed through the centuries, though it fought the darkness all alone.

Slowly, the roaring and whistling of the fire subsided

behind me, its last echoes reverberating against the canyon walls, sometimes sounding like distant flutes, sometimes, like the whispers of monsters. After six hours, the noise died completely, making the silence seem more ominous than ever. I passed four flames during that time, the third being blue and the other three green. These danced and moaned, as had the great flame, sending their weird light spilling along the gorge.

It was my seventh day's journey since entering the Great Slope. Sixteen hours had passed since I first laid eyes upon the mighty flame, and I had been too excited to eat during all that time. Since holes and crevices dotted the gorge, it was easy to find a resting place in a small cave between two boulders. I ate four of the tablets and drank my water, which again required less powder to fill the cup. After lying down beneath my cloak, I opened *Ayleos' Mathematics* to the blank pages and caught up on my journal and maps. When I finished, I thumbed through the pages and took a few moments' pleasure in the geometry section. I fell asleep staring contentedly at isosceles triangles.

It was the most peaceful slumber I had experienced since entering the Great Slope, with dreams filled with Naani. I thought I heard the Master Word beating around me once, but since I remained asleep it may have been only my imagination. Upon awakening, I pondered the dream, but could reach no conclusion. The heavy air made me so groggy I could scarcely think. I ate my breakfast numbly and set out, my diskos tied to my hip so I could use both hands to navigate between the boulders. After traveling in so much darkness, the half-twilight cast by the scattered fires delighted me.

During that journey I passed twenty-three of the dancing gas jets, five of white fire, and the others either blue or green. Despite their ghostly lambency, they gave me hope. I slept among the rocks for seven hours, then still half-asleep, rose to my scant breakfast.

I soon reached a place of relative darkness. What fires there were erupted in waves between the rocks, thousands of flames unexpectedly appearing in shudders of light, so that one moment I walked through the heart of a country of fire, the next through a land of night. The blazes broke the silence with a noise like stones tossed into a pool. More than once I had to scamper aside to avoid being burned.

Choking gases belched from the ground, leaving vile

fumes hanging in the air. I avoided the heavier clouds for fear of being poisoned, but took solace in thinking that even monsters and Evil Forces would not dwell amid such desolation.

I slept that night in a place where the air seemed fairly clear. Even so, there must have been some fumes, for I had trouble waking myself up. When I finally stumbled to my feet, I had a piercing headache that lasted until the end of the fifteenth hour, when I finally left the gas fires behind. Before me rose a grayness like mist, lit by a vague, ruddy shining.

Shortly thereafter, where the gorge turned abruptly to the left, I beheld a crimson light. I hurried forward, anxious to see its cause, and passed beneath mountainous escarpments on the right side of the gorge. The over-hanging stone blocked the ruby glow, leaving me to stumble through an area of almost total darkness, where I had to trigger my diskos several times to light my way.

Once past the shadows, I reached a second bend to the right. I was startled by low rumblings reverberating like distant thunder through the gorge. I hid behind some boulders, then began creeping among the rocks toward the source of the shining. As I turned the corner, I found myself gaping down into a land covered with countless seas. Volcanoes, rising out of the midst of the waters, filled the country with the ruddy light.

It is strange to know two existences, for as Andros I had read of oceans, lakes, and volcanoes, but had never seen one, whereas as Andrew I remembered paddling boats across ponds or watching warships pass into their docks. Whether I reacted as a man of the past or a child of the future, I stood awestruck after so much darkness, silent before the red glare.

Despite my amazement, the sheer size of the country soon wrenched a groan from my breast, for if the Lesser Redoubt, which stood in a land of darkness, lay behind this vast region, I still had many miles to go to find Naani. So I stood, troubled and anxious before the wonder and glory of that strange country. Eventually I made my way to the outermost edge of the mouth of the gorge, where I could see more clearly. I counted twenty-seven volcanoes, excluding two ranges of gargantuan hills of fire burning far away to my right. There were also myriads of smaller flames blazing across the country. A small volcano rose out of a sea little more than a mile from me, while a score of others spread out behind it. I counted three small lakes, and one tremendous body of water stretching beyond sight into the crimson glow of the volcanoes.

Some of the cones of fire rose from islands within the seas, and others rose straight out of the waters. Steam drifted over the seas, obscuring them in parts; the water boiled in various places. The low, volcanic rumblings I had heard in the gorge sounded much louder at times, as if the earth were tearing itself apart.

Perhaps, of all I saw, the thing that struck me most was the clarity of perception. Having lived all my life in shadows, I had never before looked a long distance away without the aid of a spyglass. Now the countryside rolled for miles before me. The cliffs towered on both sides and vanished into the upper darkness, for even the tremendous light of the volcanoes could not reveal where the Rift met the surface world. Neither had I ever witnessed a land so filled with energy and life.

Nearby, to the left of the gorge's mouth, rose a black mountain separate from the sides of the Rift, for I could see its peaks towering fifteen or twenty miles into the night. A volcanic cone jutted from its side about five miles up, and a second at ten miles distance, so they seemed to hang in the air, their red mouths smoking. Two others stood upon the left crest of that black mountain, so high they seemed like smoldering suns. Below these volcanoes rose mountains of ash and igneous rock, gray monuments to the dreadful glory of Time.

To my right glistened the endless sea and the red blazing of the fire-hills, but to my left, beyond the black mountain, reared tall forests of bizarre trees, with volcanoes, dead and living, rising between them.

I wandered, almost mesmerized with amazement, down the mouth of the gorge, then paused upon realizing that I had failed to plot my course. Upbraiding myself for a fool, I returned to the heights and studied the land more carefully. I soon saw but one way to go, for the sea blocked my path to the right, but a strip of bare beach straggled beside the waters to my left.

Troubled and bewildered, yet thankful for the light and splendor, I cleared the gorge in two hours and entered the Country of the Seas, as I named that land of water and fire.

X
THE COUNTRY OF THE SEAS

I walked through the brilliant light of the Country of the Seas, among rocks and water, beneath the boughs of various kinds of extraordinary trees, with leaves shaped like paper fans, diamonds, or filamented circles delicate and puffed as dandelions. Many grew impossibly tall for the size of their trunks, for without a wind to disturb them they required little support. Others spread out like immense bushes. The highest branches easily topped a hundred feet. The trees fascinated me, for I had never seen anything larger than the groves in the Underground Fields. I often paused and looked up through the branches, imagining that the red glow through the leaves was the sunlight of former ages, an easy fancy since the majority of the vegetation turned toward the volcanoes as if receiving nourishment there. In those moments my previous existence clung to me like a ghost, and I remembered with almost painful clarity tramping through forests, feeling the cool shade on my brow on hot summer days.

From the time I left the part of the gorge containing the noxious fumes to the time I stood in the forest, I had traveled almost twenty-four hours, and even my excitement could no longer delay my weariness. Searching for a place to sleep, I soon settled on what I thought an adequate spot, though one not as protected as I might have liked, a level area where three huge trees grew around a dry, stone basin.

Perhaps my memory of other lunches in other forests made my meager rations especially distasteful, for a vague recollection of sandwiches reminded me how often my stomach went unsatisfied. Despite that, I fell asleep almost immediately and dreamed of ocean waves rolling onto a beach. I climbed into the water, which was surprisingly warm.

I woke to find my dream had come true, for a hot stream rushed around me. I sprang to my feet, sputtering, the taste of salt in my mouth. Water gurgled into the basin from a smooth slit on the far side, filling it rapidly and sending steam roiling up in clouds. Because of my lack of experience in natural phenomenon, it took me several moments to realize that I was not being attacked, but was the victim of underground pressure propelling water up through the rocks. Fortunately, it was not hot enough to burn me. Once I realized I was in no danger, I pulled my pouch and scrip from the water, stripped off my armor and body vest, and spread my garments upon a hot rock to dry.

"If the water is poisonous, I'm already a dead man," I muttered. "I might as well take a bath."

I propped my diskos within reach at the basin's edge and climbed back into the pool. Up until that point I had not realized how much of my body was purple with bruises, but the heat did wonders to soothe my soreness. I soaked in the bath a long while, and it was only when the water began draining that I realized it followed a natural cycle. I climbed out and watched it slip away. Within an hour of its filling, it lay empty.

My clothing dried quickly in the heat of that country, and I dressed hurriedly. I had only slept a little while before the water had awakened me, and feeling relaxed after my bath, I slumbered another six hours beside the pool, listening to its gurgles as it filled and emptied.

Upon waking, I felt better than I had for a long time. I ate, trying not to think of sandwiches, and went on my way at a rapid pace, skirting the edge of the woods to my left and keeping the seashore to my right, though often picking my way between the trunks when the trees crowded up to the water. I enjoyed my journey; it awoke a wistfulness of bygone days, the scent of tree and leaf filling my nostrils with a perfume reminiscent of clover.

However, my happiness turned to apprehension when I saw eyes peering at me from the undergrowth, only to vanish before I could reach them. This happened several times, and though nothing attacked me, I knew I was not alone. I unslung my diskos from my belt and gripped it close.

Three times during the day's journey I heard the crackling of flames. In each instance I soon found a fire hill little taller than myself. The fires had consumed the trees, but smaller vegetation, living and dying between the bursts of lava, sprouted all around. With my preoccupation for keeping careful counts, it delighted me to note that I passed thirty-seven boiling springs, many spewing steam and roaring like animals.

I slept at the eighteenth hour with my back against a huge boulder, my dozing less easy now that I knew the forest was inhabited. I thought about Naani as I drifted off; in fact, I had thought of her all day, as if her spirit hovered close to mine. I blessed her in my heart, and vowed with renewed determination to travel more swiftly the next day.

***

I awoke abruptly, with a feeling of anxiety, and sat up on my elbow. Six squat men with humps upon their necks crouched at the edge of the tree line less than twenty paces away, watching from the shadows of the branches, their eyes shining golden as wolves'.

I leapt to my feet, weapon in hand, but though I never lost sight of the intruders' place of concealment, they vanished without my seeing them go. Having awakened so suddenly from sleep, I thought for a moment they might have been a dream, or an illusion created from the shadows and the foliage, but I quickly dismissed this as wishful thinking. I could not have imagined their staring, animal eyes.

I glanced at my chronometer; I had slept five hours. I made a hurried breakfast, draining the cup carelessly, all my attention fastened on the forest. I hoped the Humped Men had departed, their curiosity satisfied, though I knew they might just as well be preparing an ambush for me, or hurrying to their camp to return with an army of their kind. Whatever the case, I strode away, fingering the trigger of my weapon and glancing constantly from side the side. My travels had increased my endurance until I felt sure I could outdistance any pursuers.

I journeyed for thirty hours, stopping to eat every six. Never once did I see the Humped Men, but three times I heard something keeping pace with me through the woods to my left. I dared not stop to sleep until I found a place of safety.

At the end of the thirtieth hour, a wide river, flowing from my left into the sea at my right, blocked my path. At its mouth stood a small island. I thought it might serve as a refuge if I could only reach it, but the water ran deep, and I did not know how to swim. I went up-river seeking a narrower place to cross, but walked only a short distance before my way was blocked by another branch of the river feeding into the first.

I stood perplexed and uncertain. Having been raised in the Great Pyramid, where boats were unknown, I pondered far longer than might have otherwise been necessary. Only after recalling hazy memories from my life as Andrew did I think to build a raft.

Here, my interest in mathematics proved a detriment, for I was soon jotting down numbers and measurements in the back of *Ayleos' Mathematics*, creating unlikely, fanciful designs at first, then gradually modifying them to simpler forms. At last, realizing the uselessness of my grandiose plans, I shut the book and set to work. A number of fallen trees lay about, but the first I chose proved too heavy to move. Finally, I found a pair of usable trunks. I struggled a good hour with these, for they were by no means light, but at last I got them down to the water. Using my diskos to shape the wood, I made a rough pole of a sapling, then lashed the two trees together utilizing the belts and straps from my pack and scrip.

I kept a careful watch for my adversaries as I worked, which slowed me somewhat, but in the end I launched my little craft and scrambled on board. Navigation proved an unfamiliar skill; fortunately the water moved slowly, and after a half-hour of poling, I reached the island and pulled my craft partially onto the shore. I had been awake for thirty-three hours, and was almost beyond exhaustion. After surveying the island for dangers, I threw myself among the rocks and clumps of tall grass and drifted into a sound sleep.

Afterward, I breakfasted and set out for the far side of the river. This proved difficult in the clumsy raft; I had to pole furiously to avoid being swept out to sea. Oddly enough, my main worry was that if I lost the craft I would lose the belts and straps from my pack and scrip.

I finally made it to shore, feeling I had triumphed over the Humped Men, who surely could not cross the water. It eventually occurred to me that their people might dwell on both sides of the river, but if so I hoped to remain undiscovered by the clan on this side. To that end, I continued at a swift pace, past more oddities and wonders than I could ever recount. I kept to my schedule of resting and eating, and between the eighth and fourteenth hours encountered two large fire-hills that made the entire country tremble with their rumblings.

Four times, monstrous creatures at least twice my height passed me while I hid among the trees, each different from all the others, three walking on four legs, and one on two. Two of them had armored plating all over their bodies; two were covered with thick hair. I could not guess whether they ate meat, but I did not want to find out.

Often, I traveled among the trees, and often through the desolation of numerous boiling springs and fire-hills. Their roaring filled the whole land, and because of the rich atmosphere, their flames blazed with extraordinary heat. I saw many different kinds of life, all alien to me, and had no way of knowing which were lethal and which benign.

As I wandered among the trees and flourishing vegetation, breathing the sweet, rich air, it occurred to me that if I could ever return to the Last Redoubt to give my report, my descendants might find a way to reach this country to build a new refuge when the Earth Current died. Many might consider this idle speculation, since it seemed impossible for my people to bypass the monsters and Forces, but no one knows what the future may bring, and I amused myself for hours imagining the sanctuary I would design, its angles, lines and dimensions flowing through my mind in splendid procession.

A little before the eighteenth hour, I passed out of the trees into a clearing. The rocky ground had sloped upward for the last several hours, leaving the sea hidden below cliffs to my right. I found myself standing before a sharp crag, easily a hundred feet high. Something lay at its crown, an odd shape that at first glance seemed to be another stone laid across the peak, though it had a semblance of symmetry. Trees and vegetation grew upon its surface, as they did all along the ledges of the crag.

I stared at the crest without comprehension, and finally decided that whatever it was, I could probably sleep there in safety if I could only reach it. I began climbing at once, but soon discovered it was even taller than I had suspected. Being weary, I saw no point in going all the way to the summit, but set my sights upon a wide shelf of rock opening onto a shallow cave. I soon reached it, and after eating, dropped almost at once into a deep sleep.

***

I awoke abruptly seven hours later with an intense sense

of danger, though I did not see any enemies around me. I rose quietly with my diskos ready, crept to the rim of the ledge, and peered over the side.

Two Humped Men climbed swiftly and silently toward me, sniffing the air like hounds, their heads raised. I steeled myself as I watched them, keeping my head close to the rocks so they could not see me. They were not truly humpbacked, but gave that impression because of the inhuman thickness of their necks and shoulders, which were like the necks of bulls. They appeared to be powerful and moved with bestial quickness. I knew either I, or they, would be dead in the next few moments.

I stepped back a pace from the edge, holding my diskos ready, determined to kill one of the brutes instantly to narrow my odds. I waited for what seemed an eternity, every nerve quivering within me.

When the Humped Man appeared, he moved with such unbelievable speed it seemed as if he suddenly materialized. But I struck just as swiftly. At that moment, before the blow fell, when time seemed to stand still, I saw his face clearly, a brutish block, with squinting eyes and fanged tusks. Despite his massive body, he gave an impression of feline grace.

I killed him before his hairy chest ever passed over the edge. He sank back, sagged, and fell. I heard his body lumbering downward, bouncing dully from rock to rock.

A silence arose. I waited again, trying to suppress my excited breathing.

The moments passed and my second opponent did not appear. I turned rapidly from side to side, searching for my enemy, my weapon ready, my pulse pounding at my temple. Every second seemed a lifetime.

At last, I stepped softly to the rim and looked downward. The rock face stretched empty all the way to the bottom. At first I thought he had fled. I whirled around, fearing he might have slipped above me, but there was no one there.

I took a deep breath and leaned far over the ledge. A started cry escaped my lips as I spied him, crouched beneath the shelf, clinging to a rock, his whole body nearly horizontal. For the barest moment, we stared eye to eye, then he sprang, diving at a ninety-degree angle straight from the rock face. With unimaginable speed and strength, he hooked his hands upon the ledge, pulled himself up in one swift motion, and seized my diskos by its end.

Instinctively, I activated the weapon; otherwise I would either have lost it or been pulled over the edge. It blazed with power, burning the man's hand, forcing him to release it.

I staggered back when he let go, but he paused only an instant before lifting himself onto the ledge and leaping at me. I dodged to the right, avoiding the blow, even as I slashed with the diskos. My thrust fell short, barely gashing the brute's belly and scorching his thick, brown hair.

He sprang after me, but I struck full at his face, causing him to leap away from the weapon's roaring fire. He did not entirely escape, however, for I cut his arm.

Fear of my weapon shone in his eyes. I rushed at him, striking at his face again, but he eluded me with animal speed. Bounding to the point where the ledge met the rock face, he seized a boulder split off from the rest of the formation, and tore it away. It was enormous, as large as I, yet he held it effortlessly above his head.

He swung it, not sideways as a human might, which would have driven me over the precipice, but straight down. I dodged, not once but several times, dancing back and forth across the ledge, the long drop to my back. As I struck at him, I tried to avoid hitting the rock he used as a shield, fearing the impact might break my diskos. I kept expecting him to cast the stone, but he seemed to lack the concept of doing so, and continued wielding it as a club. I struck at him, but he deflected the blow with his stone, and despite my concern for my weapon, the diskos sheered away a portion of the rock without damaging itself.

The Humped Man paused and stood gasping, worn from wielding the stone. I smelled the stink of his body and saw the sweat upon his brow. Though nearly at the end of my own strength, I dared not pause. While he hesitated, I leapt to his right, trying to get past his guard, but he was less weary than I thought, for he dodged my blow and trapped me against the rock wall.

With only a moment to escape, I made a sham attack toward the left, then bounded back to the right, coming in at his side. Trusting all my fortune to a single blow, I thrust at his belly. The diskos nearly cut him in two, and he fell, half leaping as he died. The rock crashed at my feet, inches from crushing me.

I fell backward against the rock face, holding my diskos

before me. When I realized he was dead, the strength left my body and I crumbled to my knees. I tried to rise, but found I could not.

After a short while, I recovered, gathered my gear, and descended the crag. At its bottom, I found the first of the Humped Men lying dead. Killing a living creature has always troubled me, and I had no desire to see him up close, so I circled to the other side of the formation. My hands still shook from the aftermath of the battle, and seeing no danger about, I decided to halt long enough to eat and drink to restore my nerves.

I made my meal seated on a stone at the base of the crag, turning my head this way and that, watching for more Humped Men. A small fire-hill, rising to the cliffs at my back, illuminated this side of the rock, and when I glanced up at the crown I gave a cry of exclamation; from this angle I recognized the formation that had puzzled me before as an ancient flying ship similar to those found in the Museum of Antiquities.

I stood, staring at it, wondering why I had not identified it before, until I realized its farther side had lain in shadow, whereas now the warm light from the fire-hill glimmered off the dull metal of the ship's bottom, an alloy I recognized at once as the same type used in the construction of the Last Redoubt. Earth had covered the top of the vessel for so many generations that trees grew on its upper side.

It seemed so odd, seeing a creation of man upon that lonely pinnacle! I walked back and forth, trying to get a better glimpse, until at last, unable to bear leaving without investigating more closely, I climbed back up the rock. Even as I scaled the cliffside, I reprimanded myself for wasting my time when there might be more Humped Men around, though I had a vague notion of finding something useful within the craft. The truth is my curiosity overcame my judgment, for I was heartsick for anything from the place of my birth.

The battle had drained me more than I realized, and it took longer than I expected to scale the height, but once I began I refused to quit, and eventually came under the vessel's bottom. She had not landed easily; burn marks and dents scored her, and the upcropping itself had pierced her bottom, rending the metal. I climbed all around her, using the thick plants for handholds. The layers of earth obscured most of the ship, especially on top, but I found an exposed place on her side and used my diskos to try to cut an opening. The metal shrieked its defiance; smoke and sparks filled the air, and I halted, afraid the clamor would bring an army of Humped Men upon me. When I examined the side I saw my weapon had scarcely penetrated the metal.

I climbed back over the top of the craft, searching without success for another entrance. Finally, I scaled the rocks along the ship's bottom, and found, at the place where the peak had punctured the vessel, a narrow opening, just large enough for me to poke my head and shoulder through. I had to crawl under a shelf to reach it, which made me anxious, both because of what I might encounter, and because it left me helpless if a Humped Man appeared, but at last I thrust my diskos up into the bottom of the ship, and triggering the weapon, pushed myself as far up as I could go.

The interior was hot. The ship smelled faintly of metal, but not of decay, the bodies of its passengers having turned to dust ages before. I faced the front of the vessel and saw two seats overlooking a control panel. It made me nervous that I could not turn my head enough to glimpse behind me, where anything might be lurking.

I suddenly found the closeness of the place unbearable: the heat, the darkness, my head and shoulder thrust between shards of twisted metal. My courage failed. As I gave the cabin a last sweep with my diskos, I spied a sheet with writing upon it lying beside the seat. I strained, reached it, then pulled myself back out. Moving with painful slowness, I resisted the urge to panic, knowing I would only injure myself struggling to break free. I withdrew from beneath the shelf, diskos ready, fancying a hundred foes awaiting me, but the peak remained clear.

I wiped the sweat from my eyes and unfolded the sheet, which seemed to be made of the same enduring material as the gray metal book Cartesius had found in the Records. I do not know what I expected, the final scrawled words of a dying man, perhaps. Instead, it proved to be a portion of a map. At first, I could make nothing of it, until I saw symbols suggesting that it showed the Country of the Seas. It indicated mountains surrounding the entire land, with wide openings at both the north and south ends. Beyond the portal to the north lay a long passage, which ended at the corner of the page. A few letters, in ancient script, had been written there, the last four characters of what might have been the word 'redoubt.' My heart throbbed at the thought that it could indicate the location of Naani's home. I turned the page over, hoping to see more, but it was blank.

I turned and looked back at the craft. The rest of the map undoubtedly lay within it, if only I could reach it. For a moment, I considered trying, but I knew it would be useless. And what would it tell me, anyway? The portion of the map I held suggested only two ways into the Country of the Seas. And the longer I remained on the peak, the more likely my being found by the Humped Men.

Feeling somewhat dissatisfied, I began my descent. Yet, I did not consider the climb useless; the map gave me hope, however tenuous. And it thrilled me to think of the ship waiting all those thousands of years for me to retrieve that single sheet. I conjectured how the sea might have been much higher in those days, and the rock but an island in the midst of the waters. I considered the various ways the ship might have come to its fate as it flew low over the ancient sea. I thought of the pilots, perhaps dying bitter, lonely deaths far from home, their corpses keeping watch through the ages as the seas shrank and the fires rose.

When I reached the bottom I did not stop to rest, thinking I had already spent too much time searching the ship.

Despite my fears, I saw no trace of the Humped Men during that day. At the thirteenth hour I waded a small stream. Not knowing what might lurk even in such shallow waters, I kept my armor on for protection, felt my way with the handle of my diskos, and so hurried across unscathed.

Beyond the stream the forest quickly dwindled, leaving me in a country of short bushes and large boulders, where I soon met a new danger in the form of winged monsters that did not fly like birds, but bounded into the air, gliding from place to place on grasshopper wings. Three times I narrowly escaped detection by hiding behind boulders.

At the end of my day's journey, I reached another forest that grew all the way down to the seashore. By then, I was desperately sore from fighting, climbing, and walking, and had not slept for twenty-one hours. At first I could not find anywhere to rest, for I feared the winged creatures might stumble upon me on the ground, but I finally decided to strap myself to the high limb of a tree. Once again, my lack of experience kept me from thinking of the idea at once, and I imagined Andrew scolding me for my thickheadedness.

I ate my supper, then picked a likely prospect, an enormous trunk with numerous branches low to the ground. The climbing was easy, and I soon found myself high in the air, sitting with my back against a broad fork.

In stories, when people sleep in trees they always seem quite comfortable—the branches form a perfect contour for their backs, the noise of the wind in the leaves rocks them to sleep. Here, there was no wind, and if not for my armor, my bed would have been unendurable. As it was, I could scarcely relax, and kept starting awake, thinking I was about to fall. I could not hold my diskos in my hand, but had to keep it strapped to my hip, making it difficult to reach in case of danger.

A thousand worries troubled my sleep—the realization that I had not heard the Master Word in a long while, either from Naani or the Master Monstruwacan; the fact, attested by my scrawled notes in the back of *Ayleos' Mathematics*, that I had traveled twenty-five days without reaching any country faintly resembling the land of the Lesser Redoubt; the fear that I might wander the Country of the Seas a long time and still not find my beloved. I thought of what it would be like for the Master Monstruwacan if I failed in my mission. He would wait and hope, and when at last I did not return, try in vain to reconcile my loss.

After I lay upon the branch a time, unable to rest, I pulled the compass from my pouch. A yelp of excitement escaped me when I saw it no longer pointed straight north, but was now several degrees west of north, as if something, such as the Earth Current from the Lesser Redoubt, moved the needle away from the magnetic pole. I watched it a while, hoping it read true, and I thought of Naani, and of the map I had found in the airship, until my eyes grew so heavy I had to either put the compass away or drop it in my slumber.

I dozed off and on, never sleeping very well, often lying with eyes half open, staring up through branches severe and black against the crimson shining of a volcano standing far out in the sea. Its fires seethed so violently, it caused the earth to occasionally tremble, and above its red smoke pressed the black, brooding gloom of the vast night, stark, ominous, and eternal.

Watching the smoke, I was struck by the strangeness of

my journey. How odd it seemed for me to lie warm and alive in a country of light and boiling seas! I have written that the Night Land was a hundred miles below the earth's surface, while the Country of the Seas lay even deeper, but these measurements are based on legend alone, and though it was just a feeling, I often thought my homeland lay even deeper. I pondered the lost world above me, desolate, airless, a land of eternal cold and starless dark, too bitter for life, and speculated that if any human could survive long enough to look down from the heights into the Rift, he would see only monstrous depths and the dim twinkling of scattered, witchy fires.

I drifted off again, only to be startled awake by a noise. As the sound grew, I shifted on the branch so I could see more clearly. Eight Humped Men, running among the trees as if pursued, stopped not far from the tree where I lay. My whole body stiffened when I saw them, but I kept silent, daring to move only enough to unhook myself from the branch. The brutes began climbing another tree. I feared they would see me, but they kept their heads turned downward, as if watching for something.

A din arose some distance away, the loud shuffling of a creature tearing through the woods. The Humped Men crouched, motionless among the lower branches, each one carrying a heavy, bloody, sharp stone under their arm, leaving their hands free.

After some moments, another Humped Man appeared, running among the trees, passing just beneath the place where his comrades waited. When they made no sign to him I realized he was luring some creature to their position.

The beast proved to be an abominable thing, with seven legs on each side, a wide, flat head, and gaping jaws. It moved in a clumsy, shuffling gait, grunting as it went; the tree branches shook from the weight of its passing, and its roars filled the forest. Horns covered its back, and its belly brushed the earth as it ran. Clearly, it was not made to pursue its prey, but followed the man because he had wounded it, for blood flowed all down its spine. The creature's movements made its back plating expand and contract, and the wounds lay between the armored joints.

As the brute passed under the tree the Humped Men leapt from the branches and caught it by its long, spinal horns. Wielding their sharp stones, they set to work at the wounds, striking with all their strength. The creature roared and cried, but continued tearing through the forest while the Humped Men hammered at it.

After traveling only a short distance, it abruptly rolled over on its back, first to the right, so the Humped Men leapt to the left, and then to the other side, catching three of its assailants beneath its bulk. The four who survived sprang into the trees as the creature returned to its feet, and the one who had enticed the beast hurried forward, waving his arms and leaping up and down until it followed. Once more he led it beneath the others; once more they bounded to its back. They soon passed from my sight, the beast bellowing piteously, the Humped Men striking with their stones.

However many Humped Men had started the hunt, I knew few would survive to its finish. As I sat upon the branch waiting for the din to diminish into obscurity, I thought such struggles as these must have happened in the beginning of the world, and were now occurring again at its end.

I eventually descended, made my breakfast, and began my trek. Throughout the day—my imagination fired by the map—I grew increasingly anxious, and could only prevent myself from running through the woods by remembering I still had to cross the entire Country of the Seas before reaching Naani's redoubt. I also had to resist the impulse to send her the Master Word, for though I seemed to have left the Forces of Evil behind in the Night Land, I could not know that for certain, and dared not risk losing everything to a whim.

At the sixth hour I entered a region filled with steaming fountains, sprays, and boiling basins of rock, which spread a thin cloud of mist over the whole area. Since I could only see a few feet before me, I constantly mistook the boulders rising through the fog for monsters and Humped Men rushing to attack. As a result, I grew even more nervous. For orientation, I kept the sea, which also steamed, in sight to my right. I had to slow my pace in order to both watch for enemies and avoid falling into one of the many pools of boiling water.

After three hours I passed through that area. When the mist cleared, I discovered that the vast sea, which had always been to my right, ended at the base of a mountain chain. The peaks vanished into the upper darkness before me, forming an unscalable wall that blocked my path. I pondered a bit, but having no other recourse except to go back the way I had come, I turned to the left and began skirting the base of the mountains.

I continued this way until the fifteenth hour, when I discovered a far smaller gorge than the one I had used to enter the Country of the Seas, less than a hundred paces across, sloping slightly upward. Only a few dozen yards into the passage, the light faded into darkness.

After walking in so much illumination, I dreaded entering that narrow, dreary way. More than anything, I feared it might be a blind alley, for it bore no resemblance to the passage on the airship's map. I stood looking at the gorge and the compass, but the instrument could not help me decide.

Finally, I continued past the mouth of the gorge to see if there were any other way through the mountains. Another hour brought me to a black river a mile wide but so shallow the water scarcely covered the muddy bottom. Steam rose from its surface; it bubbled and foamed, and boiling waterspouts erupted in various places.

The wall of rock bounded the river to my right, and the waters passed beyond sight to my left. I suspected it was not a river at all, but a stagnant sea. There seemed no way to cross it, for this part of the country lacked trees to use to make a raft. Even if I could have built one, the boiling waterspouts posed a terrible threat. Nor could I wade across—if the heat did not boil me alive in my armor, the mud would certainly drag me under.

For the first time, it occurred to me that the way between the two redoubts might have become blocked over the ages. My stomach churned at the thought. Seeing no other choice, I returned to the gorge, praying with ever fiber of my being that it led to Naani. I stepped across the threshold, first into twilight, finally into darkest gloom.

XI
THE DARKNESS ONCE MORE

The shadows fell upon both my body and soul, filling me with fright. Odd how the land of light made me fear the dark! My chest felt hollow as I glanced back down the gorge to the dwindling illumination from the Country of the Seas. I turned and began to walk, not daring to look back for a long time. When I finally did glance behind me again, the light was gone. Despite my fright, I trudged forward at a steady, stumbling pace for six hours.

It felt as if I had returned to the Night Land, for fire-holes pocked the face of the gorge, shedding a dull crimson glare upon the black sides of the passage. Their light often revealed the lowest parts of both sides of the ravine, though its heights, which seemed to climb upward forever, remained obscured. Enormous serpents and scorpions large as my head often clustered around the fires, and though I tried to avoid the flames, the narrowness of the gorge made it difficult for me to keep my distance. Other creatures moved among the rocks as well, and I kept my diskos ready.

The gorge became steeper the farther I went, as if I climbed a gargantuan hill. This made the going tiresome, but I hurried as fast as I could, propelled by the hope of reaching the Lesser Redoubt. But every moment I feared the passage would abruptly end.

At the beginning of the seventh hour I found myself stumbling not from lack of sight, but from fatigue. I started looking for a place to sleep and soon discovered a narrow ledge a few feet up the rock face. It proved difficult to reach, but I finally crawled over its lip and concealed myself in the shadow of the rock. I wasted no time making my meal, and was soon fast asleep, for twenty-three hours had passed since my uncomfortable slumber in the trees.

The next day proved much as the last, except that toward its end I thought I sensed the weak beating of the Master Word. I listened anxiously for a long time, but when I did not hear it again, thought I must have imagined

134

it. An image arose in my mind of the Lesser Redoubt over-whelmed by monsters and Naani fleeing through the dark-ness, alone and unaided. Though I told myself it was only a fancy, it disturbed me so much I could not rest at the proper time, but hurried on through the thirtieth hour.

Finally, when I could no longer walk, I found a small cave nearly twenty feet from the bottom of the right side of the gorge. I climbed up to it, wary of an inhabitant, but the light of the diskos showed it to be clean and empty. I ate four tablets and fell asleep, thinking of nothing but Naani. Only one thought comforted me: if she and I had both been given this gift of a second life, surely it would not be in vain, surely we would find one another in all that dark world. Though a slender hope, based on nothing but faith and expectation, it helped me sleep.

Despite the length of my previous day's journey, I awoke six hours later as I had told myself I would do, though I was so drowsy I could scarcely drag myself from my den. Although I ached from exhaustion, I was soon on my way again, walking numbly through the gloom.

I made good time, pressing forward at a pace just below a run, certain I would soon reach my beloved. That day, I traveled thirty hours, stopping to eat and drink every six. A spider the size of a mastiff inhabited the rock ledge I chose as my bed that night; it sat half-in and half-out of a hole in the cliff, watching me with yellow eyes. Not feeling partic-ularly neighborly, I killed it with a swift stroke. Searching about, I found no other dangers.

For the first time since leaving the Country of the Seas, I noticed the air growing thinner and had to wrap my cloak around me for warmth. I fell asleep a short distance from the corpse, slumbering as soundly as my dead companion, and woke eight hours later, thankful that nothing had seized me while I slept.

During the day's journey, water began dripping on me even if I walked in the middle of the gorge. The air grew fetid and damp, and I realized the walls on either side must have closed together, forming a ceiling. The rocks became slippery with splotched, reeking growths stinking of decay. The fire-holes became less prominent; what few there were burned dully, their choking, sulphurous fumes turn-ing the darkness even darker.

I had to walk more slowly, stumbling as I went, half-sick from the smell. Worse, as I passed one of the fire-holes, I saw the flames reflecting off an enormous swaying form on the far side of the fire. Having seen no living thing as large since leaving the Night Land, I hid at once among the rocks.

As it passed the fire-hole, I saw it more clearly, a black, slimy creature like a giant slug, long as a warship, with waving eye-stalks, so huge its upper parts were lost in the darkness. It made no sound as it slid along and I remained in my place until it passed down the gorge. Since I could not carry my diskos and keep my balance as I made my way over the slippery rocks, I unfastened the weapon and left it swinging freely at my hip.

Because of the lack of fire-holes, most of the time I found myself walking through almost total darkness, always aiming for the distant flames, little brighter than stars, that speckled the length of the gorge. In one such lightless region I noticed something moving between me and the fires. I hid again, and after a time smelled a graveyard stench, as if something was drifting past me. When the smell subsided, I continued on my way, not knowing what the creature had been.

Three hours passed before I reached a fire-hole large enough to produce much light. As I glanced around, I became aware of the utter silence of the place, the only sound the dripping of water along the canyon's length. I wondered how many centuries it had remained that way, the silence, the dripping, the strange, quiet creatures passing back and forth.

I drew up short, perceiving another slug attached to the side of the gorge, so much like the rocks I had nearly missed it. Its head faced the floor and its tail curved so far toward the ceiling that it was lost in the darkness.

The sight of the creature filled me with loathing. I watched it a time, and when it did not move, I crawled on hands and knees among the dank rocks until I left it behind.

Three more times other slugs must have passed me in the darkness, for though I could not see them, their stench was unmistakable. Every time I drew near a fire-hole I invariably discovered at least one of the beasts lying against the cliffside. Though I doubted their speed, I still feared them, and often crawled on my belly from boulder to boulder to avoid whatever sight they might possess.

I passed a fire-hole and saw the gaping maw of a cave

on the right side of the gorge. I wondered how many such caverns there were along the passage, and whether they were the breeding grounds of the slugs.

I cleared the darkness, the stench, and the dripping water after twelve hours. The air grew fresh; the fires, which became plentiful once more, burned bright and clean, their fumes venting skyward again instead of collecting at the ceiling. With the moisture gone, I stopped seeing any more of the slugs, and could hurry along at a good pace, grateful to leave that region behind.

Three hours later, thirty-three hours into the day's journey, I looked for a place to rest. One of the difficult things about my trek was never getting enough sleep—time just seemed to go on and on—but the last few days had been the worst, for I had gone more than a hundred hours with little slumber.

I soon found a small, uninhabited cave lit by a meager fire-pit not far from its mouth. Despite my exhaustion, I no sooner sat down to eat than I realized my reeking clothing made rest impossible.

As was often the case in that part of the gorge, water flowed from a boiling spring near the fire-pit, filling a hollow in the rocks. After testing its temperature, I washed myself and my gear in it and dried with a cloth from my pouch. I then returned to the mouth of the cave, where I sat eating, my diskos beside me. I remember that moment as somewhat peaceful. Perhaps I was too weary for anything else, but I felt almost content.

Presently, several creatures, similar to rats but far larger, slipped out of holes in the rocks. Some lay around the fire-hole while others hunted among the boulders. One presently dove between the stones and came up holding a snake by the neck. It sat complacently eating its dinner, though the serpent fought until it was almost completely devoured. The display both fascinated and repulsed me. Despite my aversion, I was glad to see predators helping to control the snakes' numbers.

When the hunter finished, it drank hot water from the spring, then returned to the fire and lay down close to the edge. Wistfully, I guessed its stomach was far more full than my own.

Several more of the rats appeared; I saw them scampering among the distant shadows, killing the snakes wherever they found them. They played as well, staging mock battles and chasing one another over the rocks. I laughed at their antics, pleased that animals could find joy even in such darkness. My good humor soon passed, however, replaced by a sorrow that brought me nearly to tears. At first, I could not understand the cause, until I realized I mourned the extinction of the many wonderful creatures who had once inhabited the earth, beasts so long forgotten that their memory had not survived. With a terrible yearning, I remembered lions and bears, elephants and antelopes, hawks and sparrows, sea gulls and swans. I remembered dolphins and great whales. Most of all I remembered our finest friends, the loyal dogs and proud horses. So Andros lamented what Andrew had lost.

Not wanting to become part of the rats' provisions, I blocked the cave entrance with large stones. Once secure, I fell into a melancholy sleep, filled with dreams of riding stallions through tall grass with Mirdath.

Six hours later I rose, still fatigued, but ready to continue. Though I ate my breakfast at the cave mouth, I did not see any more of the rats.

When I say the gorge continued to be light and cheerful it shows how my perspective changed during my journey. It would seem a dreadful place to someone thrust suddenly into the canyon, but armored as I was and inured to the hardships, I found its shining fires, hot pools, and massive, misshapen boulders cozy enough, the silence broken by occasional hissing steam, the black walls lost in the upper shadows. After the slugs and slime, it seemed almost pleasant.

Eight hours later I halted, thinking I perceived the Master Word, though again it was so faint I could not be certain whether I had heard it at all. It ceased immediately, leaving me in doubt, but giving me hope as well. I strode forward, renewed, prepared to face any terror, carelessly leaping over the boulders barring my path, certain my quest would soon be over.

Two hours later the ground became level and the walls on either side abruptly vanished. I had reached the end of the gorge. I trembled with excitement.

Before me lay a new region, a second Night Land. Surely I had reached Naani's country! I peered all around, expecting to see the lights of the Lesser Pyramid shining through the darkness. To my disappointment, I found only strange fires and peculiar glows.

A heaviness suddenly filled my chest, and I had to reassure myself that even if I could not see it, the pyramid might still be nearby. It was a large country, and Naani's home was small compared to the Last Redoubt. It might be hidden in a valley or concealed by crags.

The enormity of the land intimidated me, and for a time I could not decide the best course. I took out the compass; it pointed steadily to the north. This, too, puzzled and disturbed me, for I had hoped it would indicate the pyramid's direction.

I went forward almost blindly, searching for a sign to guide my way. At first, I traveled straight ahead toward a large glaring illumination, the first of a series of lights burning in a long line to the left of the gorge's mouth. The country, which was rocky and sprinkled with moss bushes like the region around the Great Pyramid, seemed quite familiar, and I made good speed. Within a few hours, I reached the illumination. I approached it cautiously, remembering I was once more in a land of not just monsters but of entities capable of destroying the spirit.

As I drew near, the shining seemed to rise from the depths of a rift stretching for many miles, but I may have been mistaken since I could not see it clearly due to its mysterious, misty quality. It may not have been as deep, or as large, as I thought. I did not continue toward it, but hid myself among the bushes, overtaken by a sudden disquietude. Lying upon my belly, I parted the vegetation and observed it for a long while. The light swept to and fro, like shining smoke drifting on the wind, sometimes clear, other whiles obscured. Eventually, I thought I detected a monstrous head, but it immediately vanished. In a moment more, I saw it again, though whether it was an entity similar to the Watchers of the Great Pyramid or no more than a carved mountain of rock, I could not tell. Neither did I intend to find out. I went on hands and knees through the bushes until I was far from that place.

Once I was clear, I rose to my feet and surveyed my surroundings. The mouth of the gorge lay at my back, for I could see the fire-pits shining within it. To its left stood the blank darkness of the black mountains; to its right, along the mountains' feet, ran scores of low volcanoes with lights that illuminated the lower slopes. The shining area from which I had just escaped extended before me and far to the gorge's left. If it had produced a proper kind of lighting, it would have lit the entire countryside. As it was, it left only a dull glow in the distance.

Since Naani had never mentioned the pyramid being close to a glowing valley, I turned to the right, where darkness lay fragmented by shining fire-holes. It struck me then just how immense this country was, a land as great as my own. I thought of all the dangers within the Night Land, terrors of which I was somewhat familiar. Here, I did not know the perils; I had no guide on how they might manifest themselves, and I wondered if I would search until some monstrosity murdered me.

Having no other choice than to explore, I thrust my despair aside and marched to the right, keeping parallel with the rows of distant volcanoes. I continued in that direction for ten hours, agitated, hopeless and hopeful, nearly beside myself with anticipation, too concerned with searching to bother with food or rest. Eventually, my relentless pace left me lightheaded, forcing me to sit long enough to eat four tablets and drink some water. I rested only a moment before going on, however, for I could not bear to sleep with the thought of Naani so close.

After another ten hours, I tottered on my feet, heedless of my own safety, more like a man stumbling through the desert than a hunter seeking a prize. I had gone forty hours without respite, driven by the hope of topping a hill and seeing the lights of the Lesser Redoubt.

With the intention of resting only a moment, I finally lay down among the stones, but fell asleep at once. Twelve hours later, I woke, shivering and stiff, having failed to cover myself with my cloak. Only good fortune kept a predator from finding me lying unprotected.

After breakfast I set off again, aching with stiffness, cursing the cold. Seeing how foolish I had been, I vowed to act more prudently, and after six hours forced myself to eat and drink. For once I was glad the tablets could be chewed quickly, for I would have been too impatient to sit and eat a real meal. I hurried as fast as I could, probably too quickly for caution, but I did not care.

A red shining rose before me at the tenth hour, as if from a large pit. Slowing my pace, I slipped forward until I spotted tremendous figures silhouetted against the crimson light. I concealed myself in the bushes and watched them until I was certain they were like the giants of the Night Land, then I crept away into a dark region with only a few scattered fire-holes.

After that, I realized I had no right to be so reckless if I intended to live long enough to find Naani. From that moment, I kept my diskos firmly in hand and returned to eating my meals on schedule, but could not bring myself to keep to an eighteen hour day.

The land soon began to descend and the ground grew soft beneath my feet. The moss bushes died away and the fire-holes vanished. I dropped to my knees, removed my gloves, and felt the earth, which was covered with smooth stones and sea shells. I laughed aloud in delight, for Naani had told me the Lesser Redoubt stood close to the shores of an ancient, dry seabed. Seeing no sign of the pyramid upon this side, I assumed I would have to cross to the other shore.

I was so excited that I journeyed across the empty sea for thirty hours, but did not find my goal. Toward the end of the day, remembering Naani had never mentioned the size of the sea, I became discouraged. For all I knew it might takes weeks to reach the far side.

In order to avoid walking in circles, I kept the volcanoes behind me and to the right, and checked the compass often. To my distress, I began to hear the sounds of creatures running back and forth through the darkness, and a horrible, animal scream once raised the hackles on the back of my neck. Since I knew nothing about the region, I could not say what was normal or abnormal, nor could I imagine what the brutes hunted.

I heard a tremendous bellowing and the pounding of enormous feet drawing near. I dropped to the ground, holding my diskos before me, wondering if it would be better to stand and fight since there was nowhere to hide. The earth shook from the footfalls; I clutched my weapon, my whole body quivering in anticipation of battle. But the noise passed me by and died away.

As I rose, a single, distant scream pierced the night, startling me so that I raised my arm above my head as if to repel a blow. A shiver ran down my spine. Undoubtedly, a giant had caught its unfortunate prey.

I walked forty-one hours that day before reaching the far side of the ancient seabed, but when I arrived I could not see any sign of the Lesser Redoubt. Bewildered, too weary for anything but despair, I sat at the edge of the sea, staring out, not knowing what to think, overwhelmed by the enormity of the region, the vastness of the Rift, the immensity of the whole world. What a fool I had been, thinking I could find one girl in the midst of it all.

At last I roused myself, ate my supper, and made my bed among a clump of bushes. My quest seemed as far from ending as ever, and I escaped from my heartache into the oblivion of sleep.

When I woke six hours later, I found that rest had restored my courage, and I rose and paced along the shoreline of the dead sea, mentally reciting algebraic equations to keep myself alert.

My desperation returned as I walked, however, for the vastness of the land left me not knowing which way to turn. After a time I noticed a weak shining a long way off, as if faint fires spread a glow across the countryside before me and to my left. Lacking any other course, I set out toward the illumination, hoping it might be caused by the lights of the Lesser Redoubt shining up from a hidden valley.

I journeyed eighteen hours, forcing myself to eat even when the tablets gagged me, for worry had soured my stomach. My thoughts turned constantly to Mirdath walking in the woods with her hounds, or sitting in the parlor, or dancing with me at country parties, or dying the night she gave birth. I had lost her once; if I did not find again I would surely die myself.

Three times during that journey I heard running feet and screams of terror. Each time I hid, never knowing the character of either the hunter or the prey, or what balances nature had created in that country.

The shining, which had a deep red color, grew more clear, and the odor of sulphur filled my nostrils. About that time, the land began to slope upward. After several hours the ground leveled off, and I heard a low rumbling unlike any noise I had ever known before.

The roar grew ever louder as I went, until I finally came to the edge of a towering cliff. Far below me spread a sea of dull fire. The far side was hidden by the smoke rising from the sea and the smoke itself glowed crimson. Headlands wound their way out of the black cliffs into the blaze and the flames lapped quietly about them, spitting out intermittent green flames and vapors wherever they touched the land.

Clearly, this was the edge of a deep volcano, flat on the

top and covering all that portion of the country. I stood, awed and dumbfounded; its fires glowed red against my face, its fumes burned my lungs. I had reached the boundary of that region without finding my goal.

I backed away from the scorching fumes, filled with despair, astray in the night of the world, no longer certain whether I was near Naani's home, or whether it remained half a world away.

Glancing up, I realized that I now stood high above the whole countryside and might be able to view it more clearly. I scanned the area, but saw no sign of the redoubt's lights. I sat down, as close to tears as I had ever been through all my long journey.

From my new position, I suddenly became aware of something standing in the night. I blinked my eyes, straining to see, and finally recognized the black shape of a distant pyramid, barely illuminated by remote fires.

No words could possibly express my feelings at that moment. I shouted Naani's name across that dark night, and my voice echoed against the volcanic cliffs. I sprinted down the slope, heedless of anything save the end of my quest. Naturally, I stumbled and fell headlong, and for a few moments the pain was so great I thought I had broken my neck. I had to lie there several minutes, helpless and moaning, unable to rise.

At last I sat up, holding my neck with both hands, as if my head would fall off. I massaged the muscles until the agony diminished, then climbed back to my feet, humbled once more.

I proceeded more cautiously, and soon began wondering why the pyramid looked so dark. Though Naani and I had not discussed it, I thought it reasonable to assume the pyramid's builders might have shrouded its lights in order to conceal it. Perhaps this explained why I saw none of the terrible Watchers such as surrounded my own refuge. I vowed, once I returned home, to suggest a similar tactic to my people, to see if the light attracted the monsters. Perhaps some of the terrors of the Night Land would drift away if we shielded our own embrasures.

As I recovered a little more from my fall, I pressed on with fierce eagerness. I had climbed to the upper plateau of the volcano in thirteen hours; I returned to the plain in less than ten. Though the redoubt was now hidden in the darkness, the hill on which it stood hulked before me, blocking the light of the fires behind it.

I continued another four hours, passing various pits and fire-holes. I knew I was drawing closer since the hill blocked more and more of my view, but another hour passed before I reached it. I heard the sound of running and distant screams four times during that five hours, but could never see what caused the commotion. Whatever it was, it made my blood run cold.

I ascended the hill, my heart pounding with excitement, scarcely able to suppress the urge to shout Naani's name or use the Master Word. The higher I went, the more a cold fear gripped me, as if my spirit understood what my heart could not perceive.

After laboring three hours to reach the top of the hill, I stopped with a halting cry. The pyramid stood before me, not as large as my own home, but still a formidable struc-ture, rising desolate and silent into the night. For the first time I realized its lights were not shrouded, for its empty embrasures stared out at me. The Circle lay dead, its tube shattered. The huge door gaped open. Surely, if anything still dwelled inside that tremendous, dark hulk, it was not human.

At last I understood the sounds of running feet and the screams in the night.

I stumbled back down the hill, my chest heaving, my whole world torn asunder.

XII
VOICES IN THE DARK

It took me four hours to get clear of the hill. I stumbled blindly along, heedless of my way, until I found myself upon the shores of the ancient seabed. I do not know how I reached it so quickly; either the sea curved closer at that point or there were two separate seabeds in that region.

I sat beside the shore, too stunned to marshal my thoughts. If Naani were gone, my only hope was for some beast to appear so I could die fighting it. Such thinking eventually reminded me of the sounds of pursuit I had heard. As horrible as it was to think of humans being hunted through the night, it suggested that some might still survive. I decided to send the Master Word, to discover if Naani still lived. If she did not answer—if an Evil Force appeared instead to destroy me—at least it would end my heartache.

I stood, and after surveying the blackness for enemies, projected the Master Word, followed three times by Naani's name. Several seconds of silence passed. I sighed and dropped my head.

The next instant, the Master Word broke all around me, spoken in Naani's faint, sorrowful voice. *My circus strongman. I am going to die soon. I only wish you were here.*

A trembling joy filled my heart. For the first time since leaving the pyramid, after so many days of grim labor and terrible fear, I knew this was Naani calling. Though the voice was faint, it seemed to be nearby. A hundred questions ran through my mind: what perils did she face? Did she have a weapon? How could I find her in such an enormous land? Even as I tried to clear my mind so I could send an answer, I turned my head toward a clump of bushes surrounding a fire-hole about fifty paces away. Though I could see nothing through the foliage, I sensed, with inexplicable certainty, that there was some creature lurking around the flames. Without answering Naani, I slipped into the bushes and crept close enough to peer between the leaves into the clearing surrounding the fire.

145

A small figure knelt beside the flames, softly weeping, a slim woman who raised her head from side to side, listening even as she cried.

I knew in my soul, all in a single moment, that this was my own, true love. I drew in a hissing breath and rasped, "Mirdath!"

Instantly, she stopped crying and dropped to a crouch, her features suffused with terror, the tears on her face shining in the firelight.

I pulled myself to my feet, parting the reeds. I must have looked dreadful in my gray armor, for she screamed and fell back against the bushes on the other side of the fire. She tried to slip between the vegetation, but it proved impenetrable. With a gasping cry, she turned upon me, her face both fierce and frightened. The thin blade of a knife glistened in the firelight.

"Mirdath," I repeated, and spoke the Master Word aloud. "I am That One. I am Andros."

Recognition came to her, and she cried out something in a broken voice, whether Andros or Andrew, I could not tell. The knife slipped from her hand. She took a stumbling step toward me, then sobbing and shaking, fell to her knees.

I stumbled toward her in turn, but then hesitated, not knowing if I should take her in my arms, for though this was Mirdath, she was also a stranger.

She lifted her hand weakly toward me, and I saw the same uncertainty in her eyes.

"Mirdath," I cried again, and my own knees gave way. I dropped beside her, so that we knelt face to face. She thrust her hands into mine; I grasped hers hungrily. Racking sobs escaped me. For a moment I do not know what either of us said, except that they were things from the old world and the new intermixed: Andros and Andrew, Mirdath and Naani, old love names. We fell into each others' arms and wept together. In that moment, it was as if my soul, broken asunder all my life, was now made whole.

Eventually, we caught our breath and looked at one another, strangers and friends all at once. We exchanged shy smiles. Though she was much smaller than Mirdath, and looked nothing like her, Naani's appearance pleased me. Her face was thin with hunger and stress, which made her pale blue eyes look enormous. She had a petite nose and a pleasantly wry mouth that turned down when she smiled. Her hair, which lay in a red-gold tangle around her face, barely touched her shoulders. A fingernail-thin scar graced the left side of her chin.

"How long have you been alone?" I asked.

"A lifetime," she whispered.

I looked down at the wasted hand within my palm. Her skin felt ice cold; the bushes and thorns had nearly torn her clothes to pieces. Without thinking, I lifted her off her feet, causing her to give a tiny peep of surprise. I set her down with her back against a smooth rock, then stripped off my cloak and put it over her shoulders. She clutched it around her.

I took a tablet out of my scrip, crumpled it into my cup, and added the powder for water. I then heated it upon a rock beside the fire, which turned the concoction into a thin broth. When I tried to give her the cup, her hands shook too badly to hold it, so I fed her by lifting it to her lips.

After she had eaten, she whispered, "I'm sorry I'm so weak. I didn't want you to see me weak. Not after the last time. . ." She began crying, as was only natural for one who had faced so many terrors, but her words shook me to the core, for I knew she meant when she had died as Mirdath.

I reached under the cloak and held her hands to warm them. We took strength from each other, and her crying finally ceased.

After a little while, her fingers stirred within mine, and I tried to loosen my grip. Though she neither spoke nor looked at me, she clutched my hands in a weak grasp, so I kept them where they were. I sat there, mostly contented except for an apprehension that after my finally finding her, we might still be destroyed by a monster from the bushes. I realized then that though I had often feared danger in my journey, I dreaded it even more with Naani beside me.

After a time, she rose, took my hands, and looked at me as if still trying to comprehend that she no longer traveled that dark country alone. As we sat beside one another, she kissed my palms and began to weep in a soft, gasping cry of deep mourning. I took her in my arms and held her gently, stroking her hair, whispering the names of both Naani and Mirdath, and speaking words I scarcely knew I said. She wept a long time, and we held each other, two lonely people in a vast darkness.

Eventually, her weeping subsided, and while she rested against the rock, I made her more broth, then sat beside her to eat my three tablets and drink some water.

"This is good," she said, taking the cup in both hands. "What do you call it?"

"I don't know. Broth, I suppose. I just now invented it."

She studied me gravely, staring with a fixed intensity far different from Mirdath's demure manner. "With so few ingredients?"

I do not know why we thought this funny, though for me it might have been to hide an unexpected shyness at finding myself eye to eye with a woman who was, in many ways, a stranger. Whatever the case, I began to laugh, though softly because of the threat of danger. She broke into a wry grin, and had to put her hands over her mouth to suppress her own laughter. We sputtered until our sides hurt, and must have looked quite peculiar in our subdued fits of mirth.

After we recovered ourselves, we sat in silence a little while. Eventually, I gave her a serious look and asked, "Can you tell me what happened?"

She looked down, and for a moment I feared I had asked too soon, but at last she began, her voice quavering slightly: "After you and I last spoke, the Earth Current dropped to its lowest levels. Without its protection, an Evil Influence reached into some of my people's minds, compelling them to open the Great Door and enter the night. As soon as they were gone, monsters entered the redoubt. They . . . hunted us. Our weapons were useless against them. My father and I, along with the other Monstruwacans, held them off for a while in the upper stories. At last, they broke through. I saw my father . . . I saw my father—"

She broke down again. "A shaggy man," she finally managed, "A shaggy man killed him. Somehow, I reached the lifts and made it through the Great Doors before the power completely failed.

"At first I traveled with three other women, all about my own age, but we were attacked by giants while we slept. They took two of the others, and Mira, the remaining girl, fled one direction, while I ran another. I never saw her again."

"How long ago did it happen?" I stroked her palms. Her hands were much smaller in mine than Mirdath's had been.

"I don't know. Only a few days, perhaps. Or an eternity. Time doesn't exist out here. Only darkness."

"Did you ever hear me calling after the last time we spoke?"

"No," she said, "though I called to you sometimes when I grew heartsick. I couldn't do it often. Every time I did, some beast came searching for me."

I sat in silent wonder, for if she had failed to hear my calls, it must have been because she was outside the pyramid all during my journey. That was why my compass finally stopped pointing toward her redoubt. Before then, it must have been responding to the residual energies of her pyramid's dying Earth Current.

"How have you survived?"

"Running, hiding." She shuddered. "I've tried eating everything but the rocks—the moss, odd berries and growths. My only water came from the hot springs. Half the time either the sulphur in the pools or poisons in the plants made me sick. Once, my stomach hurt so much I thought I was going to die. At the time, I wished I could. I saw a woman killed once, not ten paces from where I hid, by a monster with two hands on each arm. I've often heard my people being chased through the dark, but I couldn't do anything to help. I found a group of humans hiding among the bushes once, but they refused to believe I was one of them. They ran away, and when I tried to follow, drove me back with stones.

"I lost all hope after that, though I kept as near the pyramid as I could. I don't know what I hoped for, perhaps that your people would send help. Despite the danger, I had to stay close to the fire-holes because of the cold. Monsters often chased me away or tried to take me while I slept. Before you found me, I had decided to stay by the fire until something killed me. I couldn't stand the cold any more. I sat down, while the spider-crabs squatted all around, waiting for me to die. When I heard your call, it only made me feel worse, for I thought you were still in the Great Pyramid. And then . . . you were here."

I looked around, not knowing what to say. My eyes fixed upon the circle of light, where the spider-crabs still waited, their high eyes glowing out of the shadows. That I had failed to notice them before shows how familiar such strange forms of life had become to me.

In sudden disgust, I rose to my feet, strode to the border

of the light, and kicked the creatures away until they finally fled. Unlike the crabs of Andrew's time, these did not try to pinch me, but retreated.

"They won't bother you again," I said, turning fiercely back to Naani.

She laughed, with a shadow of what I thought must be a natural tendency to levity. I made her another cup of broth. After drinking it, she became weary again, so I prepared a smooth place for her, gave her my pouch and scrip for a pillow, and wrapped her in my cloak so she could sleep. When one of her feet poked out from beneath the covering, I noticed how shredded her shoes were, and vowed to wash and bind her feet when she woke.

Occasionally she moaned or cried out in her sleep, as the memories of being hunted stalked her through her dreams. I stroked her head and whispered comfort each time it occurred, and though she did not wake, she became still once more.

While she slept, I stripped off my armor and removed my body vest. I put my gear back on, but folded the vest and laid it beside Naani.

She slept for ten hours, while I walked around the fire-hole, listening with both my spirit and my ears, determined to double my vigilance now that she was in my care.

She awoke sweetly, taking my hand and breathing a sigh. "You're really here."

"I am."

"How long was I asleep?"

"Ten hours."

She tried to rise. "So long? Were there any beasts?"

"No." I helped her to a sitting position. "All is well."

"I'm sorry," she said. "I shouldn't have slept so long."

"You needed it."

"I suppose I did." She smiled. "I'm much stronger now. How long has it been since you slept?"

I glanced at my chronometer. "Eighty-four hours . . . and . . . seventeen minutes. About three and half days." I spoke without thinking, hesitating only when I saw the pain in her eyes. No sooner had I said it than a tremendous faintness came over me, making me sway slightly. I chuckled somewhat stupidly as a thin buzzing filled my ears.

She tossed the cloak aside and rose to steady me. "What a poor friend I am! You must lie down. It's a wonder you can stand at all."

In a moment, despite my weak protests, she had the scrip and pouch under my head and the cloak covering me while she sat beside me, rubbing my hands.

"When was the last time you ate?" she asked.

"Before you went to sleep. The tablets were in the scrip. I didn't want to wake you to get them."

She gave a soft moan. "Lift your head."

I complied and she took the tablets, the flask, and the cup from the scrip, then put it back under my head. "Tell me how to make this."

I obeyed, and she laughed in delight when the powder fizzed up to create the water, though she put in too much and it spilled over the rim. I drank it with my head on her lap.

I pointed to the body vest. "You can wear that. It will help keep you warm."

"Don't you need it?"

"No," I lied, fearing she might refuse to wear it if I told her I had taken it from my own body. "It's an extra."

Tears sprang to her eyes, so I knew she realized the truth, but she took my hand, kissed it, and said, "Thank you, Andros. Or should I call you Andrew?"

I laughed in my stupor. "Call me whatever you want, my lady. Sometimes I feel like both men at the same time."

"You must sleep."

"Not yet," I said. "I need to bathe your feet first. I have ointment in my pack."

She laughed. "I can do that myself."

Seeing she had the upper hand, I did not complain any more. I turned on my right side, facing the fire, with my diskos at my breast. She looked at the weapon curiously, but said nothing.

"You mustn't touch the diskos," I said, "except in great-est need, for it responds only to its master's hand and is dangerous to anyone else. Promise to wake me the instant you see or hear anything unusual."

"I promise," she said, caressing my cheek with the back of her hand.

I meant to tell her other things, to warn her of what dan-gers might be near, but my exhaustion took me. It seemed I slept but a moment, perhaps the first good sleep I had throughout my entire journey, knowing that someone kept watch. When I opened my eyes again I saw Naani sitting beside me. She had arranged her hair with a comb from my pouch, so it fell attractively around her face. She wore the body vest, which I guessed she had washed. The suit was somewhat loose, but still revealed her figure. She blushed slightly as my eyes took her in, for if anything, the people of that time were more modest than those of Andrew's day, perhaps from living in such close quarters in the redoubts.

I dropped my eyes to avoid making her more uncomfortable, and she bent over and kissed my cheek, partially, I think, to hide her embarrassment.

"How long have I slept?" I asked.

"Twelve hours, by your chronometer."

"That long? I had no idea. I'm sorry to have left you alone."

She gave a pixie smile. "No more than what I did to you."

"When did you eat last?"

"About six hours ago. This food of yours is nourishing, but not filling. Still, its better than anything I've had for days."

We fell silent again, filled with memories of our previous lives, but still unfamiliar with one another. As she sat before me, I noticed her feet were bare, but before I did anything about that, we ate, drank, and made plans.

"We've stayed here too long," I told her. "It's a wonder we haven't been found. We need to leave quickly, to return to the Great Pyramid as soon as possible."

"Can't we do anything for my people?"

"I don't see how, unless we meet them by chance. The only ones I've heard were being pursued."

Tears filled her eyes and she took my hand. "Most of those I knew are dead—my father, my friends, but a few might still be alive. How can I desert them?" Her voice rose in anguish, and she began to cry. I held her a time, until she drew a deep breath and sat back on her heels.

"I'm all right," she said. "You must forgive me."

"There is nothing to forgive—"

"I'll be brave. But there is one thing I can do, if you have something to write with."

"I do. I've kept the hours of my journey on the back pages of *Ayleos' Mathematics*. We could take a few sheets from there."

"You brought a mathematics book with you?"

"Yes."

She grinned so mischievously I thought I saw Mirdath peering out through her eyes. "Thought you might work a few calculations in your extra time?"

I laughed, though it also embarrassed me. "No. It's just a hobby."

"Or a fixation. I have a lot to learn about you, Andros."

Her delight puzzled me, and I decided to change the subject. "What do you want to write?"

She became serious once more. "I will leave a note every time we stop at a fire, explaining the way to your country. I will also mention any possible dangers. Perhaps some of my people will read it and follow us to your pyramid."

I knew Naani's people were mostly unarmed and unarmored, and I saw little chance of any reaching my home, but I did not discourage her, for someone might indeed overcome the odds and find their way to the Last Redoubt. Besides, for the sake of her own soul, she needed to do something to try to help her people. The enormity of an entire nation, as we thought of the Lesser Redoubt, destroyed by the monsters of the night, was too terrible to contemplate. Even though it made me nervous to linger around the fire-pit, I briefly described the way to the Great Pyramid, while Naani wrote my directions down.

Afterward, I counted the packs of tablets. For the first time, I was glad I had been frugal along the way, for if we made good speed, we had enough for the return trip. As for the water, I still had two full flasks of powder and a third, the one I had used all during my journey, partially full. It never occurred to either of us to slay animals for our food, for our people did not eat meat. If I ever recalled consuming flesh in my past life, I must have looked upon it with disgust. It was a shame, since otherwise we could have kept our bellies full, but though we grumbled, we did not suffer as much as might be expected, since our stomachs had shrunk.

Before we could leave, we had to find some kind of foot gear for Naani. This puzzled me until I found an extra pair of inner shoes within my pack, designed to go inside my armored boots. I made her sit down while I fitted them on her, and we both laughed when we saw how large they were, as if we were children playing make-believe instead of adults facing terrible dangers. I took her knife and used it to shave a string off the straps of my pouch, which I then used to tie the boots around the tops.

"How does it feel?" I asked, as she walked around. She looked charming and clumsy all at the same time.

"Like walking in bags. Can you wrap cords around my feet, to keep the material together?"

I did as she said, and then she stood and tried to walk again. "This will work, though it's hardly fashionable."

"Next time I'll bring boots from the Sixty-seventh City, which is famous for its footwear."

We exchanged smiles and set off.

Despite my anxiety for Naani's safety, it amazed me how much easier it was to journey with a companion, especially since I no longer traveled on what seemed an almost hopeless mission. We steered across the ancient sea bed toward the blue shining I had first seen from the mouth of the Upward Gorge, stopping only twice to eat and rest. By the thirteenth hour I noticed Naani stumbling as she went, for she had not yet regained her full strength. Without a word I scooped her up and carried her like a baby.

"Andros, you mustn't!" she cried. "I'm too heavy!"

I bent down and kissed her lips. "No, you were tall as Mirdath; now you weigh little more than a feather. I could carry you forever."

"I see." She stopped protesting, but after a time said, "Do you wish I were tall again?"

I chuckled.

"Why are you laughing?"

"I'm sorry. I didn't mean to. You were tall, now you are petite. It's neither better nor worse, only different. I think you're lovely."

"Oh," she said, laying her head back against my chest. "Andros, what is a *feather*?"

"I don't know. The expression just came to me."

We went on in silence, until a nagging thought made me speak, though I tried not to sound too pathetic. "I don't look the same, either."

It was her turn to laugh. "You're not entirely different. You were always tall and powerful. You're a little more lean. Your face and voice have changed. But it's a good face—a handsome face."

I grinned like a boy. "So you don't think us ill-matched?"

At this she hugged me tightly around the shoulders and buried her face in my chest. I soon realized she was crying.

"What's wrong?" I asked.

Her voice broke as she said, "You've come for me through all the darkness and dangers, and you ask if we are ill-matched. Oh, Andros!"

For a time we walked, she softly weeping, I feeling her love surrounding me. It was one of the sweetest moments of my life.

"Try to sleep," I told her at last. She fell silent, remaining so until the eighteenth hour when we stopped to rest, but she never slept all during that time because she wanted to help me watch for danger. Since she, too, possessed the Night Hearing, she could be as useful at it as I. Without the protection of my body vest the metal armor against my skin made me terribly cold, nor were there any fire-holes in the ancient seabed to warm me. I kept my cloak around Naani as I carried her, taking comfort in her comfort, but when I started to shiver she ignored my protests and wrapped it over my shoulders. I gave in, knowing it would be unwise for either of us to get chilled, though I pulled it forward so it partially covered her, too.

After we rested, I tried to pick Naani up again, but she refused. "We can make better time if I walk. I'm strong enough now."

We went side by side once more, sometimes touching one another's hands, though mostly I kept my arms free so I could reach my diskos. We searched diligently for a fire-hole, for the cold seemed especially bitter to both of us, and we continued what I came to call The Battle of the Cloak, I insisting she wear it, she insisting I wear it. At last she threatened to give me my body vest back and don her old rags, which she had brought with her in a bundle that I kept in my pouch. I continued to refuse until she won the struggle by bursting into tears. Few men can withstand this particular weapon, especially when it involves a woman's self-sacrifice, and I would rather have fought a thousand monsters than see her cry.

I wore the cloak. I did convince her to trade off every hour, so the battle ended diplomatically, although during her turn she asked me the time every fifteen minutes.

We traveled five more hours, and though she denied it, I realized she was exhausted. Since there were no fire-holes,

I looked for a cave. We found a series of cliffs, ancient islands once rising from the dead sea, among which we discovered an entrance about six feet off the ground. While Naani watched, I climbed up to it and triggered my diskos to see if it was safe. It proved to be empty, but as I turned I found her scrambling up the cliff, knife in hand. Being unfamiliar with the power of my weapon, she had mistaken its spinning for the sound of a beast.

"What a strange device," she said, once she realized what had happened. "I thought a monster had you."

"Your people didn't carry diskoi?"

"No. We have nothing like them."

That seemed odd to me, especially if her ancestors had migrated from the Great Pyramid. Of course, almost anything could have happened in the intervening centuries to deprive them of their weapons.

I helped her into the cave, then followed after. I was glad to find a shelter, for I knew we both needed to sleep at the same time if we wanted to complete our journey before the food ran out. The interior darkness left us blind, and we made our meal together by touch alone.

As we ate Naani said, "I just had the strangest thought. When we reach the Great Pyramid I could cook you a meal like in the old days. I use to dismiss the servants and make it with my own hands."

"Yes," I said, somewhat hesitantly, for her words sparked my memory. "You use to . . . make my meal . . . while I sat by the fire smoking my . . . what was it . . . my pipe?"

She clapped her hands together. "Yes! That was it!"

"You would work," I said, straining to recall, "while I did nothing."

We both sat there, puzzled. Finally, Naani said, "Why wouldn't you help me? You weren't injured."

"I don't know," I said. "Those were strange, barbaric times. Yet there was a certain gracefulness to them as well."

She patted my arm. "It was so long ago. It's like looking down a long tunnel into the sunlight."

It had been twenty-six hours since I last slept, and thirty-eight for Naani, so when we finished eating, we were both ready to lie down. As I have written before, our people were modest, and not wanting to dishonor her in any way I had her lie a short distance from me with the cloak over her. But she said, "This is silly, Andros. We were once husband and wife. If we don't sleep close together, we'll both freeze."

I agreed, though honor required that the suggestion come from her and not me. In many ways, women are more practical than men.

We slipped into one another's arms beneath the blanket of the cloak. After some debate I removed my armored shirt, so we could share some measure of warmth, but the morals of our people restrained us from becoming more intimate. Beyond mere custom, I respected and revered Naani, even as she did me, for such is the real meaning of love, and I fell asleep, warm for the first time that day, her sweet breath against mine.

When I woke seven hours later, I slipped from under the cloak and wrapped it gently back around her, leaving her sleeping. She moaned slightly and reached for the place where I had been, but did not wake.

I watched the night through the cave opening for a long while, making certain nothing stirred, then I searched through my scrip in the darkness until I found two tablets to eat. When I made the water, the fizzing woke Naani, who called to me in a whisper. I answered at once to relieve her of any anxiety.

"Good morning," she said, for those words of greeting had survived even the ages of darkness. "Where are you?"

"Here," I answered, reaching to take her hand. She rose and kissed my forehead, then ran her palm along my left arm until she found the cup, which she took from my grasp. When I gave her two tablets she took one of them and held it to my lips in the gloom. "Bless it with your kiss."

Sorrow and joy froze my heart, for Mirdath had often done the same thing when we ate together. In that moment the walls of eternity rolled away and a thousand memories overwhelmed me, but I kissed the tablet without saying anything.

Getting our gear together, we set off across the utter silence of the ancient sea bottom. We stopped to eat at the sixth and twelfth hours, and arrived at the long slope of the far side of the sea during the fifteenth hour. After ascending it, we reached higher regions overlooking the entire country.

XIII
FORCES

After the gloom of the ancient sea bottom, the country before us seemed much brighter. We came out in a region of scattered fire-holes west of the place where I had originally descended. Naani and I stood close together, she gazing up at me, our faces lit by the faint red glare of the distant flames. She looked beautiful and noble, but pale with exhaustion, and I mentally scolded myself for overtaxing her. After traveling for so many days I felt strong as iron; sometimes it seemed I could walk forever. I tended to forget that it would take some time for her to reach my level of conditioning.

I put my arm around her and kissed her. "We have to decide how to get back to the Upward Gorge."

I pointed to the blue glow blanketing the west. "I don't know what that is, but I don't trust it. We should be able to go to the left of it. We should also avoid that large fire-pit. I've seen giants there. The Upward Gorge is to the south, but it's too far away to see from here."

"We can't go that way," Naani replied. "See the way the fire-holes glow green? According to our Records, that's a sign of poison gas."

This caused me some concern, for the emerald-tinged flames stretched in a band all the way to the blue glow. "I wonder how I avoided it on my way to the sea bed?"

"You must have passed between the poisonous fields and the Red Pit. You were lucky."

"What do you call the blue light?"

"The Shine. You're right to fear it. It's one of the most dangerous parts of the country. When the burning mists roll, the Fixed Giants can be seen staring out of it. They're terrible, evil creatures."

"I saw one. A monstrous face through the smoke."

Naani shuddered against my arm. "If it had turned its will on you, you would not have survived. They destroy both body and soul."

"We have similar creatures in the Night Land, called

158

Watchers, but they do not bother to hide themselves."

"We must avoid them," she said, biting her lip in thought. "I think we should go back down to the seabed and follow the shore southwest past the gas fields, then ascend again. We will have to be careful after that, to avoid the giants of the Red Pit."

Listening to her think aloud helped me see the way her mind worked, and I liked how quickly she planned our course. Her voice had a slight, pleasant rasp surprising in one so small.

"Very well," I said. "That's what we will do. You know this country. I don't."

"I have studied it all my life. I was always drawing maps."

"So was I. I suppose most children do. We should rest before we go on."

"How long have we walked?"

"Seventeen hours."

She slumped as I said it, as if the information sapped the last of her strength. "That fire-hole is close," she pointed at a flame a little to our right. "Let's find someplace warm."

A weary hour passed before we reached the flames. It proved farther away than we thought and much larger than we suspected, for it was a fire-pit rather than a fire-hole, its red flames shooting out of a deep hollow. As we approached, I signaled for silence, and holding my diskos in hand, crept on hands and knees to the rim. The light nearly blinded me and I felt the heat on my face even from where I crouched. Though I did not see anything dangerous lurking in the hollow, I grew uneasy, fearing that a fire that large could not help but attract every predator in the country. I wished we had never come.

I studied the area a long time, torn between our need for warmth and my fear for Naani's safety. While I debated, she startled me by appearing at my elbow. Momentary annoyance crossed my features.

"You're angry," she whispered.

"No . . . I . . . We should stay away from the fires; it's too dangerous."

"We're freezing. We can't survive unless we get warm. Even if we don't sleep here, we have to rest a while."

I knew she was right; the cold wore on me more than the walking. It may seem strange that we had traveled so far to find the fire only for me to voice such misgivings,

159

but the need to protect Naani lay heavily upon me. I had made decisions easily on my outward journey; now I found my will almost paralyzed. I became like a man trying to hide a valuable jewel, unable to find security anywhere.

Despite my misgivings, we finally descended. I searched the rocky floor and spied three serpents and two enormous scorpions watching me from their dens. These alone convinced me not to sleep there, but I did not mention them to Naani. She had already told me she did not like snakes, and I wanted her to rest comfortably.

We sat together by the flames. How good it felt to be warm again! I would have given much for another body vest and heavier clothes for Naani. More than once I wished I had packed something of the sort, but I had started my mission with little idea of how it might end, and one can scarcely think of everything.

When our hands thawed enough so we could open the scrip and pouch, we made our meal and ate it in vigilant silence. As we sat there, it occurred to me that many of the monsters might find the brilliant light of the hollow intolerable, making it safer than I had first suspected.

As we finished our supper, a serpent slithered across the rocks, startling Naani. "I'm warm enough," she said. "We can go."

"This isn't as bad as I thought. We might stay, after all. There's a cave along the sides. I'll check to see if it is safe."

"We don't have to."

Now that I was warm, I hated to return to the bitter cold. We had no guarantee of safety there or anywhere else, and the deserted condition of the hollow suggested that the monsters avoided it. Indecision struck me again; it suddenly seemed foolish to take Naani away from a safe place, to sleep—perhaps unprotected—in the dark.

The hollow was large, and the cave stood a hundred feet from the fire and twenty feet above the floor. I clambered up to it, and was able to see by the firelight that it was empty. I hurried to help Naani up, for climbing the rock face made me feel vulnerable. She showed complete confidence in me, a trust I would have relished if not for our danger. We retreated from the cave mouth, out of sight of spying eyes, and slept beneath the cloak as we had done before, except that I left my breastplate on so I could be ready for battle. It had been twenty hours since we last slumbered.

We woke seven hours later to shouts and shrieks, gripping one another in terror, for the screams were human.

A tremendous roar erupted from one quarter of the night and another answered from a different direction. The whole country boomed with gargantuan, husky voices, as if men as big as houses ran shouting through the darkness.

Naani, having heard many such noises during her month of wandering, began to tremble violently in my embrace, so I drew her deeper into the cave. But I was no less frightened than she; it sounded like an army of giants approaching.

A dreadful, wailing scream rose and fell, the sound of a woman being brutally slain. My heart sickened; rage filled my breast. If not for my concern for Naani, I would have bolted after the monsters. When the girl's screams abruptly ended, Naani covered her face with her hands and broke into desperate sobs.

Other screams followed, accompanied by the hoarse shouts and thudding feet of the giants stalking their prey. The whole land echoed with the sounds of pursuit, the din increasing until the chase seemed right at the edge of the hollow. I crept forward and peered out from a position where I could see over the far side of the fire-pit's rim. A cluster of humans, either naked or in rags, passed beside the lip—weeping, screaming, and panting—like wild animals fleeing the hunter's bow. Though I saw them for but an instant, the memory remains burned in my mind.

Only my fear of abandoning Naani kept me from leaping after them, but no sooner did the humans pass than four giants thundered by, three a dull gray in color and covered in thick hair, the fourth a pale white, his naked body scored with livid blotches, and I realized I could do nothing to help those poor souls. Out in the night, the giants' bellows mingled with distant screams followed by silence.

My heart ached at seeing the fleeing victims, too terrified and broken in spirit to turn and defend themselves. I knew, from what Naani had said, that her people had grown listless from being starved of the Earth Current for thousands of years, but even if they had possessed my people's vigor, they might have done little better in such a hopeless situation. Still, I always thought Naani an exception to her race, for regardless of the danger she kept her courage.

As I watched these events unfold, Naani wept in the back part of the cave. "Oh, can't we do something?" she whispered. "Can't we do something?"

I was about to turn to comfort her when a half-clad woman clambered over the edge of the hollow. She slipped and slid her way to the bottom, gave a quick glance over her shoulder, and hid herself by crawling under a rocky ledge. No sooner had she done so than a squat, hairy man, with shoulders broad as a bull's, scaled gracefully into the hollow. He turned his evil head from side to side, sniffing the air like a beast. Sharp tusks curled out of his mouth. He seemed to know exactly where she was, for he scurried, silent as a fox, toward her hiding place.

Cold anger filled me. Though I could not aid the others, I resolved to save this one woman. Without hesitation, I leapt the twenty feet to the bottom of the hollow. I rolled to cushion the blow as I landed, but the Squat Man was so fast he reached the girl by the time I regained my feet and dragged her from her hiding place by one leg. She gave a shriek and I shouted a challenge, but in a split-second the hunter ripped her nearly in half, cutting her scream short.

I was so blinded by rage I could hardly see the Squat Man as I hurled myself toward him. The roar of the diskos filled the hollow, as if it, too, yearned to gorge itself upon the hunter.

My opponent turned toward me, no doubt thinking to deal with me as easily as he had the woman. He attacked silently, without so much as a growl. I swung the diskos at him as he sprang toward me, but he ducked beneath my blow with animal speed, then caught me by the legs and tried to tear me apart as he had his first victim.

I slashed at him, severing one of his taloned hands. Even then he did not cry out, but threw me halfway across the hollow. I hit with a tremendous impact, my mail clanging against the rocks, my diskos ringing like a bell. But my armor protected me and I bounded back to my feet, still holding my weapon.

The Squat Man reached me in two quick strides, still silent but frothing at the mouth in fury, specks of foam gathering around his tusks. I sprang forward to meet his charge, first feinting to the left, then swinging to the right with all my strength. The weapon shrieked as it took off his head and shoulders. The momentum of his charge knocked me backward and we fell together in a heap. I rolled away to escape his thrashings, then jumped up to strike again, my brain not yet registering his death.

A movement to my left caught my eye, and I pivoted, thinking it another foe, but it was Naani rushing to help me, her knife in hand, her face pale but determined. As soon as she realized I was safe, she turned and helped me look for other dangers.

Once we were sure that there was nothing else that could harm us, I said, "Go back to the cave. I'll give the woman as much of a burial as I can."

Instead, she walked past me, avoiding the body of the woman, but going straight to the Squat Man's corpse. A dozen emotions flashed across her face as she stared at the broken form.

"I didn't believe anyone could kill such a creature," she finally said, looking at me with a touch of awe. "No one from my redoubt could have done it."

I shrugged. "Your people don't have diskoi."

The ferocity in her expression surprised me. Her voice was hoarse, her breathing heavy. She stared at the dead man a long time, her eyes shining with disgust, hate, and, above all, triumph. She abruptly kicked the body, and then began lashing at it, kicking it over and over, her face suffused with rage.

"I'll . . . never . . . fear . . . you . . . again!" she cried, striking the corpse between each word.

I rushed to her in alarm and seized her arms. For a moment, she flailed against me and I had to call her name several times before she finally stopped, her face red, her eyes wild. She broke into sobs against my shoulder.

With the danger past, we trembled in each others' arms. I will always remember her defiance and the way she looked when she saw how I had killed the Squat Man.

We dared not stay in the hollow much longer. I cast the torn body of the woman into the fire-hole while Naani waited a short distance away, her eyes averted as if in prayer. When I returned to her side, sorrow etched her face, as if I had given everyone she ever knew to the flames.

Together we climbed back into the cave to catch our breath and eat. My battle left me parched, and I drank more water than usual. For an hour we sat listening, without hearing any more noises. While we waited, Naani pre-

163

pared another sheet describing the way to the Last Redoubt, which she placed on the floor of the hollow,
weighted down by a stone.

We left the fire-pit and headed back toward the ancient
sea bed. It took two hours to reach it, for we crept from
bush to bush in case the titans were still searching the land.
Once there, we felt safe enough to increase our pace,
believing the giants would stay close to the fire-holes to
hunt the humans seeking warmth. We traveled an hour into
the sea, then turned slightly southwest and began skirting
the shoreline, steering by Naani's knowledge of the country and the light of The Shine. By the seventeenth hour
Naani thought that we had passed the fields of poison gas.

We began looking for a place to sleep. I was particularly
exhausted from my battle, which had left me bruised and
sore. But after searching through the gloom for an hour
without finding anywhere to rest our heads, we decided to
build a shelter by gathering some of the smaller boulders
scattered along the shoreline.

During our discussion we both said the same words at
the exact same time, and without thinking, caught our little
fingers together in the dark of that grim land, even as we
used to do in the early years. Solemn as children, we made
a silent wish, the way a lad and lass might once have done.
Then we laughed and kissed each other. In that moment it
seemed that the world and time could not alter the heart.

Naani carried the thin, flat boulders and I rolled the
larger ones until we constructed a fortress big enough to
sleep in, with the flat stones placed along the sides to keep
creeping creatures from reaching us. When we were done,
we climbed in and sealed the entrance with rocks. It was a
poor shelter, for it left us trapped if a beast found us by our
scent. Though I said nothing to Naani, I felt as if I had
crawled into my own coffin.

We ate in complete darkness, then slept with the cloak
over us. I could not bring myself to remove my armored
shirt, though it would have helped us conserve warmth. As
it was, I spent a restless night between the cold, my aching
body, and my fear of discovery. Every time I drifted off I
dreamed of fighting the Squat Man again. But Naani slept
in my arms peaceful as a child.

At the seventh hour, my soreness became so intolerable
I could scarcely move, and I gave up trying to sleep. I
slipped out of Naani's arms, intent on letting her rest a lit-

tle longer, and after listening for several minutes, rolled the entrance stone away and crawled outside, where I walked back and forth swinging my arms, trying to loosen my joints. It seemed hopeless; my muscles were all but locked in place, and I did not know how I could defend us from danger when every movement made me groan in pain.

Without waking Naani, I crawled back into the refuge and retrieved my ointment from my pouch. Once outside again, I stripped off my armored shirt and began rubbing the salve wherever I could reach, though I moaned from my efforts. I began to realize just how far the Squat Man had thrown me. Despite the pain, I had to rub fiercely to keep warm.

In the middle of my work, I heard a stirring. Naani poked her head out of the shelter. "Andros, what are you doing?"

"I didn't want to wake you."

"I thought something was killing you out here." Her knife glistened in her hand.

"Sorry. I tried to keep quiet."

"Where's your shirt? Do you want to die from exposure?"

When I explained what I was doing, she said angrily, "Why didn't you call me? You have no business trying to do this alone. Take your diskos and give me the ointment. You'll freeze."

She hurried back to our sanctuary, brought the cloak and put it around me, then massaged my back with the ointment while I rested on my knees. When I could move a bit better, she sent me back to the refuge and had me lie down. There she spent a long hour rubbing me down, speaking gently but seriously as she worked.

"You're not alone any more, Andros, and I'm not a child. I can't do what you can, but I can help. We have to work together. It hurts me that you tried to do this by yourself. Promise you won't do anything like it again."

"I only wanted you to sleep a little longer."

"It won't do. We are partners. What use is our being together if I can't help you? You have done so much, finding me in the darkness—"

"I only did what my heart commanded."

We both fell silent, while she continued my massage. Finally, I said, "Do you remember when Mirdath disguised herself as a villager to go to the dance?"

"I do. You tried to stop me, but I was too stubborn. You had to fight two men who wanted to take advantage of me. You were magnificent."

"You are still stubborn, Naani."

"I am still stubborn. Don't forget it."

We both laughed.

"Does it ever bother you, the two lives?" I asked.

Her hands slowed their ministrations. "It did at first, but not now."

"Even though I know it's all true, I still find it hard to believe."

"If you know it's true, why is it hard?"

"I don't know. I feel pulled sometimes. Stretched. Don't you?"

"No. I feel Mirdath behind me. She was beautiful and she knew it. I'm not as lovely, but I have always felt beautiful, even as a child. I think that was her. Believing I was pretty made me seem prettier than I am."

"You are beautiful, inside and out."

She bent down, kissed my cheek, and continued the massage.

"It wasn't *all* confidence with her, you know," Naani said after a while. "She desperately needed someone after her parents died. She wanted a man to take charge of her. Sir Alfred did his best to give her security, but she never forgot that it could all be taken away. It made her needy, despite her beauty."

"Don't you need anyone?"

She laughed. "We all need someone. But that was a different time, a day of lords and ladies. What a world it must have been! Men going about, free to do anything they wanted; women, as captive in their houses as we are in our pyramids."

"Were you unhappy, then?"

"No, because I was a creature of that day."

After the massage I felt better. I dressed and we sat eating breakfast, talking of ancient days, feeling the love between us. I remember that sanctuary as a holy place, a shelter from all the terrors of the world.

We departed, leaving the ancient sea behind for the last time. When we reached the crest of the shore, we surveyed the land again. The Red Fire-Pit stood nearby in the southwest and monstrous figures moved against the glow of the flames. We dropped to the ground at once, thinking we might be revealed in the light, but were actually too far away to be seen.

Fire-holes covered all that portion of the country, mostly red in color except in the field of poison gas far behind us. The Shine blanketed all the west, and in order to avoid both it and the Red Fire-Pit, we needed to travel west by southwest. This would also allow us to bypass numerous other dangers, of which there were so many that when Naani described them, it amazed me that I had survived my original journey. We would have to avoid the low volcanoes as we approached the mouth of the Upward Gorge, for though no one from the Lesser Redoubt had ventured into the night for thousands of generations, the Records indicated a tribe of wolf-men dwelling among the peaks.

I asked her countless questions about the country, and under my prodding she said that The Shine was considered the source of every Force of Evil working against her people's spirits. Her grief overcame her as she told me this, and I took her gently in my arms, vowing to myself to ask only for those details necessary for our survival, to avoid arousing her sorrow merely for the sake of my own curiosity.

We traveled northwest a while longer to give the Red Fire-Pit a wide berth. Its light illuminated the countryside for miles around, forcing us to crawl over the barren regions between the clumps of vegetation. We did not stop to rest until we felt we were far enough away from the realm of the giants, and when we resumed we turned southwest to avoid getting too close to The Shine, only to encounter a broad valley filled with a deep darkness. After some debate, we decided to cross it rather than go around, in order to save several hours.

It soon seemed we had made a mistake, for though the valley appeared shallow from above, it proved tremendously deep. We descended three hours before reaching the bottom, and I became so nervous that except for Naani's insistence, I would not have even stopped to eat and rest. It helped that when I grew uncertain she kept calm, and when she became anxious I remained steady. So we balanced each other, as is the way of love between a man and a woman.

However, we decided not to stop to sleep at the seventeenth hour, for we both urgently wanted to leave the valley behind. This was partially due to a lack of fire-holes, since the only ones we saw emitted an uncanny blue glow. But from the first hour of our descent we had both sensed an aura of evil within the vale.

Two hours after we ate, we were halted by a vague sound. Without a word, we dropped to the ground and listened. Though we remained there for several minutes, we did not hear anything else, and eventually rose and continued on our way.

We passed two places where blue flames licked out of the earth. A gas hung around them and their fires burned with an even, smoldering light, clear as a star's. A stench accompanied the flames and the bitter gas burned our throats so badly we feared being overcome. After that, we avoided the fires whenever we could.

An hour past the second fire-hole we heard a soft rustling behind us. We glanced back and glimpsed what seemed to be humans running through the night, their faces pale. They made so little noise among the stones I thought they had to be barefoot. So shadowy they seemed, so much like lost spirits among the blue shining, I hesitated to attract their attention, for more than one monster possessed human traits.

Even while I debated, a noise arose, far in the distance, but in the direction where the figures ran. We recognized it as the mysterious sound we had heard before, though this time we perceived it more with our spirits than our ears. It became gradually clearer—the din of something spinning high in the air, as if at the valley's edge—and we both suddenly knew, beyond doubt, that it was a Force of Evil.

Now that it was upon us, I realized that its presence had affected me from the time we first entered the valley. Despair filled my heart, for if it found us, how could I protect Naani?

We heard the spinning descend into the vale and begin drawing closer. I looked around, trying to think of a way to escape, but there was nowhere to hide. In desperation, I drew Naani behind some boulders. To my eternal shame, I hoped it would find the other figures we had seen rather than us. Perhaps if Naani had not been with me, I would not have thought such a cowardly thing. But I will never know for certain.

The sound came closer, its volume increasing. I could make out two distinct tones within the spinning, and a third resonance, heard only in my spirit, the sound of Darkness Incarnate, whispering of the Void and the Abyss.

Without speaking, Naani drew her knife from its sheathe and handed it to me, so I could save her soul by slaying her. I raised my diskos, thinking it might be a cleaner death, but she whispered, "No, not with that. Don't cut me to pieces. A quick stroke with the blade."

It became ever more evident that we were the Spinner's target, for it was almost upon us. I stood heartbroken and helpless, trembling. My mouth went dry; my heart hammered against my chest. I gripped Naani close to me, and could scarcely restrain a sob rising from my soul. I did not kiss her, nor she me, but we clutched each other while I held the knife ready. Despite the many dangers we had faced, I realized Naani and I had been happy in our short time together. Now death, and worse, had come.

The spinning pulsed through the air, echoing off the boulders. I bared my forearm, where the Capsule of Oblivion lay embedded beneath my skin. A wave of blackness passed across my eyes, blacker than the darkness around me. I wondered if I had the courage to do what must be done.

As the noise of the spinning increased, Naani pulled my face down to her's and gave me a last, enduring kiss. But whether I kissed her back, I cannot remember, for a sickness filled my heart.

May you never stand where I stood that day, without hope, your only courage flowing from the love between you and your beloved. Perhaps you see me there and love my Naani as I loved her then.

The noise increased. I felt a terrible presence unfolding before us. I raised the knife, aiming for her heart. Naani squeezed my arm one last time. I dared not wait too long; she had not undergone the Rite of Preparation and the Evil Force could seize her from a greater distance that it could me.

The sound of spinning abruptly ceased directly before us, and a pale, horrid light rose, revealing the trunk of a tremendous Tree moving toward us through the darkness, its branches whipping back and forth like a cat-of-nine-tails.

I turned Naani from the Tree, and her hands fluttered against mine. With my body between the Evil and my love, I prepared to strike before it was too late. The knife trembled so violently in my hand I could scarcely control it. A mist covered my eyes; I could hardly see. I looked down, measuring the distance between the blade and her heart, desperate to make a clean blow so she would not suffer. Naani had shut her eyes, her mouth drawn taut. I took a deep breath, willing my hand steady. A moan escaped my lips. I glanced back at the Tree.

To my surprise, it had halted its approach and was beginning to withdraw. At first I could not believe it, thinking it a trick of the eye, or worse, a delusion brought on by the Evil to give us false hope. But it receded quickly, the pale light fading until the thing vanished back into the darkness.

"It's gone!" I whispered hoarsely. Naani did not answer, but clutched me as if she had not heard, her eyes still shut. We remained so a long time, trembling and terrified. I looked in every direction to see if the Evil Force would return. Finally, I glanced up, thinking it might be above us, and gasped in wonder.

"Look," I rasped. "Look."

Naani raised her eyes. Above us hung a clear, burning Circle. We both laughed in child-like wonder.

"Thank you," she whispered to the Circle.

"Thank you," I echoed.

Then Naani fainted in my arms.

I could not blame her. I nearly fainted myself. She must have imagined the knife stroke a thousand times while she bravely waited. Only after our rescue did she allow herself the luxury of losing consciousness. But she revived almost immediately and gazed up at the light.

I cannot adequately describe my feelings as I stood beneath that mysterious Power of Good. It burned with a soft, holy glow, filling my heart and soul with an unspeakable joy. Why it chose to stand between the Forces of Evil and the human spirit I do not know, save I felt a love beyond comprehension emanating from it. My heart leapt with gratitude; all fear of the Tree slid away.

It may have been only my imagination, but I had the distinct impression that this Power was able to save us because we showed strength of spirit, as if our willingness to sacrifice our lives for the sake of our souls somehow enabled it to aid us. Whatever the case, my experience with the Circle changed my whole perspective of creation. I now believe humanity has always been protected from the

Forces too powerful to be withstood by mortal flesh. I also think steps were taken measure for measure, so as the Forces of Evil took physical form in the Night Land, the Powers of Good did likewise to oppose them.

We pressed on, bathed in the soft light of the Circle. For twelve hours it burned above us, so we knew the Evil Force hovered nearby, waiting for its chance to destroy us. During the time we journeyed beneath that radiance our limbs felt light and we never grew weary; our hearts sang within our breasts and we could not keep from holding hands.

Only once did anything disturb our serenity, when we heard, far away in the shadowed vale, a dreadful scream-ing and the faint sound of something spinning. We paused, shaken, clasping one another again, imagining the victims' fate. Guilt swept over me as I remembered how I had hoped for them to be taken rather than us. Though I felt unworthy of the Circle's protection, it remained faithfully overhead.

Eventually we climbed over the rim of the valley back into a country of dim light that seemed dazzling after so much darkness. Though thirty-three hours had passed since we had last slept, other than Naani having tired feet, we remained refreshed. Still, common sense told us we should rest.

I began looking for a hot pool to bathe her feet, and we soon reached a fire-pit with two flames burning at its bot-tom beside a bubbling spring. The spring was warm with-out being scalding, and we did not find any creatures lurk-ing around the hollow. Naani lay with her head on my knee, using my palm as a pillow against my armor while putting her feet into the hot-spring. I draped my cloak over her while I made dinner.

After we had eaten, I rubbed ointment on her feet to soothe them.

"That feels good," she said.

"Do you think we could go on a bit more?"

"If we need to."

"I want to get as far from here as possible. The sooner we reach the Upward Gorge, the less chance of something finding us."

She shuddered, obviously thinking of the Tree.

As if in answer to a question we did not ask, the light from the Circle suddenly flickered and died, leaving us staring up into the darkness. Naani gave a little gasp.

"I'll miss it," she said, wistfully.

I did not reply, but its loss left me feeling naked, de-fenseless. Still, my gratitude did not diminish; it had saved us when nothing else could. The stamina it gave us van-ished with it, however, and though I was not as weary as I would normally be after so long a trek, I felt my vitality drain away.

Nonetheless, we had vowed to continue, and after an hour's rest, we pulled ourselves up the hollow. We man-aged a good pace, and soon left the Red Fire-Pit of the giants behind us, though not nearly far enough for my comfort. A dark ridge rose before us, eclipsing the lights and flames. The low volcanoes stood to our left. To our right, across all that region, hung the cold, baleful glare of The Shine.

When the ground began sloping up toward the ridge, I eagerly increased my pace, for I remembered descending it at this point when I had first entered the land. I strained my eyes, searching for the mouth of the gorge. In my excite-ment I failed to notice Naani pausing to remove a rock from her shoe.

She screamed behind me, a cry just as quickly extin-guished. Fear poured through me as I whirled around and saw my beloved struggling against a Yellow Man with four arms—two wrapped around her waist, two clutching her throat.

Without even pausing to take the diskos from my hip, I leapt forward. I became little more than an animal at that moment, for I seized the man's two upper arms with in-human strength, pulling them backward until they broke at the shoulders with a grinding shriek.

The creature screamed in agony, then turned and tried to seize me with its lower appendages, which were huge, hairy, and much larger than its upper arms. It caught me by the thighs; its fingernails, long and sharp as talons, clicked against my armor. It was broad-shouldered and easily twice my weight, and had it intended to do so, it could have torn me apart. Instead, it caught me around the body, while I grasped it by the throat. If I caused it any harm I could not tell; I know I never cut off its air, for its neck was hairy and muscular as a bull's.

Its fetid breath raked over me as we struggled. Its fanged mouth, too small for chewing, seemed meant for drinking blood. It sought my throat, and I strained to hold it off.

We swayed back and forth in our struggle. It would have killed me at once except it seemed unable to use its lower arms for anything except holding its prey. It never released its grip on me to try to tear my hands from its throat, but wagged its ruined upper members uselessly, unable to adapt to their loss.

Suddenly, it gripped my body with greater ferocity; I felt my armor straining almost to the breaking point as I fought to keep the monster's teeth from my throat.

It abruptly released me and leapt away, ripping my hands from its neck. It dove back toward me, giving me no chance to reach my diskos. I used all my wrestling skills in that moment, and finally slipped beneath its arms long enough to deliver a solid blow with my armored fist. I evaded it again by stepping to the side, and struck it a savage stroke to the side of the head. I was no longer angry; a cold cruelty filled my brain. I would either kill the Yellow Man or it would kill me.

It tried to grip me from the side, and I had to use all my speed to slip away. I sprang toward it, my body straight as a spear, and struck a blow with all my strength to its jaw.

It fell backward, leaving me momentarily free. In that instant, I pulled my diskos from my hip. The Yellow Man, looking somewhat dazed, grunted and rose, screeching at me like a monkey, as if crying unknown, half-shaped words.

It attacked again, but I killed it with the diskos. When its last struggles ceased I tottered toward Naani, who lay huddled on the ground, her hands to her throat. She looked dead.

I scrambled to her as quickly as I could, and with trembling hands, removed her fingers from her throat. I gasped, seeing blood, but when I examined the wound, realized it was only a slight cut. With some effort, for my whole body trembled both from fear and the exertions of battle, I managed to remove my gloves, but I could not steady my hands enough to feel her pulse.

I sought to quiet my breathing, which still came in labored gasps, and I put my ear above Naani's heart. A sob escaped me as I heard a steady beating.

I pulled the scrip from my back and made enough water to bathe her face and throat. Her body quivered slightly in reaction. No knowing what else to do, I continued wiping her brow until her eyes gradually opened. She moaned softly.

"Don't try to move," I ordered. "Keep still."

"What . . . oh! That creature!"

"It's dead. How is your neck?"

She moved her head slightly and winced in pain. "I thought it had killed me. It hurts, but I can move it."

Gradually, I helped her rise to a sitting position. She turned her head again and massaged her neck with her hands. "That horrid face! I'll never forget it. And Andros, I —why, Andros, are you weeping?"

I drew her close to me, partially to hide the tears streaming down my face. "I thought I had lost you . . . again." My voice broke. "I never want to lose you again."

So we sat together a moment, swaying back and forth, holding one another.

"You won't lose me," she said. "I'll never go away. Not with my brave warrior beside me."

In that moment it was as if all my grief for Mirdath returned to me. I wept like a child, and she comforted me as a mother soothes a small boy.

"I'm sorry," I said at last, when my sorrow was spent. "I should be consoling you."

"Never be sorry," she whispered.

We left that place behind as quickly as we could. When Naani first tried to walk, her knees trembled terribly, the attack having taken a dreadful toll on her small frame. Ignoring her protests, I scooped her gently into my arms and carried her, her head cradled against my shoulder.

After such a terrible scare, we were both so thankful for one another's survival that we teased like carefree lovers, whispering private, sweet words together. This sudden exhilaration soon passed, though, replaced by my fear for her safety. I began studying every bush and stone, for the Yellow Man had come within a few feet of us without my seeing, and I rebuked myself for my lack of vigilance. Since the vegetation grew in huge clumps in that area, watching for danger kept me busy.

A short time later, we reached the top of the ridge. I gave a chuckle of surprise, for the lights of the Upward Gorge, which I thought still many miles away, glowed before us. I pointed it out to Naani, who gazed thoughtfully at the baleful fires, her emotions flickering across her face. To me it meant escaping this land of giants into relative safety—to her, following an unknown path, leaving her childhood home behind.

Still carrying her, I set off at a fair pace and soon reached the gorge. My weariness hung on me like a stone; we had not slept for thirty-six hours.

"Put me down here," Naani said.

When I complied she turned back toward her homeland. I kept my arm around her, to support her as she stared into the gloom.

Presently she spoke in a hushed voice. "Everything looks so different from here. Where is it? Can you tell?"

I pointed across the darkness to the north. "There, I think, but we can't see it from here."

She nodded but did not reply, and I knew she was saying goodbye to all the world she had ever known.

Finally, she said, "When the last of my people are hunted down, no one will ever see this country again."

She turned, her head down. We clung together, and eventually she lifted her eyes. "We have to go."

Still she did not move, but stayed another moment, her gaze shifting all across that weird landscape. Then she turned, and side by side, we entered the gorge. As we walked, her body began to shake in soundless sobbing, and she stumbled as she went. I lifted her once more, while she wept with her head against my armor.

For another hour, I carried her down the gorge. Eventually, her weeping ceased, and she fell asleep in my arms.

So we said farewell to that dark land, leaving it to Eternity.

XIV
DOWN THE UPWARD GORGE

I carried Naani until I started stumbling as I went. At one point, when I glanced up at the sides of the gorge, nothing looked familiar, and I could not recall any of the last hour's journey. This frightened me, for I had nearly been walking in my sleep. It was a wonder I had not fallen headlong with my beloved in my arms.

I cleared my mind by an act of will and soon sighted a ruddy fire-hole a short distance away. From my original journey I knew caves probably surrounded it, and I searched the left side of the gorge until I sighted seven such just beyond the fire.

After our experience with the Spinning Thing and the Yellow Man I made certain to pick a cave both habitable and high enough to be difficult to reach. I only wished we were several miles down the gorge, farther from the dangers of Naani's country.

I kissed Naani to rouse her, and she kissed me back, but did not wake. I held her against my harsh armor, shaking her tenderly, my whole exhausted heart filled with love for her.

At last, she opened her eyes and I set her on her feet.

"I'm sorry I slept so long."

I chuckled. "We were both asleep for a while."

She was too weary to understand my comment, and I was too exhausted to explain. While I climbed to the cave, I made her walk up and down a bit, to rouse her enough so she could scale the cliff. Since the ascent was fairly rigorous, I knew our enemies would have difficultly reaching us in the face of my diskos. Though the mouth opened in a narrow slit, the cave itself was tall enough for me to stand upright, and proved surprisingly warm, as if underground lava coursed behind its walls. By the glow of the fire-hole, which lit the entire chamber, I could tell it was uninhabited.

When I returned to help Naani climb up, I found her pacing nervously back and forth.

"Is something wrong?" I asked.

"No," she said, looking up at the cave. "Is it safe?"

"Quite comfortable. The glow from the fire-hole lights the entire chamber. There's nothing dangerous."

She continued pacing. After a moment, I said, "Are you ready?"

She stopped, glanced up the cliff again, and murmured, "Andros, I'm afraid of heights."

"You are?"

She bit her lip. "Yes."

I laughed.

"What's funny?"

"You lived at the top of the Lesser Redoubt."

"That was different. Don't laugh at me."

"It is funny, don't you think?"

Apparently she did not. She abruptly stamped her foot and turned her back to me.

"Naani, wait," I said, still chuckling. "I didn't mean—"

"It is not funny. I can't help it."

I restrained my mirth. "You're right, of course. But we need to reach the cave."

"I know." She kept her back to me, but turned her head slightly to the side. "I just . . . I don't like to be weak. I have never liked heights. I don't even like looking down from the lifts."

"Did it bother you when we climbed into the hollows? They were as deep as this cave is high."

"It terrified me. I just didn't want to say anything. But at least there were bushes to hold onto. This looks so sheer."

"Naani, we—"

She waved her hands before her. "I'll be fine if you'll help me. I'm just scared."

Without saying anything else, I led her by the hand to the cliff. "I'll be right beneath you, to catch you if you fall."

We climbed together, Naani feeling her way, her eyes sometimes shut. When at last we crawled over the lip, her ashen face made me regret laughing at her. Before we slept I removed the straps from my scrip and pouch, and returned to the bottom of the Gorge, where I strapped as large a boulder as I could carry onto my back. I made no slips returning to the cave, though my ascent kept Naani gravely anxious. I balanced the boulder lightly on the lip of the cave mouth, where a touch would send it rolling.

177

Though it blocked the bottom part of the slit, it did not cover the upper portion, leaving the light from the fire-hole dancing against the walls.

"Our blind sentry," I said.

"At least he doesn't eat much." She seemed to have regained her cheerfulness. "Let's name him Vigilance."

"Or Stoneface." Later, we laughed at the things we said that night, though at the time we were both too stupefied to find humor in anything.

Since the cave was so warm, Naani spread the cloak upon the rocks as a cushion. She made our couch in such a sweet manner, especially after I had teased her about her fear of heights, that I lay down without mentioning that the cloak gave me little comfort through my armor. At her bidding, I turned on my side, and she knelt and kissed me very soberly, then lay down on the cloak beside me, where we both immediately fell asleep.

Due to our exhaustion, it was fourteen hours later before we awoke. I roused to the fizzing water and opened my eyes to find Naani preparing our breakfast.

"Good morning," she said, smiling.

"Good morning. What a trek we had."

"I believe I walked farther yesterday than in all the rest of my life."

She rose to a kneeling position and kissed me lightly on the lips. Then she sat beside me and we gazed at one another.

"This is the first time we've really seen each other in the light," she said.

"I trust I pass muster. Remember, I've been many weeks on the road."

"Actually, you're quite handsome," she replied, as if making up her mind. She suddenly blushed and turned her head down.

"And you are a beautiful woman."

"As beautiful as Mirdath?"

I laughed to cover my uncertainty, for Mirdath had been exceptionally lovely, but Naani was very pretty, and given leisure to prepare herself, might have been beautiful indeed. More than that, though neither of us looked our best at that time, she had a beautiful soul.

"Why are you laughing?" she demanded.

"You're the only woman in the world in competition with herself."

She grinned and reached over and kissed me again. The truth was we could not stop staring at one another. For myself, I was filled with awe at finding my love through all the ages and darkness. To look upon her face, so new to me, and see expressions and mannerisms so familiar, made me both shy and bold at once. The experience was like meeting a stranger with whom one feels immediately comfortable.

"I watched you while you slept this morning," she said.

"I know."

"You know? Were you awake?"

"No. But somehow I knew you were watching me. Next time, I'll wake up and catch you at it. I suppose that's when you made your decision about my looks."

Her laughter was light and lovely. "Yes, it is. You think me wicked."

"I think you holy."

Her eyes glowed with an almost supernatural light, as if her soul glistened through those lovely blue windows. I think mine did the same. After a while, she lay beside me and we held one another a long while, though my armor must have been uncomfortable for her. Finally, she went back to where the water and tablets lay.

"I should check the boulder," I said, starting to rise.

"I already have, several times. I haven't seen any monsters in the gorge. Sit back. Let me spoil you with this elaborate breakfast."

Because she was so adorable, I laughed and did as she asked. She brought me the cup of water, placed my head on her knees, and helped me drink. One at a time, she took the tablets, kissed them, and gave me two to kiss and eat, while she ate the others.

"A six-course dinner," she said, "Two tablets for you, two for me, and two cups of water."

"A meal well-served," I replied, using a saying from the old days. Often, we seemed to move back and forth through time, using first one manner of expression and then the other. It felt both familiar and strange, for the language the people of the pyramid used was alien to any tongue of the past.

When we were done, Naani said, "You should probably try to stand."

I laughed. "I'll do more than try—ah!" The moment I sought to rise, my whole body was racked with pain from my battle with the four-armed man.

"I thought you might be stiff," she said. "I have the ointment ready."

She helped me off with my upper armor, then made me lie down again upon the cloak. As she rubbed in the salve with the care of a mother with a child, I listened to the low muttering of the fire-hole and slipped back into a doze. By the end of the hour, when she woke me, much of my soreness had vanished, and I felt I could handle myself again against any dangers that might come.

"You're more powerfully built than the men of the Lesser Redoubt," she said. "I can scarcely put my hand around your biceps. Are all your people like this?"

"Not all, but some. Being so long with so little Earth Current probably affected your people's size. But I've always enjoyed exercise."

"That hasn't changed from your time as Andrew."

"No, I suppose not, though I doubt I'm as strong as I was then."

"Who did you say was in competition with themselves?"

I laughed. "Serves me right."

We descended from the cave to the bottom of the gorge, Naani struggling with her fear of heights all the way down. We journeyed for six hours before halting to rest and eat. During our stop, I bathed her feet in warm water in a stone basin, and rubbed them with ointment, for her makeshift shoes never completely protected her.

The fire-holes burned and muttered all around us during that part of the journey, their red glow sending our shadows dancing against the rocks. The air grew warmer and steam spurted, whistling, from between the boulders. We caught whiffs of sulphur, though nothing overpowering enough to affect our breathing. The grim walls of the gorge rose measureless on either side.

Naani took delight in the numerous fires. "It's like a lighted lane, leading us home," she said. "And there aren't any Evil Forces here, Andros. I feel nothing at all."

"Really?" I stopped and listened. "I sense a vague lifting of my spirit, but nothing more. I've long suspected that your Night Hearing was more powerful than my own, though. Perhaps this proves it."

She was in such good humor I did not tell her we were approaching the country of the slugs, but after we had gone another six hours, I insisted we stop to sleep, for I wanted to travel straight through that dismal portion.

By coincidence, we came upon the same cave where I had slept after escaping the slugs' domain. I recognized it at once, though how I distinguished it from all the other burrows and holes I had slept in, I do not know. For some reason, finding it delighted me. Having waited there a hundred thousand years or more, it was unlikely to have moved—but I pointed it out to Naani, along with the fire-hole and the spring where I had washed.

She took this in with great interest, as if I were relating a story from my childhood. Standing beside the fire, she said, "It must have been lonely."

"The thought of you sustained me."

She reached up and hugged my neck, her eyes suddenly moist with a gratitude I could scarcely bear, for I felt unworthy of it.

Since the cave was close to the ground, we did not have to deal with Naani's fear of heights. We again blocked the opening with boulders, and even filled in the spaces with smaller stones to keep any creeping creatures out. Though this left us in total darkness, we felt quite secure.

She fell asleep almost at once, her breath rising and falling softly, but I lay awake for a while. Every day, as I recognized more and more of Mirdath within her, my love for Naani grew, along with my fear of being unable to protect her. In a single moment, some evil like the Yellow Man could take her from me. My chest tightened; I could scarcely breathe.

Sleep is the friend that carries us away from the unbearable, and at last, when I could stand the terror no more, I plunged into slumber.

***

We woke eight hours later, and when I removed the boulders the region lay unoccupied except for a rat-creature, gorged from eating serpents, sleeping beside the flames. After breakfast, I led Naani to the hot pool beside the fire-hole, and she exclaimed when she saw the beast.

"Consider it a friend," I said. "It eats snakes and avoids people."

"I can do without those kind of friends." She shuddered, but ignored it from then on.

I made her sit beside the pool while I bathed her feet, for though she was starting to develop calluses along her heels, her soles were still tender in places. Her feet, scarcely longer than my hands, were so slender and dainty, and I was so taken with love for her I kissed them reverently, which made her laugh. After drying them with my pocket cloth, I rubbed them with ointment while Naani sat silent.

We set off again, traveling at a good pace. I estimated it would take three hours to reach the dank region of the slugs and twelve to pass through it. Without making too much of it, I told Naani of the coming trial.

She squeezed my hand. "You came through it to find me. We'll make it back through together."

Toward the middle of the third hour the air grew heavy with fumes, and we found ourselves groping through an endless, smokey gloom, our throats raw, our only beacon the occasional, dim glow of a fire-hole. We went in silence, Naani walking behind me, I often reaching back to make certain she was there. I wanted to keep her hand in mine, to know if something tried to seize her, but I could not do so and still respond to dangers from the front.

As terrifying as the darkness had been when I had first gone this way, it was nothing compared to the fear I now experienced at the thought of losing Naani. Time after time I forced myself to concentrate on my path, to avoid thinking of her being spirited off into the gloom, for I knew if I ever did lose her that I would never be able find her again.

After two hours I caught a whiff of the terrible stench signifying a slug. My chest tightened in apprehension for my beloved, and I removed my armored glove so I could feel her touch. I reached back, found her hand, and drew her down among the boulders.

"We have to wait here," I whispered.

Gradually, the reek grew to an almost smothering intensity. Naani struggled to avoid gagging; I could feel her hand trembling slightly in my own. The bitter fumes made us so breathless that I feared I might pass out, leaving my love to shift for herself. My eyes watered and my head grew light; the darkness took on a dream quality. In order to remain conscious, I concentrated on my surroundings, listening to the water dripping on my armor from the heights, running my ungloved hand over the slime covering the surrounding rocks. The moments seemed to drag by.

Finally, after what seemed a lifetime, the scent diminished and we continued on.

After having come this way before, I mistakenly thought it would be easier the second time. Strange, the mind's capacity to forget past terrors. Even when no slugs were near, the place smelled of the open grave, and the few fires we passed gave us little comfort, for we had to keep concealed to avoid being seen in the light.

As we passed a pit burning crimson from a hole deep in the earth, I reached back and caught Naani by the arm.

"Look," I whispered, pointing beyond the fire toward the right side of the gorge. She stared momentarily, then gave a muffled gasp. Her hand flew to her mouth as she saw the slug, its hide glistening with moisture in the firelight, its head moving back and forth, its body, huge as the black hull of a ship, stretching silent and slow through the darkness. Despite its eye stalks it moved as if blind. Regardless whether it could see, it was horrible, and I feared it could smell us.

I pulled Naani down among the boulders, and she clutched both my hands, not so much to be comforted, but to keep me from doing anything rash, as if she feared my rushing out to try to kill that tremendous beast. No doubt she remembered Andrew's brashness and quick temper, not realizing that Andros, though still headstrong, possessed more restraint. Besides, the only thing I wanted was to get as far from that place as possible.

As we peered between the cracks in the boulders, the slug gradually swayed its tremendous head toward the wall and climbed upward, its muscles carrying it forward in a rippling wave. It soon became motionless except for an occasional lifting of its tapering tail, its head lost in the upper darkness, its body, a black ridge of soft, dreadful life flowing out of the shadows. Eventually Naani and I crept between the boulders and slipped away.

We traveled unmolested another two hours before Naani halted me with a touch.

"There's something coming," she whispered.

Since I now knew her senses were more sensitive than my own, I listened, and realized she was right. We were in an utterly black part of the gorge, without a fire-hole in sight, and I made Naani crouch behind a boulder while I huddled over her, covering her with my armor.

We waited a long time, I holding my diskos ready the whole while. The stench gradually increased until it became so dreadful we could scarcely breathe. We sensed some creature, no doubt one of the slugs, passing before us, silent save for what seemed to be the slow, enormous pumping of its lungs. We could not absolutely identify the sound, however, since the passage diffused it into horrid, whispering echoes that made it impossible to tell if it originated directly before us or high in the night where the mountains joined over the gorge to form the gargantuan roof.

The noise slowly subsided and the odor lessened. I imagined the slug making its way down the gorge toward some lonely cavern. It occurred to me that if Naani's people came this way when they left the Great Pyramid to establish the Lesser Redoubt they showed tremendous courage in entering the gorge without knowing what lay on the other side. It seemed to me that either the canyon was less terrible then, or they had taken another route.

After the monster had been gone quite a while, we padded onward, always listening, ever wary of the slugs' scent. In the fifth hour we reached the mouth of the intersecting cavern I had passed during my original journey, only faintly visible in the dim light of a fire-hole. I paused and pointed the opening out to Naani.

"Do you know where it goes?" she asked.

I shrugged. "I think it must be the slug's home. Perhaps they use it to come up from the lower regions of the earth."

Naani kept close to me as I whispered, for the gaping opening filled us both with fear. Still, coming as we did from a people who had glimpsed many mysteries through the embrasures of the redoubts, we were drawn by curiosity, and looked upon the cavern with a mingling of dread and fascination. The light of the fire-hole lit its nearest portions, leaving its monstrous bowels deathly dark.

Abruptly, detecting the movement of an enormous head, I realized that there were slugs gathered around the fire, some coal-black, others pale white, all obscured by the darkness. The one that had raised itself began crawling in our direction, as if it had somehow sensed us. We slipped away with all the speed we could manage, and soon left the fire behind. Nothing dangerous approached us for the next hour, but though we did not mention it to one another until later, an uneasiness fell upon our spirits.

We traveled mostly through complete darkness. Any time we heard murmuring echoes we knew it would not be long before we encountered the dull glare of a fire-pit, looking weird and unworldly in the haze of the fumes. We anticipated these eagerly, though when we finally reached them, we always passed at a distance and drifted quickly back into darkness. I longed to linger within the glow of the light and dreaded our return to the night more each time. But we dared not stop until we won past that terrible vale. We went as quickly as the darkness, the dangers, and the boulder-strewn way allowed, our eyes, throat, and lungs burning from the fumes. Not all the fire-holes produced sound, however, so we were sometimes delighted to see an unsuspected illumination rising before us.

Our uneasiness grew as we went along, until Naani whispered something my spirit had already perceived, though I was loathe to admit it. "Something is following us. I've sensed it for a long time, but it's closer now."

"You're right. I've felt it, too." I thought of the slug that had woke beside the cavern.

I set Naani in front of me, to put my armor between her and danger, and we went on our way. I kept glancing over my shoulder and smelling the air for signs, but I neither saw nor scented anything. Our lack of speed worried me, for between our groping along and bruising ourselves against the boulders, we made poor time.

We soon reached the red glare of a fire-hole, a place I recognized by a jagged stone rising above the flames. At first, I welcomed it like an old friend, but as we drew closer, I remembered that the slugs liked to gather around it. I pushed Naani down among the stones and we crept along as fast as we could.

As we came abreast of the fire-hole, we spied seven slugs lying against the cliff on the far side of the gorge, their heads hidden in the upper darkness, their soft tails spreading across the boulders along the canyon floor. Naani touched my arm and indicated the wall closest to us. I gasped. Three of the brutes rested against that side as well, and a fourth sprawled across an enormous ledge. My heart sank, for they lay all around us, but Naani squeezed my shoulder and gave me such a determined look that I regained my courage. We crept among the boulders until, after what seemed an eternity, we passed between them. None stirred, and we left them to their slumbers. However, the lack of odor was disturbing, for it meant that some of the slugs did not emit a scent. Knowing we could no longer trust our noses to warn us when one of the creatures drew near left us anxious indeed.

At the edge of the circle of light I looked back up the gorge to try to see what followed us. To my relief, I spied nothing. If we could only get past the country of the slugs, I thought we would be safe.

We passed three fire-pits in the next hour, and paused on the far side each time to look behind us. Though we did not see anything, we both admitted that we sensed something drawing closer. The sensation, coming through my Night Hearing, manifested itself as a gray shape vibrating a few feet from my head, felt rather than seen.

For a long while, we did not see any of the slugs; the air of the gorge grew free of their smell, but remained bitter from the fumes. During the tenth hour, while traveling in a region of almost total darkness, we detected a faint trace of their odor. Somehow, we knew instinctively we were not approaching a monster, but that our pursuer was drawing near.

We pushed forward, suffering numerous falls and bruises for our efforts. We were so afraid that we ignored the pain. Often we paused to listen, but heard only the dismal dripping of the water, until we finally perceived the murmur of a fire-pit. This raised our hopes, but even as we hurried to find the light, the stench grew, and we did not know whether this was the scent of our pursuer, or if more slugs awaited us at the fire. Despite our desperation, we were forced to slow down, to avoid rushing blindly into death.

We soon saw the fire looming dully in the distance. Though the flames lay half-shrouded in smoke and fumes, they gave us enough light so we could move more quickly. We broke into a trot, driven by the fear that our enemy was closing the gap. When we reached the fire-pit, we did not find any slugs, though the stench was now nearly unbearable.

The pit, which was enormous, glowed with red-hot flames. We looked around, first behind us, where we did not see any indication of the approaching monster, then to the sides of the gorge.

"We have to climb," I said.

Naani nodded bravely, though her face went deathly pale. I remembered her fear of heights, but could not think of another plan.

I studied the nearest wall of the gorge, then darted a few yards beyond the flame and scanned the other side. There was no time to make a proper decision, but the closer wall seemed to offer the most protection. I ran back to Naani.

"Can you do it?" I asked.

Her face was smudged with slime from the boulders and the dripping water; I had never seen her so pale. But she managed a wan smile. "If you help me."

She went first, so I could catch her if she fell. The sides of the gorge were wet and slippery, and slimy growths blotched the stones. Her feet slid when she first tried to climb, but she found a firm footing and pushed herself up.

"Do not look down," I told her, when she tried to turn her head.

"All right." Her voice quavered.

I was unable to follow my own advice, however, and kept glancing over my shoulder, expecting to see the monster entering the circle of light.

For a few minutes the climb went well, until Naani reached a difficult way where an enormous ledge jutted out from the cliff. Boulders had lodged on it, and a huge one stood just at the edge, looking as if it might tumble at any moment. I suddenly realized that if our efforts disturbed its equilibrium, we were right in its path.

Even as I thought of this, Naani reached a place lacking a handhold. Because it sloped slightly inward, it was not particularly steep, but she looked up at the boulder, apparently seeing it for the first time, then looked down at me. When she saw how high we were, her eyes widened and her face turned white; even in the dim light I could see her hands trembling. She sobbed and pulled her body flat against the rocks. Once or twice, she tried to get back on her haunches, but her courage failed.

"I can't move!"

In my concern about our pursuer I had fallen slightly behind. Now I scrambled up to help her. My haste almost proved my undoing, for I missed a handhold, lost my footing, and slid down. I clutched vainly at the rocks, my armor rattling as I fell; I thought I was about to plummet all the way to the bottom. At last, almost twenty yards down, I stopped my descent by catching my foot between two boulders.

Once I had a firm hold again, I looked up and gasped. The boulder above us seemed to totter, as if disturbed by

187

my fall. Naani lay stretched over the rocks right beneath it, quietly sobbing and calling my name. She must have thought I was about to die.

"I'm all right," I called up to her, hoping my voice sounded steady. "Naani, listen to me. You need to move to the left, away from the boulder."

"I can't!"

"You can. The ground slopes in where you are. You won't fall. Raise yourself up and pull to the left."

Even as I spoke I climbed back toward her, going as swiftly as I dared, but more cautiously to avoid sliding again. Her eyes were closed; I could see her shuddering.

"I can't! I'm sorry. I'm sorry. I can't."

One never knows the fears of another; such things are impossible to judge. Because heights never bothered me, I had foolishly scorned Naani's terror. We never know when we will meet something that sends us into panic, something another might think inconsequential.

"I'm coming," I said. "I'm coming. Just stay where you are."

I could not tell if the boulder still teetered, but I moved as efficiently as possible to keep from disturbing the formation.

It seemed an eternity before I drew up beside her. She clutched the stones so hard her shoulders shook. I tried to take her hand, but she refused to release her grip.

"I have you." I slipped my arm around her wrist. "You can let go."

She clutched the stones. I glanced up at the looming boulder.

"Naani, you have to let go. I have you. Relax."

I reached over and kissed her cheek. Gradually, she opened her eyes. We lay almost face to face.

"I'm here. Let go."

I felt her whole body slacken as she finally released her grip.

"I'll help you up. I've got you."

Together we moved to the left, out of the boulder's path. A moment later we climbed onto the very ledge where the stone perched, a broad way, with more than enough room for both of us to stand. Naani got as far away from the lip as she could and sat with her back to the cliff while I dropped to my knees a foot from the edge. Our exertions had left us breathless. She tried to speak once or twice, but could not get the words out.

"I'm sorry," she finally managed, running her hands over her eyes. "I panicked. I feel so foolish."

"Don't be embarrassed. We made it."

She glanced up. "Is it coming?"

I looked over the edge. It surprised me how small the fire-pit looked. Our fear had propelled us to a great height in a remarkably short time. The bottom of the gorge lay partially obscured by the haze of fumes, the smoke rising even to where we were.

"I don't see it," I said. "We should be safe."

"No, we're not. We have to defend ourselves. The slug can climb. It has followed us this far; the cliff won't stop it."

I became suddenly angry. "It can't climb this high."

"We don't know that."

"Do you think," I asked, my voice rising, "my diskos can stop something the size of a warship?"

"I think we need a plan."

Our anger, borne of stress and fear, flamed in our eyes, and died just as quickly, leaving me feeling like an oaf.

"You're right," I said. "What can we do?"

I glanced back down the cliff and my breath froze in my lungs, for something was moving on the far side of the fire-pit. The monstrous head of a white, blotched slug came into the light. Its eyes, which were on stalks long as poles, jutted forward and down, so that it seemed to be looking at the cavern floor. We were so high up it seemed as if I gazed upon a shell-less snail moving among a vegetable garden. Even from this distance I could smell its stench.

Naani, who had crawled up beside me, clutched my arm, startling me. I glanced at her, but her eyes were locked on the beast.

As it moved into the light, we saw its body was the same blotched, unhealthy shade of white. Why some should be black and others white, I do not know, but that was the way of it. As it advanced, it moved its eyes among the boulders, searching, its gargantuan head swaying from side to side. No doubt it was looking for us.

The haze kept us from seeing it clearly. Sometimes it disappeared, only to rise again out of the smoke. I cannot convey the sheer size of the creature and the horror it instilled.

Despite the obscurity, both Naani and I saw when it abruptly opened its maw—a mouth large enough to drive a wagon through—revealing a white tongue wide as a barge. It lapped up a snake from among the boulders like a frog snapping up a fly. The serpent, which must have been enormous to be visible from such a height, writhed in vain, and vanished in a moment.

The slug continued its search without pausing. Its crawling seemed slow when seen from such a height, but it crossed the gorge floor so rapidly that I finally understood why it had been able to overtake us. Its head, as it swayed, was so large it literally moved from one side of the canyon to the other. Its breath, the source of the stench, puffed out in drifting clouds.

It set its tongue among the boulders and licked up another snake thick as a man's body. The thought struck me, even in my horror, that Naani and I were fortunate not to have stumbled onto one of the serpents in the dark, and I knew if we ever escaped the slug, the gloom would hold a new terror.

The beast passed so close to the fire-pit we could see the massive wrinkling muscles of its skin. It brought its head around to our side of the gorge, gathered its tremendous body, then thrust itself upward, climbing toward the ledge where we crouched. As it scaled the cliff, its eye stalks moved back and forth, searching the crannies and caves pocking the cliffside. The smell grew as it approached; this close its skin resembled a white, mildewed hill. I glanced at my diskos, which suddenly seemed a puny weapon compared to the monster's bulk, as if I was an ancient knight, pitting my pitiful sword against the leather hide of a dragon. Despite the diskos' power, I knew it could never harm such a primitive beast. Nor would our shelter protect us from its terrible tongue.

Looking around in desperation, Naani and I both fixed our eyes on the tottering boulder at the same time.

"We have to push it over!" she said.

I scrambled to the rim of the ledge, right beside the boulder, and looked down. As near as I could judge, the slug crawled directly beneath the stone.

Together, Naani and I braced ourselves against the rock and heaved, but it was far too massive. We flailed away at it while the slug drew ever closer. Clearly, my earlier fear of the boulder crashing down upon us had been unfounded.

"We've got to work together!" Naani said. "We're wasting our strength. We need to be as high as possible against the stone."

I saw she was right, for we had been pushing from a position on our hands and knees, to steady ourselves against the fall. "Very well. Together. We'll push beginning right . . . now!"

We stood and struggled against the boulder, straining with all our strength. For a long moment nothing happened, and I thrust so hard I felt the blood pounding in my forehead. We roared together in our efforts, snarling like Night Hounds.

Just when it seemed my arms and legs would give way, the rock moved with a loud grinding that drove us to new efforts.

Abruptly the stone fell, and Naani and I clutched at one another to keep from tumbling with it. We collapsed at the lip of the ledge, then pulled ourselves back, but I managed to catch sight of the boulder as it careened down. For an awful instant, it took a tremendous bounce, and looked as if it would miss the slug, but it struck on the humped portion of the monster's back, just behind the head, driving through its soft skin like an arrow, vanishing into its vitals.

The slug bellowed with a noise like the sound of rushing wind. Its expelled breath sent blood and matter rising in a steaming, reeking cloud.

Crying in pain, it released its hold and sank backward, even as the echoes of the boulder thundered through the gorge. Its death screams reverberated like a hundred monsters dying at once, resonating out of the depths of the Rift into the eternal darkness of the upper world. After walking though the silent canyons for so long, that terrible cacophony astonished me. Naani pressed her hands against her ears and I bent my head down to my chest.

As the last reflections died away, we knelt on the ledge, trembling in each others' arms, looking down at the white mass of the slug's quivering corpse. With the returning silence, Naani, cradled against my chest, undoubtedly remembering the ancient world, said, "How embarrassing it would have been to be eaten by a snail."

It took a moment for me to comprehend, but then I broke into laughter. "A terrible thing. What would they put on our memory tokens?"

We knelt, laughing and holding one another, our hearts still hammering from exertion and fear.

"You realize we have to climb down from here?" Naani finally asked.

I moaned and looked at the canyon floor. It would not be easy.

***

All during our descent, I marveled at the way the power of desperation had allowed us to scale the cliff so quickly without falling to our deaths, for the climb took more than an hour and required us to rest on ledges three times before we reached the bottom. Naani demonstrated great courage, despite being ashen-faced throughout the entire ordeal. Once, when she seemed to reach the end of her strength, I thought for a terrible moment she was about to fall, but even then, as I rushed up to steady her, she did not cry for help.

We reached the canyon floor a hundred paces from the horrid heap of the slug's corpse, and hurried away at once, for its body still twitched and the stench was almost unbearable. But now that I knew about the enormous serpents, I became doubly anxious for Naani's safety.

"I should carry you," I said.

"I'm strong enough."

"You look exhausted," I reached over and tried to pick her up, but she slapped my armored wrist.

"You need to be able to reach your weapon."

"I don't want you getting too weary."

"You don't want me eaten by a snake, you mean."

"That's true. My armor can protect me against bites, but you haven't any defense."

"But if you pick me up and we meet a snake, you will need to free your hands for fighting."

"I still think I should carry you."

"I think you're wrong."

I stopped and we stood glaring at one another, she fiercely stubborn, my pride slightly wounded.

"I am right, aren't I?" she said. "Isn't it sensible?"

"It . . . I suppose—"

"I'll walk close behind you. Will that be good enough?"

The battle with the slug and the arduous descent had been a terrible ordeal, and both our nerves were frayed. I wanted to shout that I was supposed to be her defender.

How strange it is to love a woman so desperately, to feel two souls as one, and wish to strangle her at the same moment. No doubt she felt the same.

Still, she spoke quite mildly, and Mirdath had always been the practical one, while I led with my heart and counted the consequences after.

"Very well," I mumbled. "Follow closely."

I went sulking along, half wanting a snake to appear to terrify her, half terrified I would fail to protect her if one did. Unwilling to tolerate my moping, she hooked her fingers in my belt and began to tease me.

"Yah," she whispered. "Get along, mule."

She did this until my ill temper vanished, partially because our people had forgotten both the horse and mule hundreds of centuries before, and it seemed to me as if it was Mirdath rather than Naani who said the words. It made me realize how foolish I was acting at a time when I needed all my concentration to lead us through the dark. I reached back and squeezed her hand.

"I'm a cretin," I whispered.

"You're my hero."

***

Two hours later we passed beyond the darkness, fumes, and stink of the enclosed portion of the gorge, back into a region of numerous fire-holes. With the return of more light, my fear of the serpents lessened somewhat, but I still kept Naani close behind me.

Despite our weariness from over nineteen hours of travel, we were elated to escape the land of the slugs. We joked softly with one another, and her sweet laughter echoed among the stones. It may seem strange, our jesting amid so much terror, but we were young and learning to love each other all over again. Besides, we had seen enough danger to grow as callused to it as anyone can.

Our search for a resting place took another hour. With a grimace, Naani pointed up toward a cave fifty feet off the ground. "We could go there."

"Can you stand another climb?"

She tilted her chin up and managed a brave smile. "It can't be as bad as the last one. I don't like it, but I'm nearly asleep on my feet."

Two fire-holes lay close by a warm spring that formed a water basin. We looked on the water with longing, for we

193

reeked of the scent of the slugs, and knew we would have to bathe before we could rest. I searched the rocks, but did not find anything harmful.

"Keep watch while I investigate the cave," I said.

"All right."

The climb proved an easy one, and the cave was clean and dry, without any holes to hide creeping things. When I poked my head back out, I saw Naani below me, head up-turned, minding me instead of the gorge.

"You're not watching," I called.

She grinned. "Sorry. Will it do?"

"It will. You aren't much of a sentry." Despite my attempt at humor, I hurried back to her, nervous at leaving her unprotected.

Upon examination, the pool turned out to be the right temperature for bathing. Though the water was so clear that I could see all the way to the bottom, just to be safe I checked its depth with the handle of my diskos, and found it shallow enough for wading. I sniffed the water, then tasted it.

"Eaugh! Not the best for drinking, but clean enough, I think. You can wash while I keep watch."

When she hesitated I clasped her hand. "I'll be right here, with my back turned."

She smiled shyly. As I have said, we were a modest people, and our having been married before left us more than a little confused.

"Hurry," I ordered needlessly. "It bothers me to have you out of sight."

She took the cloak from my shoulders to wash it, and I stood leaning on my diskos, watching and listening, facing the gorge. Presently I heard her splashing in the water. She hummed an ancient song, the words of which I could not quite recall. Something about lilies, I thought. I was struggling to remember when her scream pierced me to the heart.

I spun around and saw her scrambling toward the side of the basin, while a serpent thick as my arm rose out of some hidden cavity in the depths.

I leapt into the pool, scooped her wet and naked into my arms, and turned my back to the serpent so my armor could protect her from its fangs. It struck at my thigh, the jar of its heavy head nearly knocking me over. I let the blow carry me forward, so I could set Naani down away from the monster, then turned, my chest burning with fury, and seized the serpent's head with my gloved hand even as it tried to strike again. In one motion, I tossed it to the opposite shore, then waded across and killed it with my diskos, taking a divot out of the rocks with the force of my blow.

As it flapped helplessly in its death throes, I waded back to Naani, who had wrapped herself in my cloak.

"Are you all right?" I asked.

"Yes. It startled me. Did it bite you?"

I pulled myself beside her and hugged her to my armor, probably hurting her somewhat in my fervor. We sat holding one another a moment, both trembling, our hearts pounding. I could not help but think, with terrible remorse, how I had wished her to be frightened by a snake only a few hours before.

Gradually, we composed ourselves, and then laughed a little in elation. She actually recovered first and prepared a meal of tablets and water to give us some comfort. Before she went to work, she belted the cloak about her waist, and looked very pretty, with her hair wet and lovely at her shoulders.

"At least the cloak is clean," she said, "though it's soaked. It isn't as cold here, is it?"

"No. The fires help, but the air is getting warmer."

As we sat there, I realized how beautiful Naani had looked in the bath, though I had seen her only during a moment of stark panic. Though the image stirred my desire, I felt more than mere lust: I had never known before how a woman could be so beautiful and yet so holy. Even with Mirdath I had not realized this until after she died. Yet love hallows all things.

Naani brought me from my reverie by wrinkling her nose. "Something smells." She sniffed the air experimentally. "Ah, its you. Your turn. I'll keep watch. Hand me the diskos."

"Be careful with it," I said, giving it to her grudgingly. "Use it only if you can't get it to me. Remember, it can turn on those other than its master."

"I remember."

She helped me undo my armor, then stepped away. As she took the watch, she leaned on the diskos as I had done and cast a roguish glance over her shoulder. She spoke in as deep a voice as she could manage, "You need fear nothing. I am on guard." The oversized cloak and the weapon, which was too large for her, made her look both sweet and ridiculous.

Not knowing if any other snakes would appear, I did not enter the pool, but cleaned myself by dipping my helmet into the water and pouring it over me. I washed in haste, hating to remain defenseless for long. The water felt soft and filmy beneath my hands, no doubt caused by the minerals within the basin. When I finished, I rinsed my pocket cloth, which was fairly large, then wrung it out and wrapped it about my loins.

"I'm more or less proper," I said.

She turned, and I could not help noticing as her eyes ran over my body. She smiled slightly, suppressed it, and turned quite red. To hide her embarrassment, she hurried to kiss me and hand back the diskos. I grinned in response. I have always prided myself on my strength and athletic ability, but to see that pride reflected in her eyes meant a great deal. Having no fear of harming her since I was not wearing my armor, I swept her into my arms and hugged her to my chest. She kissed me once passionately, and then I set her down before I could be overcome by desire.

To dry ourselves, we stood as close to the fire-hole as we dared, for its flames scorched our faces. I held the diskos and kept watch while she washed first her body vest, then the rest of our few garments. Afterward, she set them to dry upon some hot boulders.

When all was dry and we were dressed, Naani took my hand and set my arm about her waist. She leaned her head against my breast and demurely raised her lips to me. I kissed her tenderly, and she looked up at me from beneath her long, fine lashes and gave a dainty growl, like a wolf intent on devouring me.

We laughed together, and I kissed her again. Carrying our gear, we climbed up to the cave. As was our custom, I placed a boulder at the mouth of the opening to warn of intruders. We slept eight good hours, though sometime in the night, through the haze of slumber, I thought I felt Naani kissing my cheeks and forehead. I meant to open my eyes, to catch her at it, but fell back asleep instead.

***

I woke to find the boulder still securely anchored in front of the opening and Naani making breakfast. Seeing me, she grinned, came over, and gave me a kiss. She had managed to arrange her hair somewhat with the comb from my pouch, and though I suppose we both looked ragged, at the time I thought her radiant. When she smiled, she smiled with her whole soul; that was Naani's way.

"You should have woken me. I could have helped with breakfast."

She laughed and stuck her tongue out at me. "Such an arduous task. Here is the main course."

She put her tablets to my lips so I could kiss them, then kissed mine and gave them to me.

We kept a good schedule throughout the day, stopping to eat and drink at every sixth hour. By the fourteenth hour, despite my walking a little slower than normal, Naani began to stumble as she went. Without speaking, I scooped her into my arms.

"Andros, don't! We've already had this discussion. I can walk behind you if you're concerned about snakes."

"I'm not."

"You'll overexert yourself." She kicked her legs up and down helplessly. "Put me down!"

"As small as you are, I could carry you for miles. You're worn out and I don't want to stop yet."

She must have been truly weary, for she quit protesting at once. The truth is I loved to carry her; it cheered me knowing I could cradle her like a child from all the dangers of the night. And I think she loved being in my arms.

After traveling four hours we spent a peaceful night's slumber on the ledge where I had killed the spider on my first journey.

The next three days passed without incident. I always carried Naani part of the journey, for her month alone and our continuous traveling took a terrible toll on her endurance. More than anything, my carrying her spared her feet, which were always tormented by blisters. The more I learned about her, the more I loved her; she had the sweetest spirit and the sunniest personality, much like Mirdath but different as well, both more thoughtful and more direct.

We began encountering scorpions the size of small dogs. Some fled from us, but many were fat and lazy, and rose to bar our path. Their stings could not penetrate my armor, and I kicked a good number of them out of the way, some bursting when I did so.

We also saw several snakes, but they mostly ignored us, and I picked my path as carefully as I could, avoiding as much as possible the dark places between the boulders where such creatures liked to lie. When I was not carrying Naani, we kept to our plan of my walking in front of her.

Sometimes, as I carried her, Naani spoke of the ancient days, though we never discussed this as much as might be imagined. Often it was merely because we had to remain vigilant, but it was also because we were creatures of that future age, and our memories of our previous lives were like the memories of childhood, or the dream of a paradise where the sun shone in the sky and wind and rain were the friends of humankind. Though we knew the truth of it, it seemed distant and a little unreal. When we did speak of it, it was sweet to our souls, holy and far off, like a mist shining on golden lights, full of pleasure and bittersweet pain.

Once, when Naani spoke of her life in the Lesser Redoubt she grew somber, curled her head on my shoulder, and wept. I said nothing, but held her close, knowing how natural such grief was for one who had lost her whole world. That, I understood quite well.

When I could recognize them, I pointed out the caves and crannies where I had slept on my original journey. This fascinated her, as if I spoke of deeds done ages before.

We often caught glimpses of strange things lurking among the boulders. None approached us, but I knew where my diskos was at every moment. I remained constantly alert, though the monotony of the journey sometimes made it difficult.

During that time, we often passed fire-holes and fire-pits, and the flames sputtered at random along the gorge, making the walls leap into sight for an instant, only to fall back into shadow. Sometimes we walked among the muttering of the fire-pits, sometimes among the silence.

The air gradually grew warmer and more thick, and it took time for us to adjust to it. We had to learn, as I had the first time, not to put as much powder into the cup to keep the water from foaming over the lip.

I began to tell her of the Country of the Seas. She listened with fascination, the way a child listens who has never seen the ocean, and she asked many questions about it. Most of my answers were undoubtedly incorrect, for like herself I knew more of pyramids and metal halls than of seas and volcanoes.

In the sixth hour of the fourth day I showed her the ledge where I had slept when I first entered the gorge, and in the eleventh hour, after traveling through a deep gloom, we perceived a distant shining.

"Look," I told her, pointing. "We've reached it. It's down there."

With a burst of laughter, she suddenly sprinted toward the glow. At first, I was anxious for her safety, but I soon caught up with her, and we ran together, occasionally stumbling but never halting, like two mad children, rushing for the light.

XV
THE ANCIENT WOODS

We halted our headlong flight between the base of the mountains, just beyond the mouth of the Upward Gorge. Naani looked all around her, her eyes bright with wonder, her breathing rapid, but as she glanced back into the entrance to the gorge, her expression filled with such fear that I whirled around, thinking something approached from behind. Though I saw nothing, I understood her dread, for the maw of the ravine loomed so black and foreboding it seemed impossible for us to have won our way through it.

"Come away," Naani said, taking my hand.

Together we trotted farther into the warm glow of the Country of the Seas, then paused again. Naani glanced back only once more, her face suffused with awe and relief, before turning to inspect the new land. Her eyes darted this way and that, her breathing came labored, heavy in the thick air.

"*Oh,* Andros. I never knew there could be so much light! And the distances! I can see so far. Would my voice carry all that way?" To my astonishment she suddenly shouted with all her might, "Hello! We are here!"

After so much time spent whispering in the dark, she could hardly be blamed for wanting to yell, yet it startled me terribly. Our upbringing in the pyramids generally made us soft-spoken, and her outburst seemed out of character. I certainly did not want to alert the land to our presence. Before I could hush her, an echo resounded from the dark mountains to our backs, causing us to whirl around in alarm. Having so little experience with reverberations, the sound of Naani's returning voice dismayed us. Her face turned pale and she clamped her hands over her mouth.

"Let's get out of the open," I said.

We hurried down the slope, away from the gaping gorge, and climbed breathlessly onto a flat rock rising a few feet off the ground to rest and eat. I kept a sharp lookout for almost half an hour, to insure Naani's shout had not

200

roused an enemy, but when nothing dangerous appeared, we relaxed a little and sat close together, enjoying seeing one another in such radiance.

She asked many questions about the country which I could not answer, and she pointed out many curious objects roundabout. But her eyes turned more and more to the fiery illumination of the sea to our left, and she soon grew uneasy.

"What is it?" I asked.

"I remember—" she began, but her voice failed. I took her hand and she continued. "I remember moonlight on the ocean, like shining silver, the surf washing against the rocks, the cries of gulls. I remember tremendous trees, their leaves spreading overhead while I lay in tall grass, the scent of clover all around. I remember—" Again she hesitated, then threw herself against my armored shoulder, weeping while I stroked her hair.

"Oh, Andros, it's all gone! It was so beautiful! Could there ever have been such a world? Am I mad to believe it?"

"Not unless we both are." Her words filled me with the full loss of that former life, and we held each other in silence.

Finally, Naani spoke. "But why us? Out of all the millions who have ever lived, why should we be given another chance?"

"I don't know. Perhaps because we weren't finished. Whatever the cause, it is a tremendous gift, to be able to see you again." Tears sprang to my eyes.

"But to be here, when we could be there! Mirdath and Andrew lived in such a beautiful world. It was paradise. If only we could go back."

"I don't want to go back," I said firmly, a lump rising in my throat. "I don't ever want to go back, because you aren't there any more. When you . . . died, everything ended. I was so lonely. Once it might have been paradise, but it became a torment for me."

I broke down then. "Oh, Mirdath! I have missed you so."

So we wept together, and I am not ashamed of weeping, for if a man cannot mourn such a loss, what sort of man is he? Afterward, we held each other close and talked for a long time, trying to recall all we could of that previous existence.

***

Beyond the mountain to our left, beside the shore of the sea, rose the steaming mist I had passed through on my outward journey. We set out for it along the base of the mountains with the intention of eating and resting before crossing. Our way seemed effortless compared to the gorge, and we kept a good pace. After six hours, while still some distance from the beginning of the mist, we stopped, having journeyed almost eighteen hours. We camped on a tall, flat rock with a twelve foot radius; the climb proved steeper than I anticipated, but Naani handled it bravely. We ate, drank, and fell quickly asleep, for we were both exhausted from travel and excitement. Because the country was so warm, we slept with the cloak beneath us.

Seven hours later we woke, still delighted at the sheer amount of light. Naani came into my arms and we kissed. I loved her so desperately. "I wish I had a breast pocket big enough to put you in," I said, "to keep you close to my heart."

She laughed mischievously. "If you did, I would tickle you until you couldn't stand me."

We kissed again, and she retrieved the comb from my pouch. She arranged her hair while we talked, and though I kept a careful watch, I felt light-hearted as a child. I still feared the Humped Men and other dangers, but I did not believe any Evil Forces lived in the Country of the Seas.

When Naani finished combing her hair, she started to tie it up on her head, but I told her how pretty I thought it was lying on her shoulders, so she left it down. We ate a leisurely breakfast, but ended up hurrying to pack our gear out of guilt at our dawdling. As we prepared to descend from the rock, we looked out at the mountains surrounding the Upward Gorge. From this distance, we could see their true enormity, monstrous walls rising beyond the volcanic light into the dark night of the deadly upper world.

I experienced Naani's amazement with her, for though I had seen all these wonders during my original journey, my mind had been focused on my quest to the exclusion of all else.

"The world is a mysterious place," she said at last. "I wonder which is more alien, the sunlight and forests of the past, or these stark walls of stone?"

We descended the rock easily enough and were soon on our way. After traveling only a brief while, we heard the far hissing of steam and the eruptions of the geysers, sounds that frightened Naani until I explained what they were. We soon entered the clouds of steam, where we traveled more than three hours. I kept my love behind me to prevent her from stepping into a boiling pool, and we tried to steer by keeping the seashore to our left. This proved difficult since we could only see about a dozen feet in any direction and were often confused by the innumerable, scattered pools.

The shrieks and whistles of the geysers startled us constantly, for they sounded like leviathans rising from the depths, and the earth often quaked beneath us, only to subside to a deathly hush. The steam rolled all around like ghosts of the dead.

Finally, the air cleared and we left the roaring waters behind. The gargantuan trees of the great forest sprawled to our right, and Naani clapped her hands in admiration.

"I was wrong," she said. "The trees aren't all gone. Can I pluck a leaf?"

"Who am I to say?" I laughed. "Help yourself."

Hand in hand we walked into the forest, and for an instant Naani's smile was so much like Mirdath's it took my breath away.

"They aren't the same as the old ones," she said wistfully, "but they are still trees." She went to the nearest trunk, put her head among the leaves, and smelled them.

"I don't know," she said. "I can't remember, but the scent seems right."

She led me from tree to tree, until she had collected a leaf from every type we saw, of which there were at least a dozen.

"They're giants," she said. "Like guardians of the earth. Were they always so tall?"

"I think so, though I can't remember clearly. I have forgotten so much. But I miss them."

***

At the sixth hour we ate and rested. Naani washed in a warm pool while I stood guard, then we traded places. One of the most wonderful things about that Country was that we could keep clean while we traveled.

Afterward, we walked until we drew opposite the volcanic island I had watched while sleeping in a tree during my original trip. Naani and I traveled much slower than I had then, partially because of our fatigue from the journey down the gorge, partially because this land seemed a paradise to us. When I told her of sleeping in the trees, she insisted we climb one to eat our meal.

"I haven't climbed a tree in a million years," she said.

"Perhaps longer, but what about your fear of heights?"

"After all the climbing I've done lately, I won't let it stop me."

Nor did she. Perhaps our frantic flight from the slug gave her new confidence, but she made a graceful ascent to the lowest branches. We ate sitting in a forking of four boughs, I slightly below Naani, looking up at her. For a moment, it seemed as if sunlight gleamed off her hair, though it was only the volcanoes' glow. When we finished eating, she drew her knife, cut a small portion of the bark, and put it in my pouch.

"A keepsake, and a memento to show your people," she said. "At one time I wanted to be a gardener in the Underground Fields."

"What changed your mind?"

"Once we learned I had the Night Hearing, my father said I had a higher calling to work in the Tower of Observation. He was right, of course."

"Did you like it?"

"At times. It was an important position and everyone said how lucky I was. I still went down to the Underground Fields and worked, to get the earth between my hands. I could think there."

Her face turned bleak. "I suppose it will all die without the Earth Current. All the flowers." She looked around at the branches. "We should get down. We need to be on our way."

As we went, I talked about my original journey to take her mind off her grief, and she began to ask questions. Her inquiries made me realize that though it seemed a lifetime ago, only seventeen days had passed since I had first crossed this country.

We left the trees and entered that barren, rocky region where the hopping bird-monsters dwelled, and it was not long before we spied one of them. Naani and I hid at once between two boulders and kept still until the creature bounded by, half-flying, half-leaping, too heavy to ever take to the air. This was the first time I had glimpsed one up close, and I shivered as it passed, for it had no feathers and seemed more bat than bird.

"I've seen pictures of these in books," Naani whispered. "They once nested around our redoubt, before the final night fell. We thought them extinct."

"They must have migrated here for the warmth."

"Do you think your people could ever do that, Andros? Could they someday start a new life here?"

"I suppose, though I don't know how they could ever make it through the Night Land."

"Are the monsters so terrible?"

"Yes, and much more numerous than in your country. But the Forces of Evil are worse."

Naani's face became pensive. "It seems a shame to waste all this light."

When the bird-beast had passed, we set out, but an hour later saw a score of the creatures bounding in flocks among the boulders. These were followed by several single birds, and we were often forced to hide.

Despite my vigilance, while traveling what I thought a deserted way, I heard a noise behind me and turned to discover one of the monsters bounding over the rocks, its mouth open, its forked tongue darting in and out. No doubt it had been hidden or resting among the stones as we passed. It hissed and poked its head forward, so that it resembled a lizard as much as a bird.

I looked around, but we stood in a clearing, too far away to seek the protection of any boulders. Naani leapt to my side, her knife drawn, while I steadied my grasp on my diskos. Though I admired her courage, I could never fight my best if I thought her in danger.

I caught her quickly by the waist, and pulled her down to the ground between my feet.

"Andros, no!"

I grasped her shoulder more fiercely than I intended. It must have bruised her, for she gave a cry of pain. "Stay down!" I ordered. "Let me do what I was trained for. Lie flat, face down!"

I must have looked ferocious, for she obeyed instantly, and I threw my cloak over her, hoping to hide her from the bird by confusing its sight. There was only enough time to raise my diskos before the creature was upon me.

One instant it was a hundred paces off, the next, with two lumbering, monstrous bounds, it attacked, using a bill long as my arm. The flashing roar of my diskos, which caused the beast to pause, kept me from being killed; otherwise it would have taken me with its first stroke. Instead, it missed my head by inches and struck a blow to my left side. If not for my armor, it would have gone through my body instead of making my breastplate ring. It struck again, staggering me. But as it drew its head back for a third jab, I hit it at the point where one of its leathery wings joined its shoulder.

It squawked, hissed, and fluttered backward, its wings beating along the ground, its bill striking at its injured joint. Fearing its cries might bring others, I rushed in to finish it off.

It jabbed at me, but I withdrew, avoiding the blow, then dashed back in and split its skull. It twitched only a moment, as the last impulses of its nerves faded, then lay spread across the stones. With its body extended, it looked as large as a colt, its bill glistening like the blade of a scythe.

I rushed back to Naani, who was already rising to her feet. Without speaking a word, we hurried across the clearing and hid among the boulders for a good half hour before going on.

We saw only two more of the creatures, and those from a distance, before we reached the shallow river I had crossed during my first trek. I carried Naani over, sounding my way with the handle of the diskos as I went, an easy crossing until I stepped into a hole and slid up to my neck in the water, soaking us both. I clambered out unharmed but embarrassed, and Naani giggled like a girl and teased me for an hour after.

Beyond the river, the fields of boulders met the edge of another forest. We looked for a fire-hole where we could dry off, and soon found a volcanic hill no higher than a man's head, with warm rocks all around. Naani helped me out of my upper armor, and we sat together on the stones while wisps of steam rose off our clothing.

We talked about all the things we would eat when we got home, but soon gave it up, since it only made us hungry. Besides, despite our yearning for solid food, I believed the tablets kept our bodies and spirits in a condition that prevented the Forces of Evil from exerting an excessive influence over us. Whether this was my own idea or a rigorous teaching of the Great Pyramid, I cannot recall; it may well have been a peculiar belief of that age or a scientific certainty based on some fact I no longer remember.

I dressed as soon as my armor was dry. Naani helped me back into my breastplate, and with it on, I felt much more secure. We then searched for a ledge or cave where we could sleep. Finding nothing, we settled into the branches of a tall tree set somewhat away from its fellows. I chose it because it did not have as many lower branches and could be easily defended. I had to boost Naani up, supporting her feet in my palms, for the first boughs grew nearly twice her height. For some reason, the ascent bothered her more this time, but she soon found a perch. I took the strap off my pouch to use as a rope, which I threw to her. She tied it around a branch, and I pulled myself up.

We climbed a little higher into the thickest branches, where she made us a bed by laying the cloak across several intersecting boughs. She remained a little dizzy until we were both lying down together, each with one of our wrists strapped to the tree to keep from falling.

Having journeyed nearly twenty-two hours that day, we soon fell asleep, but it was not a restful slumber. Four times I woke to find Naani whimpering in her sleep: calling out to her father, crying out names I could not recognize, or writhing to escape some phantom monster. Each time I gently shook her until she woke, though she went immediately back to sleep.

I woke eight hours later with the distinct impression someone had been kissing me in my sleep. Naani was already up, looking mischievous, and once again I vowed to wake next time and catch her at it.

"Good morning," I said. "How are you?"

"Since I didn't break my neck, I would say good. I kept imagining I was about to fall. I could have sworn the trees were swaying."

"Trees have that effect, I suppose, though there hasn't been any wind here for centuries. Next time we will sleep on the ground so you don't have nightmares."

"I didn't have any nightmares."

"Yes, you did. I had to wake you four times. Don't you remember?"

She looked puzzled. "Really? I don't recall. Probably dreams of falling. I'm sorry I disturbed you."

I decided not to say anything about her calling to her dead family. "It was nothing. I went right back to sleep. After breakfast, I think I will climb a little higher and take a look around."

I did so, but though I scaled as far as I could safely go, I spied no sign of anything living either near or far.

***

We climbed down the tree and continued on our way. Naani, seemingly lost in thought, drifted a few steps from me and soon began softly singing, swinging her hips slightly to the tune. I could not help but watch her, for she seemed to have forgotten anyone was about, as if I had caught her unawares. I noticed everything: the way she placed her feet, the poise of her form and the tilt of her head, the look in her eyes, the red-gold of her hair, the way she idly brushed a curl from her brow.

Abruptly, she sang another song, an ancient air I had not heard for thousands of years. I could not quite place it, but it shook me to my soul, as if all the silence of the ancient moonlit world stole about me.

Naani faltered a little as she sang, trying to recall the words through the veils of memory. My blood heaved in my veins; a tightness rose in my throat, the beginning of a sob, the ghost of forgotten tears. Yet the sorrow, falling so swiftly upon me, was also steeped in golden mists and the glamour of love, and I remembered many things I had not recalled before.

I looked at Naani through eyes misty with tears, and saw that she, too, wept as she walked, not so much with pain, but with the tenderness, sorrow, and love of all that was and would never be, of words spoken and unspoken, of years lost and found, of forgotten glory and dreadful part-ings. I saw in her eyes the treasures forever hidden in the darkness and heard the distant music of neglected songs— all this, built of years and remembrances, descending over shadowed mountains into the valley of the spirit, seen through the light of memories shrouded by hushed shad-ows.

As Naani went, tears in her eyes, still singing, she did not hold her head downcast, but up, as if she walked in glory. Her concentration was so deep, I do not think she even knew she sang. The tune came sometimes broken, her voice quivering, and other times as clear as if the eternity since she had last heard it was but a moment past.

Listening to her, watching her face, both pure and trium-phant, troubled and overjoyed, I imagined I heard faint echoes surrounding us, the voices of my long-dead loved ones. My breath came sharp against my chest; tears rolled down my face, and though I knew I walked beside Naani in that boulder-strewn forest, it seemed I also stood beneath the light of ancient sunsets, in other forests, with Mirdath by my side.

I do not know if I truly experienced a vision or not; it certainly seemed real, but it passed in an instant, leaving me watching Naani. She halted suddenly and turned to me, holding out her arms, her eyes pale blue, her face transfigured with love.

We stumbled into each others' embrace, clinging as tightly as my armor allowed. Tears streamed down both our cheeks, but we held each other in silence, unable to express what lay in our hearts.

Presently, we moved apart, each filled with the ecstasy of knowing that our beloved, once lost, was now found.

***

An hour passed, and in that time Naani fell into an uncharacteristic brooding. She grew pensive, and more than once a look of anguish passed over her features. When I asked what troubled her, she only said she was thinking of the past. Since she appeared to be dealing with personal matters, I said no more, and we spent the next two hours in silence.

I, too, had a change of mood, perhaps brought on by Naani's introspection. My joy left me, and I began thinking that we should escape this country as quickly as possible, for the longer we stayed the more chance of our encountering the Humped Men. It seemed to me that since entering the Country of the Seas, I had acted like someone under an enchantment. Despite the region's beauty, my battle with the bird-beast clearly demonstrated the dangers surrounding us. Feeling both foolish and guilty about our leisurely pace, I vowed to act more prudently from that time on.

We came to a rock basin hidden among the trees with a warm spring bubbling into it.

"This would be a lovely place to wash," she said. "Would you mind?"

Despite my need for haste, I wanted to humor her, especially since she seemed so melancholy. "Go ahead, I'll keep watch. But be quick. We need to hurry."

I think my tone stung her, though I was aggravated at

myself, not her.

"Keep your back turned," she ordered.

I soon heard her washing in the pool, though she did not sing as she had done previously. Gradually the noises subsided to an occasional splash.

"What are you thinking?" I finally asked. More than anything else, I wanted to hear her voice to be sure she was safe.

She replied in a mischievous tone, "I was thinking what a lovely country this is. And I was wondering if we should stay here."

"Do you really mean that?"

"Certainly. Where else is there so much light and warmth?"

"We would starve when the tablets ran out."

"There were once other ways to survive. We could remember them."

I nearly turned around to face her, for I thought I detected Mirdath's old, familiar way of teasing me to the point of anger.

"It's too dangerous. I told you about the Humped Men."

"We could find someplace far from them. They would learn to respect your weapon."

"My people are waiting for us. I want to show you the Great Pyramid and introduce you to the Master Monstruwacan. Besides, we couldn't remain here forever, just the two of us. Don't you miss having the millions around you, the cities and the people?"

"My people are dead. Sooner or later, the Earth Current will fail in your redoubt, and your folk will be forced to come here anyway, tomorrow or a hundred thousand tomorrows from now."

The mocking despair in her voice pierced me to the heart; it was so unlike her, and yet reminiscent of Mirdath's stubbornness. I turned around without thinking.

Naani sat fully dressed upon a rock, splashing the pool with her toes to make me think she still bathed. She looked at me and laughed, but with a trace of anger.

"You little fraud," I said, trying not to sound annoyed. It was only a prank, and my irritation seemed unwarranted. "Hurry up and let's be on our way."

In answer she stuck her tongue out at me. "I'm staying here. This is where we are going to live." With that she put her fingers in her ears and began to sing.

210

I laughed, though it made me more angry than I wanted to admit. Going to her, I kissed her on the mouth, and removed her fingers and gently kissed her ears.

"We better go, Naani. There might be danger."

"I am, as I said, staying on this rock."

At this I became truly annoyed. While waiting for her to bathe, I had grown increasingly concerned for our safety. I glanced around anxiously, to insure that nothing approached.

"Very well," I scooped her up and began making my way through the forest.

"Andros, put me down! You are a cave man."

I was still young and had my pride, so I only laughed, determined to show her who was in charge. I felt quite manly carting my woman away, her beautiful hair flowing across my armor. She eventually quit protesting, and I stumbled along the forest's edge for at least a mile before Naani sedately raised her lips to mine. I kissed her, feeling I had won the day.

"Dear," she said, "if I could make a suggestion, you might want to go back for my shoes."

I halted and looked down at her bare feet.

On reflection, it seems unreasonable for this to have made me so furious, but she gave me such a triumphant look that if I had not loved her I would have dropped her on her head.

I did not reply, and if Naani saw the rage in my eyes she pretended not to notice. I carried her back to her shoes, sat her down, and began putting them on her as if she were a child.

"Why, Andros, are you angry?"

"You don't care about our safety. You think this is a game, but it isn't."

"I think nothing of the sort."

"Yes, you do." I finished binding her shoes. "Will you walk, or should I carry you?"

She leapt up and set off through the woods, walking a little apart from me. As she went, she tied her hair into a tight ball around her head, knowing I liked it when she wore it down.

We spent a quiet morning walking together, and at the sixth hour I announced a rest. We ate in silence. By this time I began to feel remorse. Naani, like Mirdath, was, after all, mischievous by nature. She meant nothing by it.

And it broke my heart for us to quarrel after everything we had been through.

"Naani," I began, "I didn't mean—"

"It doesn't matter," she replied, her face pensive. "There are more important things in the world."

"What do you mean?"

She only shook her head and stared at the forest.

"What's the matter? Is something else wrong? Back at the pool you mentioned your family. Did—"

Again she cut me off. "No, it isn't that. It isn't anything. I just like to tease."

That was all I got from her. I tried to take her in my arms, but she drew away, so I knew this was more than a lover's spat. At last, I left her to her brooding. She did put her hair back down, which I took as a good sign.

She walked somewhat before me and to the side, saying nothing, but keeping a good pace. I tried to cheer her by pointing out curiosities that I had noticed on my first journey. She listened intently and nodded to show she heard, but her expression remained morose.

At the fourteenth hour, we came to the rock of the ancient flying ship. Naani seemed to wake from her moodiness when I told her about fighting the two Humped Men on the peak. The battle roused her sympathy, and she wanted to know all the details, especially whether I had been injured. For a few minutes her sweet spirit returned, and we held one another at the base of the peak.

"Naani," I finally said, "what troubles you?"

"All the ages. All those who lived and died and have gone before. Yet I remain."

"Through a miracle. A miracle you should accept."

"A strange gift," she said. At once, she fell back into her melancholy.

I grew dejected, for it seemed that after traveling so far to find the twin of my soul, she did not love me, after all. Even though I did not really believe this, the thought made me withdraw, and we spoke little for several hours.

Toward the end of the day, I tried to lift her into my arms, to carry her a time as was our custom. At first, she resisted with an expression of irritation, but then allowed me to pick her up.

We saw nothing to fear during that time, and heard little except the occasional muttering of the scattered volcanic cones. The thick, warm air, coupled with Naani's mysterious silence, left me listless.

We descended from the high hills where the ancient ship stood, into an area where the trees grew right up to the sea-shore, forcing us to pass among them. The smaller cones were more active in that region, and the whole country seemed alive with the sounds of tiny, bubbling eruptions and the noise of boiling springs. We passed in and out of the woods, keeping along the shore line.

At the eighteenth hour the roar of the volcanoes grew more terrible, and the earth began to tremble.

"What is it?" Naani asked.

Glancing around, I pointed to two large cones overtopping the trees. Though we had seen these for many hours, we had scarcely noticed, for despite their size they were but two in a country filled with volcanoes. "The same thing happened when I passed through here the first time," I said. "The underground forces cause tremors."

"Put me down. I want to see! It's so dreadful! Like a roaring monster. Is it dangerous?"

"Not as long as we avoid lava, steam, or falling rocks," I said with a smile.

Her eyes glistened brightly, her wonder overcoming her melancholy. "How wonderful!"

Our path took us within several miles of the volcanoes, which were nothing less than mountains. Naani and I gazed at their heights with both awe and trepidation.

"Isn't it odd the way vegetation still covers the area?" she asked, "Wouldn't the lava destroy it?"

"One would think so. But there isn't any falling ash like at some of the other volcanoes, and the air is clear. There also aren't any volcanic hills forming around these. They probably haven't erupted for years. When I first came through, the fires made me think of torches, lighting the way to you."

She smiled and touched my arm.

Since there seemed no danger of falling lava, we sought for a refuge until we found a cave twenty feet above the ground in the side of a hill. It proved dry and comfortable, and once we were inside, Naani prepared our meal while I carried boulders from below and placed them at the entrance. I tried to joke about our blind sentry, but she no longer found it humorous.

Her wonder at the volcanoes had passed, and she ate her tablets quietly, her eyes moving listlessly around the cavern. I sat beside her, overcome by a sudden despair. Ignoring my pride, I blurted, "Don't you love me anymore?"

This seemed to surprise her, for her expression softened. "Oh, Andrew, you know I love you."

Her use of my old name shocked me, as if all her thoughts were focused on the past. "What is it, then?"

"I can't explain. You must give me time. So much has happened."

I tried to take her hand, but she withdrew it. "I am very tired. I would like to sleep now."

With that she curled up on the cloak, her back to me.

Not knowing what to do, not understanding what bothered her, I rose and stared out over the boulders I had placed at the mouth of the cave. From my position I could see the countryside quite well, including the two volcanoes, which I guessed stood no more than twelve miles away. The country between looked like an enormous park, spread around the volcanoes' feet, bare patches interspersed with ancient forests, glistening hot pools, and serene lakes. A slight mist covered some parts, giving the whole a romantic, mysterious look. Beyond that, the land ascended in a monstrous sweep to great terraces in the heights, with trees growing all along the slopes. The two volcanoes rose to meet the everlasting night, their upper peaks ghostly in the vast glow of their fiery crowns, which seemed to burn halfway between the known world and the lost, ancient empires of the surface.

The sight of the terraces, standing so high yet far below the burning crests of the volcanoes, left me transfixed. As the mystery of the red shining and flickering shadows fell upon them, they looked vague, somber, and dreadful. It seemed a place where no life could ever dwell, or a region where a man might wander forever lost.

Presently, I broke my reverie and searched the landscape closer to our cave, looking for signs of the Humped Men. Seeing nothing that troubled me, I turned back to the cave. Naani's breathing was already steady and slow, and with my diskos close by, I lay down beside her without touching her, wounded that she had not kissed me goodnight.

I fell asleep to the constant trembling of the earth, a slight shuddering, comforting in its way, like being rocked to sleep, but I dreamed of fire-breathing monsters rampaging outside the cave. Naani's slumbers were also broken once more by nightmares; six times I had to wake her while she cried and moaned in her sleep, calling the names of her lost kin.

***

Naani did not wake before me the next morning as she normally did, and I let her sleep an extra hour before rousing her with the noise of the fizzing tablets. I tried to be jovial, but she would have none of it, and I saw her soul had not yet climbed out of the pit into which it had fallen. I tried to hold her, and though she allowed it, she scarcely returned the embrace at all.

"You had nightmares again last night."

"It's nothing," she insisted. "I will be fine. I don't remember dreaming."

"You don't remember my waking you?"

Her brow furrowed. "A little. But I don't remember what I dreamt."

"I can't help if you won't say."

"And I can't say if I don't know. It will pass."

We ate in silence. Afterward I looked out across the countryside, where a herd of strange, four-footed creatures ranged far to the northwest, near the base of the volcanoes. Otherwise, I detected no danger.

Perhaps because Naani remained so pensive, leaving me time for reflection, I saw the country with new eyes that day. When I had first passed through, I had been so intent on my mission I had failed to notice how this whole portion seemed like a huge park. Fires burned cleanly in many places, and spewed rocks in others; hot lakes bubbled and fountains of steam whistled their eternal, lonely songs. We wound through patches of woodland or walked beside a single, enormous tree standing in a clearing apart from its fellows. Volcanoes dotted the landscape, each over twenty feet tall; we passed seven of these in three hours. Two smoldered, scarcely burning at all, but the other five sent up smoke and ash, making the area around them desolate. One of the five occasionally discharged stones that burst in the air with a roar, scattering shards all around, leaving fragments caught in the tree branches. I wondered how long the vegetation could withstand such an assault. We kept as close to the sea as we could to avoid being struck.

Presently, we heard a dull boom, originating from a boiling water spout rising from the midst of a formation

215

between us and the mountains. The jet varied in height from a hundred to three hundred feet and a boulder big as a house danced on the stream. The booming occurred whenever the boulder fell to earth. It must have been caught in the jet for several decades, for it was completely round, polished by the water until it reflected the volcanoes' crimson light.

Though I had heard the noise it made on my original journey, I had not seen the cause. This told me that we were at least half a mile farther from the shore than I had been before.

We watched the fountain playing with the rock, but did not approach it too closely, since it occasionally threw off a ferocious spattering of stones. We did get near enough to hear its pressure building: a coughing roar from deep within the earth followed by sobbing gurgles, then the water spout shooting upward. When the stone fell, it descended into a cup-shaped pit. I suppose the water cushioned the blow, preventing the boulder from breaking.

It was a strange sight, and after watching it a while, I turned to go, thinking Naani would follow. After a dozen paces, I noticed her absence and turned back and found her walking toward the boiling fountain.

"Naani! Come away! Don't get too close."

If she heard, she ignored me, beginning to run instead.

I shouted again. When she disregarded me, a dread filled my heart that an Evil Force had seized her mind; I thought of the youths rushing into the House of Silence. I tore after her, while she drew ever closer to the fountain. I could hear the pressure building beneath my feet.

Running with all my strength, I caught her as she climbed the pile of rocks surrounding the jet. The pit gaped before us, the boulder lying in its center.

Even as I reached her, the fountain erupted, surging in a tremendous column, as if the sea lifted itself into the shape of a pillar, its thunder shaking the ground. It hung in the air directly above us, seemingly ready to collapse on our heads. A fine haze of scalding water rose around us.

I scooped up Naani and fled, crowding her against my breast so my armor could protect her from flying stones. Even as I sprinted beyond the shadow of the column, a rock struck a boulder at my back, shattering it and sending shards ringing against my armor, nearly throwing me off my feet.

When we reached safety, I put Naani down. The fragments had knocked the wind out of me, so for a moment I could scarcely breath, much less speak. Not knowing I had been hit, Naani laughed like a child, as if it were all a game.

"Are you insane?" I cried, when I found my voice once more. "Has some Force possessed you?"

Seeing how angry I was, she grew more somber. "No, I'm not. I wish I were."

She stalked away, while I gaped at her back.

"Naani!" I called, but she ignored me.

Her actions thereafter baffled me completely, for she seemed more determined than ever to taunt me. She walked some distance away, humming sometimes, sometimes dancing as she went, until I began to wonder if our trials had really unhinged her mind. One moment, she seemed completely despondent, the next she bounced along, happy as a child, but in an almost frenzied state. During her animated phases I tried to convince her to calm down, but she refused. I tramped along, feeling I had lost my beloved, after all.

We soon left the rumblings of the two volcanoes behind, while Naani's mood vacillated between bleak and exuberant. At times she seemed almost drunk; she talked incessantly about various parts of our journey—the flying ship, the fountain and the boulder, the slugs of the Upward Gorge—a thousand things, but she spoke as if to keep from thinking, and paid little attention to my replies.

So we went through much of the day, until I grew dull from worry. To add to my distress, I began to sense something watching us, and more than once, though I was never certain, I thought I glimpsed figures moving behind the trees. I kept asking Naani to lower her voice, but though she complied, the danger did not seem to make an impression on her. Neither would she walk close beside me, regardless of how I begged, and I found myself constantly trying to keep near enough to protect her. More and more I feared she had fallen under the sway of an Evil Force. If so, it was like none I had ever encountered, for my Night Hearing detected nothing.

Finally, when I found it unbearable, I scolded her, calling her selfish and thoughtless. Tears sprang to her eyes, but instead of replying she sulked. This lasted for two long hours, but at least she stayed closer after that.

We made good speed toward the river, for I wanted to press on and build a raft as quickly as possible, so we could sleep safely upon the small island in the middle of the stream. Naani showed some interest when I spoke of it, though she soon returned to her brooding.

When we reached the river, we stumbled upon the same two trees which had previously served as my raft. We searched until we found another tree a hundred paces away, which I carried back to the others. I also cut several branches from live trees with my diskos, to use for cross-pieces. With our belts and straps tying the parts together, I quickly reconstructed the raft. While I worked, Naani watched me listlessly, as if even the thought of assisting lay beyond her strength. Because of the raft's weight, I coaxed her into helping me carry it to the water, though I had to ask several times before she complied. I drove a sharp branch into the shore for a stake, and moored the craft to it using another limb as a hook.

I could not find the pole I had cut on my original journey, which troubled me somewhat, since some creature had obviously taken it. I put my script and pouch upon the raft, then looked for a sapling to suit my purpose. I found one beside a flat-topped rock only a few feet away and began trimming the branches while Naani watched.

Her despondency, which seemed worse each moment, terrified me. All my attempts at humor failed completely, and I soon fell silent, concentrating on my work. When I glanced up a moment later, I saw her walking toward the forest, head down, her movements almost furtive.

Even as I watched, it seemed I saw something moving among the thickets. I dared not even call out a warning, but sprinted after her, still carrying the pole. She broke into a run, so that several precious seconds passed before I caught her.

Furious with fear, I dropped the pole, took her by the shoulders, and shook her. "Naani!" I hissed, pointing toward the trees, fearing to speak too loudly. "There's something in there! What is the matter with you? The Humped Men might be near."

She struggled a moment, then was still, and when she looked at me the torment in her eyes shocked me. "You will not shake me," she said. "You will not touch me that way or I will run into the woods so the Humped Men can protect me from you."

Her words stunned me so much that I loosened my grip. Before I knew it, she twisted out of my grasp and dashed straight toward the area where I had seen movement. I caught her in a moment, and she struggled furiously, beating my armor with her fists as if I were an enemy.

I pulled her back out of the shadow of the forest and half-dragged her to the flat rock. She sobbed and fought, shrieking as if she did not know who I was, her words garbled and incomprehensible.

Abruptly she fell silent. At first I thought she had come to her senses, but then I realized she was staring wildly toward the forest. At the same time I heard the noise of something bounding through the foliage.

I turned to find a Humped Man almost upon us, his hands stretched forward as he charged. Lacking the time to reach my diskos, which lay where I had been trimming the sapling, I pushed Naani behind me, and picked up the pole and braced it against the ground. The assailant, unable to halt his charge, ran right onto the point, impaling himself through the chest, his momentum driving him halfway down the shaft's length, the force pushing me to the ground.

He howled and clutched at me, while Naani scampered to the side on hands and knees. I rolled to my feet, scooping up my diskos as I went. So powerful was the creature that he did not die at once, but sought to pull himself off the shaft. Even as he struggled, I swung my weapon, ripping him into two parts from the head down.

As he fell, I heard the sound of more running feet. Glancing up, I saw a number of Humped Men rushing toward us, carrying heavy stones as weapons. I turned to Naani. To my relief, she stood with knife drawn, ready to aid me. If she had still been irrational, I do not know what I would have done. I grabbed her by the hand, and in two quick bounds, pulled her up with me to the top of the flat rock.

I did not have time to number my adversaries, but there seemed to be at least a score of them, and though I was certain we were about to die, I would not give them Naani easily. Strangely, I did not despair. I say this not as a virtue—I was certainly afraid—but after dealing with Naani's bizarre behavior for the last few days, I finally faced an enemy I could understand.

The rock gave me one advantage: it fell steeply away on

two sides, and a sheer stone wall rose ten feet high at my back, leaving my assailants only one direction of approach. Neither were they familiar with the power of my diskos.

They attacked in complete silence, swarming up the rock face with the speed of panthers. They were overconfident at first, for four of them thronged so close together that I split three of their heads with a single slash of my weapon. The fourth froze in astonishment at the sudden destruction of his fellows, and I dispatched him with a kick in the face that sent him sprawling to the ground.

With prodigious leaps over the backs of their comrades, three more sprang to the rock from below. One, carrying a heavy stone, struck me a terrible blow, driving me back against Naani. I thought he had cracked my armor, but even while falling I managed a killing stroke to one of his friends.

Naani braced me from behind, helping me stay on my feet. I slew the stone-wielder with a horizontal slash, then regained my balance and sprang at the remaining foe. The rock was too narrow for him to avoid me, nor did he try. Instead, he leapt right at me.

I met him in mid-bound, catching him in the midriff with a two-handed swing, and he seemed to explode from the power of my weapon, which cut him in half. But my battle had taken me close to the edge of the rock, lying now behind me, and even as the Humped Man's body flew through the air, two of his brothers grasped me by the ankles, pulling me back and down, bringing me hard to my knees. Though I lost track of it, the hurling body must have passed completely over me and tumbled down the side.

I struck at my foes, but only managed to chip the rock. Fortunately, it did not damage my diskos. They nearly pulled me over the edge, but I landed a lucky blow that severed the shoulder of one of them. He let go, and I used my free foot to smash the other one's hand.

I was somewhat dazed, but Naani appeared at my side and helped me up. We stepped back from the edge as more Humped Men reached the top. I braced myself and fanned the diskos in a quick circle. It roared like a beast, its flames blinding my enemies, driving them back with its fearsome thunder. I ran at them and killed the foremost man with a blow to the neck. Then the creatures leapt at me from three directions at once, pounding me on the helmet, back, and breast with their stones. I reeled from the blows, but did not fall, though I thought I was about to die.

Through my confused senses I heard Naani's anguished cry. My head cleared at once, replaced by a red fury. I fought, in those next moments, as I had never fought before. Neither can I give an account of it, for I do not remember what I did, but it seems the battle lasted a lifetime.

When the gray haze of rage left me, Naani held me in her arms, and the dead lay heaped all around us on the rock. My armor was battered and broken; blood covered my body; I could feel it pouring from my wounds.

"Naani," I said, slowly, as if drunk. "They didn't hurt you?"

She was crying, touching me here and there. "Where are you injured?" she kept asking.

"I don't know. It . . . hurts all over."

For a few moments I could do nothing, then I regained enough of my senses to stand. "We have to get to the raft, Naani. The raft."

I was so weak I could scarcely walk, but with her help I made it to the edge. When I did not see any Humped Men, I managed a ragged smile, though it must have looked dreadful with so much blood running down my face.

My triumph died when I glanced down and to the right, and saw four more of my enemies creeping up the rock. I pushed Naani back, though the effort staggered me. I knew I had to fight them before my strength drained completely away.

I gave the first a weak blow in the head, but the diskos did its work well, and he toppled, dead, to the ground. I swayed upon the lip; my legs abruptly gave way beneath me, dropping me to my knees. Still, I wielded my weapon as best I could. Even as I fought, Naani sprang down from the rock and darted past the Humped Men. I tried to shout, to tell her to run for the raft, but my voice came out as a gurgle. Black despair filled me as I realized I would soon be dead, leaving no one to protect her or lead her to the Last Redoubt.

But Naani did not run away. Instead, she shouted at the men and darted back and forth, trying to draw them away from me. They ignored her, however, and one of the creatures reached me and delivered a blow to my armored chest that surely cracked his hand, for it drove me back against the rock wall at the far edge. Everything grew dark. I must have momentarily fainted. Then my sight returned.

My enemy made the mistake of trying to seize the diskos, and lost a hand in the effort. In response he struck me again, a terrific blow to the side.

Suddenly, Naani was there, running right in among them. She drove her knife twice through the arm of my attacker before the creature turned and caught her by her garment.

Seeing her thus gave me new strength, and I lurched to my knees and killed the Humped Man. Even as my limbs failed, I shouted at her to run to the raft. Blood washed across my vision, blinding me, and I fell back, but I did see Naani bolt away. The two remaining men paused, uncertain whether to follow her or finish me.

I heard her calling them, even as she danced toward the forest, but some silent communication must have passed between them, for they turned their attention back to me. Wary of me now, uncertain if I were dead or alive, they approached with slow, sly cunning.

My vision faded, but came back as I heard Naani's piercing scream. The next moment she tore beside the Humped Men, eyes blazing, face set, stabbing one of them in the shoulder as she passed. The man howled and turned. I thought he was about to kill her, but she leapt so rapidly from side to side even those swift creatures could not seize her.

They both approached her then, but she had already bounded back to the ground and into the trees. They sped after her, moving in their swift, lumbering manner.

By an act of will, I managed to clear my head a little. I pulled myself into a sitting position, but immediately tumbled over on my face. As I raised myself to my knees and crawled after her, I could hear my own breath pumping in and out like a faltering blacksmith's bellows. I tried to shout, but it came out as a rasping whisper.

I soon glimpsed her, a distant figure running among the trees, knife in hand, her enemies in pursuit. I thought one of the creatures staggered as if injured, while the one Naani had stabbed, who was in the lead, ran easily despite his wound. I saw them only an instant before they vanished into the thickets, leaving me alone.

The world became an empty horror; I could not hear anything except my blood pumping in my ears. I think I fainted again. Then I found myself on my feet, stumbling among the trees, trailing my diskos behind me. How I descended the rock I do not know; I have no memory of it. The ground seemed to shift beneath me; I could not feel my feet striking the earth, but I kept searching for my love. Strangled sobs escaped me. A thundering abruptly filled my ears, and I could no longer stand.

I awoke moments later, not wholly aware of having been unconscious, though I must have been, as I did not recall falling. I lay face down, but managed to lift my head to look among the trees. I saw no sign of Naani or my foes; a strange preternatural silence filled the whole world.

I knew Naani must be dead. Noticing my blood stains on the ground all around me, I chuckled grimly. If she were gone, I would welcome my own death.

I swooned again.

When next I woke I tried to lift my head, but it was too heavy. I turned my neck until my cheek lay flat against the earth so I could look around. Nothing crossed my vision for what seemed a long time—all appeared hazy as a dream—but then I saw a slender figure moving among the trees.

Naani ran slowly toward me, staggering as she came.

Somehow I got to my hands and knees, though I felt the blood seeping out as I began to crawl. I tried to call her name, but could not make a sound.

She drew near, stumbling, crashing into trees, half-blind from running. She saw me, still alive and trying to reach her. Her strangled cry was the first sound I had heard since leaving the rock. But when she was nearly upon me, she slowed, swaying, and dropped suddenly to the earth, overcome by exhaustion.

I crept to her as quickly as I could, though the ground seemed to move to avoid my hands. I had to look down as I went, because I could not lift my head.

I dropped to my stomach and slowly raised my eyes to see how far away I was. Beyond her fallen form, which lay yet a few yards from me, I saw the Humped Man Naani had stabbed slip out of the shadows, sniffing the ground as if tracking her. His wounds must have slowed him, for bright blood covered his shoulder and breast. Strangely enough, it occurred to me that I admired his tenacity.

I can be tenacious as well, I thought. I suppose that gave me the strength to rise to my feet, for I had to reach Naani before my enemy did. I ran forward, a stumbling gait, but made it only a few feet before I fell rolling to the ground. I pulled myself back to my hands and knees, while the Humped Man lumbered forward, moving like an ape.

It was a dreadful race, but I reached Naani first. No doubt the Humped Man thought me finished, for he came at me quickly, as if to end my struggles. Somehow, I got a grip on my diskos, rose up on my knees, and struck him even as he ran in upon me. His momentum took him past me, where he fell face down, dead. I would never have had a chance except for his injuries.

I could do no more. Blood poured from my wounds; my head lolled upon my shoulders. I looked down upon Naani, but could see no sign of an injury, though her blundering through the trees had bruised her.

When I tried to put my ear to her chest to listen for signs of life, I half-fell upon her. Still, I heard her steady heartbeat.

I have to get her on the raft, I thought, before darkness took me.

So Naani lay unconscious, as I, in my broken armor, fell senseless, my head upon her breast, while the far noise of the burning volcanoes rumbled through eternity.

XVI
THE ISLAND

Searing pain brought me back to my senses. At first I could not marshal my thoughts, but eventually I realized I was lying on my back. I wondered why I could not rise.

I heard a noise nearby. With an effort that sent excruciating waves of pain down my back and sides, I turned my neck an inch or two. Naani stood beside me, gasping for breath, furiously stroking with a pole, determination etched in her jaw line.

At first, I could not understand what she was doing, until I realized we were on the raft. I tried to speak, but her attention was focused on the shore behind us and the sound of something howling masked my words. With an effort, I tilted my head down until I saw a Humped Man standing upon the shore, staring stupidly and shrieking, as if he either did not know how to swim, or feared some creature living in the water. As Naani poled us away, his wails gradually dimmed.

"Naani," I managed.

She glanced my direction, but said, "Lie still."

"Naani," I insisted, "I fought a good fight, didn't I?"

For a moment I did not think she heard, until tears swarmed into her eyes. "You fought a good fight," she managed hoarsely.

I tried to rise to help her, but I fainted again, and so lay helpless as my brave beloved saved both our lives.

***

My memories are a vague jumble, filled with pain and discomfort, half-wakings and incoherent dreams, yet I always recall Naani's love around me, even through the black mists of swirling weakness.

I awoke once, feeling better, though my whole body still ached. Something soft lay beneath me and Naani knelt by my side, concern burning in her eyes. Her tears wet my face as she bent down, kissed me on the mouth, and cradled my head in her lap so she could give me some water. My throat was so parched I drank three cups, though the effort exhausted my strength. When I was done, she kissed me again, light as a breeze blowing across my lips, and I fell back asleep.

Three times this occurred, and on the third occasion I

felt strong enough to move my hand enough to reach for her. She took it in her own small hands and kissed it. I looked into her loving eyes and slept again. On my fourth wakening I whispered that I loved her, and she broke into desperate weeping, holding my hand against her breast.

So I moved in and out of consciousness, but finally roused enough to become aware of my surroundings. We camped beside a rock formation surrounded by ancient trees and clumps of tall grass. The rock formed a natural alcove, and its overhanging lip concealed us from being seen from more than ten feet away. I lay naked beneath my cloak, my body bandaged all over with the bundle of clothes Naani had brought with her from her home country. She sat beside me, dressed in the body vest. I touched it gingerly, remembering how it had been ripped in the battle. "You fixed it."

Her eyes filled with tears again, but she said, "I am surprised you remember it being torn. I used threads from my old clothes and made needles from thorns growing on the island. It was hard work, borrowed from Mirdath's time, but I managed. Even your bandaging is hers, for I would not have known how, otherwise."

"Thank you for saving us."

She squeezed my hand, saying nothing.

"How did you get us to the raft?"

"I woke and found you unconscious, your head on my breast, and until you moaned I thought you were dead. I stopped the bleeding as best I could and dragged you to the raft. It seemed to take hours. The surviving Humped Man had dropped behind while chasing me, and I kept expecting him to appear. I suppose his wounds slowed him. I found the pole you cut and pushed the raft out just as he came out of the woods."

"I remember," I said. "I saw him. You were very brave."

"I was desperate."

***

My strength increased from that point on. Naani fed me tablet-broth at frequent intervals, and washed and changed my dressings regularly. Lacking any other cloth, we had to use the same bandages over and over.

By the fifth day, though my pain had subsided, Naani would not let me even so much as speak, but sat by my side and entertained me with stories. By the next day my mind cleared for what seemed the first time, and I stubbornly refused to keep quiet. It pained me to see how thin and haggard she had become during my ordeal, and I did not want to distress her, but I needed to understand why she had acted so erratically before the attack.

"Naani, I love you," I began carefully, a little fearful of causing a relapse by mentioning the subject. "Thank you for saving my life. You seem to be yourself again."

She dropped her head, tears springing to her eyes. "I can't explain what happened. I acted like a fool. I began thinking about how all my family was dead—I had two brothers, you know."

"I'm sorry. You didn't say."

"They were killed when the monsters first entered the redoubt. I couldn't stop thinking about them, and of all those I ever knew. So many good people. I kept seeing their faces."

"I thought a Force of Evil had possessed you."

She looked up and gave a bitter smile. "It felt as if it had, but it was all my own doing. I remembered those I knew as Mirdath: my guardian, Sir Alfred; my maid, Clara; Mistress Alison—all my old friends from dances and teas. I have survived them all. I don't know what happened to me; I just couldn't bear it. Some part of me seemed to just go away, as if I fled to some distant place. I watched myself treat you so badly, but it didn't seem real. I knew I was acting childish, but I couldn't help myself. Everything became so bleak. All I wanted was to die, to join them. I . . ."

Her voice faded into tremendous sobs. "They're all gone, but I'm alive! Oh, why did I live? My folly nearly killed you, too!"

I have never seen anyone mourn as Naani did then. For an hour she wept with such tremendous, gulping sobs I thought she would make herself sick. Being too weak to cradle her in my arms, I offered what comfort I could by holding her hands.

When her grief was finally spent, I said, "You are not the last. The ancestors of those we knew in Mirdath and Andrew's time still live in the Great Pyramid, your cousins, thousands of generations removed. And you must not be ashamed of how you acted. You couldn't help it. There was just too much sorrow. I understand it now. I should have realized before. And if you had not led the Humped Men away, they would have killed me."

She did not reply, but nodded her head. Then she brought me dinner, kissing the tablets as she had always done and letting me kiss hers in turn. She made mine into a broth and we ate in silence.

Afterward, I asked her to place my diskos by my side, though I doubt I could have lifted it. She did so, and lay down beside me, her head in the hollow of my arm.

"Does this hurt you?"

"No. I'm getting stronger."

"I felt so responsible," she said. "When my people learned I had contacted the Great Pyramid, they put all their hopes on me. They thought your people would be able to help us."

"We tried." I told her the whole story of the youths who had left the pyramid to come to her aid. When I was done, she said, "Then there was nothing you could have done."

"No. The Forces of Evil were too strong. And there was nothing you could have done, either."

Without another word she fell into the sweet sleep of oblivion, perhaps her first real rest since the battle. For a time, I stared down on the goodness of that lovely face. Seeing her thus, a holiness surrounded my heart, uplifting my spirit in a quiet glory of love and gratitude. Once more I had thought her lost to me, once more I found her by my side. I sighed and soon joined her in slumber.

At the third, sixth, and ninth hours I awoke and drank part of the broth Naani had made. The perpetual glow of the volcanoes lit the gray stones of the alcove with a comforting red light. After eating, I fell asleep again with my hand on my weapon. More than once, in my fading reflections, I thought of the diskos much as the ancient knights viewed their swords, as a true comrade that loved me. Such is the way when weapon and wielder become nearly one.

At the twelfth hour, Naani woke with a cry of alarm, but once she saw I was well, she nestled back against me. "I'm sorry I have slept so long," she murmured. "I should be keeping watch."

I laughed. "Indeed, how dare you sleep instead of standing guard? You should be ashamed. What kind of sentry are you?"

For a moment she took me seriously, but then raised her small fist against my nose. "I could take your head off with a single blow."

She looked so pretty and stern I chuckled again.

"Don't laugh so hard," she ordered. "You will start bleeding again. It isn't that funny."

"No, it isn't," I said, restraining myself, for it did make my wounds hurt. "You have been the best of watchmen. My little warrior."

"My circus strongman."

She eventually rose and made more broth, and we slept again.

***

I remember the seventh day on the island as a happy time. We woke and ate, and Naani washed my wounds. I began taking my tablets whole. Perhaps it was my imagination, but they seemed to satisfy my hunger more than the broth did. Naani insisted I eat often, but I complied only after counting the tablets to make sure we had enough to complete our journey.

We spent our time like children, talking and laughing, eating and sleeping. I still lacked the strength to stand, but was weak enough not to care. The despair that had overtaken Naani before the attack did not return, and her true, cheerful disposition reasserted itself. She loved to quip and tease and sing; I adored her sweet spirit; she made every moment a joy.

When she went to wash herself in a nearby pool, her being out of sight distressed me so much I called every few minutes to see if she were well. She returned, her hair a lovely cloud around her head, its tips just touching her shoulders.

I glanced at her pretty, bare feet. "You have forgotten your shoes."

"You are so impatient I have to do half my dressing in front of you."

She sat down beside me, took the comb from my pack, and began straightening her hair. I reached up and plucked a single red-gold strand.

"Ow!" she said. "Was that necessary?"

I took the hair, put her ankles together, and wrapped the strand around her toes, binding them together. "Now you are my prisoner."

"You, sir, are not a gentleman." She pulled her feet away, though she kept them close enough so as not to break the cord.

When she finished combing her hair she took her knife,

229

and with a threatening look, cut a lock of my hair and a lock of her own. These she plaited together and hid in her bosom. I insisted she do the same for me, and I slipped mine under the bandage covering my heart.

We did many such foolish things, that are not foolish to those who remember being in love.

Exhaustion soon overcame me. Naani quickly saw I had overtaxed myself, for my hands turned white and began trembling from a lack of blood. She ordered me to rest, then clenched her fists, placing them into my right hand until I fell asleep.

***

I woke, startled, to find her stroking my brow.

"What is it?" I asked.

"You were moaning in your sleep. Were you having a bad dream?"

I could not remember for a moment. At last I said, "It was like dreaming in a dream. Though it was about me, it seemed to be about someone else, as if I watched it all from a distance. I dreamt of a young man in the ancient days when the sun shone bright and pure upon the earth. He met a maiden, a woman who was his one true love, and they walked together beneath boughs of spreading oak and elm under the blue sky. They married, but she died in childbirth. His grief nearly destroyed him, until he found himself awake and alive in the far future, with his love alive as well.

"He tried to find her, and when he did, discovered she was different in form, but still lovely in body and soul. He revered her, who had been his wife in the ancient times, so that his reverence for her was like an anguish of sweet trouble, of holy thoughts bred of her lovely companionship and his memories—"

Naani, kneeling beside me, looked intently into my eyes, and I realized I was speaking more as Andrew than Andros.

"Oh, Naani!" I suddenly burst out. "Am I a madman, sitting in a chair in an ancient manor, dreaming this life, deluded by grief? Or am I deceived in this existence, imagining I once lived? In my dream, I wasn't certain. None of it seemed real."

"It's real," she said. "And if I am an illusion, I am a very persistent one. It's hard, living two lives at once, especially when one of them seems all shadows and phantoms. But it

230

is real."

"Naani," I suddenly said, as the whole memory of the dream returned to me. "The baby died. You died; and then the baby died, and there wasn't anything I could do. I had forgotten, put it out of my mind. It wouldn't have been so lonely if she had lived, because I had named her Mirdath."

Naani put one hand over her mouth, the horror of recollection in her eyes. "I remember the baby! Her cries have tormented me all my life."

I wept in great, gasping sobs then, as the whole weight of the memory came back; and Naani wept with me. After scores of centuries, two parents huddled together, mourning for their lost child, with only one another and the Country of the Seas surrounding them. But there was a sweetness in that mourning, as if we had both carried the weight of our sorrow forever, buried and unknown until that moment, waiting hidden throughout our lives for us to weep together.

***

We talked much that day of things ancient and new, and laughed as well as mourned.

"Here's a very old one," I said. "When does a man neigh?"

"Neigh?" Naani said. "A strange word." Then as if reaching far into the past, she said, "When he is a little hoarse?"

We laughed as if this were quite clever. Naani, unlike myself, scarcely recalled what a horse was, and could only conjure an image of a tremendous beast, towering and bulky, more a monster than anything else, but we laughed because we remembered it together. The words we used for *neigh* and *hoarse* were not in our own language, but in the English of Andrew and Mirdath.

I told her various things about the Great Pyramid, while she listened, enthralled, as if I reported sailors' tales of far wonders. When I mentioned the millions dwelling there, she said, "So many? And so crowded? How strange. With the lack of Earth Current, our redoubt was always underpopulated, like a rambling house. My peoples' spirits seem so thin compared to yours, so lacking in vitality. I don't think we loved properly, though we spoke of love often."

"I think that is always the way," I said. "Even in the Great Pyramid, thousands pass their lives without knowing true love. They do not see how two spirits can live together as one, lost in the mystery of perfect peace and desire, their bodies a natural delight, a splendor surrounding them even on the darkest days—the man with the woman, the woman with the man, he both hero and child before her, she a holy light and true companion. If one dies, the soul of the other fails. That is love. Anything less is just a borrowing of its name for animal desires. Any marriage not born of it, made for such pitiful ends as wealth, ambition, or attraction have no more part of it than the greed of a merchant or the appetite of a glutton.

"Why, Andros, you are a poet," Naani said.

I sighed. "I am a young man a million years old."

"We are becoming melancholy. Tell me more about your pyramid."

So I told how millions of laborers had excavated for many ages to carve the Underground Fields a hundred miles deep, and how countless villages, filled with numberless inhabitants, were spread throughout its many levels. I also told of our scientific discoveries in chemistry, monstruwatry, and metaphysics, of our rolling migrators, of the underground pipes criss-crossing the Night Land, drilled twenty miles and more into the earth to provide a natural water supply, and of the air ships and terrible weapons housed in our Museum of Antiquities.

"Our Underground Fields went less than five miles deep," Naani said, "but there were tremendous, natural caverns beneath those, that we called the Country of Husbandry. It was a lonesome, dimly lit region where we buried our dead. There were only a few inhabitants. Those I met lived solitary lives and went about that land quiet as ghosts."

"We give our dead back to the Earth Current," I said, "in the Country of Silence, the lowest field. A hallowed place, really. To me, it expresses all that is noble and everlasting in humanity. I have always been drawn to it, especially to the Hills of the Infants. I thought it was because of the death of my parents. Now I know it was a hidden yearning for you and our daughter."

She kissed me and looked deep into my eyes. "I love you with all my soul."

I also told her what I had learned about the history of the world from the gray metal book. When I spoke of the desolate, frozen world two hundred miles above the Rift, she became thoughtful.

"All that emptiness and darkness," she said. "It makes me feel insignificant. But I won't give in to it."

"Nor I. Size has nothing to do with significance. I think there is no true death, but the dying of days, and God watching, waiting to take us when our time is done, if we have served Him well."

"And did He throw us back?" she asked, "like fish tossed into a stream?"

It took a moment to remember what a fish was, but at last I said, "We were returned for a purpose, to find one another, to finish what we started."

"He must look favorably upon love, then."

"I think He does."

"Your mention of the metal book reminded me of something I read. Have you heard of the Moving Cities?"

"No. Tell me."

"According to an account my father found in the Records, the cities once continuously followed the sun west upon tremendous metal roadways, keeping just ahead of the night. No one lived in the darkness because of the unbearable cold. Those cities in advance of the others planted crops which were harvested in turn by those behind, then sent forward."

"The rotation of the earth must have slowed," I said, "so a day lasted a long time."

"I don't know," Naani looked a little puzzled at my reply. "You must be right, though. The cities could not have traveled quickly, but staying in one place would have meant freezing to death, so they lived always in the sun, as we live in the darkness."

We reflected on this a bit, and Naani said, "Andros, did you ever love another woman?"

I laughed at this, because she looked so serious. "No, I never did. I have lived a solitary life, as if even before my Awakening I remembered our love and knew no one I met could be you."

I felt a twinge of jealousy known to all lovers, as I asked in return, "And you? Did you love anyone else?"

She shook her head slightly, so her hair stirred against her shoulders. "I felt the same way. A kind of emptiness that left me uninterested in other men, even during the flirtatious years of girlhood. I always knew my one true love waited for me, and someday I would meet him. I never kissed a man, not once, except for my father or brothers."

"Nor I a woman," I said. "As if we knew."

"We did know."

We hugged, and my momentary uneasiness passed. But I pitied those who, not having met their beloved, play lightly with that which is a treasure, not keeping their heart for their darling, but squandering its holy glory on others. I think it must cause constant regret when they finally meet their true love and realize their failure. Yet I suppose in the end, if at last they find real love, that love eases their pain, as love does. Then, perhaps the pain of their regrets, which can cause either growth or decline, makes their love even stronger. I also believe if everyone met the love of their soul, debauchery would pass from the earth, leaving only love dancing through the years.

We fell asleep that night in each others' arms.

***

The next day we woke, both basking in our companionship. Naani changed my bandages after breakfast and eased me to a sitting position for the first time, with my back against the rocks. She rested in my arms, her hair more red than gold in the crimson light. We laughed like two children, and I have never been happier.

Later, I withdrew *Ayleos' Mathematics* from my pack, so I could bring my journal up to date.

"Andros," Naani said, placing her hands on her hips. "I really must know. Out of all the things you could have brought with you, why did you choose a mathematics book? I cannot think of anything less useful."

I looked down at the scarred, yellow cover. "I wanted to use the blank pages to chronicle my travels. I am always behind on my entries, though. If not for my excellent memory for numbers I could never put down how many hours we have journeyed."

"You remember the number of hours we walk each day?"

"Absolutely. It is a gift, and it only works for numbers. Otherwise I am just as forgetful as anyone."

"But why the book?"

I hesitated, feeling somewhat foolish. "I have always had it with me. I suppose I brought it because it gives me comfort. Nothing is more changeless than numbers. The monsters roar; the Forces of Evil surround the redoubt, but numbers remain the same."

"You are different than Andrew in that way. More thoughtful."

"Andrew had the fields and the forests. Perhaps I would spend less time in books if I could walk the English lanes again."

That whole day was as good as the one before, except when we spied a few of the Humped Men upon the shore, close to the flat rock where we had fought. We could not see what they were doing, but they soon departed, seemingly without thought or knowledge of us. Neither did they return.

***

By the tenth day I was strong enough to walk a bit, though Naani kept close to catch me if I fell. Either the powdered water held special healing properties or the people of the future recovered more quickly than men of ancient days, for a normal man with such wounds would have been forced to stay in bed a month or more.

Because of my bandages, I could not wear my armor, so I used my cloak for a garment instead. Naani had stored my mail in a niche in the rocks, and at my request, she brought it out. During my illness, she had polished it to a fine shine, but I felt sick when I saw how broken and bent it was.

"It can't be fixed!" I moaned. "But we have to have it."

"There must be a way," Naani said. "Could we use a stump for an anvil and heavy stones for a hammer?"

"I don't know. I'm no blacksmith."

"We can try."

It took a few moments for Naani to persuade me, but she persevered until I agreed to attempt it. We picked out the stones together and worked on the armor throughout the day, though my weakness forced me to take frequents rests. Naani hammered on the armor as much as I, though she could not strike as forcefully. We beat the broken parts smooth and took the dents out. When we finished, I was finally appeased, but the work had taken its toll, and I fell asleep early.

***

The next day we discussed the best way to continue our journey, for though I had not completely healed, we needed to reach home before our supplies ran out. Travel seemed impossible in my injured condition, but we both thought of a solution at the same time. We were talking about all the bodies of water in that country, which in turn reminded us of boats and lakes from long ago. We soon struck on the idea of floating through the land on the raft, where we would be free of the Humped Men and could sleep at our leisure.

I had no experience at boating, but we were soon standing over the raft, discussing what we could do to make it safe, for it was too small to use for very long. Mainly, we wanted to put something solid between ourselves and any monsters that happened to swim beneath us. To that end, we searched the tiny island for fibrous bushes to bind more logs together. We did not find any, though we discovered many small saplings to use for braces.

"We could cut my hair and plait it into cords. You wouldn't mind me being bald, would you?" Naani asked.

"I will not let you cut your beautiful hair."

"Because it would make me look like a boy?"

"Because it would make you look like a bald-headed girl. We could-"

I stopped abruptly and ran my hands through the long grass which grew all across the island. Much of it was as tall as my thigh. "If we could braid these into cords, it would work. It is certainly tough enough." I grinned at her and added, "I thought of this idea first."

She put on a pouting face. "Only because I gave you the notion by talking about my hair."

I kissed her and we began cutting arm-loads of the grass. These we took back to our camp, where Naani showed me the art of plaiting. In this way, we could create cords of any length. We worked happily all through the day, but when it came time to sleep, Naani had done three times as much as I. She kissed me gravely. "Don't fret. We can't all have the needed skills. It's nothing to be ashamed of."

I wrestled her to the ground and would have tickled her soundly if not for my wounds.

***

The next day, I used my diskos to cut down six trees. I felt almost whole again, though still slightly weak. We plaited the cords the rest of that day and the day after, and I announced to Naani that since I felt much better, I would stop eating more than my ration of tablets. She tried to talk me out of it, but I held firm, since by my estimation we had just enough to get us home.

On the fourteenth day upon the island, while Naani sat plaiting beside me, I cut seven more trees for a total of thirteen, which I trimmed down nicely with the diskos. I then cut twelve saplings, two of which I sliced thin to use for paddles. Using Naani's knife, I carved a foot-long crosspiece that I fastened with pegs and lashed to one end of the paddles. I then took a large piece of bark, shaped broad on one end and pointed on the other, and after making holes in it, tied its wide end to the crosspiece and its narrow end to the shaft. I made holes down the length of the bark and secured it to the shaft, also, thus making a decent paddle about ten feet long and two feet wide at its head.

I shaped the handle small enough to fit Naani's grasp, all the while teasing that she made my work more difficult by having such tiny hands.

Those hands she presently placed over my mouth to stop the mocking. I mumbled on a bit, and then she went on with her plaiting.

I made the second paddle larger for my own use, and when I finished, I was pleased with my work.

***

On the fifteenth day Naani thought my wounds were nearly healed, and we danced a slow waltz across the beach. Neither of us remembered the steps properly, but we turned gaily to that ancient dance, until we fell laughing in a heap upon the shore.

It took us nearly six hours to roll the trees down to the water, where I began adding them to our existing raft, lashing the saplings across the trunks, with the center tree farthest forward and the others tapering back like a ship's bow. I finished the last of the lashing the next day and completed our craft by setting up two rests for the paddles. We put our gear on board, along with the pole Naani had used in her flight from the Humped Men. I kept my diskos on my belt at my hip, but placed my armor in the middle of the craft.

Naani took my arm as we stopped for a last look at our little campsite. I sighed, and she stood on tiptoe and kissed me on the cheek. "If there were never any more," she said, "this would be enough."

Arm in arm we turned to the water and launched the raft.

XVII
THE DARK AGAIN

Steering the raft proved much easier than we had imagined. The paddles worked well and balanced nicely in their rests. We stood to row, Naani at the front paddle, I at the back, both of us pushing steadily, the raft traveling at a speed slightly faster than we could hike over the broken landscape. Standing did not bother us since we were used to walking, and our only complaint lay in the monotony of paddling, which consisted of little more than rocking back and forth on our heels.

At the twelfth hour, we let the raft drift while we stopped to eat, but soon returned to our labor. Because we felt safe, we talked continuously. Naani often glanced back at me with love, sometimes pursing her lips with a kiss to tempt me, then ordering me back to my work when I tried to desert my station to approach her.

At the eighteenth hour we pulled in the paddles, set our cloak beneath us for our bed, and let the lapping of the waters rock us to sleep.

***

We woke at almost the same time eight hours later, and for a moment could not remember where we were. We sat up and grinned, filled with joy at the sight of one another's faces, then kissed, washed in the seawater, ate, and returned to our paddling.

All that day we traveled the coast in peace. The only incident was when we saw an enormous beast lumber out of the sea onto the shore. Since the creature was a considerable distance away, it did not frighten us, especially when it seemed content to browse the forest. Still, I would not have wanted the raft to be in its path when it left the waters, for one of its gargantuan feet was easily broad as our vessel.

Despite its size, it seemed natural enough, like all the animals in that country. I think the prehistoric world must have been filled with such beasts, born of circumstance and environment. But I do not think chance is the only factor. I also believe some spiritual energy may control the

238

shape of all living forms. Even though this Force may sometimes be perverted by foul or foolish breeding, as in the case of the monsters of the Night Land, it still provides direction. I picture it as an exacting principle, as constant as a mathematical table. Having seen spiritual forces within the Night Land, it seems reasonable to me that the human spirit is peculiar to itself, either as the cause of human life or its result. I believe humankind may be fundamentally consistent in certain ways, undeviating in those regards despite modifications in form. I also think this was true even at the first, when humans were undeveloped in the things of the spirit. Perhaps the spirit affects the flesh with an energy confined only by humanities' peculiar limitations. Our development may lie between two points that are not so far apart, for despite their differences, the people of the future were quite similar to those of the past. Perhaps humans can change quickly from one point to the other, moving from brutality to refinement and back within a few generations.

I speak not, of course, of the afterlife. For who knows how much or how little we will be transformed? For myself, I hope for beautiful things, for a sweet advancement into a world of which we behold the shores always in the light of love.

Our voyage took four days of twenty-four hours each, for we loitered along so I could gather my strength. Other than the sea beast, we saw little of note except when we passed close to one particular volcano rising out of the waters. The sea boiled in various, seemingly random places all around it; the release of subterranean gases near its base made the waters bubble and groan. Scores of jets shot high into the air, roaring as they went. Long after we passed the volcano, we stared back at its terrible power, thankful at avoiding its boiling spray.

Our only other concern came when we reached the place where the sea broke off into smaller lakes, but we always found passages where we could cross.

As we went along, I pointed out various parts of the country that I remembered from my original journey, for Naani never seemed to tire of hearing of my adventures.

At the end of the fourth day we beached our raft beside the shore, where the ground sloped up to the mouth of the gorge leading to the Night Land. Despite our peaceful journey, my mind had often turned toward our next step. If we could win through the gorge and the Night Land to the pyramid, we would have our whole lives before us, but our greatest dangers lay ahead.

We stepped off the raft carrying our meager bundles.

"I wonder," Naani said, "if anyone will ever see this craft again? Or will it remain here, forgotten through the ages?"

"A wooden monument to our journey? It will rot, of course, long before anyone returns. If anyone ever does."

Naani drew her knife, cut a piece of wood from the raft, and placed it in my pouch as a memento. She knelt and kissed the craft.

"Thank you, good boat." I did not laugh, for I was grateful to that vessel as well. I also knew that with every step of the journey, we were moving farther from Naani's home, and this was another way for her to say goodbye.

She helped me into my armor; it felt heavy after going without it for so long, but I took comfort in its weight. With my scrip and pouch at my back, my diskos in hand, and Naani with her knife-belt wrapped around her waist, we climbed toward the gaping darkness of the gorge.

Some miles to our right rose that towering mountain where perched the four volcanoes that I had seen on my outward way. Below them lay the enormous hills of ash that had been building for thousands of years.

We soon reached the foreboding mouth of the gorge. Though we had traveled far that day, and the canyon's darkness seemed terrible after so much brilliance, we continued our journey, for I thought it wiser to leave the light behind rather than chance meeting any more of the Humped Men. When we came to the place where the gorge cut off the illumination by a sharp bend to the left, we paused and turned to catch one final glimpse of the Country of the Seas.

It is impossible to describe our feelings. We, who were born into darkness, were leaving forever the only lighted country we had ever known. Perhaps recalling our previous existence in the sunlit world made the parting even more difficult. In those last moments, we stood listening to the far mutter of the volcanoes, the bubbling of the seas, and the clamor of life. Naani clutched my arm as we looked our last into the red glow of that deep, hidden country.

It occurred to me that perhaps in some far distant future

the Humped Men would find their humanity and build a civilization there, for though they were cruel, I thought them human enough. The thought comforted me, but when I suggested it to Naani, she did not seem to hear.

Presently, I turned, and she slipped her hand into mine. Tears rolled down her cheeks.

"We will tell our children," she said.

"Will they believe, I wonder?"

We turned the corner of the gorge and stumbled into the gloom.

***

Sixteen hours later we found a place to sleep where the dim glow of the Country of the Seas cast dull twilight on the stones. We rested well enough among the boulders and woke to the safety of silence.

While we ate our breakfast, I consulted my journal to see how long it had taken to travel the gorge the first time. According to my account, if we went no more than sixteen hours each day we should reach the bottom of the Great Slope in five days.

We soon left the twilight behind. The darkness oppressed me, for I feared something attacking Naani from the shadows. Occasional fires gave a little light, though the gases they emitted left us struggling to breathe.

My strength increased every day. At first, after my two weeks of idleness, walking made me sore, but my stiffness eased by the second journey. We went along at a good rate, for we were both anxious to reach the Great Pyramid, I more than Naani because of my fear for her safety. Only an effort of will kept us from reckless haste or from walking past the sixteenth hour. Despite my anxiety, we did not see a living creature during our travels. It was a lonesome place, all boulders and stark stones, filled with a silence broken only by the spectral moaning or whistling of the burning gas echoing up and down the gorge. We kept close to one another, often touching hands, as if to reassure ourselves against the solitude. I could not help thinking that if we died there, we would lie unburied and unmourned, with none to know our fate.

On the fifth day, at about the seventh hour, we heard the rising and falling of a rushing noise. I drew Naani close, and with my diskos ready, crept cautiously through the twilight. We passed three dancing gas fires singing their eldritch song among the rocks; distant flames seemed to catch the refrain and send it darting along the gorge.

"I should have realized," I finally whispered to Naani. "It is the echoes of the giant gas fountain I told you about."

"Is it close?"

"Not yet, but it makes a tremendous commotion. We will be out of the gorge soon."

We tried unsuccessfully to see the fountain, for it was so far away it looked the same size as the other fires leaping along the canyon, but after about an hour we perceived its distant, slow pulses of blue flame. The noise grew more steady and gradually turned into a vast piping with a constantly changing tone. We passed the last of the lesser fires, leaving only the gas fountain rising before us.

The noise, which lifted and fell to the dance of the monster flame, was even more thunderous than I remembered. We stood staring at it, my arm around Naani, her hands to her ears. The tendrils of fire lifted and twisted, blue and gold, rising for hundreds of feet, while our shadows ran behind us, long and thin, tall as towers. The sides of the gorge sprang into sight with each surge of the flames. Speech was impossible, but we turned and looked at one another and exchanged a sober kiss in the blinding light.

Eventually we turned and looked in our intended direction. The titanic boulders surrounding the fountain blocked our sight, but I managed to show Naani a glimpse of our way when the flame rose to its pinnacle.

Though it was past the sixteenth hour, we walked another mile to escape the deafening blare and made our bed among the boulders. All through our slumbers the flames roared, and I dreamed I walked beside an ancient ocean, listening to the pounding surf.

***

We woke, saying little, and watched the fountain dance as we ate our breakfast. I suppose I will never find the words to truly describe that monstrous, solitary fire, surrounded by the guardian stones.

Soon, with our gear upon us, we set off toward the emptiness of the Great Slope. For most of the first day the gas fountain gave us some illumination, and when we glanced back, as we often did to see how high we had climbed, we found the flame shuddering below us in the night. I was surprised at how quickly the slope brought us above the level of the fire; it did not seem that steep, though our legs told us we were constantly climbing.

As we left the fountain behind, the light gradually faded, so that by the end of our trek we stumbled numbly through the gloom.

On the second day we entered total darkness and had to crawl on hands and knees. This proved a terrible ordeal for Naani, who had neither gloves, nor armor to protect her legs. At first we traded off using the gloves, but her hands grew so sore that wearing them hurt as much as the stones did. Finally, we thought to wrap the rags from her bundle around her hands and knees.

I led the way, my diskos at my hip. I used my pouch strap and tied one end to my wrist and the other to Naani's belt, so we would never lose contact. I tied the other strap from my scrip to a stone, and cast it in front of me as I had done before. Since we climbed this time instead of descending, and since I had traveled the slope before, I did not feel this to be absolutely necessary, but I continued the practice because of the memory of the Pit of Hands. I also kept to the right side of the slope to avoid encountering it again.

For eight days we ascended through that terrible darkness, the only sound our shuffling steps and the echo of the stone I threw. To us, wanting to go as silently as possible, its reverberations seemed tremendously loud. I grew sick of tossing the rock and groping among the boulders. At times we seemed no more than phantoms, doomed to creep along that endless way. A gnawing fear of wandering in circles beset me, for often I could not tell if I crept upward or downward. In those moments I had to pause, draw Naani close, and for at least an instant, let the diskos emit a flash of comfort through the eternal desolation. Our faces shone pale and alien in the luminous glow; we exchanged ravenous glances, devouring the sight of one another, each glimpse sustaining us until the next burst of light.

Sometime during the fourth day Naani crept to me and kissed me on the cheek, her face wet with tears.

"Why are you crying?" I whispered.

"I want you to know that I am forever indebted to you. For you to dare this awful darkness for my sake, not knowing what lay at its end, fills me with awe, and humility, and deepest gratitude."

I kissed her on the mouth, both out of love, but also to silence her, for her words made me both proud and embarrassed. Loving her as I did, with a love that drove me to dare anything, I never considered myself especially heroic. I treasured her words, though, since I had been feeling particularly low at that moment, and her praise gave me the strength to go on.

That became the way of it during that leg of the journey, that we took turns fighting despair—it was so dark; it seemed it would be dark forever. And beyond the darkness lay the horrors of the Night Land. But whenever I could no longer bear the shadows, Naani would whisper a few words of cheer, and when it seemed she could not crawl another step, I comforted her as best I could.

At the beginning of the fifth day we finally admitted to one another that every time we woke we thought we sensed some creature nearby, even as I had done on my original journey. Whatever it was, we felt its presence all the time we traveled the Great Slope. Though it filled me with foreboding for Naani's safety, she did not fear it, for her Night Hearing told her it intended no harm. Whether it was some kind of animal, or a dispassionate Force, or even something giving us protection and aid, we never knew.

The air became colder and we kept the cloak about us when we slept, though we did not need it when we journeyed because of our exertions. Our breathing grew more difficult, and the powder bubbled less when we poured it into the cup.

I kept track of the time by glancing at my chronometer whenever I triggered my diskos for light, but I also learned the number of stone throws in an hour, a talent for which there is little demand. Naani was actually the one who discovered it, and she became as accurate as any timepiece, while I tended to lose count. Surrounded as we were by the eternal darkness, having only each other, our spirits grew even closer. Adversity either draws lovers together or tears them apart. If the love is strong enough, and if they are determined to cherish that love, they will prevail, for love is more than an emotion; it is an act of will. In those times when we feel neither lovable nor loving, we should set our sights upon our love, resolving that nothing will move us. Many have erred in thinking love a passing fancy, rather than a continuous, eternal goal.

On the eighth day, about the end of the ninth hour, we caught a glimpse of light far above us. We had finally reached the Night Land.

XVIII
FORCES OF EVIL

After being so long in darkness, we hurried toward the light, which gradually became clearer until we saw it as a high, looming glow. We continued our ascent, and at the fourteenth hour, stood at the end of the Road Where The Silent Ones Walk.

We followed the Road until we topped the Great Slope and at last stared out over the wonder and mystery of the Night Land. Despite the dangers I knew we must face, I was ecstatic with pride. I had returned home even as I had vowed, bringing Naani back out of the unknown world. But my conceit vanished as I looked across that country, replaced by a dread of our ever reaching the pyramid through all the Forces, monsters, and beast-men.

I searched eagerly for the Great Pyramid, and upon spying it, put my arm around Naani and pointed. Only the highest lights on the Tower of Observation were visible, yet a flush of joy ran through me.

She studied it a long time, then turned to me, threw her arms around my neck, and burst into tears. I was close to weeping myself, and we held each other in the darkness.

"How far is it?" she asked. "What will we have to cross to reach it? Will those within be able to help? Can you contact them?"

"Which question do you want me to answer?"

She stopped and put her hand over her mouth. "I'm sorry. It's just so wonderful. When you told me about it, it was as if you spoke of heaven. Yet there it is, so bright and shining. I can see the Earth Current pulsing inside it, even from this distance! I just can't believe it."

"It will take several days to reach it, and there are many dangers, the greatest of which is the first, the House of Silence."

I pointed to the House. Upon seeing it, Naani shrank back, as if physically struck.

I clutched at her. "What is it?"

"It's horrible!" she said. "Can't you feel it? I wish I had

245

never looked at it. We have to hide."

Since her Night Hearing was more acute than my own, I did not question her, but obeyed at once. The sight of the House, with its aura of brooding, vigilant evil had always affected me, as if some fate awaited me concerning it. We threw ourselves among the moss bushes growing in clumps beside the Road and waited until Naani's fear subsided. It crossed my mind that despite the terrors surrounding the Lesser Redoubt, more Forces of Evil had gravitated toward my pyramid, drawn by its many souls.

The House of Silence stood upon its low hill, relatively nearby and to our right. Since I had been forced to travel on hands and knees to escape its notice the first time, it had taken me many hours to pass from under its shadow to the top of the Great Slope. We would have to be careful again, and the thought of approaching it filled me with dread. I wished the task was over and done.

After some discussion, we decided to eat and find a place to sleep, so we could be fresh to face the dangers before us. We searched until we discovered a mammoth boulder surrounded by moss bushes, and lay down beneath the vegetation. The chill of the Night Land fell upon us immediately. We huddled in the cloak, sharing what little body heat my armor allowed, keeping quiet, sobered by the House of Silence; I slept fitfully, waking often to listen for danger.

Nonetheless, nothing disturbed us, and after eight hours we rose, ate, and set out again. I made Naani wear the cloak. At first she refused, until I explained that I needed my limbs free to fight, and dared not be hindered by it.

The Road Where The Silent Ones Walk bent around the bottom of the hill where the House of Silence stood. In my original journey, it had taken eleven days from the Last Redoubt to the top of the Great Slope, because I had traveled around to the northwest of the Plain Of Blue Fire. From where I now stood, I saw a shorter route that might take us out of danger in four or five days.

I showed Naani how the pyramid stood right behind the House of Silence, so that the most direct path would be in a straight line. Whichever way we went, we could not avoid passing close to the House, since in that area barren rock covered the country to the northwest and the only concealment lay in the vegetation along the Road. We would have to cross the Road Where The Silent Ones

Walk twice, but we agreed it was worth the risk.

I did not have to warn Naani of the danger of the House; she sensed it quite well, and we left the top of the Great Slope and descended into the Night Land, crawling from bush to bush until we intersected the Road. For several anxious moments we looked for signs of the Silent Ones, but seeing none, we bolted across. Its surface shimmered like gray glass and our footfalls echoed strangely on its surface. It seemed miles wide, though it was probably less than a hundred paces. I was terrified, but the next moment we were across, scampering into the foliage to the east. Once concealed, we lay quiet for several minutes, watching to see if anything approached.

When nothing arrived to destroy us, I led us away, feeling buoyant at our successful crossing. We stayed on the southeast perimeter of the bushes, to put as much distance between us and the House as possible, which now lay ahead and to our right. In this way, we would never be nearer than a mile from it, though truthfully, that was dreadfully close.

We traveled six hours before resting, creeping on all fours, or stooping like apes. We did not speak, but listened continually. By the tenth hour we had drawn relatively close to the House, though as far away as the vegetation allowed. To our left stretched bare stone, glowing fire-holes, and also one of the Silent Towers scattered across the land, which were thought to contain strange Watchers.

This Tower stood tall and thin, far away among the naked rock, gray and dim except when the flare of distant fires shed light upon it. We dared not ignore it; such Towers were believed to be outposts of the House of Silence, so we tried to keep hidden from both it and the House. It was hard to remember the Tower, however, with the windows of the mansion peering down on us like vacant eyes.

By the eleventh hour we had to creep from bush to bush, shadows passing between the darkness and light, for the House loomed huge and silent above us, directly to our right, its lights shining as deathless and steadfast as they had through all the dreary ages. We could feel the evil emanating from it, as sharp and bitter as acid on the tongue. Our attempts at remaining concealed from that probing Force seemed utterly futile, as if we were children playing hide and seek, thinking ourselves secure while the adults watched, knowing our every move.

By the twelfth hour I grew less anxious, for we were beginning to draw clear. But as I turned to Naani, to give her a kiss of encouragement, she suddenly cried in pain and crumpled to the ground.

"Naani!" I hissed, reaching for her. She lay unconscious, her eyes closed, and I sensed the House attacking her spirit. I swept her into my arms and set my body between the wretched structure and her. The moment I touched her I sensed a dreadful energy coursing through her, drenched in the essence of Silence and bleak desolation. I knew then that the House could slay me on whim, but chose to concentrate all its energies on Naani instead. I do not know why it selected her in place of me; perhaps because she had not gone through the Rite of Preparation. But how can anyone understand the motives of such evil?

I marshaled my thoughts, imagining my spirit and will as a shield, which I set around her. Though I had never done such a thing before, it was not much different than sending a call into the night.

Since concealment was now useless, I stood up, Naani in my arms. My choice was clear. Only speed could save her from the Force's malice. I had to either carry her immediately to the physicians in the Great Pyramid or die of exhaustion in the attempt.

I freed my diskos from my hip and took it in my arms with Naani. A dozen strides brought me out of the bushes. I broke into a desperate trot, while the silent power of the House hammered against us.

"Mirdath!" I cried as I went, and "Naani!" but she neither responded, nor even seemed to live. A sob broke from me; despair coursed through my heart; the fires of madness burned in my brain. I could think of nothing but saving her. But even as I ran I realized I could not carry her all the way unless I conserved my strength.

I halted long enough to warm a broth of the tablets and water upon a hot rock, which I tried to pour between her closed lips. It proved useless, as in my heart I knew it would, but all the while I worked I kept my body, my will, my spirit, and my love between her and the horror of the House. I made a little more water and rubbed it on her face and hands, but it did no good. I put my ear to her breast and listened for her heart. The blood drained from my face when I could not hear it, but then I caught a slow, faint beat. As long as she breathed, I knew the House had not stolen her soul.

After wrapping her in my cloak, I disregarded my churning stomach long enough to force myself to eat. I lifted my mute love again, trying not to think how merry she had been only an hour before, and set out at a long trot, determined, if necessary, to run through all eternity. I saw the world as if in a fever dream, born in the madness of intention and despair.

At every sixth hour I stopped only long enough to eat and drink, but I always tried to bring my dear one to her senses. Her heart grew ever more feeble, until I no longer dared to listen.

Why no Power of Goodness came to my aid, I do not know, but though I called on God and any Forces within the land to aid me, I received no answer. In my frustration, I was tempted to fall into cursing, but was restrained by the fear that bitterness of spirit could weaken my shield around Naani.

I traveled the land blindly, recognizing almost nothing. I can recall my journey only as vague gray shapes intermixed with flashes of light and the glare of fires; nothing seemed real except the woman in my arms, who was everything.

I sped through the dreadful hours, neither deviating my course to evade any evil nor striving to conceal myself; Naani was slowly dying, and there was no gain in life save by speed. I vaguely remember creatures coming at me out of the darkness on three different occasions. I do not recall the combat, except that I killed them in the heat of a boiling anger. At the end of one encounter, I remember blood running down the diskos into my hand.

At some point, I felt the ether stirring around me, as the millions of the Great Pyramid spied me carrying a woman out of all the world's night. To them, it must have been as if a man had entered the land of the dead and returned to the world of the living. A continuous, spiritual murmur filled the air. I knew that all the millions must be watching from the embrasures and View Tables as I rushed across the Night Land, though only those with the strongest spyglasses could see me since I was still a long way off. No doubt, millions stared vainly at my reported location while the Hour Slips related every detail. Humans remain human, whatever the era.

Though I noticed the stirring of the ether, I ignored it, for all my will, powered by the madness of despair, remained bent on driving headlong through the miles of the night.

***

Later, in what seemed an enormous space of hours, I reached the place where the Road bent toward the Vale of Red Fire, not far from where the young men had fought the giants. As I sped across the glassy slickness of the Road, not even pausing to look for the approach of the Silent Ones, many of the watching multitudes saw me for the first time. The ether shook with their emotion, and the Night Land awoke.

Out of the east rose the faint and dreadful Laughter, as if a monstrous being chortled to itself from dreadful, lost regions. The Laughter echoed over the plains, rolled around the darkness of the west, and wandered among the far mountains of the Outer Lands before dying into silence. I felt a chill in my heart, but did not truly care, for if I could not save Naani, I wanted only death. I did have the presence of mind to pause long enough to draw her knife from her belt and to bare the Capsule of Oblivion, so I could slay us both if an Evil Force found us. Even this tormented me, though, for the House of Silence had attacked my beloved's spirit, and I did not know if even death could spare her from its clutches.

I went like a machine, stopping every six hours, never resting between, scarcely able to stomach eating the tablets. Through my fever, I grew increasingly aware of Forces of Evil, traveling abroad, restlessly searching. Monsters roamed through the shadows and roars filled the land from night sky to night sky. I kept my eyes upon the pyramid.

The Vale of Red Fire soon lay far to my right, and that mountain of vigilance, the Watcher of the Northeast, rose before me to my left. Above it, the blue halo of the luminous ring shed its light over the upper portion of the behemoth's head, as the brute stared across the plain at the Last Redoubt, its sprawling back toward me.

Out of a bush leapt a tall, gangly, man-shaped creature. I became so furious I did not even think to set Naani down, but launched myself at him when he was still half-hidden in the shadows. He died in pieces. The diskos' roar, and the act of striking down one of those who had harmed my darling, gave me momentary comfort. I sped away, my heart seething within me. Other creatures came at me from the darkness, but they died quickly, and I remember no more about them.

***

The hours passed in spaces of terror, numbness, and ever growing desperation. At the last, I burned with tireless energy. Weariness departed from me, and I swept easily across the land, anxious for its denizens to attack me, so I could ease my heart by drawing their blood.

The cacophony of the country increased, so that along with the roaring I heard deeper, more dreadful noises. Later, I discerned the far thudding of the earth, and a giant man ran past me, his bulk so immense he shook the ground. By a sweet mercy, he did not see me, and was lost to the night in an instant. As he swept by, the ether boiled first with the fear of the millions, and then with their relief and gratitude. I sensed, through my haze, that they sent their sympathy and encouragement to me and surrounded me with their love and prayers. If, as we sometimes believe, such groanings of the spirit pass outward to the Everlasting, surely their anguished pleas broke upon the shores of Eternity in a foam of supplication. Perhaps this, added to the fierce wine of my own desperation, kept me running through the darkness. I know it wrapped me in a veritable shield of protection, for the Force emanating from the House of Silence lessened around Naani's form.

Soon, I heard a sound that raised my hackles: the dreadful, distant baying of the Hounds. I knew then that without a miracle, we would die. I looked up through the ebony heavens at the light of the pyramid and murmured in utter anguish, "Help me. Someone please help me."

Even as my eyes turned to the highest light on the crest of the pyramid, I saw the sharp, flashing code of the Set Speech. I had to stop and wipe the sweat from my brow to read it. My heart warmed a little, for I knew Cartesius would do whatever he could to aid me.

Be of good courage, the message said. *We have prepared three of the ancient distance weapons. We will save you, even if we have to turn the Earth-Current loose upon the land. A hundred thousand men are Prepared and in their armor. They are descending the lifts to aid you when they can.*

Hope rose within me. For the first time I did not feel completely alone. Still, the baying of the Hounds drew closer, and when I glanced in fear at the Northeast Watcher, now behind me, the bell of its ear quivered continually, as it silently spread the alarm across the Night Land. No other part of it moved; it stared at the pyramid, a silent hill of life, leaning always toward the last millions, like a dog straining at the leash, while the light from the Ring flowed down upon the vast folds and wrinkles of its neck, the chain holding the beast.

The ground trembled with the beating of the Earth Current, as my people prepared for our defense.

XIX
IN THE COUNTRY OF SILENCE

Even through my despair and exhaustion, as I looked up at the pyramid, rising vast and enduring into the everlasting night, its sheer enormity astonished me. I was now much closer than I had realized, and that mountain of life and safety, standing among the desolation, gave me new reassurance.

As I hurried past a fire-pit, something slipped over its rim. The creature, a broad, hairy man, nearly twice my height, rose from a crawling position, gaped at me, and rushed forward, his arms stretched eagerly toward me. As the light from the fire fell upon him, I saw how huge his hands were compared to his body, with ripping claws like a wild beast's.

I quickly set Naani on the ground. My own life meant nothing to me at that moment; I only cared that this thing intended to delay me. Cold anger filled me; I leapt furiously at the giant, striking with a two-handed stroke, but he avoided it by slipping to the side. The shadows cast by the dancing flames partially hid him, and I did not see his arm come around until he caught my helmet. He tore it from my head with so much power it threw me a dozen feet away onto my back. The impact jarred me, but ignoring the pain, I leapt to my feet and came at him again. The diskos roared and blazed as I caught my adversary above the waist. Despite his size, my weapon passed effortlessly through him, glutting itself on his blood. He turned his shoulders as he died, and his upper torso fell to the ground, leaving the legs and trunk standing in the firelight, the blood fountaining upward.

I already had Naani in my arms and was running away before the lower portion of the giant crumpled with a ghastly sound. All around me, the ether roared with the sheer, astonished joy of my people. No doubt my weeks of conflict had honed my warrior's skills and taught me techniques unknown within the redoubt.

Before another mile passed, two vague forms scampered

out of a dark upcropping of stones. I killed them and went on, never knowing what they were.

After that, all became a haze, for as creature after creature rose from the bushes and rocks, it seemed I fought continuously against a country crawling with brutes. I struck as one in a dream, with the ferocity of growing despair, for surely we had reached the end of our lives, and I could not save my own true love.

The whole Night Land echoed with the roaring of its denizens, and once I heard the noise of running giants. Why a Force of Evil did not slay me, I do not know, unless my journey had burned away any weaknesses such a Power could use to gain a hold on my life.

The baying of the Hounds rose, ominous and deep, out of the southeast again, but much nearer. I knew my strength could not protect my love against the entire pack.

From the pinnacle of the pyramid, an eerie blue light flashed toward the region where the Hounds howled. It struck again and again, perhaps twenty times in all, each burst accompanied by a crackling louder than any sound I ever want to hear again. From the southeast, I heard the yelping of animals dying in pain.

My heart rose within me, for I knew my people fought for me, to bring me home again. But if the Night Land had seemed awake before, it grew doubly so. The roaring of the monsters and the stirring of great Forces rocked the land; the strange, awful Laughter rolled continuously from the hidden country in the east.

Through it all, I perceived, once more, the hoarse baying of the Hounds, no more than a mile to the southeast, and I knew the energy weapon had failed to kill them all. I suddenly felt utterly alone, save for the woman dying in my arms. I looked vainly for the promised hundred thousand warriors, but saw only the lights and shadows of the land and the movement of monstrous life in sundry places. Death was near, and I knew it.

Despite my despair, or perhaps because of it, I broke into a dead run. I was within two miles of the pyramid and could clearly see The Circle shining around it, but the Hounds were drawing nearer. A bitterness rose in my throat, that I should lose my dear one within sight of the safety of my home. I cried out in my despair, my voice coming in gasps, "Please. Please."

Almost instantly, as my people, watching through millions of spyglasses, read my look of desperation, I was surrounded by the sweet, strengthening power of their anguished sympathy. I ran faster, braced by their support, even as I spied the Hounds to my left, less than half a mile away. By the growing excitement of their baying, I knew they had my scent.

From the pyramid's pinnacle, the eerie blue light flashed again, striking among the Hounds as my people took desperate measures to save us. I glanced back where the bolt landed, and saw scores of the brutes between patches of shadow and light, still loping toward me, tall as horses, their heads low.

I hesitated; I paused; I stood still. There was no use in running any more. If my people could not aid us, we would be dead in mere moments. I looked from the Hounds to the Last Redoubt, and again to the Hounds. My spirit sank, for the beasts, that numbered in the hundreds, were scarcely four hundred yards away. I never thought there could be so many of them.

I set Naani down, raised my diskos toward my foes, and gave one final glance at the pyramid. Even as I looked, I heard a mechanical grinding noise, and a tremendous flame poured from the sealed lower portion of the redoubt, covering the entire region where the Hounds ran. The dreadful glory of the fire blinded me, and even from where I stood, I had to crouch, head down, over Naani, to protect her from its withering heat.

So had the Masters of the citadel turned the full power of the Earth Current loose upon the Hounds. The Night Land erupted in thunder, as the energy sundered the air and ruptured the earth. Even the roaring of the monsters was lost in that cacophony, and only fortune spared me from being killed by the shards flying all around.

The flames died, and save for the sound of burning, the Night Land lay silent. My eyes gradually adjusted to the darkness again. Where the Hounds had been, only fire, blasted boulders, and shattered terrain remained. I shook myself from my daze, scooped up Naani, and ran again, for it seemed we might yet reach safety. No danger approached; the power of the pyramid had quelled the monsters. The country lay silent save from far in the dead east, where the maniacal Laughter gradually rose once more.

As I ran, I stared hungrily up at the pyramid. Its lights seemed to have dimmed. At first I thought my eyes were still dazed by the flash of the weapon, but I soon realized that using so much energy had drained the Earth Current. The thought chilled my heart, for if the current fell too low, the entire pyramid would be endangered. They dared not use the weapon to aid me again without risking the lives of all the remaining people of the earth.

I looked in vain for the hundred thousand warriors, while the clamor of the monsters rose all around me again, accompanied by new, peculiar sounds, as if things were waking in the Night Land that had never been roused before. I spied living creatures creeping between me and the light of The Circle, and I knew I faced a bitter fight to bring Naani home.

Suddenly, I sensed tremendous emotion from the multitudes, as if a new peril approached. I glanced up at the Tower of Observation, to see if Cartesius was warning me of the danger with the Set Speech, but the lights remained dim. I looked all around until I spied a pale circle, silent and steadfast, hovering above Naani and me, a holy Power undoubtedly standing between our souls and some terrible Force seeking our destruction. The sight of it gave me a surge of strength. I ran on.

I came within four hundred paces of The Circle, its light burning so dimly it was nearly invisible. Though I feared that it might not serve as a barrier until the Earth Current was recharged, I could only sprint toward it with all speed.

Three beast-men rose out of the shadows and came at me, growling like dogs. The first was so close I had no room to swing my diskos, so I gave him a violent blow to the head with the handle. Even as he fell, I leapt to the side and brought my weapon back into position. A cold, deadly fury filled my heart, so that Naani seemed no more than a baby in the crook of my arm. As I rushed the other two creatures, a clarity of thought engulfed me, a terrible wisdom in the art of slaying. They ran at me as well, but despite their swiftness, I made two quick, light strokes with the diskos, killing them as if they were no more than rodents. They never even touched me.

A shout of wonder answered the attack. I looked around, and saw warriors in gray armor crowded within the Circle, roaring their encouragement. I hurried toward them, wondering why they did not help me.

In a moment I knew the answer, for enormous Black Mounds rocked and swayed all along the boundary of The

Circle. My soul recoiled in horror, for these were living manifestations of Forces of Evil. No one could help me, for the soul of any human venturing outside The Circle would be instantly and utterly lost. Only the hovering halo of light protected Naani and me from destruction.

The hundred thousand warriors shouted, urging me on. I pressed to within four score paces of the Circle, where a herd of squat, brutish men rushed out of the shadows, creatures no taller than my chest, but powerfully built. They mobbed around us and caught at Naani, trying to tear her from my arms.

For an instant I was trapped, unable to both guard my love and use the diskos. I kicked with my metal boots, to create a space, then whirled swiftly around and wrenched free. I leapt backward with the brutes after me, but now had room to use my weapon. I rushed among them, striking swiftly to the right and left in a circling motion. The diskos spun and roared, shining its eerie light upon the men's faces, revealing animal eyes and the tusks of pigs.

I raged through them, laying to every side, while they struck at me with heavy stones, so my armor rang and broke. More than once, the jarring blows nearly overwhelmed me. Naani was spared only because the beast-men were short enough that I carried her above their reach, draped over my shoulder.

Though I plunged always toward the light of The Circle, my foes' numbers seemed endless. The growls of the beast-men and the fierce shouts of the hundred thousand roared all around me. Many of the warriors tried to reach me, but their comrades held them back from dying a useless death.

I was less than fifty paces from The Circle, but was so wounded and dazed, so ill with weariness, and the despair and madness of my journey, that I began to stumble. At that moment, all the sleepless miles fell upon me at once. As I dropped to one knee, a single thought swept through my mind: *I'm so tired. Soon I will sleep.*

The brutes rushed toward me. I rose and lifted my diskos to give final battle, but oh! how bitter it was, the thought of failing so close to my goal.

Suddenly, the beasts screamed as lances of flame struck them from behind. Those before me gave back. I looked around. To my astonishment, a wise commander within The Circle had ordered his warriors to hurl their diskoi like spears. Such a plan showed tremendous ingenuity; our weapons were too precious to throw away, so no one had ever used a diskos in such a manner before. Under the on-slaught, the herd thinned out in front of me. I gathered my strength and gave a last, despairing charge, striking, never ceasing to strike, leaving dead brutes in my wake. I broke through the herd and stepped over The Circle.

A hundred hands reached out as if to help me, but none touched me. Rather, the warriors gave back, as if over-awed. I stood in their sudden silence, the diskos running blood down its handle. I must have rocked unsteadily, for many raised their hands as if to help, but then drew back again, hushed.

We stared at one another. With gasping breath I tried to tell them I needed a doctor for Naani.

"I need . . . I need . . ."

I heard the sound of giants running in the night. The company began to all speak at once.

"Call a physician!"

"Get him inside."

"Beware the giants!"

"The Halo has vanished."

"So have the Black Mounds."

The Night Land roared its frustration and pain. The Laughter rolled from the east. I heard it all through a haze. At last I became aware of a constant, murmuring from above. As if in a dream, I glanced up, recognizing the shouts of the millions flowing down the lofty miles.

"A physician," I managed at last to the man nearest me. "She needs a physician."

The Master of the Diskos, being of the rank we would call a commander in the present age, appeared before me. He made the Salute of Honor with the diskos. "The physic-ians are coming. They were trapped when the lifts failed, but are on their way. All the power faltered after we used the weapon: the air pumps, the lifts, everything. Let me take her."

He tried to lift her from my arms, but I clung to her. I said, very slowly. "I need a physician. She is dying. I need a physician."

Someone tried to reach their hand out to steady me, for I swayed back and forth on my heels, but I glared at them so violently they withdrew, not daring to touch either me or Naani.

At that moment the warriors parted, opening a lane between myself and The Portal. A team of physicians rushed out, a short fellow, the Master Healer, foremost among them.

"We need to lay her down," he said.

Someone produced a cot, and I laid Naani upon it. The Healer made a sign, and the warriors around us turned their backs, forming a protective curtain between ourselves and the others.

Using his instruments, the healer examined Naani. The whole pyramid fell silent, so only the rumblings of the Night Land were heard.

The physician looked up, his eyes filled with pity. He shook his head.

My Naani was dead.

He bowed his head above her and slowly covered her face with a white cloth. He offered no words of comfort; he knew none would help. He rose quickly from kneeling beside her.

"Gondril," he said to the Master of the Diskos. "Help Andros into the pyramid. I need six to carry her as well."

He looked keenly at me, while I fought to breathe, but when the warriors came to help me I waved them off and stood above Naani's body, glaring at them. I must have looked dreadful, with blood running down my face and my armor, for no one dared approach. They looked at the doctor, who said, "Very well. Leave them be."

I stooped, kissed Naani on the forehead, and lifted her into my arms for our last journey.

As I passed down the lane of the hundred thousand, all dressed in their gray armor, each gave the silent salute of the reversed diskos, their empathy and anguish burning in their eyes. No one spoke. For myself, I scarcely knew anything except that the world lay quiet and empty. I had failed my task, and my Naani lay dead in my arms.

A hundred of her sweet acts of love poured through my mind. I suddenly remembered I had never awakened to discover her kissing me in my sleep as I had meant to do. A mad anguish swept through my numb brain; I could scarcely see. I must have faltered, for I suddenly found the Master Healer steadying me, though he released me at once when I straightened and recovered my way.

As I approached The Portal, the lights flickered, then began burning brighter, as the Earth Current returned to its former levels. The lifts and the air pumps came back on with low hums. The Portal, which had been shut, now rumbled open.

A number of the Masters of the Great Pyramid came out to greet me, the Master Monstruwacan hurrying before all of them. He did not know of Naani's death until one of the warriors told him, and then he slowed his approach. Seeing the look on my face, he refrained from rushing to embrace me, but stepped back, the other Masters with him, and watched in silence as I went by.

A continuous murmuring fluttered through the night, as the millions of inhabitants sought news. With the opening of The Portal, the report of Naani's death sped upward through the miles. I felt in my spirit, as if in a dream, the grief of the multitudes as they learned her fate, but this gave me no comfort. Neither could I yet grasp the depth of my loss. I was too stunned.

As I entered The Portal, I found the Full Watch arrayed in their armor, standing in silent respect, giving the Salute of Honor as I carried my love.

Those around me guided me to the main lift, while the Masters walked behind me. Once on the lift, Cartesius stood to my left, the Master Healer to my right. I remember the lift passing many staring multitudes, though I paid them no heed. A hush fell upon them as they saw me, so that a silence swept up the pyramid, save for the sounds of weeping.

Cartesius and the Master Healer exchanged worried glances, and I suddenly realized I was standing in my own blood, which was seeping from dozens of wounds. Still, the physician hesitated to help me. Perhaps, knowing my heart was dead within me, he did not wish to wake me too quickly to my dreadful pain. When my head began to whirl, he tried to ease Naani from my grasp, but I held her dumbly while my blood spilled to the ground. I looked at Cartesius, who was speaking to me. I could not understand what he said, but it struck me that his face seemed very kind and human. A peculiar humming filled my ears; the Monstruwacan held me up while beckoning to those behind me.

Just before the blackness took me, gentle arms wrapped themselves around my broken armor.

***

I drifted in silence and half-dreams, where I seemed to be continuously carrying Naani in my arms, though sometimes it was Mirdath. At last I opened my eyes to find Cartesius sitting beside me, holding my hand. We were within a chamber of one of the Health Centers of my own city. For a long time I said nothing, and he watched me in silent concern.

"She's dead," I finally murmured, feeling the full weight of her loss.

"Yes," my friend said, "but she died in your arms, rather than in the darkness, alone. Surely your love brought her comfort."

"I always meant to wake," I said, "to catch her kissing me."

I began to sob so violently Cartesius feared I would re-open my wounds. A burning pain spread through my chest, and the Master Monstruwacan summoned the healer, who held an elixir under my nose. Eventually, it eased me back into the comfort of sleep, but before I drifted away, I heard Cartesius ask the physician in a low voice, "Is there any hope?"

"Little, I think. His spirit is strong, but from the moment I saw him carrying her, I knew he would never survive if she died. He bends all his desire toward following her, and his wounds, which should heal, do not. I am nursing his strength, trying to get him through her funeral, but after that . . ."

His voice fell away and I tumbled into a dreamless sleep.

I remember waking and slumbering several times, and then waking more fully to find the Master Healer standing before me with two of his assistants.

"Andros," the physician said, "it is time to send Naani back to the Earth Current."

One of the assistants, a woman, brought me a loose garment, but I shook my head, dumbly, and looked about in confusion. The healer watched me intently, and then gave one of the men an order, though I did not hear what he said.

In a few moments my broken armor and a body vest were hurried into the room.

"Will you wear these?" the healer asked.

I nodded and rose to a sitting position so they could

261

dress me. Even as they did so, I sensed the grief of the multitudes making their way down toward the Country of Silence.

After I was dressed, I tried to walk, but the doctor would not allow it. "You need to conserve your strength," he told me gently.

At that moment Cartesius entered the room, adorned in his own gray armor, carrying his diskos. He took me by the shoulder, squeezing it gently. I had never seen such sorrow in his eyes before.

"We have to send her off," I finally managed, my tone dull and dead. "It is the last thing to do."

"Yes, it is. I'll be right there with you."

They placed me on a sling, and carried me to the main lift, where a bed had been prepared. My old mentor bade me lie down, which I did. I think he and I both knew I would never return in the lift, or need a bed again.

The pyramid looked deserted, for almost everyone had gone down to the Underground Fields, leaving only the Stress Masters standing guard at the lifts to supervise the movement of the masses. I watched them pass, one by one, as we slipped down the miles to the Country of Silence, lying a hundred miles deep in the world and stretching a hundred miles in every direction, consecrated to silence and the dead.

The healer's assistants helped me from the lift, but when they tried to use a sling to carry me to The Last Road, I refused. Though trembling from weakness, I stood and held out my hand for my diskos. Cartesius took it from the man who carried it and gave it to me.

Holding my old, trusty companion gave me strength as I walked steadily down the way leading to The Last Road, the Master Monstruwacan and the physician close behind.

Surely, all the people in the world stood in that country. They spread across the rolling hills as far as I could see. When they sighted me, the ether stirred with their pity, and a murmur grew, like low, rolling thunder that passed back and forth across the country before dwindling into silence.

I had been brought to a rise beside the beginning of The Last Road, which wound its way through a white metal gate, down to the vast golden glow of the Dome, the pulsing well of the Earth Current. A slight figure lay before me, dressed in a white robe stitched with all the colors of the sun, the loving work of many women. A white cloth covered her face. I rocked upon my feet, steadying myself with the diskos, and Cartesius grasped my arm to aid me. The healer tried to give me more medicine to breathe, but I refused after the first whiff; I knew I could bear the pain for the short time I had to live, and I wanted to remain alert in the precious moments left for me to be near my love.

Cartesius and I left the others and walked down to the place where my dear Naani lay. Two maidens, dressed in white, knelt to the right and left of her. These, maidens because they watched over a maiden, represented Faithfulness. Had Naani been wed, they would have been married women. The place at the head of the bier, which represented Love, remained empty. The Master Monstruwacan led me there, then took his own position at Naani's feet, the place representing Honor. He reversed his diskos in silent salute to her. So we assumed the four positions which had been the custom for countless generations. I kept my eyes on Naani's funeral robe, embroidered with what we called yellow Flowers of Weeping, because she had died in love.

Just then, a faraway sound rose and drew steadily closer, as all the people sang the Calling Song, millions chanting softly to millions, the sound passing toward us, then over us, then onward in hushed breaths, as if all the love in the world called in soft anguish to a lost beloved. The sound passed away over the Country of Silence, leaving only the noise of the weeping multitudes.

The crowd stirred again, as a strange, low sound rose from beyond the Hills of the Infants, a noise like a wandering wind. This was the Song of Weeping, and it, too, passed around us and fell away into the dim distances.

Cartesius glanced up at me, for the moment had come when I must part with Naani forever. I held no hope that she and I would ever meet again in this world, nor did I understand why we had been given a second chance at love, only to lose it in the end.

I gathered my courage and stooped to lay my diskos beside my little darling there upon the Last Rest, and the two maidens drew back the white cloth covering her face. She looked so sweet, as if merely asleep, like a little child, her beautiful red-gold hair lying on her shoulders the way I always liked it. The pain in my heart told me that I died even as I looked. And that was well.

I laid my head against her shoulder and wept.

"I will find you," I whispered hoarsely, "if it is allowed. I will find you. Wait for me there."

The Master Monstruwacan, with tears flowing down his own cheeks, left his place to clasp my shoulder.

I struggled with myself, not wanting to leave her, but the sympathy of the millions gave me strength, and at last I pulled myself away, and the maidens covered her beautiful face.

The Master Monstruwacan returned to his place, and raising his reversed diskos, said in a trembling voice, "Naani, last daughter of the Lesser Redoubt, our sister lost to us through all the darkness and ages, I commend your spirit to eternity and the hand of God."

The Road began to move toward The Gateway, carrying my beloved away. I had to fight to keep breathing, for I did not want to die before she vanished from sight. Blood was running inside my armor; the strain of walking had re-opened my wounds. I wondered dimly, after Naani was gone and I died, whether I would return to the empty existence of Andrew Eddins.

A low moan and a whistling like a dree wind filled the air, as the multitudes wept, for though they guessed only a little of my story, it moved them greatly.

I stood still, mustering all my remaining strength to finish this last vigil before I died, drawing my breath as evenly as I could, watching the small form now far away, moving along the roadway. I scarcely noticed the Master Monstruwacan and the two maidens as they helped support me. I saw only my own darling, dwindling away.

The bier reached the place where the Road passed into the luminous vapor surrounding the Earth Current, a faint, shining smoke drifting all around the base of the Dome. When the dead entered it, the light gave them an uncertain quality.

I stared, holding on to the last, for in a minute she would enter the Current and be gone forever. The shifting vapors clung around her body, making her seem unreal. My eyes grew heavy as she began to fade from sight, and the pain in my chest worsened. I did not expect to survive her disappearance long.

A strange, hoarse noise rose from those around me. At first, I could make nothing of it, but it grew until all the Country of Silence was filled with a thunder unknown since its inception. I roused myself from my pain and suddenly saw what they saw, for Naani seemed to move.

"It is only the whirling of the vapors," I muttered, shaking my head. "The vapors."

But Cartesius ordered the Road halted, and I clearly saw Naani raise herself from the bed.

My strength returned to me in a rush, and all the power of the rejoicing spirits of the millions filled me with vitality. I sprang onto the migrator and ran like a madman, staggering as I went, shouting Naani's name, while the roof of the Country of Silence boomed with the exclamations of the people. At Cartesius' order, the road rolled back toward me, returning my love.

Others ran behind me, but despite my wounds, I reached her first. She sat upon the conveyance, holding the face cloth in her hands, her eyes bright with wonder.

When she saw me, she smiled.

I fell beside her, then climbed to my hands and knees and raised myself to her side.

"Andros," she said, her voice weak. "I woke to a golden mist and thought I was in heaven. Isn't that funny? Why is everything so bright?"

My voice failed, and all I could do was clutch her hand.

She looked down and gasped. I followed her gaze and saw blood rilling down my armor; my running had re-opened all my wounds. She dropped to her knees beside me, fear in her eyes. "Andros!"

"We're home, Naani," I finally managed. "I brought you home."

A haze covered my vision. She cradled my head in her breast, there upon the earth. The air shook all around us with a tremendous noise, and a mighty spiritual stirring rocked the ether.

"I love you," I said. "I won't die now. I'll fight and not die."

Even as I spoke, I fell into darkness.

XX
THE VISION ENDS

I returned to life to find myself once more back in my bed at the Healing Center, a bed I had thought never to need again.

I remained somewhat disoriented, but heard, rising out of the depths of the world, the deep thunder of the underground organs accompanied by a rolling chant, as of multitudes singing beyond far mountains, or even beyond death itself. Sometimes it sounded like a blowing wind, only to rise golden and recognizable as the ancient melody of the Song of Honor.

By this, I knew the inhabitants of the Great Pyramid rejoiced over Naani's revival, but everything seemed faint and far away, and I did not have the strength to open my eyes. I felt as if I drifted on the deep waters of an endless sea.

I think I moaned a little, for I heard the Master Monstruwacan's kind voice above me, repeating over and over, "You must live, Andros, for Naani is well." He must have repeated it for hours, for every time I neared the surface of consciousness, I heard his hoarse, whispered voice reassuring me, and each time I descended back into slumber more determined to survive.

For days I dwelled in that half-waking, half-sleeping state, always remembering my mentor's words, fighting with all my will to live.

Other days came, when I lay quietly, thinking of nothing, but looking out with open eyes. I remember the Master Healer bending over me at various times, studying my face. And always the kind face of the Master Monstruwacan hovered above me, reminding me that my love waited for me on this side of life.

After a long time, the dear face of Naani appeared, her eyes shining with love. I must have fumbled my hands a bit, for she reached out and held them. The warmth of her spirit surrounded me, and though she did not speak I felt a great contentment, and soon drifted into a peaceful slumber.

A day came when my attendants helped me up and carried me to a quiet, dimly-lit garden, where they set me down and left me alone. I thought of my journey, and of other days, centuries past, when I had sat in such a garden with the sunshine upon my face.

After a while I heard a rustling and Naani stepped out from behind a bush, looking somewhat shyly at me, but with love shining in her eyes. She wore a garment blue as the ancient sky, and her hair shimmered in the light of the lamps.

"I have never seen you properly dressed before," I said. "You are even more dainty than I thought."

She raised one small fist close to her nose. "I am strong enough to deal with you."

I tried to rise to go to her, but she dropped all her playfulness and rushed to my side. "Andros, you mustn't," she said, scooting onto the bench beside me.

We kissed beneath the light of the lamp.

For a pleasant hour we talked, and I asked her about her revival, for the healers had not yet explained it to me.

"They tell me the attack from the House suspended my life signs, leaving my spirit dormant until I passed into the cloud of the Earth Current, when its power woke me. They have searched the ancient Records—you know they would —until they found a similar occurrence several centuries ago. I suppose in all the ages if something could happen it has. But I'm afraid I made a terrible disturbance."

"You did, indeed," I said, running my hand over her wrist. "I didn't know it at the time, but Cartesius told me it nearly caused disaster, for everyone who watched rushed toward The Last Road. Many would have been trampled, including you and I, except the Master of the Watch kept his head and lined up the regiments to hold everyone back."

"All for one person," Naani said.

"A brave and special person. I remember you coming to my bed and holding my hand. The Master Healer said you were extremely weak yourself, at the time."

"I was. He only allowed it because he thought you would die unless something strengthened your spirit."

"He was wrong; I couldn't die, not after finding you again."

Her eyes grew moist. She looked down, running her fingers along mine, and for a while we sat in mute happiness, still both far from recovered.

Finally, I said, "When I thought you. . . dead, all I could remember was that during our travels, I never woke to find you kissing me while I slept."

She blushed slightly and smiled a mischievous grin. "Perhaps you will soon get another chance."

The Master Healer, looking quite satisfied, returned with the attendants to take us both back to our rooms.

***

I saw Naani every day after that, and nurtured by our shared love, we both soon returned to health. The Master Healer eventually allowed us to take short walks in the Underground Fields, though we always followed obscure paths to prevent the multitudes from thronging around us.

Three weeks later, Naani and I were married in a private ceremony with a Minister of Matrimony, the only other guests being a few close friends and the Master Monstru-wacan, for neither of us were strong enough to handle a public service. We would have to have one later, for the pyramid would not be denied honoring us, and there has never been a more glorious wedding than that, when the multitudes formed an Honor Guard eight miles high from the top to the bottom of the redoubt.

Naani and I, unable to bear being apart, stayed almost constantly at one another's sides, and we soon grew to perfect health. I now think of those times as the Love Days, which are the most beautiful days of all if the love is true. We wandered along the paths of the Underground Fields through the numerous villages of that deep country. Often, we withheld our names to avoid being approached by the kind and curious, for we wanted only one another. We frequently carried food with us and slept among the grass, though sometimes we ate in the villages. Naani teased me once, saying, "This is a lot like our journey together, eating and sleeping out in the open, but the food is better. Don't you miss the bubbling powder?"

I patted my stomach, which was quite full at the time. "No, I don't. I never want to feel that gnawing emptiness again."

We went down to the Country of Silence once, but did not stay too long, for the memory of the time when I thought Naani dead overwhelmed me. But later, we often walked there, talking of the ancient days and of our journey together.

***

After being married a few weeks and going through the public marriage ceremony, Cartesius visited us.

"I have a surprise for you," he said. "Put on your best and come with me."

He led us down the lifts into the Hall of Honor, which we found filled with all the great and influential inhabitants of the pyramid, a tremendous multitude, all standing in waiting silence.

The Master Monstruwacan led me to the center of the hall, where a structure stood in the Place of Honor, veiled by a curtain. My mentor said a few words about my journey into the Night Land, and the curtain was thrown back, revealing a statue of a man in broken armor carrying a woman in his arms.

Naani and I were dumbstruck, for I was still a young man, and this honor was usually reserved only for those already dead. I did not believe I had done some great deed; I had only loved with all my heart and spirit, which made danger a small thing by comparison. I was humbled, proud, and awestruck that they would give us such a tribute.

Naani broke into tears of joy and held me close while the audience kept a sweet, sympathetic silence, which was their way of doing honor in that day. But Cartesius beamed with pride.

We left the hall quietly, holding each other as we went.

***

So ends my tale of the Night Land, and of the vision that came to me in my sorrow after Mirdath died. I do not expect those who read these words to believe them. Sometimes I can scarcely believe them myself, as I sit in my quiet hall in the heart of the English countryside. Sometimes I wonder if it is all the delusion of a man made insane by sorrow, a man who wanders the dark fantasies of an alien future to comfort his own terrible loss. Yet I have strange evidences as well: I understand mathematics now, which I did not before. I can speak the language of the Last Redoubt, and I know how many times a stone attached to a strap of a certain length can be thrown in an hour.

No, I do not believe I am mad. I think rather that I have been granted a tremendous gift. I do not understand why this should be, but I believe, out of all humanity, I was given the chance to find my true love again upon this mortal coil. And though I will die, as men always do, I will live again in that far future.

I have had love. In finding my love I have gained honor, but have learned that honor without love is but the ashes of life. Having love is having all, for true love is the mother of honor and faithfulness, and those three together build the House of Joy.

A FINAL NOTE

So ends the strange narrative of Andrew Eddins found within the ruins of the ancient manor upon the high hill. No corroboration exists for his story, yet one single fact remains. Not far from the desolate house lies a small family cemetery. Among the markers, three particular headstones can be found. The first is for Mirdath Eddins, with the inscription *Beloved Wife*. Upon the second, that of the Eddins' infant daughter, is written simply *Baby Mirdath*. The third epitaph, etched upon the gravestone of Andrew Eddins, is more mysterious:

> *Do not think I died of grief*
> *Why do you seek me here?*
> *I am not dead, I have but gone*
> *To find her in the Night*

According to the dates on the stones, Andrew Eddins died five years to the day following Mirdath's passing.

THE END